MIGHTY JACK
and the GOBLIN KING

Ben Hatke
color by Alex Campbell
and Hilary Sycamore

:01
First Second
New York

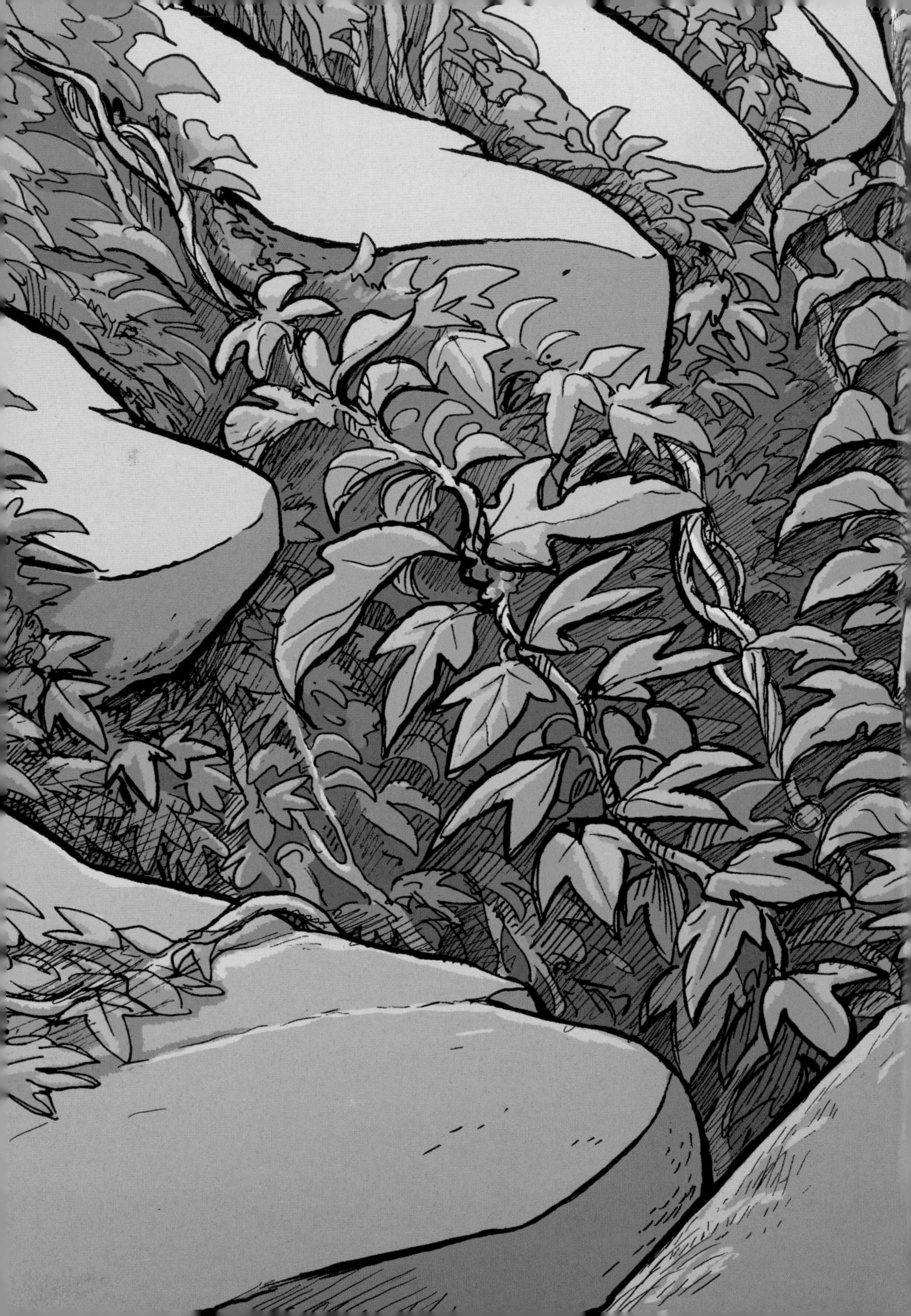

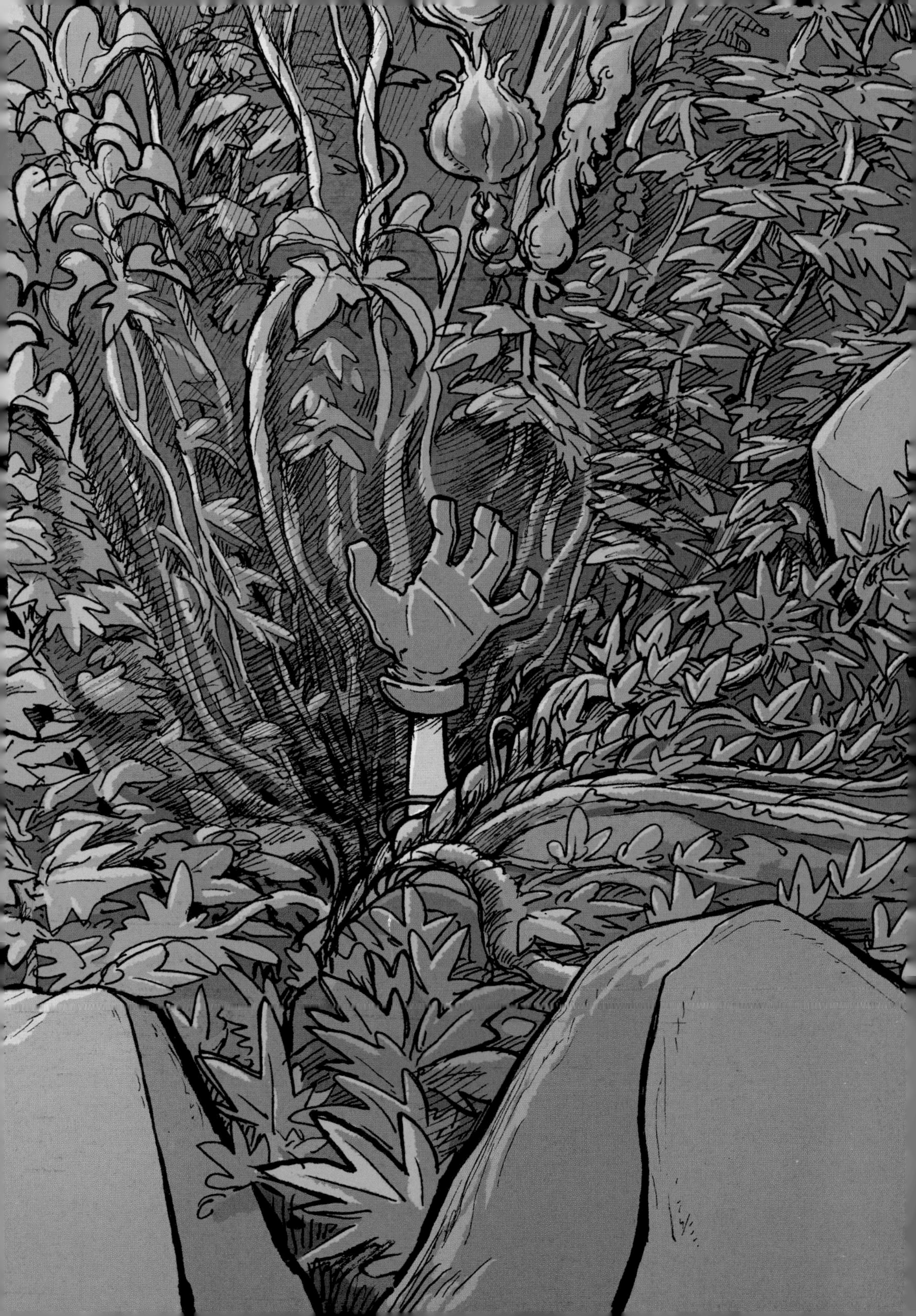

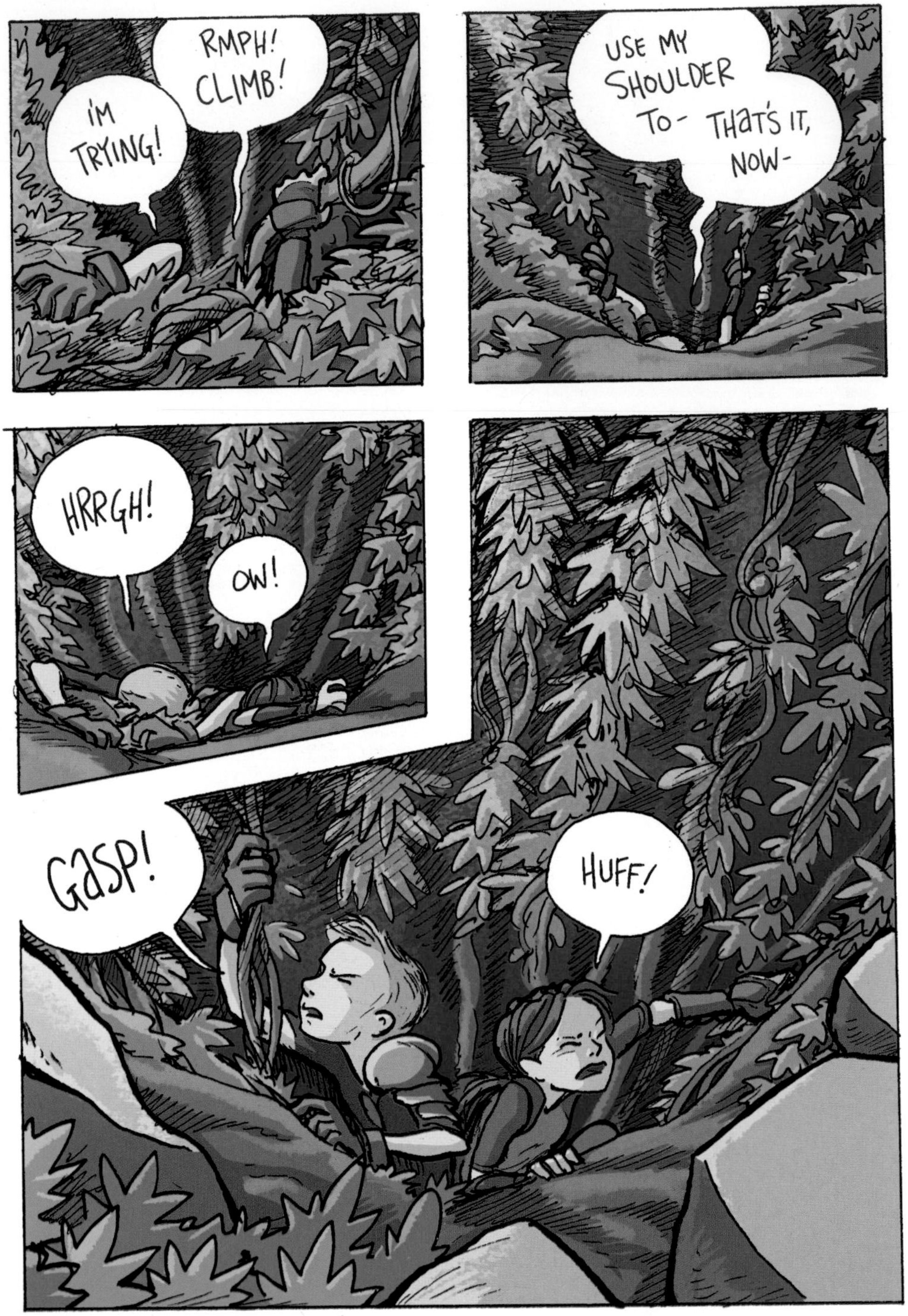

RMPH! CLIMB!
I'M TRYING!
USE MY SHOULDER TO-
THAT'S IT, NOW-
HRRGH!
OW!
GASP!
HUFF!

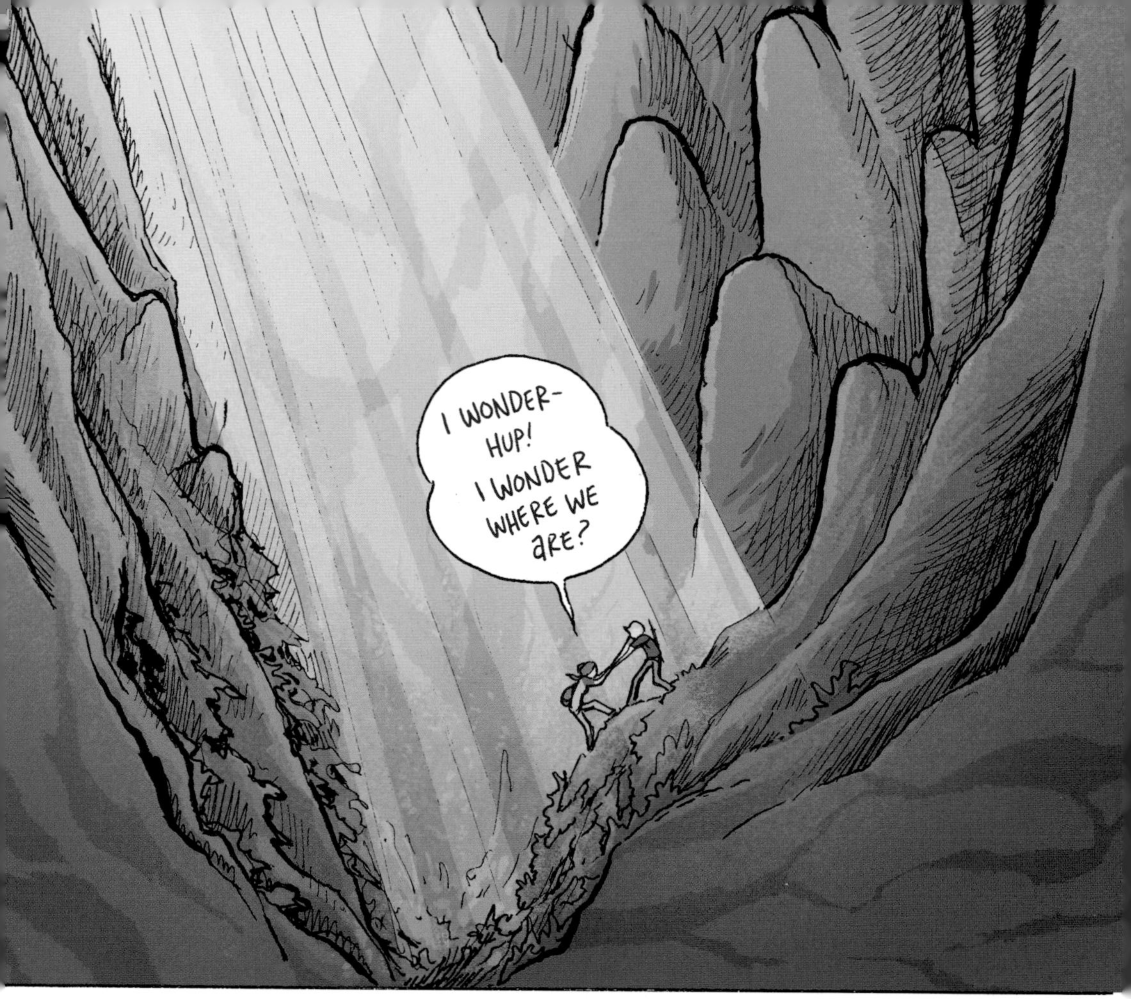
I WONDER-
HUP!
I WONDER WHERE WE ARE?

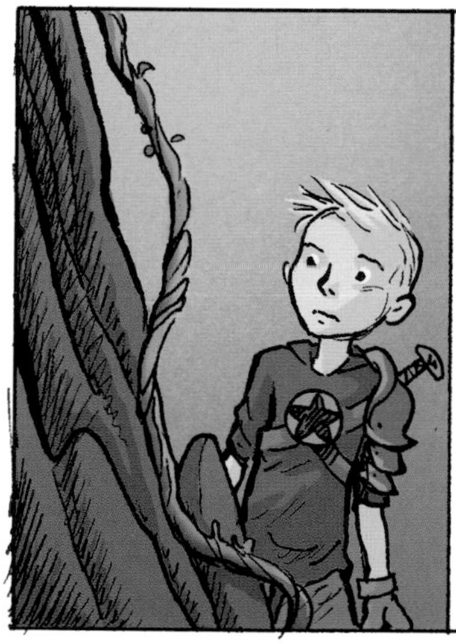

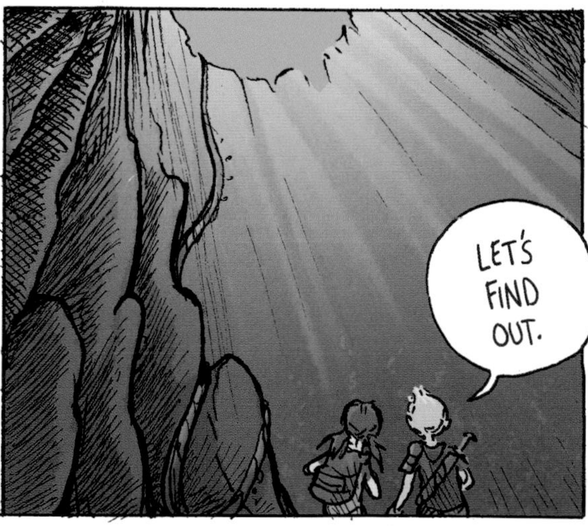
LET'S FIND OUT.

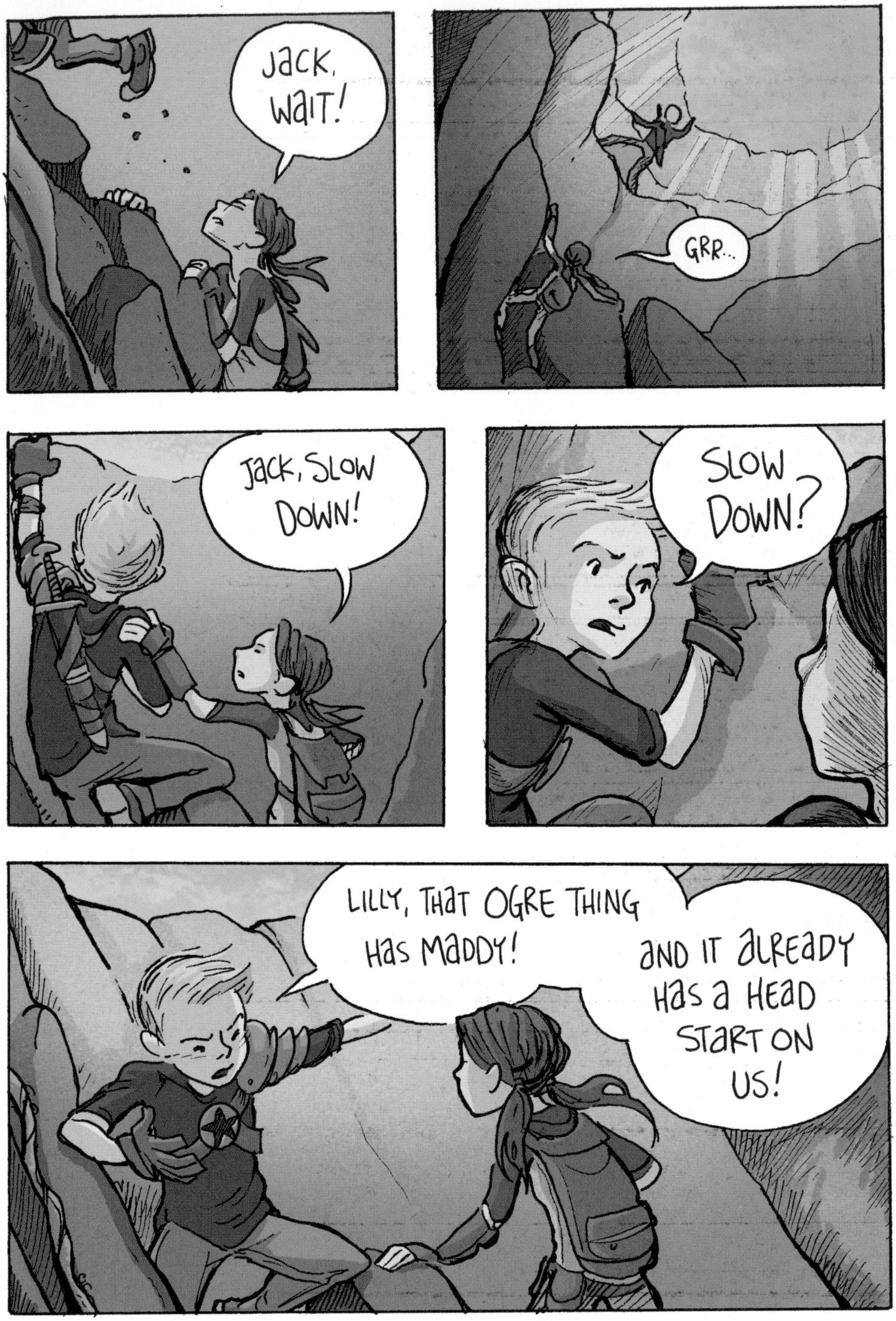
JACK, WAIT!
GRR...
JACK, SLOW DOWN!
SLOW DOWN?
LILLY, THAT OGRE THING HAS MADDY!
AND IT ALREADY HAS A HEAD START ON US!

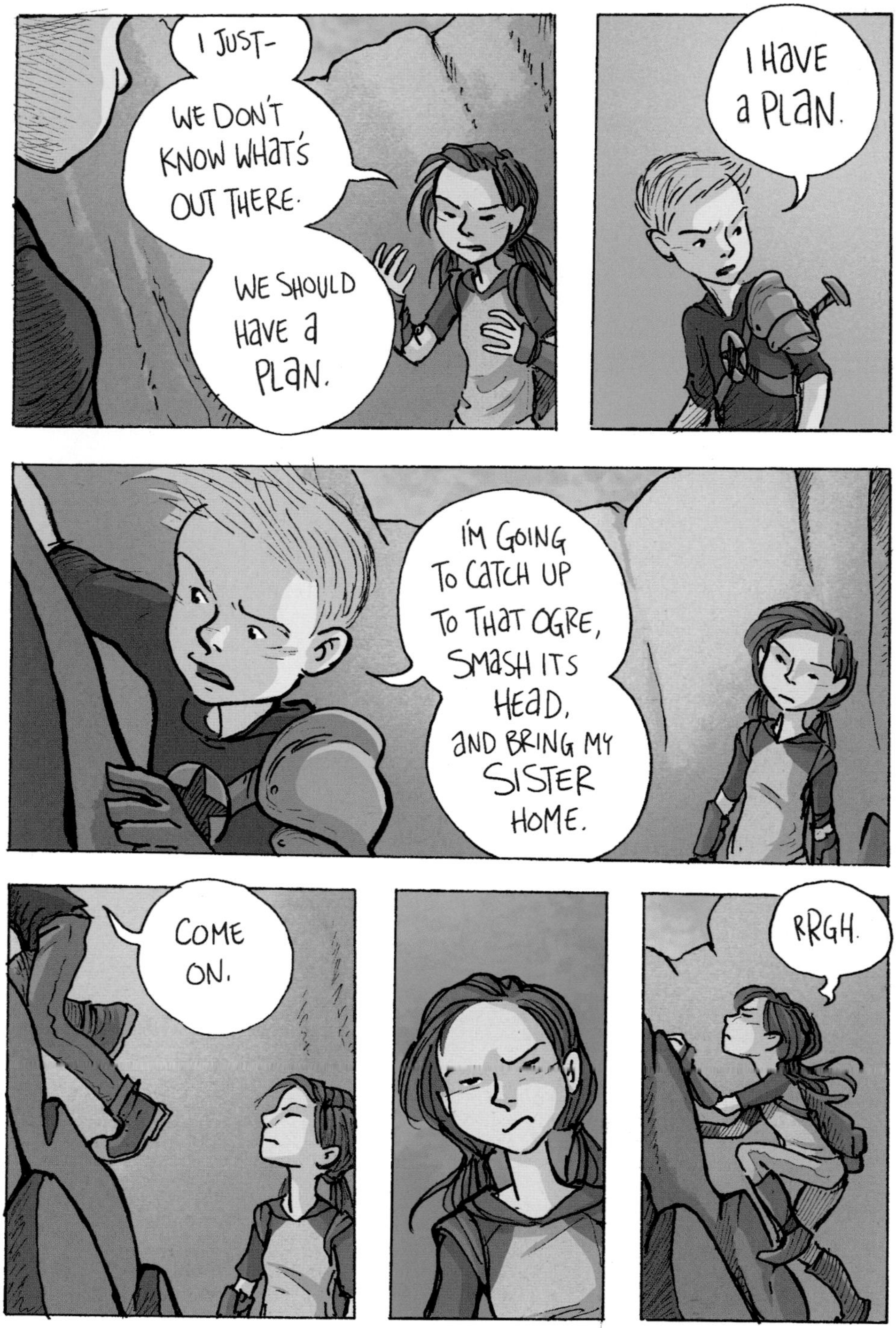
I JUST-
WE DON'T KNOW WHAT'S OUT THERE.
WE SHOULD HAVE A PLAN.
I HAVE A PLAN.
I'M GOING TO CATCH UP TO THAT OGRE, SMASH ITS HEAD, AND BRING MY SISTER HOME.
COME ON.
RRGH.

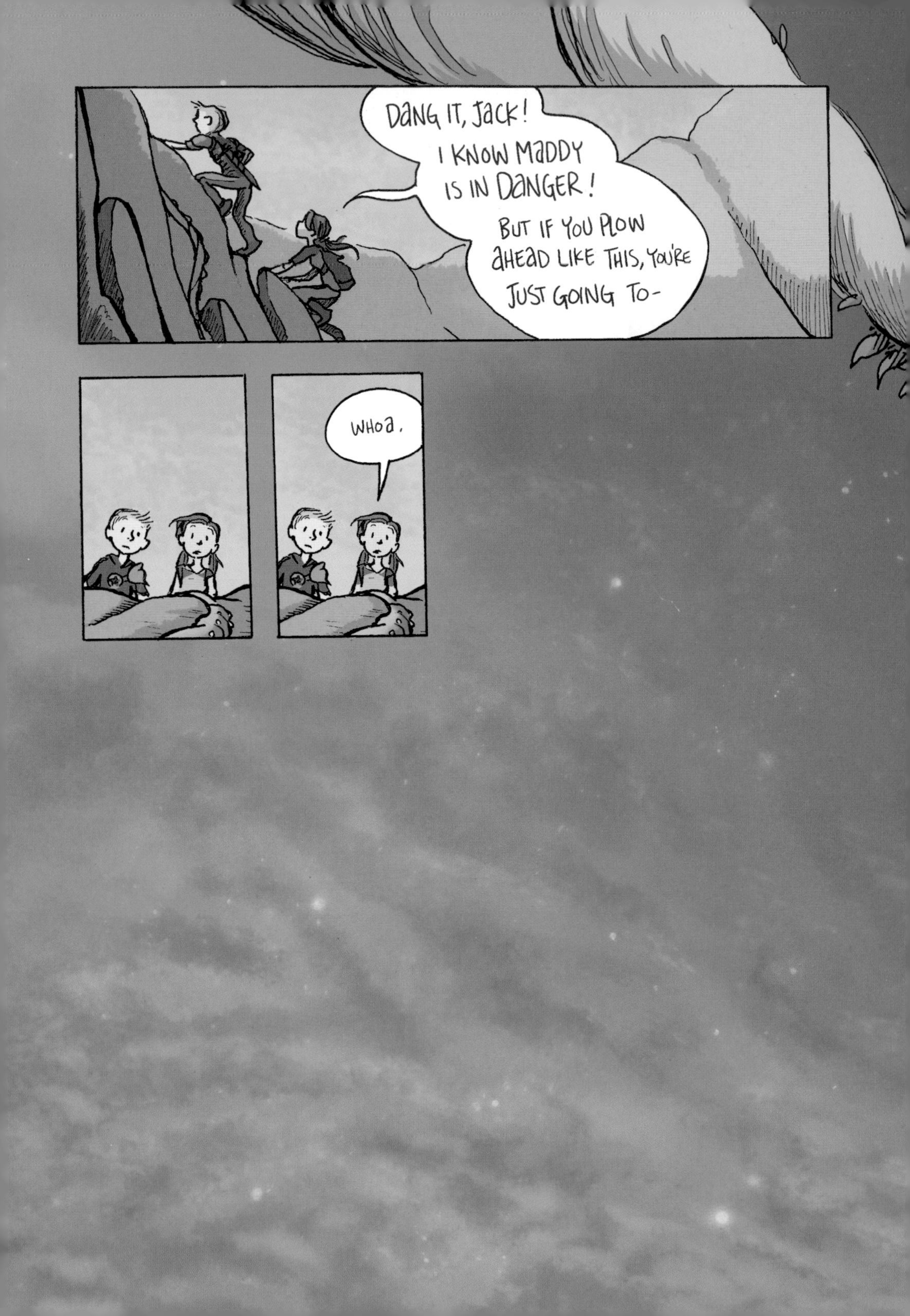
DANG IT, JACK!
I KNOW MADDY IS IN DANGER!
BUT IF YOU PLOW AHEAD LIKE THIS, YOU'RE JUST GOING TO-
WHOA.

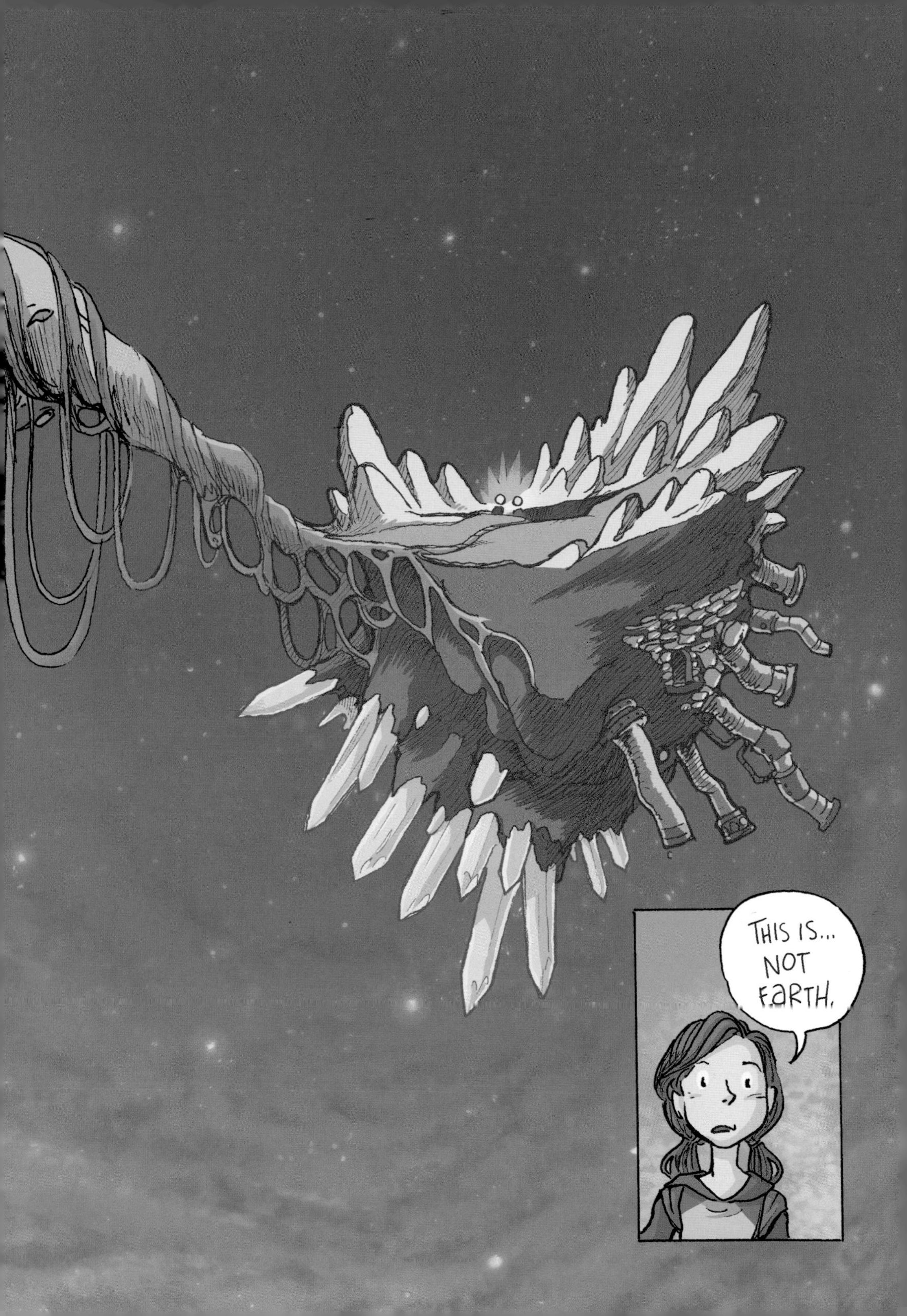
THIS IS... NOT EARTH.

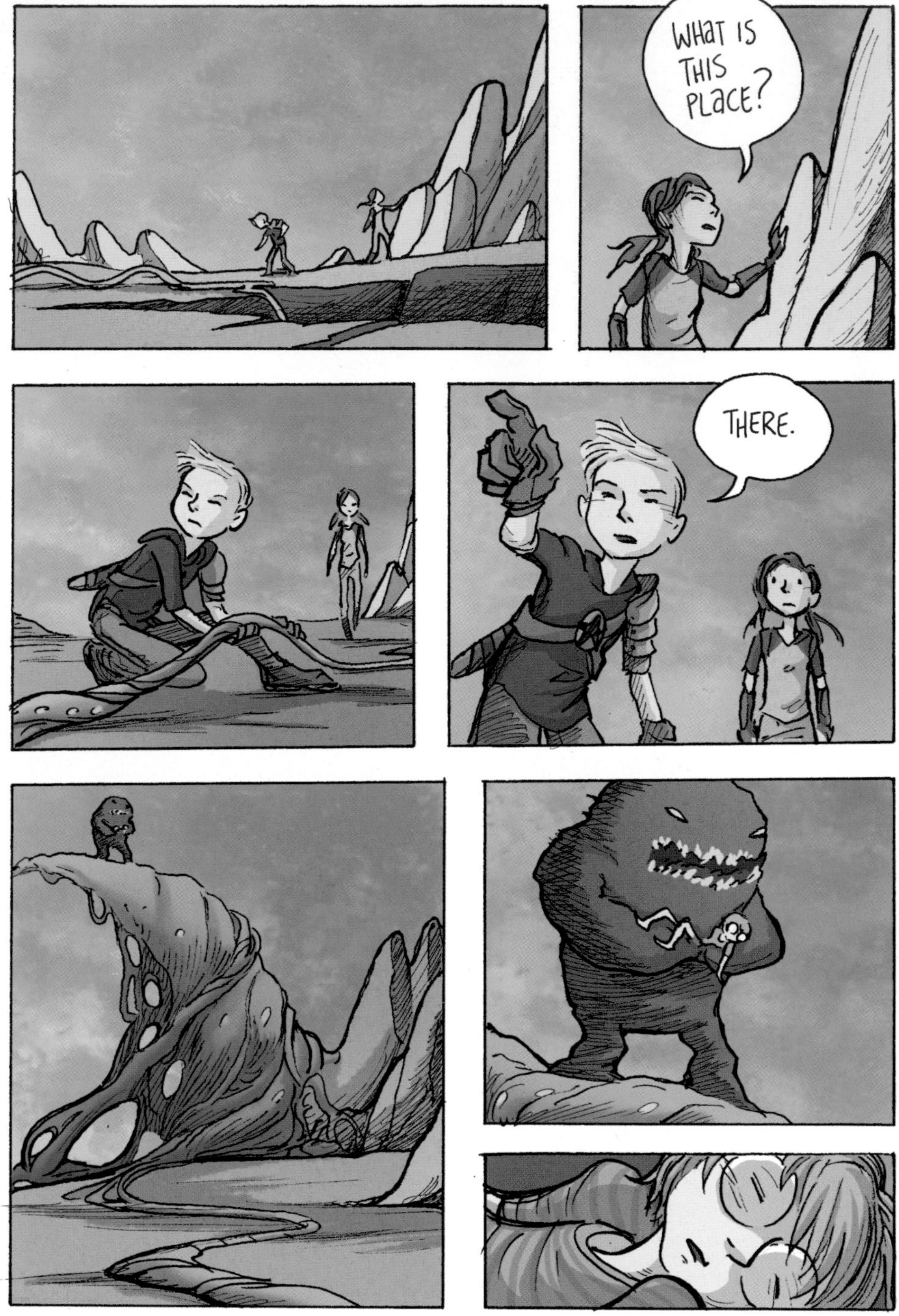
WHAT IS THIS PLACE?
THERE.

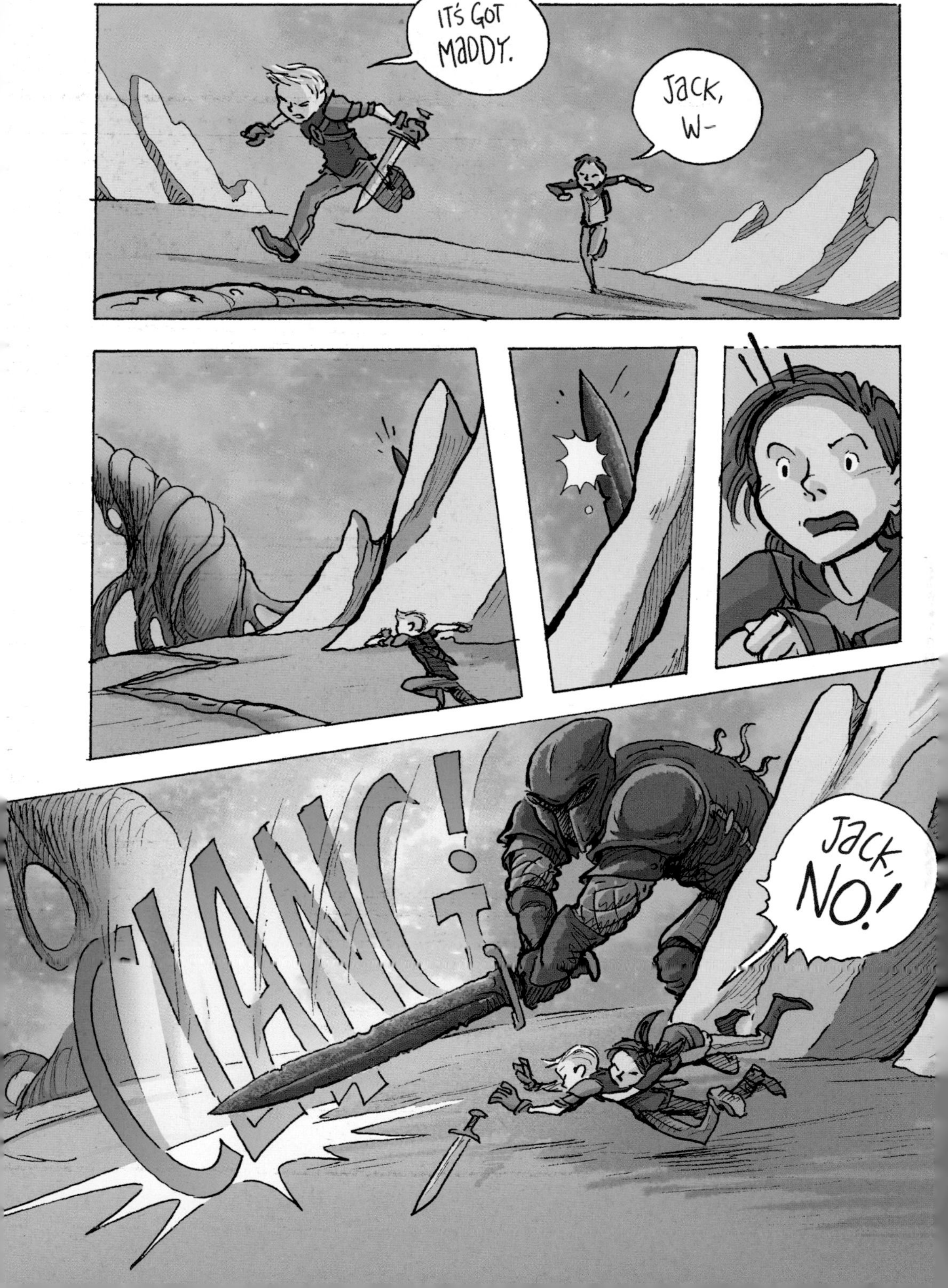
IT'S GOT MADDY.
JACK, W-
CLANG!
JACK, NO!

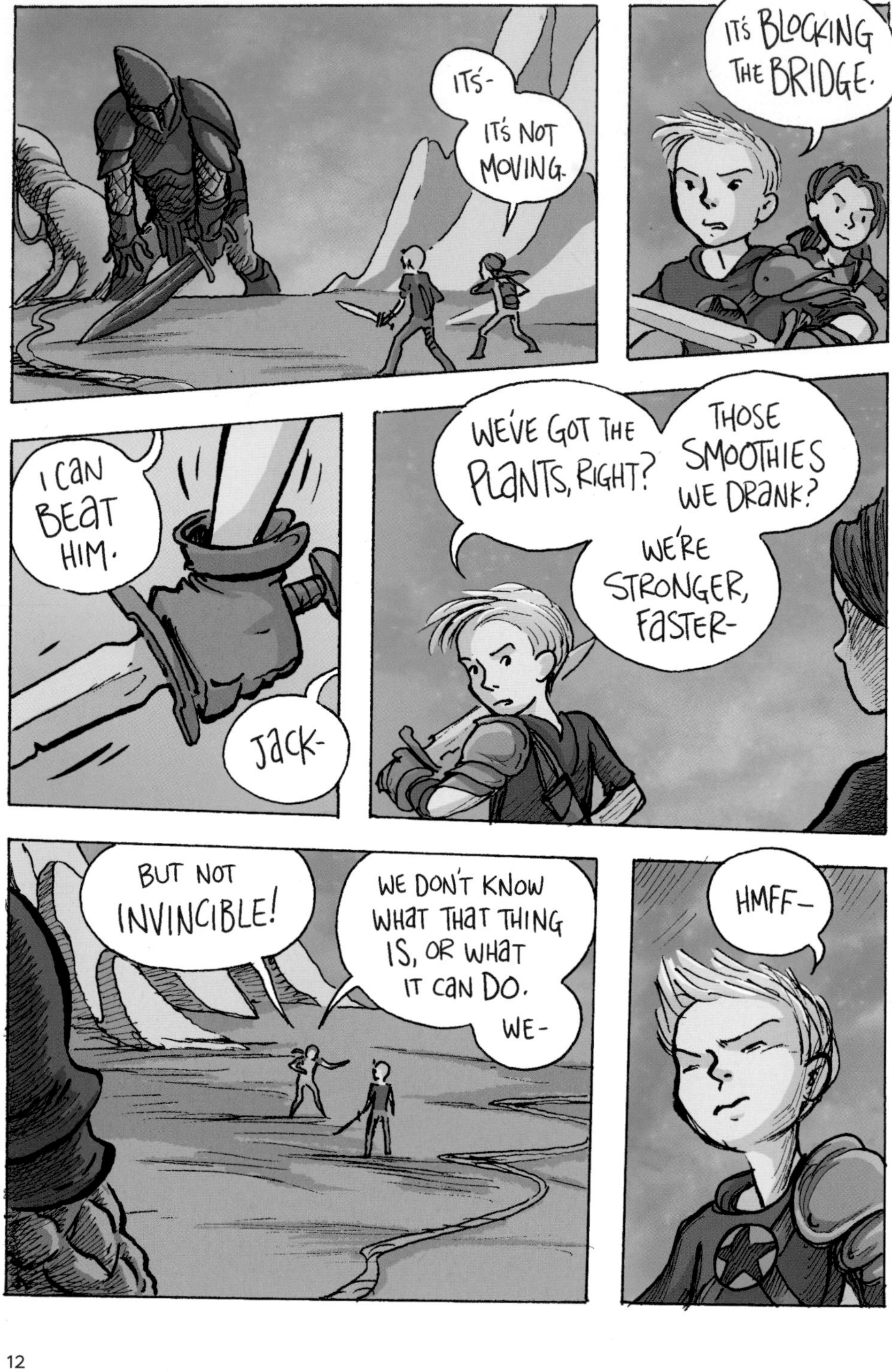

ITS-
ITS NOT MOVING.
ITS BLOCKING THE BRIDGE.
I CAN BEAT HIM.
JACK-
WE'VE GOT THE PLANTS, RIGHT?
THOSE SMOOTHIES WE DRANK?
WE'RE STRONGER, FASTER-
BUT NOT INVINCIBLE!
WE DON'T KNOW WHAT THAT THING IS, OR WHAT IT CAN DO.
WE-
HMFF-

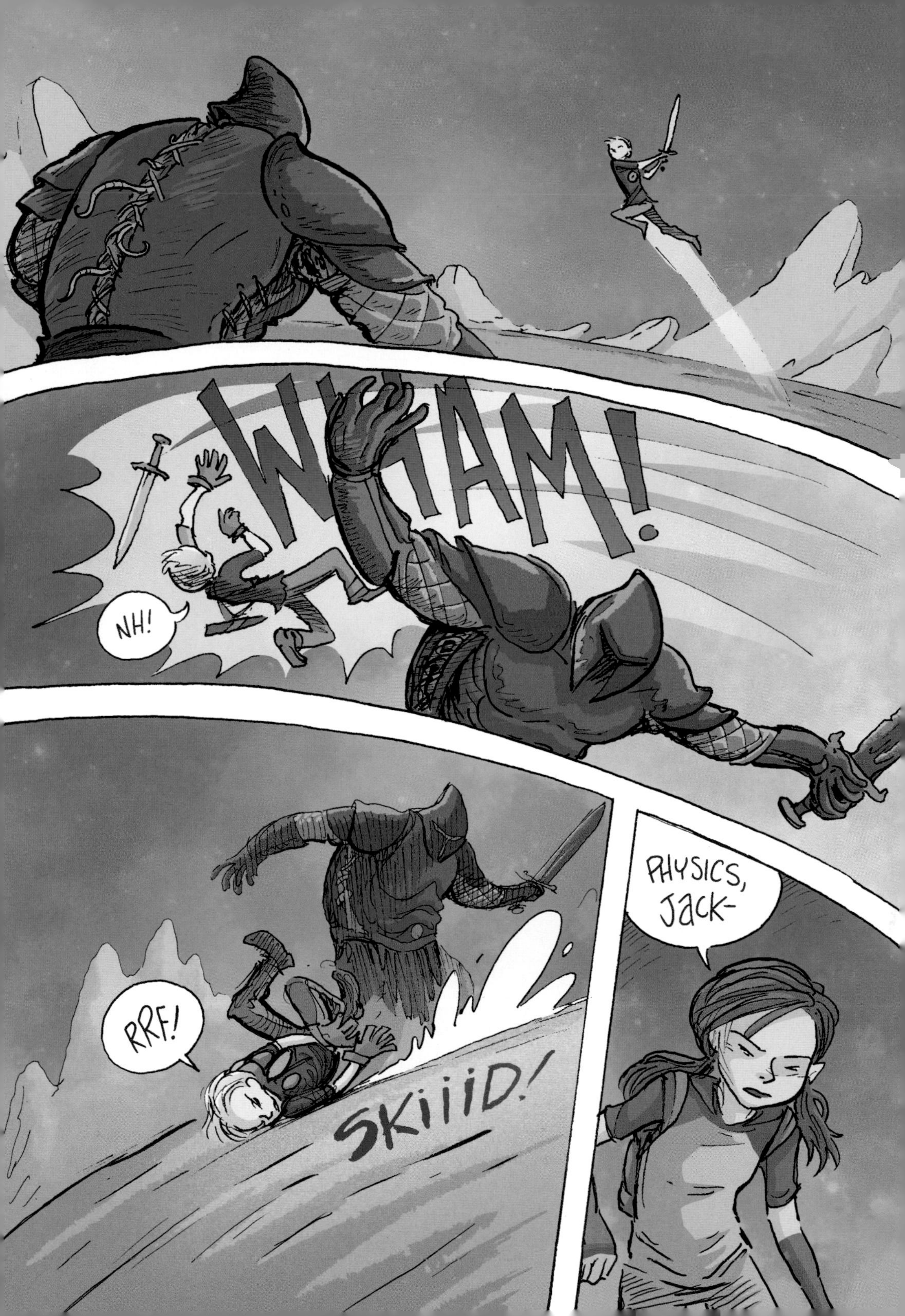
WHAM!
NH!
PHYSICS, JACK-
RRF!
SKIIID!

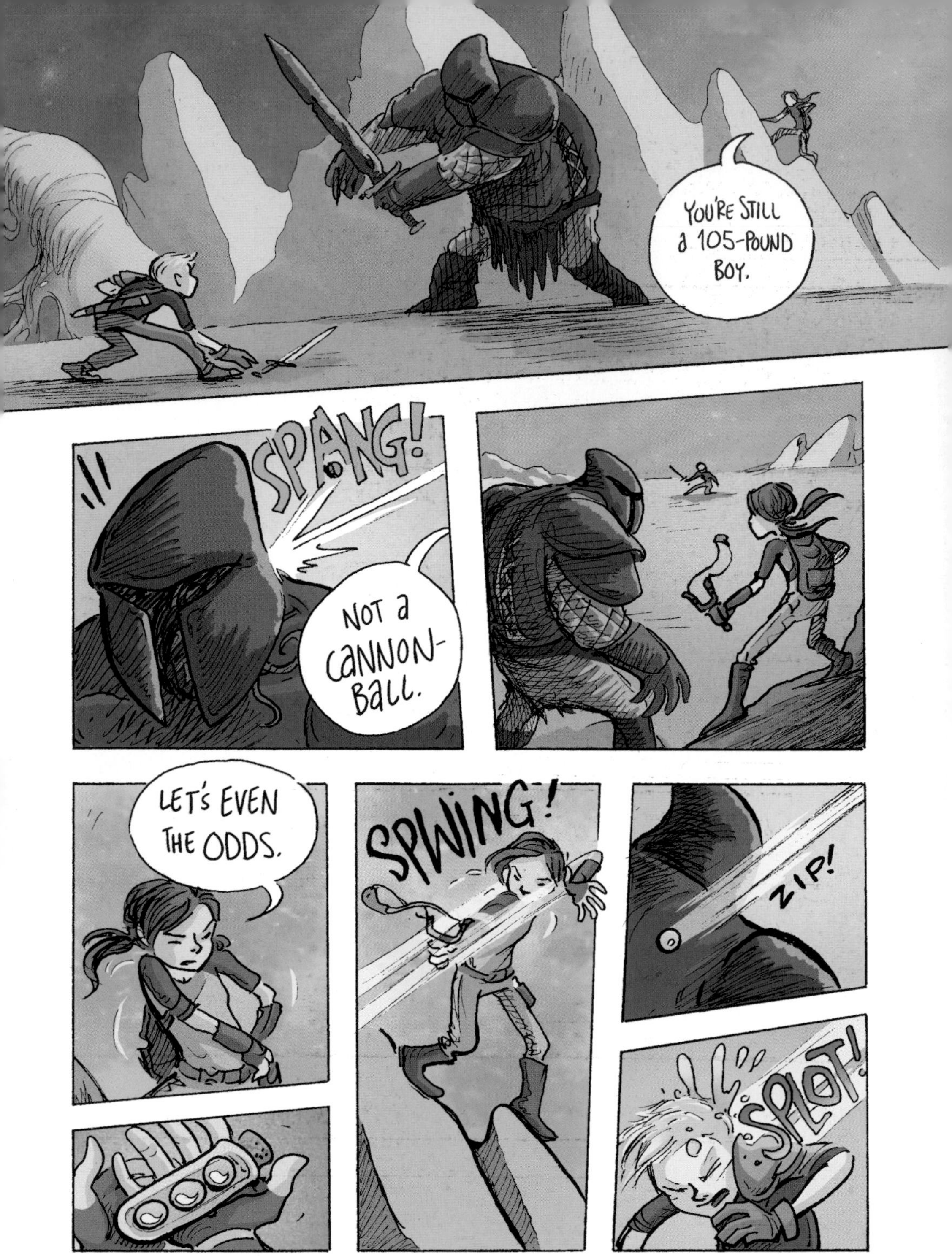
YOU'RE STILL
a 105-POUND
BOY.
SPANG!
NOT a
CANNON-
BaLL.
LET'S EVEN
THE ODDS.
SPWING!
ZIP!
SPLOT!

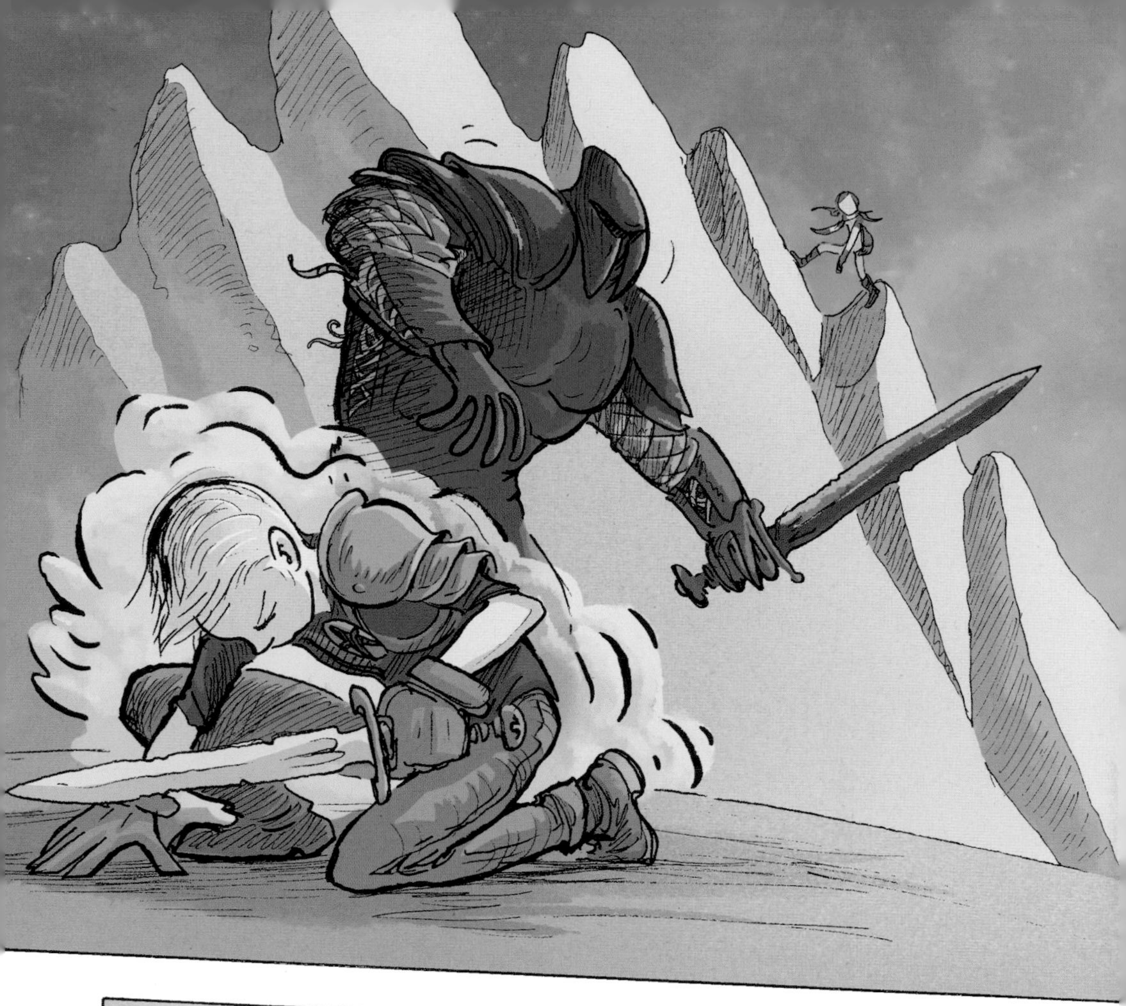

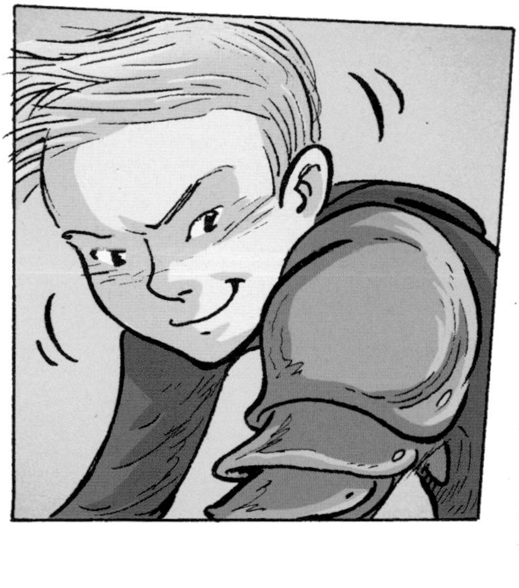

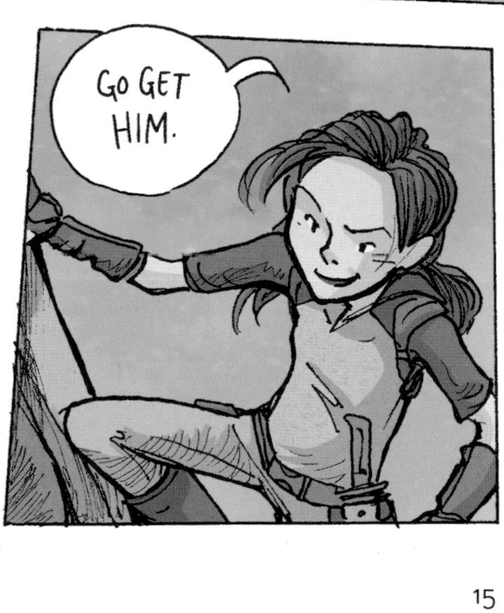
GO GET HIM.

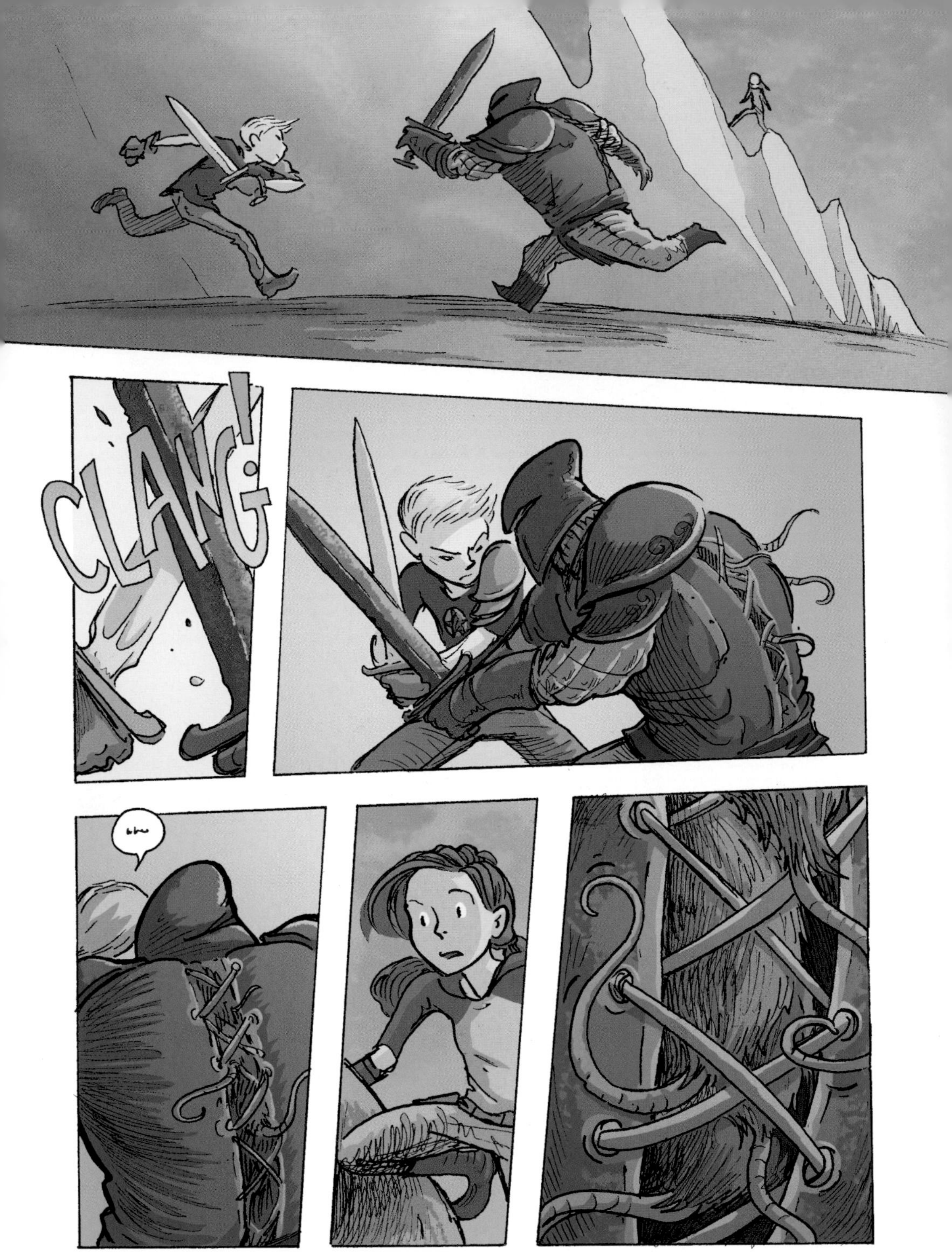
CLANG!

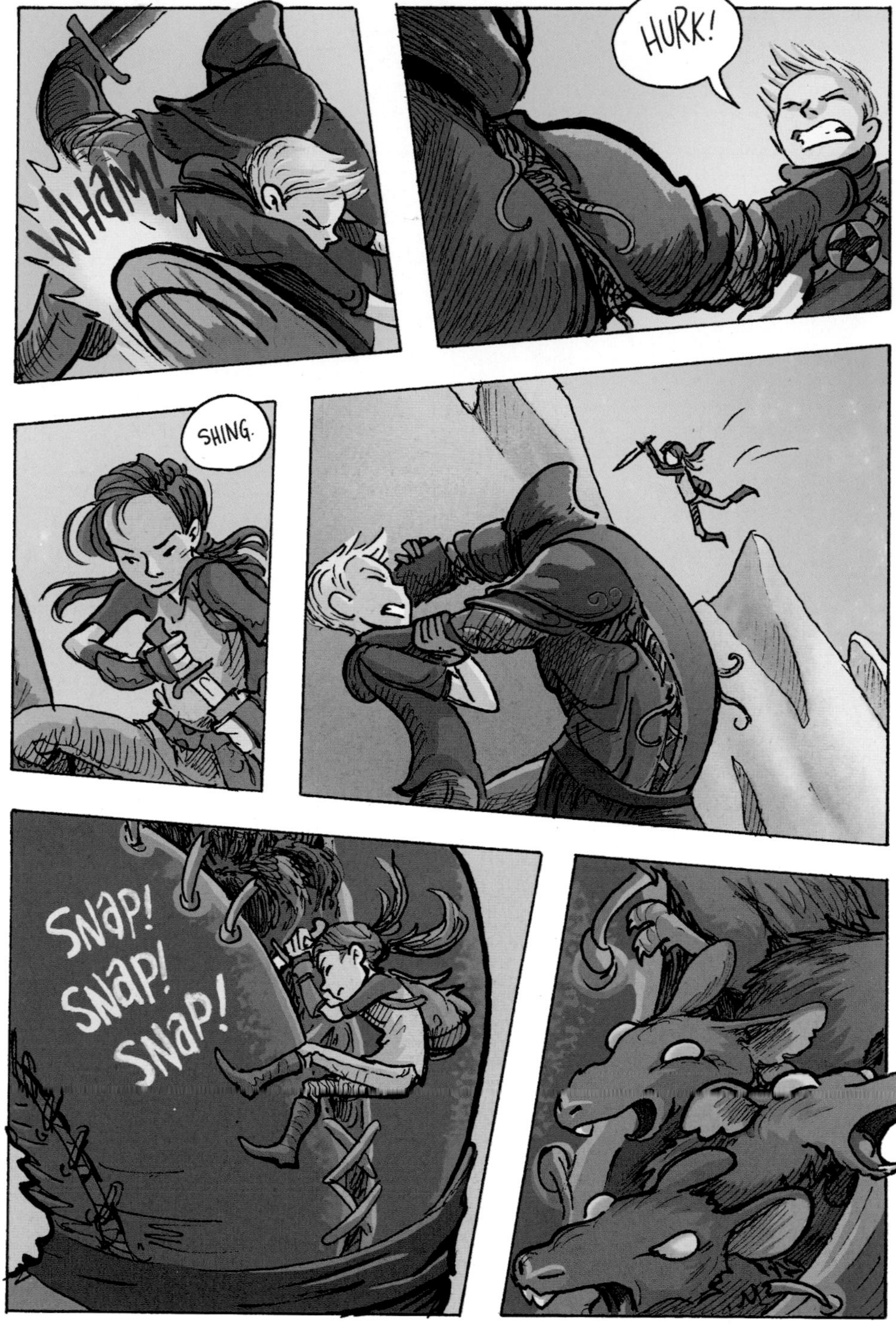
WHAM!
HURK!
SHING.
SNAP!
SNAP!
SNAP!

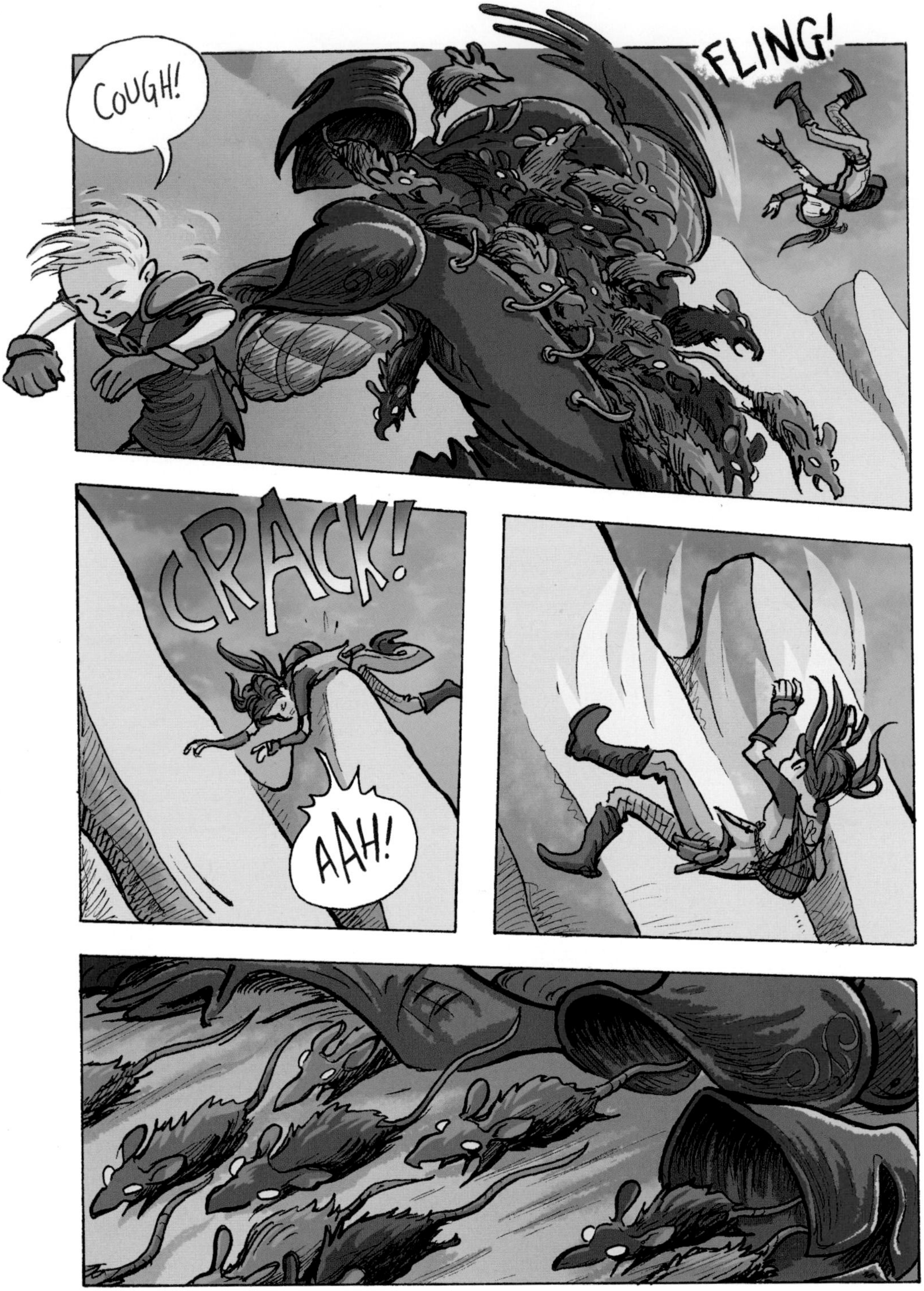
COUGH!
FLING!
CRACK!
AAH!

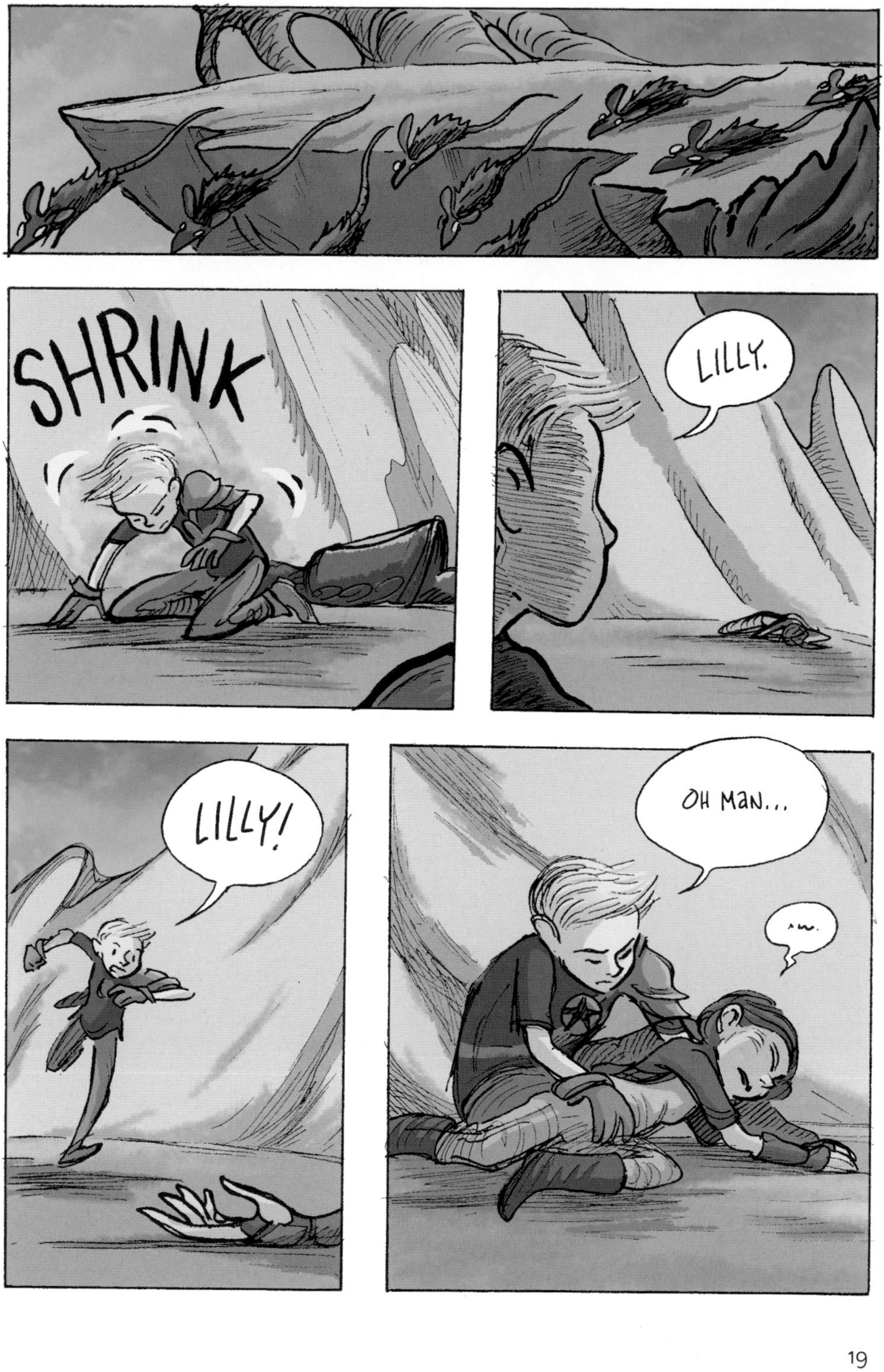
SHRINK
LILLY.
LILLY!
OH MAN...
aw.

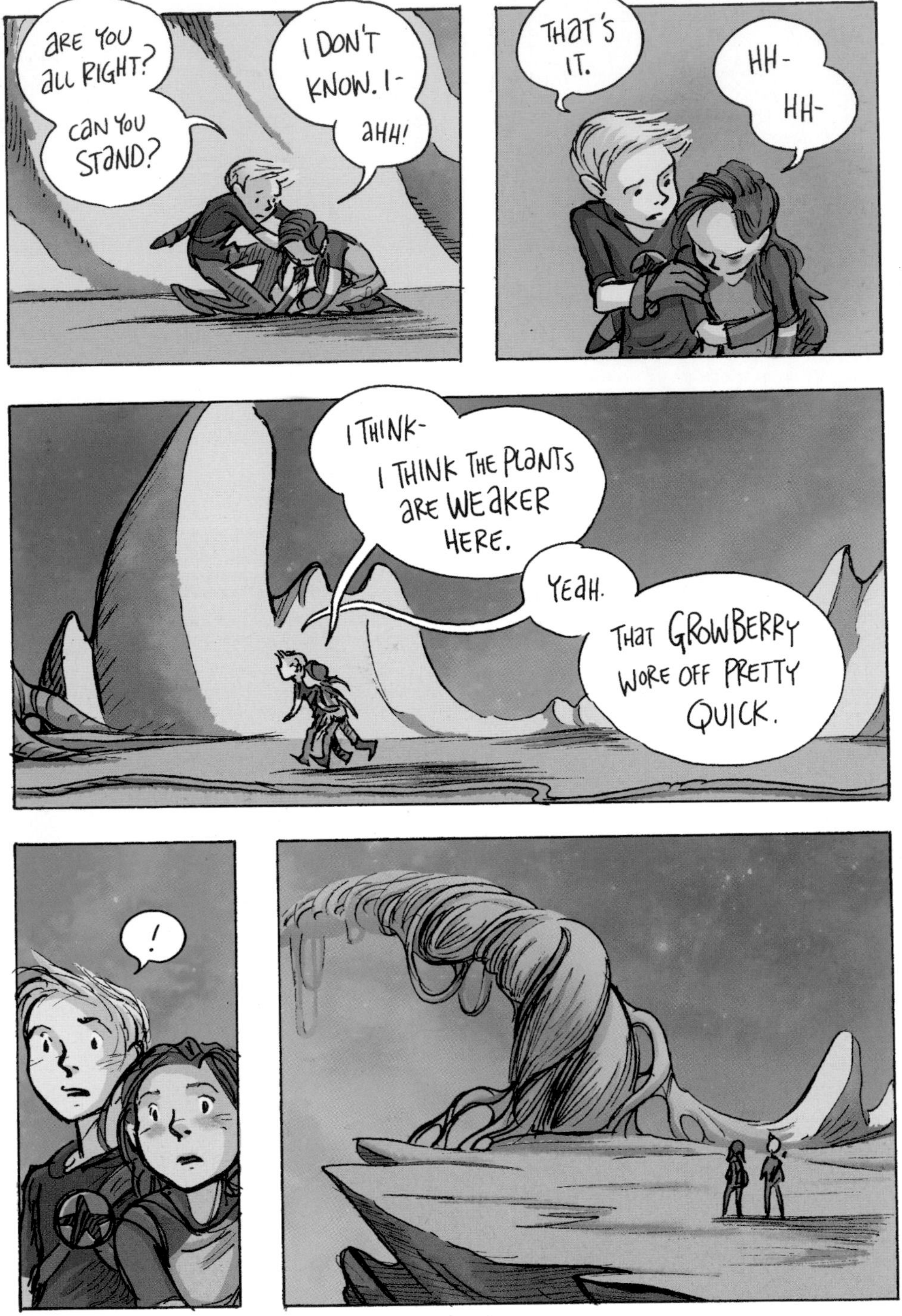
ARE YOU ALL RIGHT?
CAN YOU STAND?
I DON'T KNOW. I-
AHH!
THAT'S IT.
HH-
HH-
I THINK-
I THINK THE PLANTS ARE WEAKER HERE.
YEAH.
THAT GROWBERRY WORE OFF PRETTY QUICK.
!

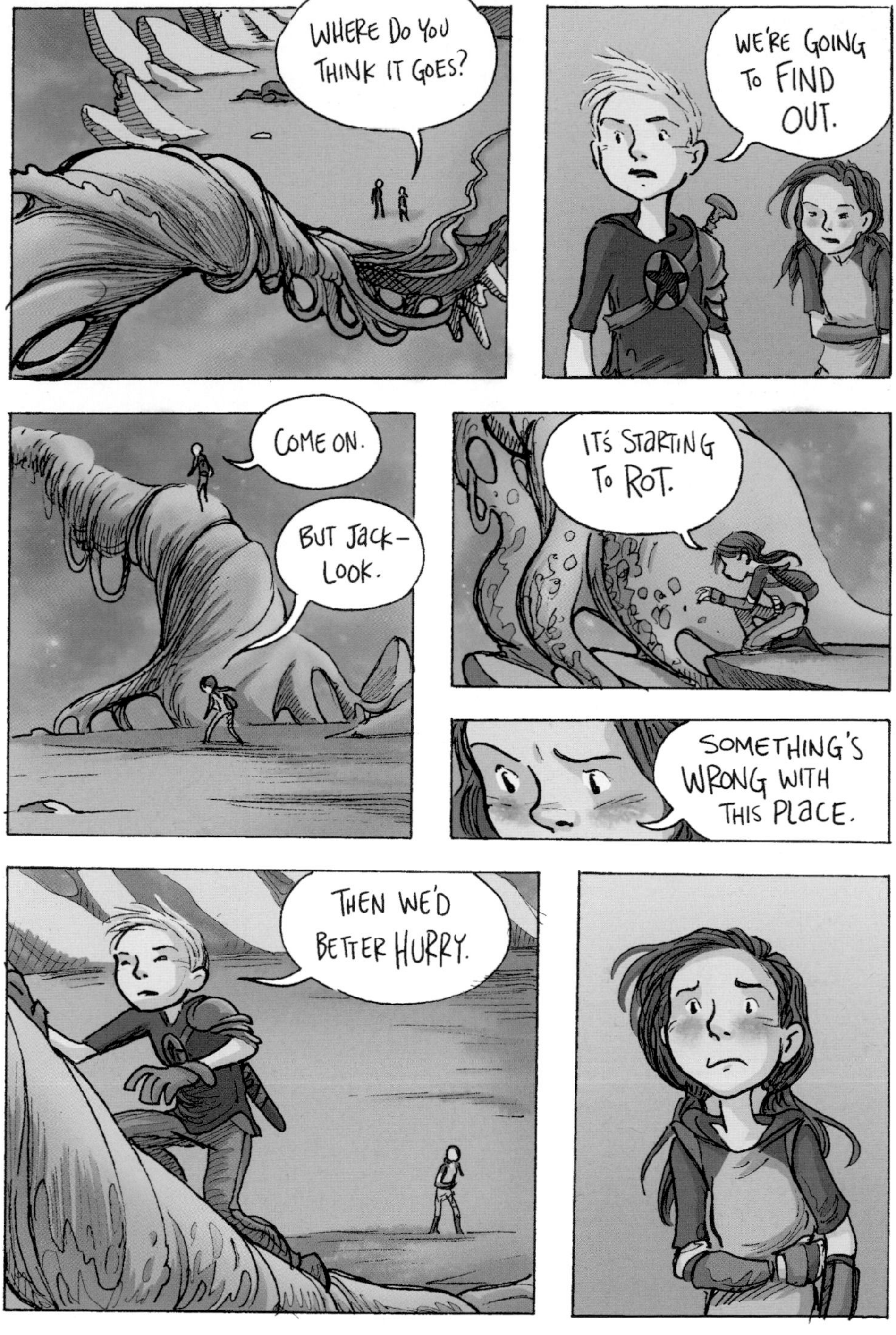
WHERE DO YOU THINK IT GOES?
WE'RE GOING TO FIND OUT.
COME ON.
BUT JACK-LOOK.
IT'S STARTING TO ROT.
SOMETHING'S WRONG WITH THIS PLACE.
THEN WE'D BETTER HURRY.

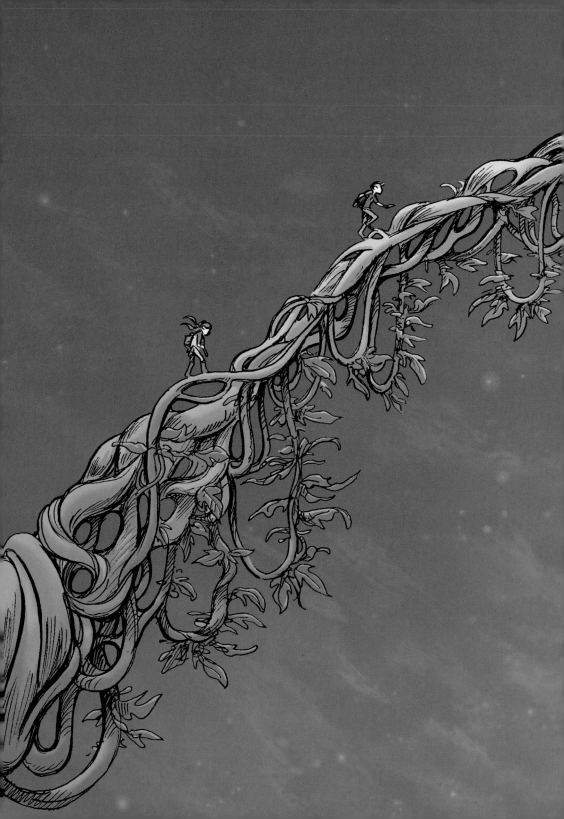

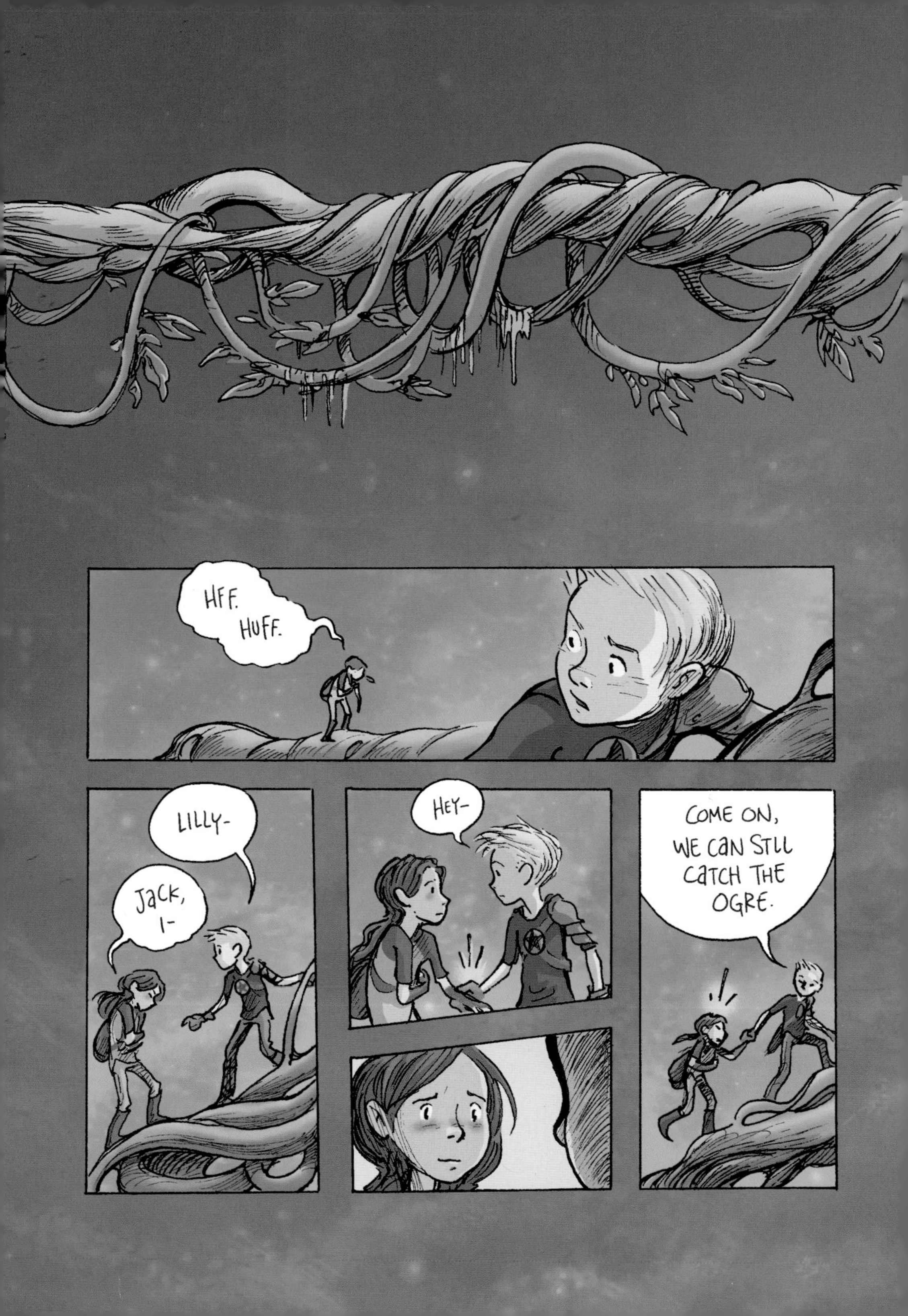
HFF. HUFF.
LILLY-
JACK, I-
HEY-
COME ON, WE CAN STILL CATCH THE OGRE.

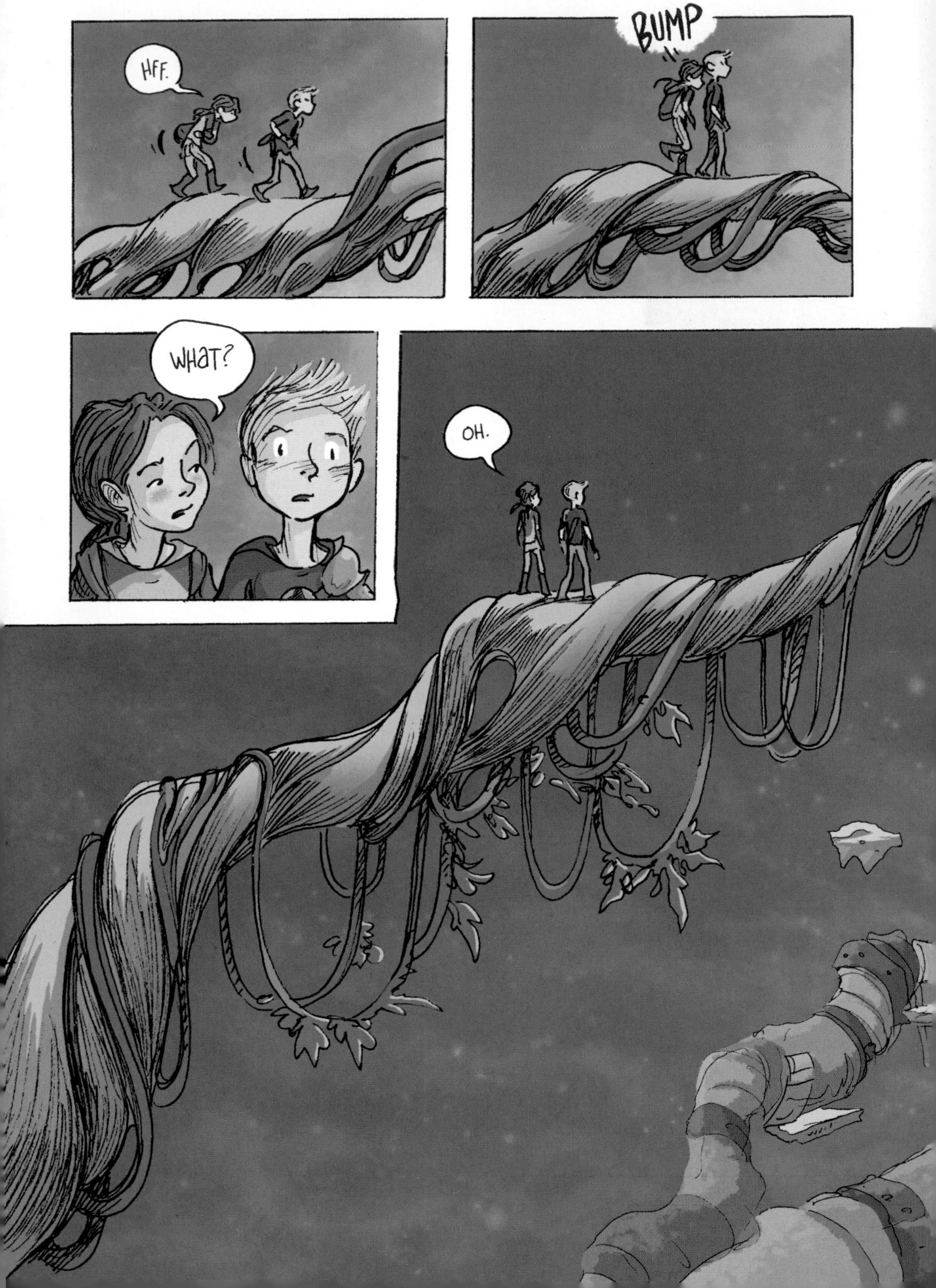
HFF.
BUMP
WHAT?
OH.

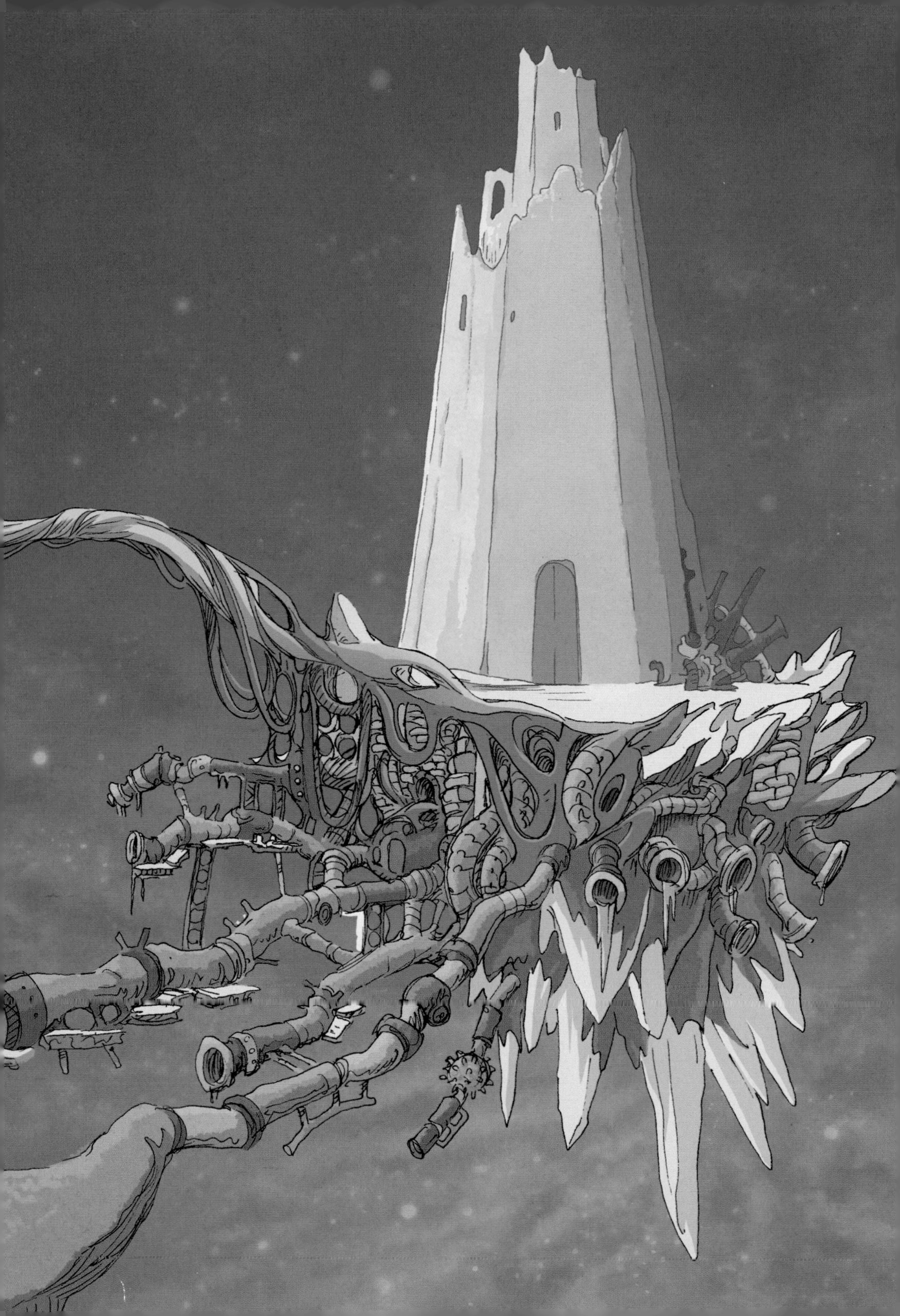

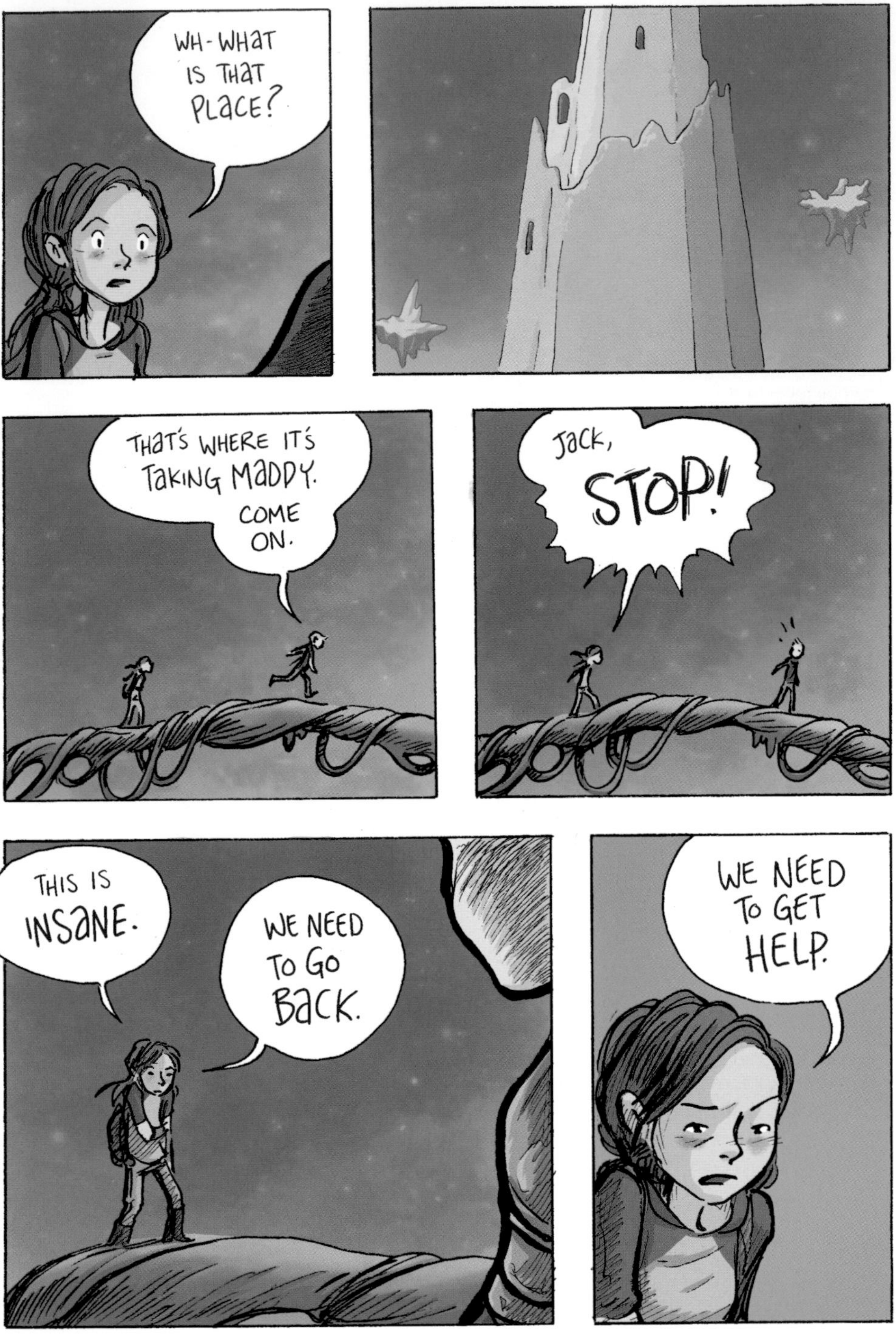
WH-WHAT IS THAT PLACE?
THAT'S WHERE IT'S TAKING MADDY.
COME ON.
JACK, STOP!
THIS IS INSANE.
WE NEED TO GO BACK.
WE NEED TO GET HELP.

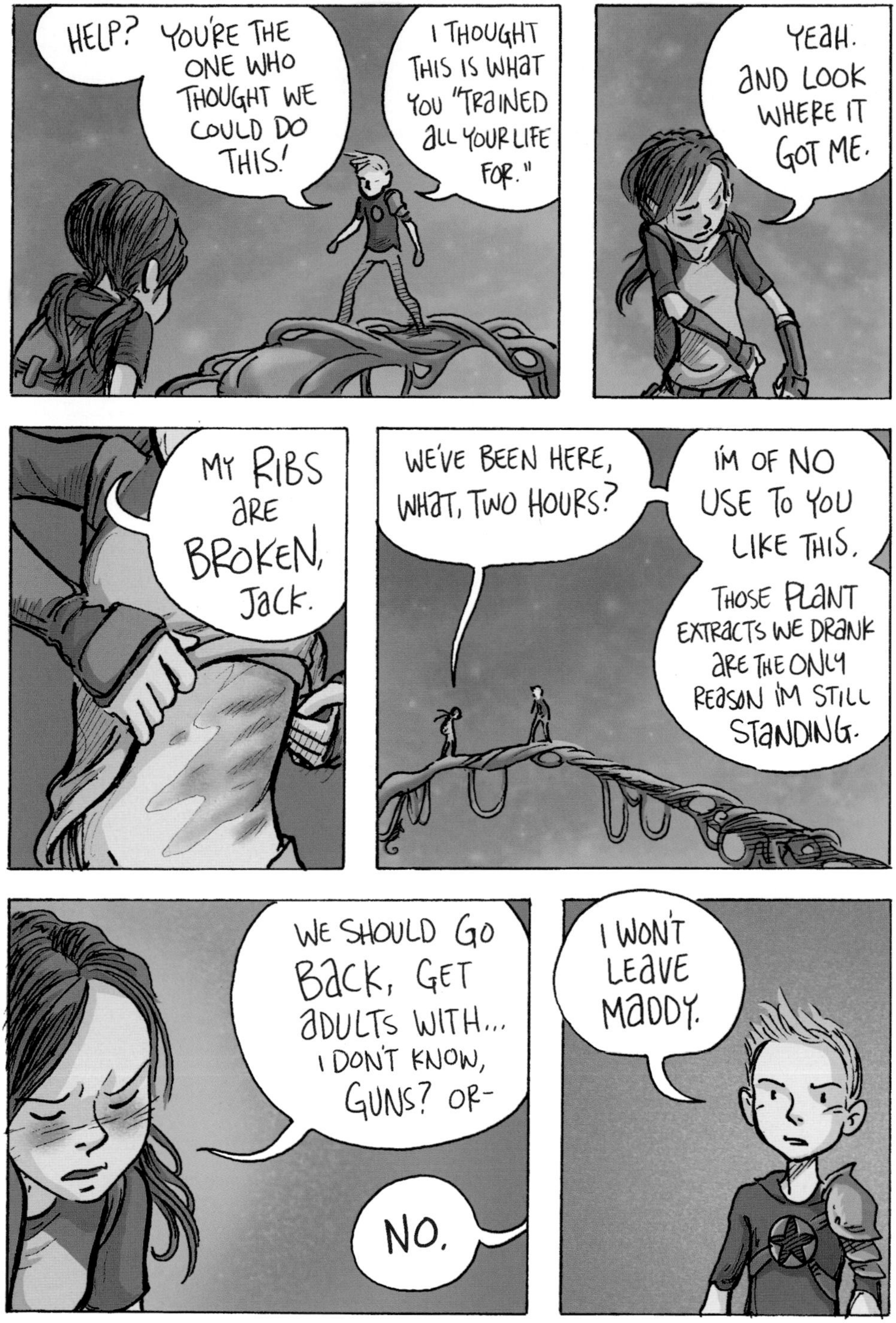
HELP? YOU'RE THE ONE WHO THOUGHT WE COULD DO THIS!
I THOUGHT THIS IS WHAT YOU "TRAINED ALL YOUR LIFE FOR."
YEAH. AND LOOK WHERE IT GOT ME.
MY RIBS ARE BROKEN, JACK.
WE'VE BEEN HERE, WHAT, TWO HOURS?
I'M OF NO USE TO YOU LIKE THIS.
THOSE PLANT EXTRACTS WE DRANK ARE THE ONLY REASON I'M STILL STANDING.
WE SHOULD GO BACK, GET ADULTS WITH... I DON'T KNOW, GUNS? OR-
NO.
I WON'T LEAVE MADDY.

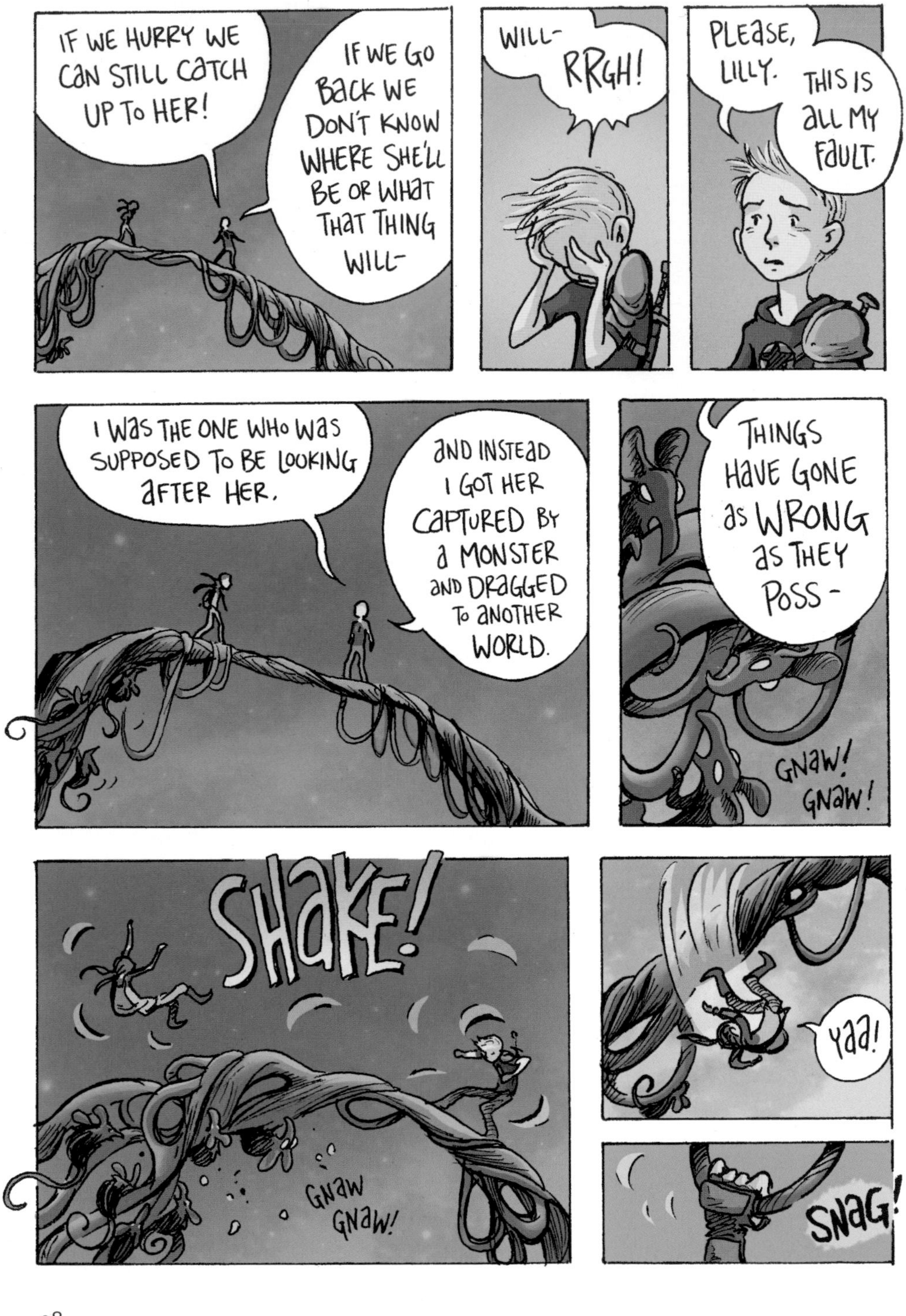
IF WE HURRY WE CAN STILL CATCH UP TO HER!
IF WE GO BACK WE DON'T KNOW WHERE SHE'LL BE OR WHAT THAT THING WILL-
WILL-
RRGH!
PLEASE, LILLY.
THIS IS ALL MY FAULT.
I WAS THE ONE WHO WAS SUPPOSED TO BE LOOKING AFTER HER.
AND INSTEAD I GOT HER CAPTURED BY A MONSTER AND DRAGGED TO ANOTHER WORLD.
THINGS HAVE GONE AS WRONG AS THEY POSS -
GNAW! GNAW!
SHAKE!
GNAW GNAW!
YAA!
SNAG!

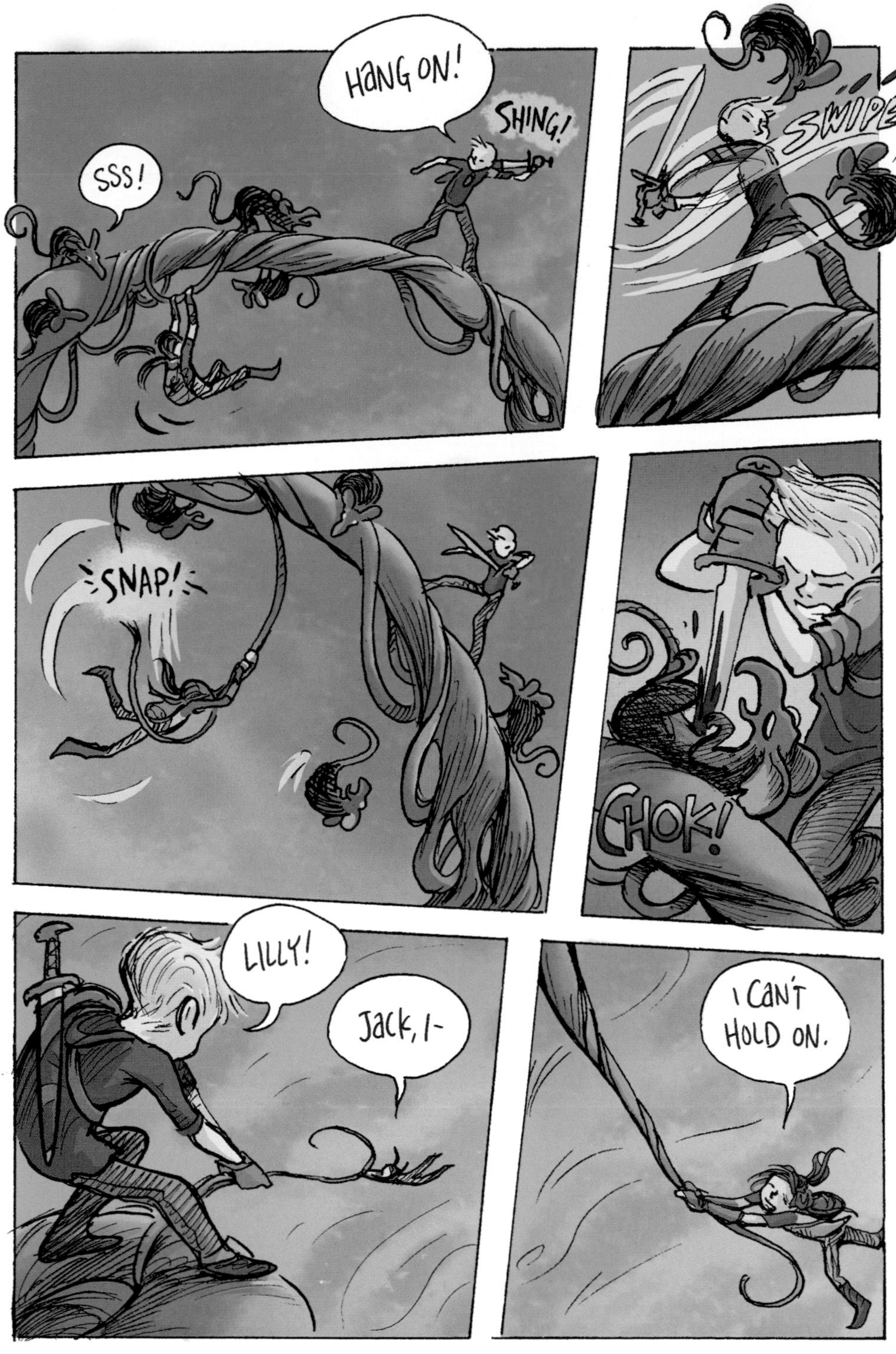
HANG ON!
SHING!
SSS!
SWIPE!
SNAP!
CHOK!
LILLY!
JACK, I-
I CAN'T
HOLD ON.

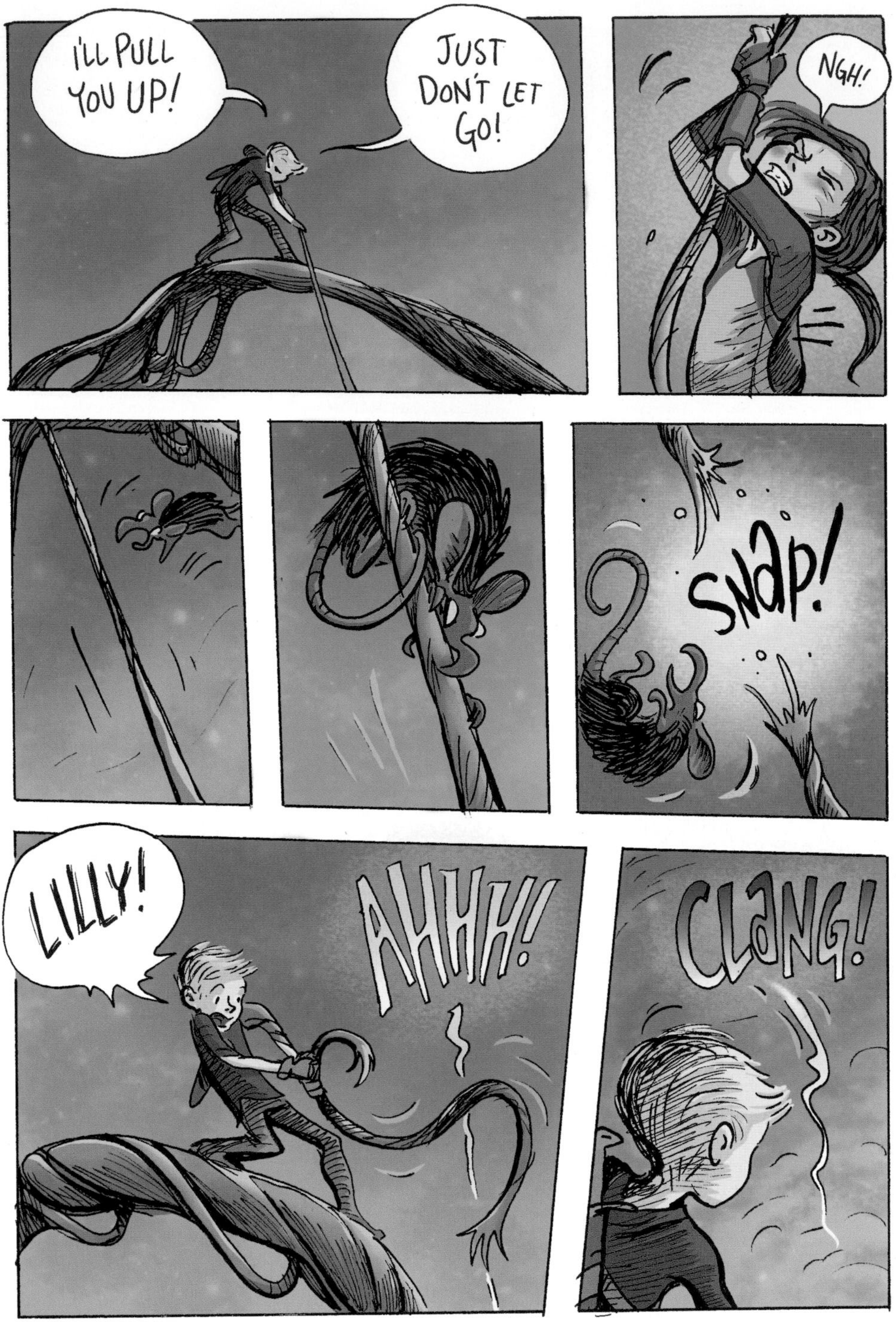
I'LL PULL YOU UP!
JUST DON'T LET GO!
NGH!
SNAP!
LILLY!
AHHH!
CLANG!

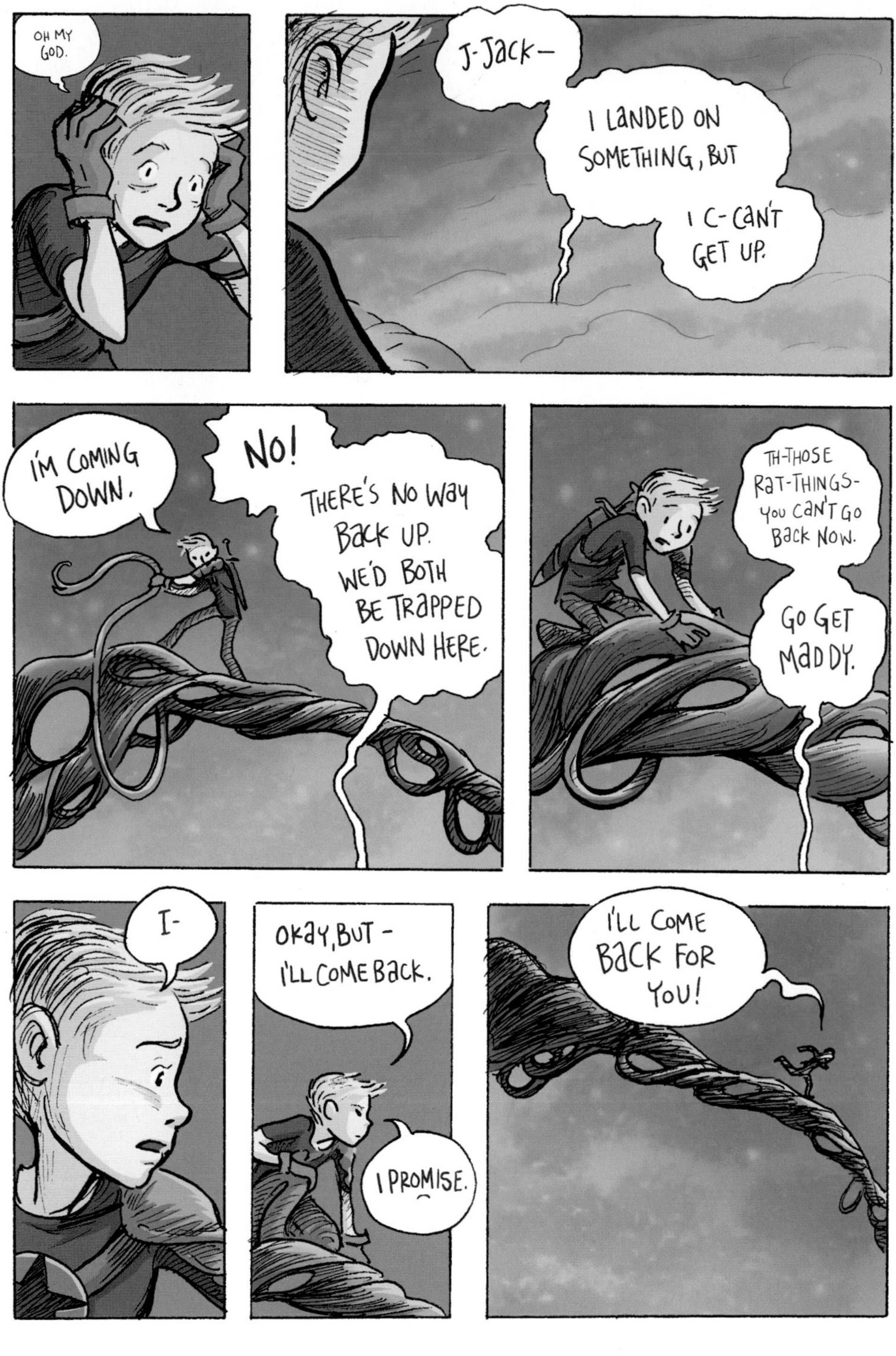
OH MY GOD.
J-Jack—
I LANDED ON SOMETHING, BUT
I C-CAN'T GET UP.
I'M COMING DOWN.
NO!
THERE'S NO WAY BACK UP. WE'D BOTH BE TRAPPED DOWN HERE.
TH-THOSE RAT-THINGS- YOU CAN'T GO BACK NOW.
GO GET MADDY.
I-
OKAY, BUT - I'LL COME BACK.
I PROMISE.
I'LL COME BACK FOR YOU!

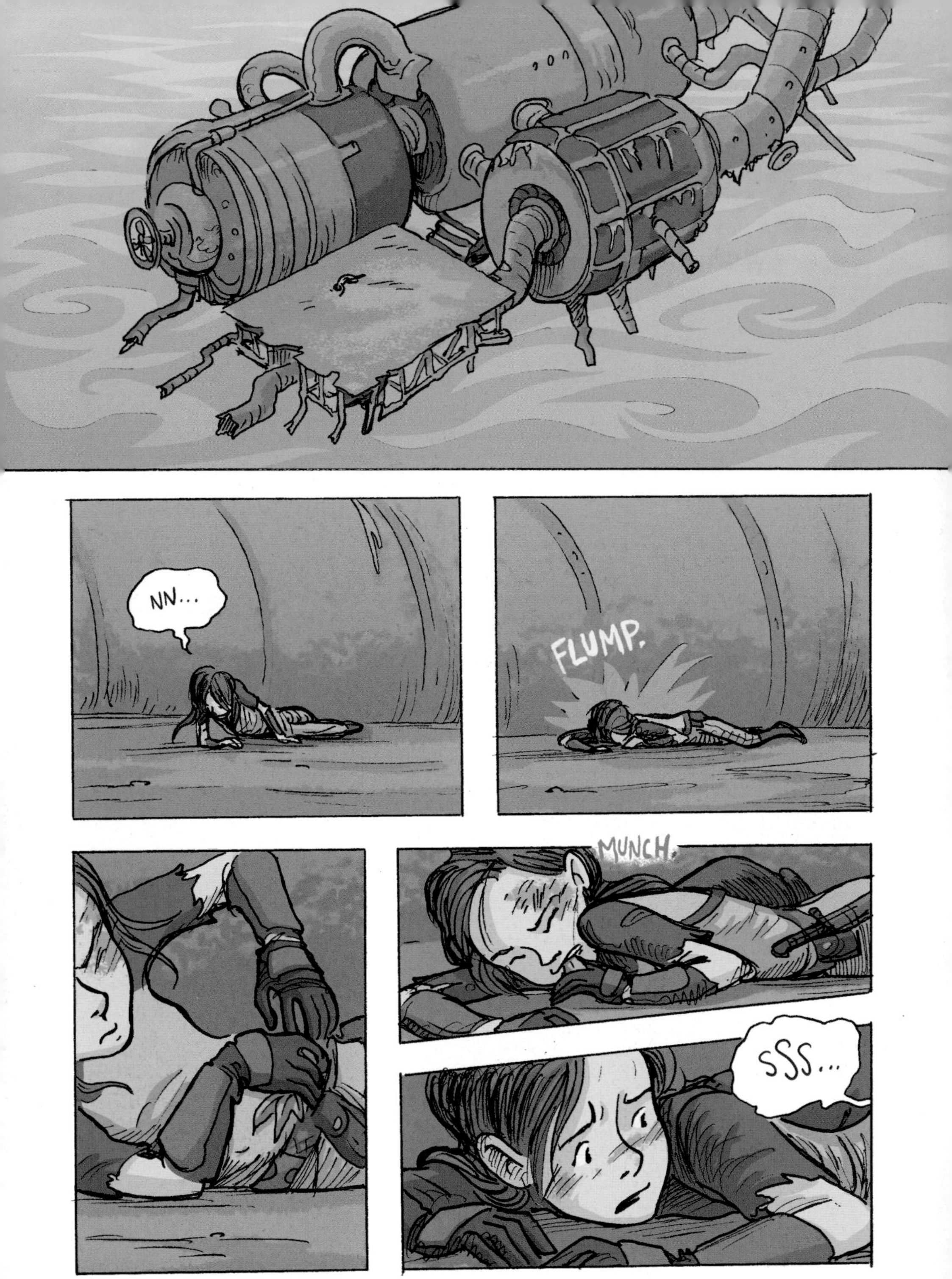
NN...
FLUMP.
MUNCH.
SSS...

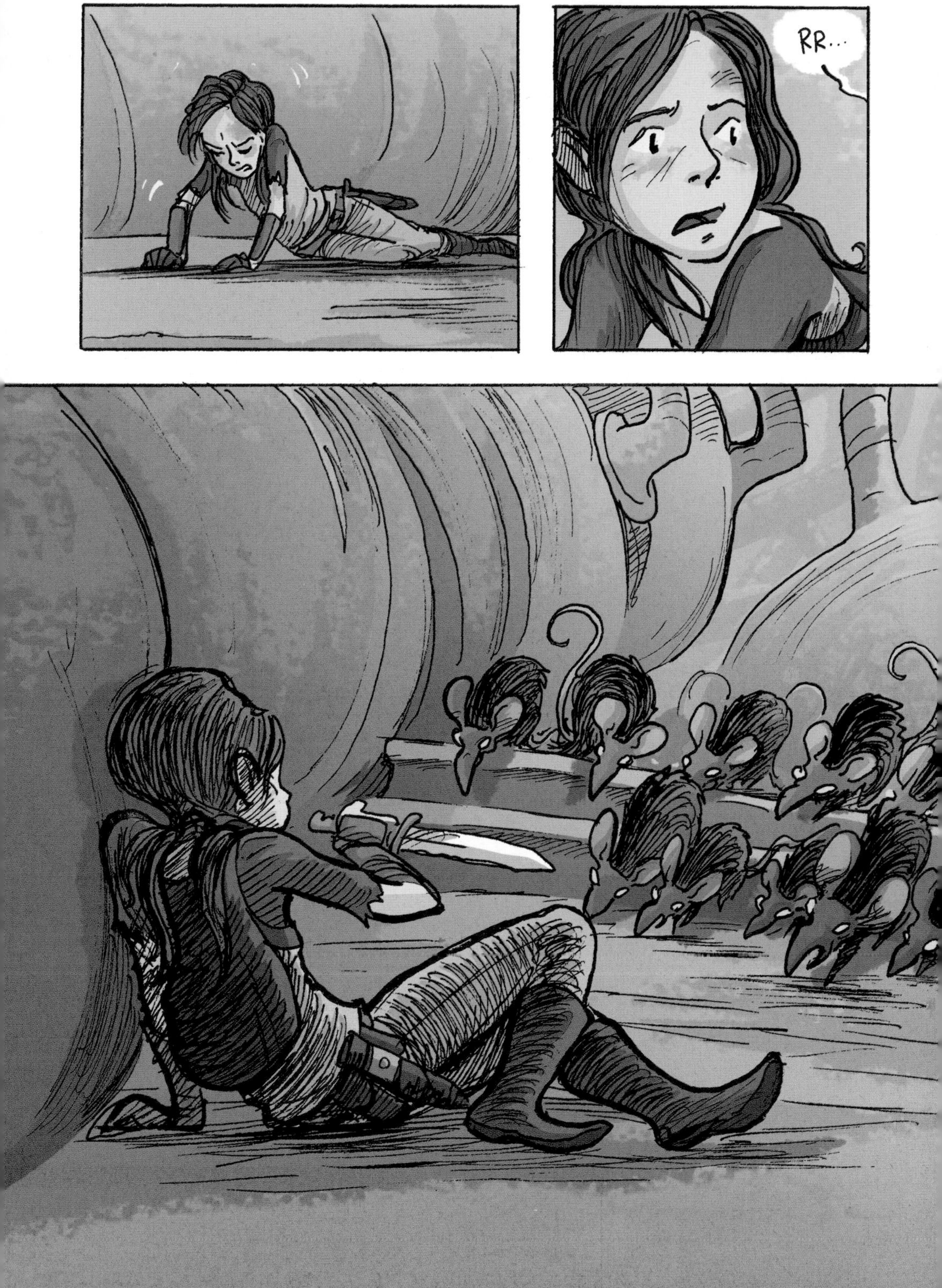
RR...

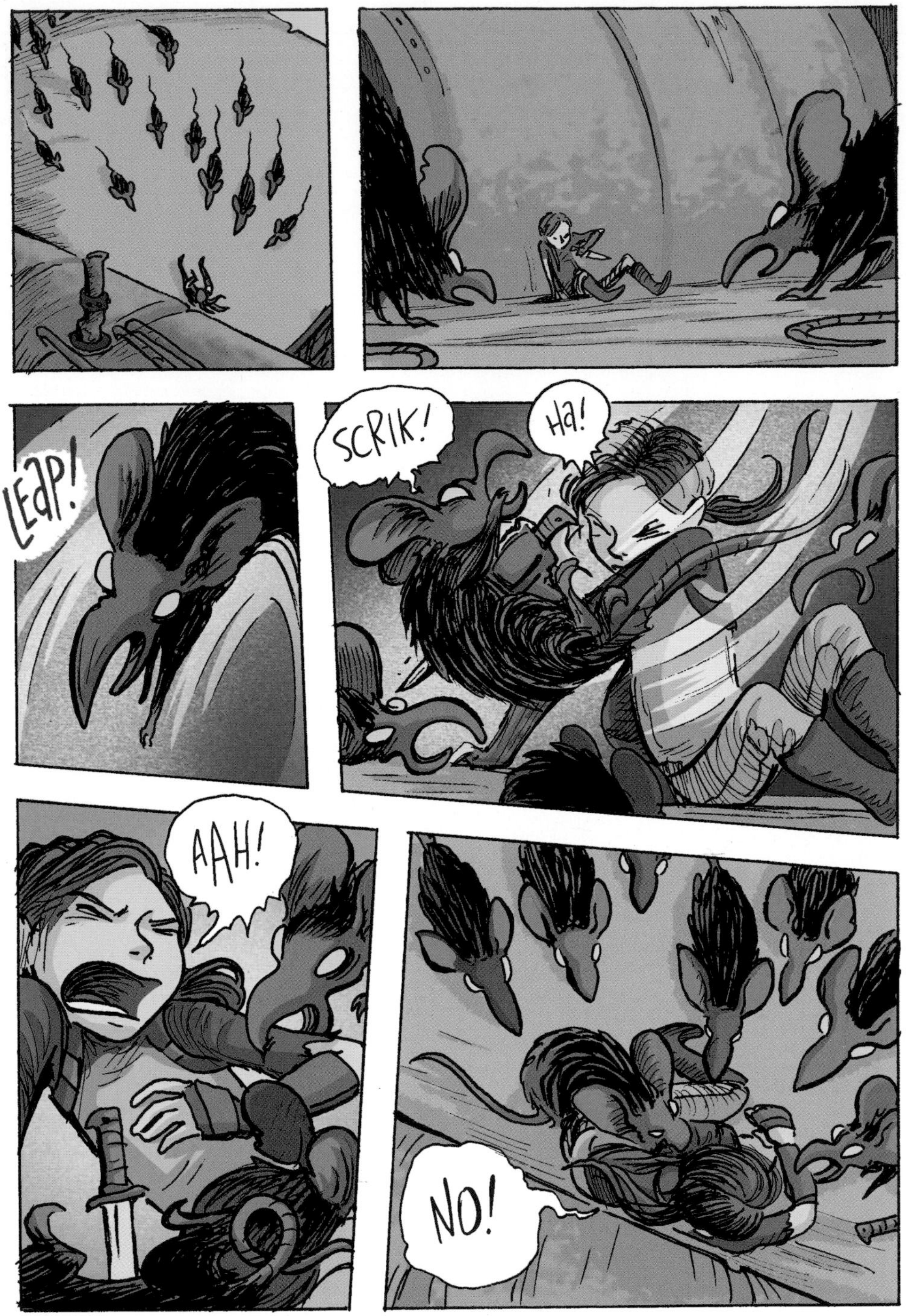
LEAP!
SCRIK!
HA!
AAH!
NO!

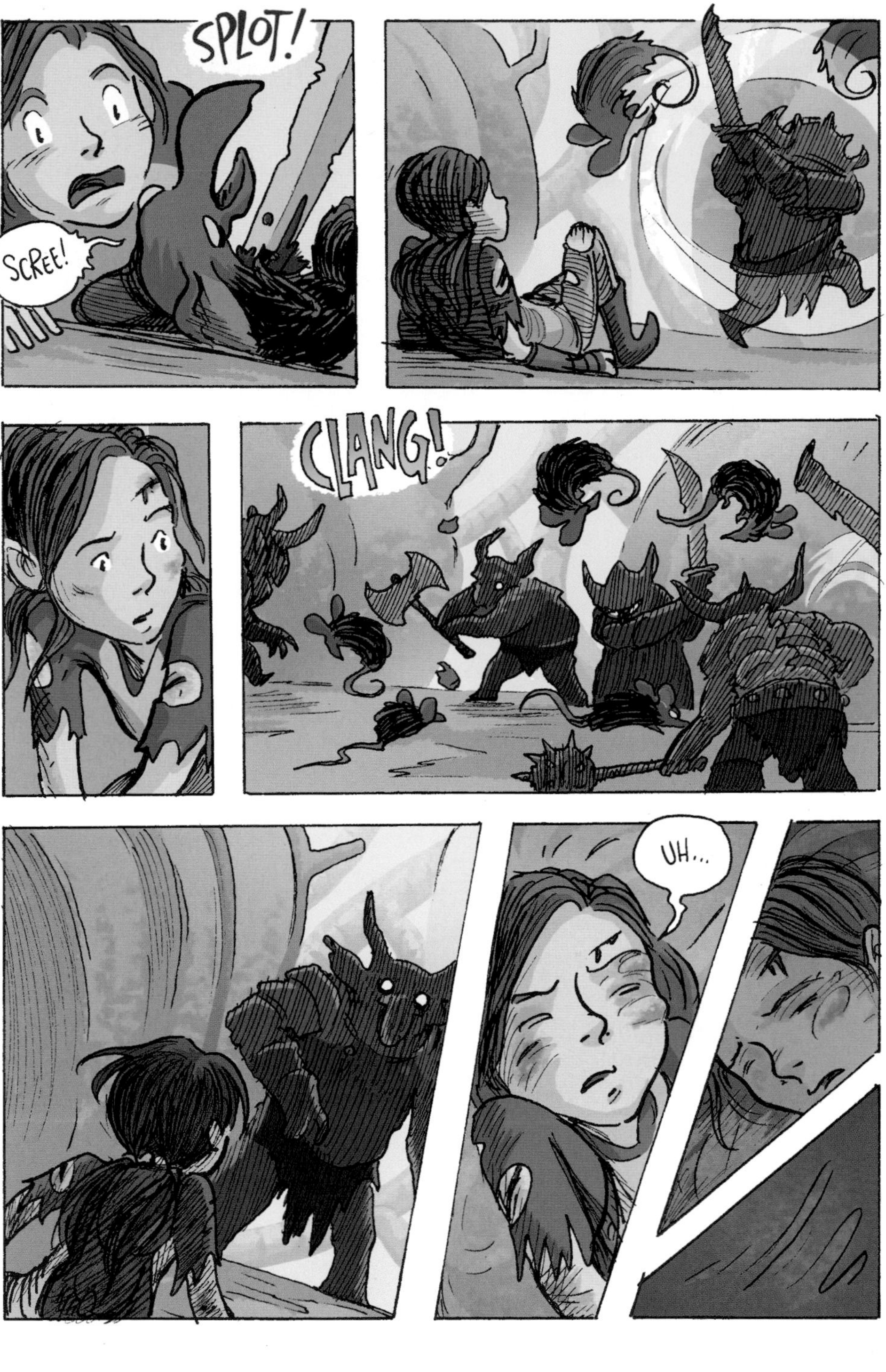
SPLOT!
SCREE!
CLANG!
UH...

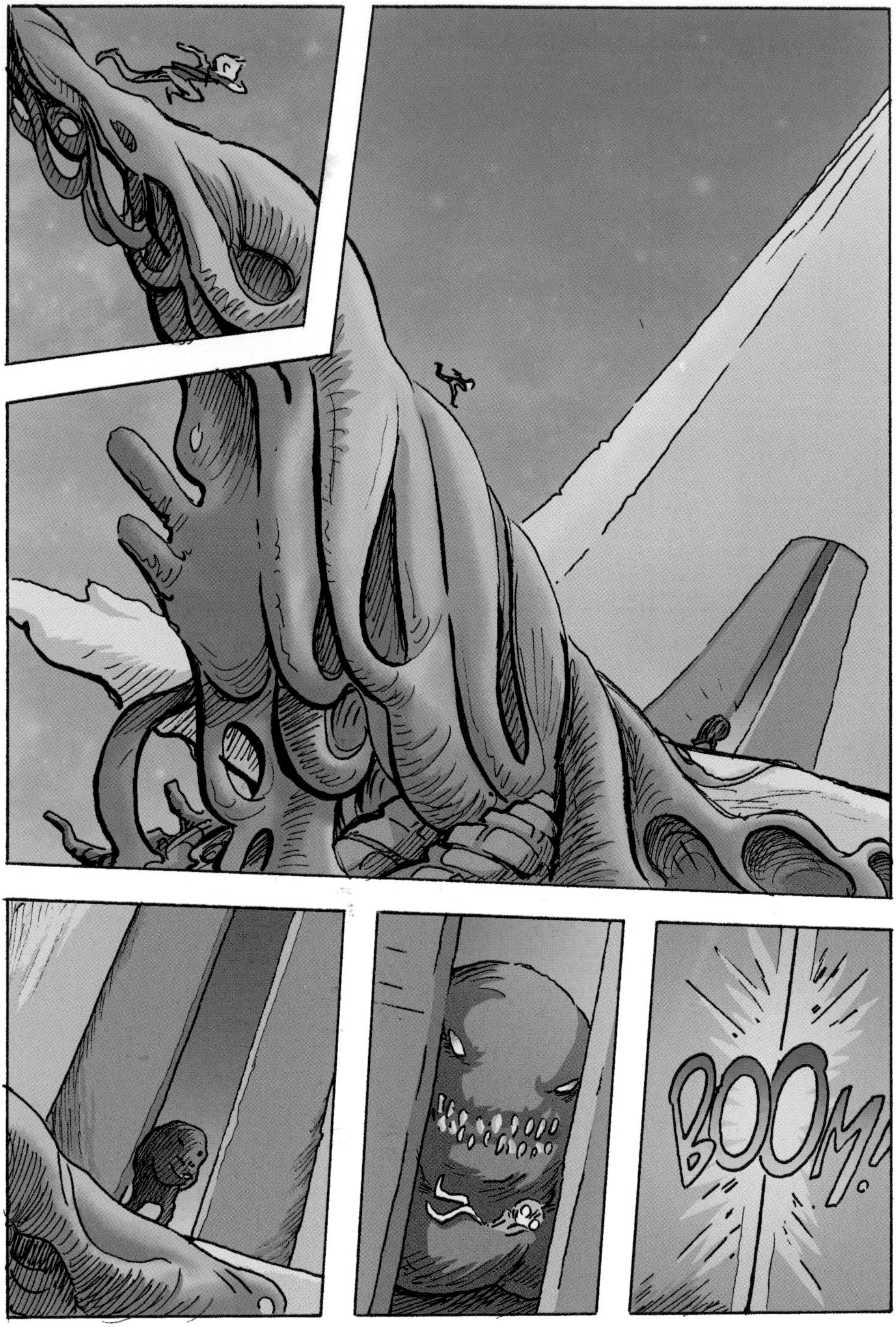
BOOM!

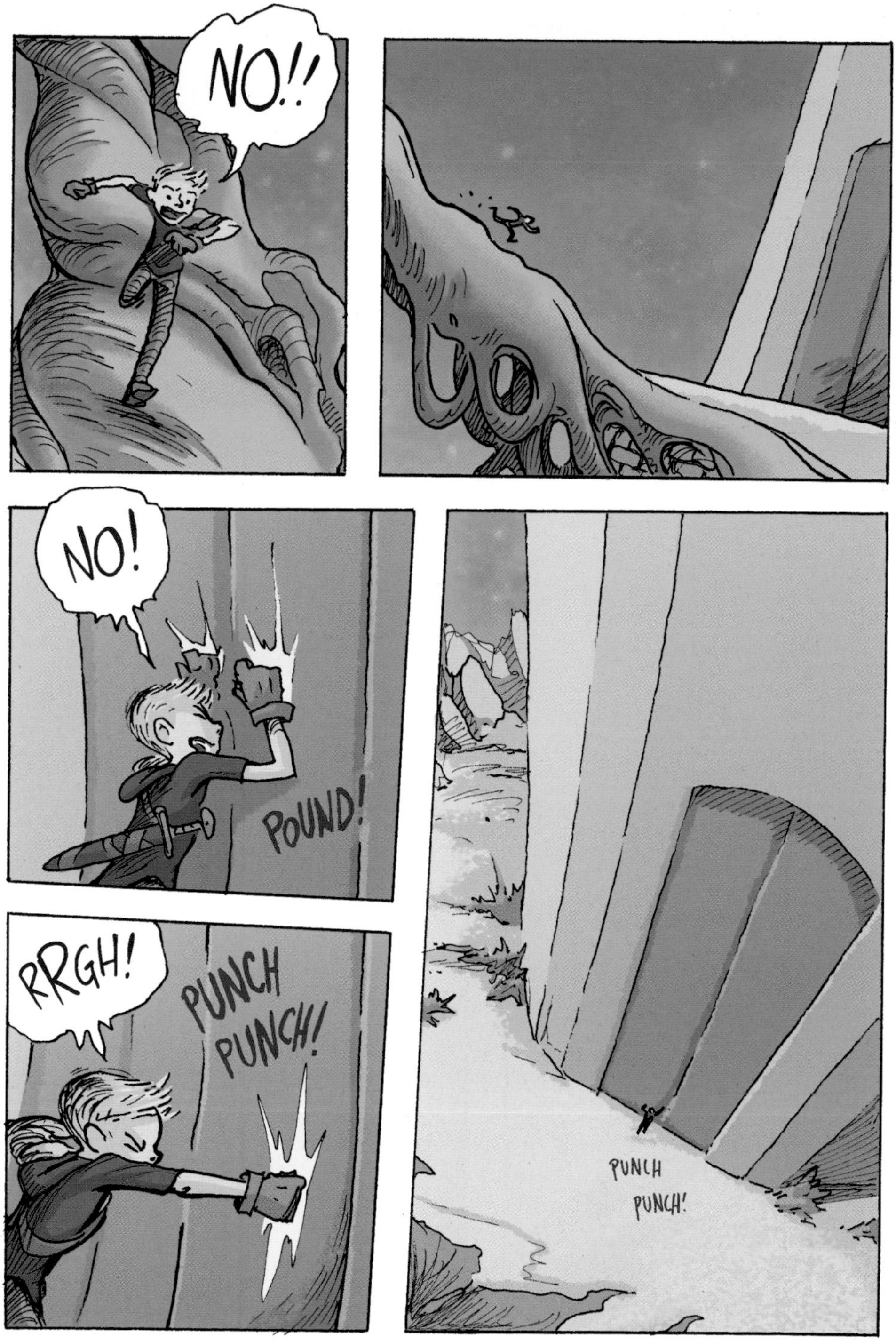
NO!!
NO!
POUND!
RRGH!
PUNCH PUNCH!
PUNCH PUNCH!

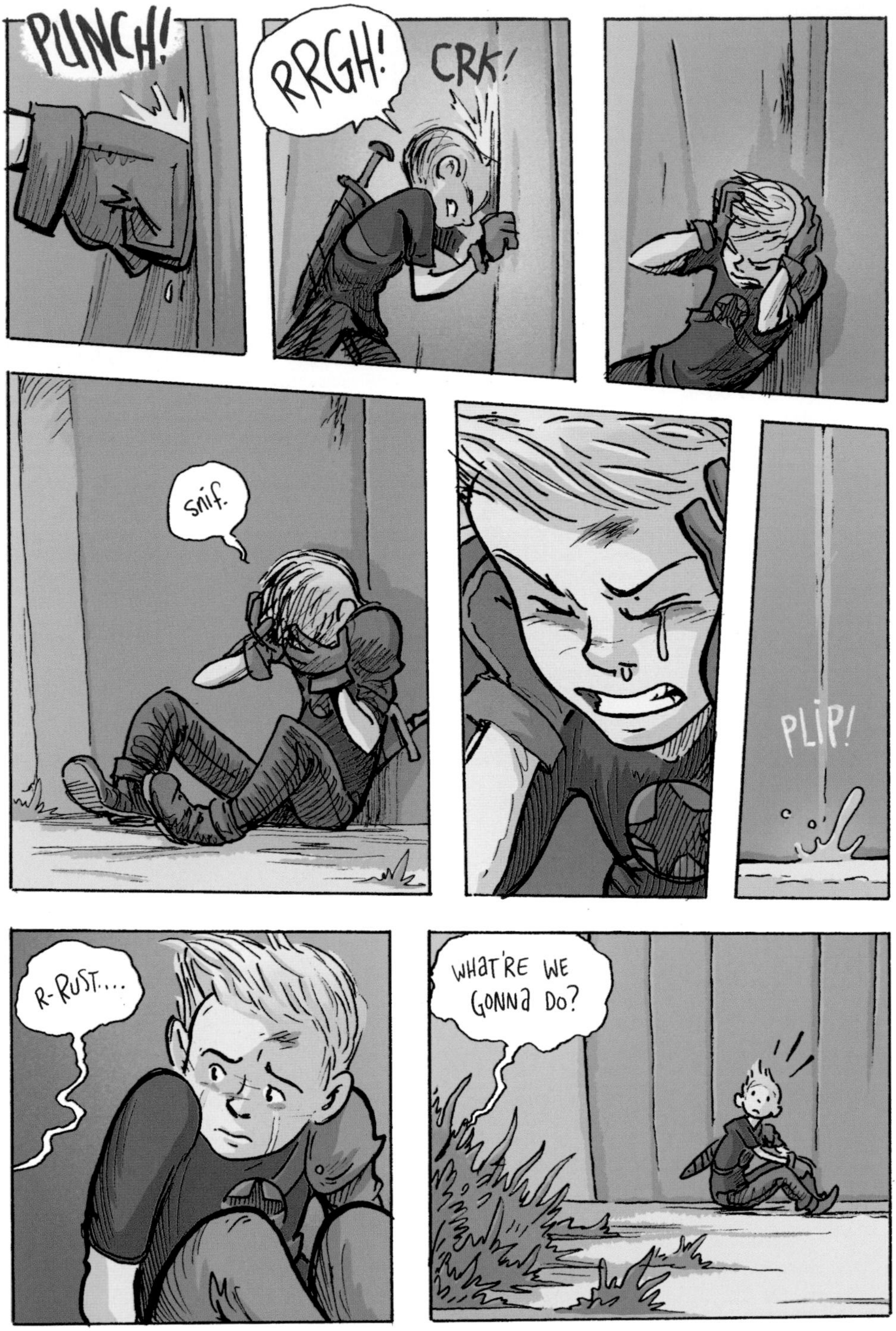
PUNCH!
RRGH!
CRK!
snif.
PLIP!
R-RUST....
WHAT'RE WE GONNA DO?

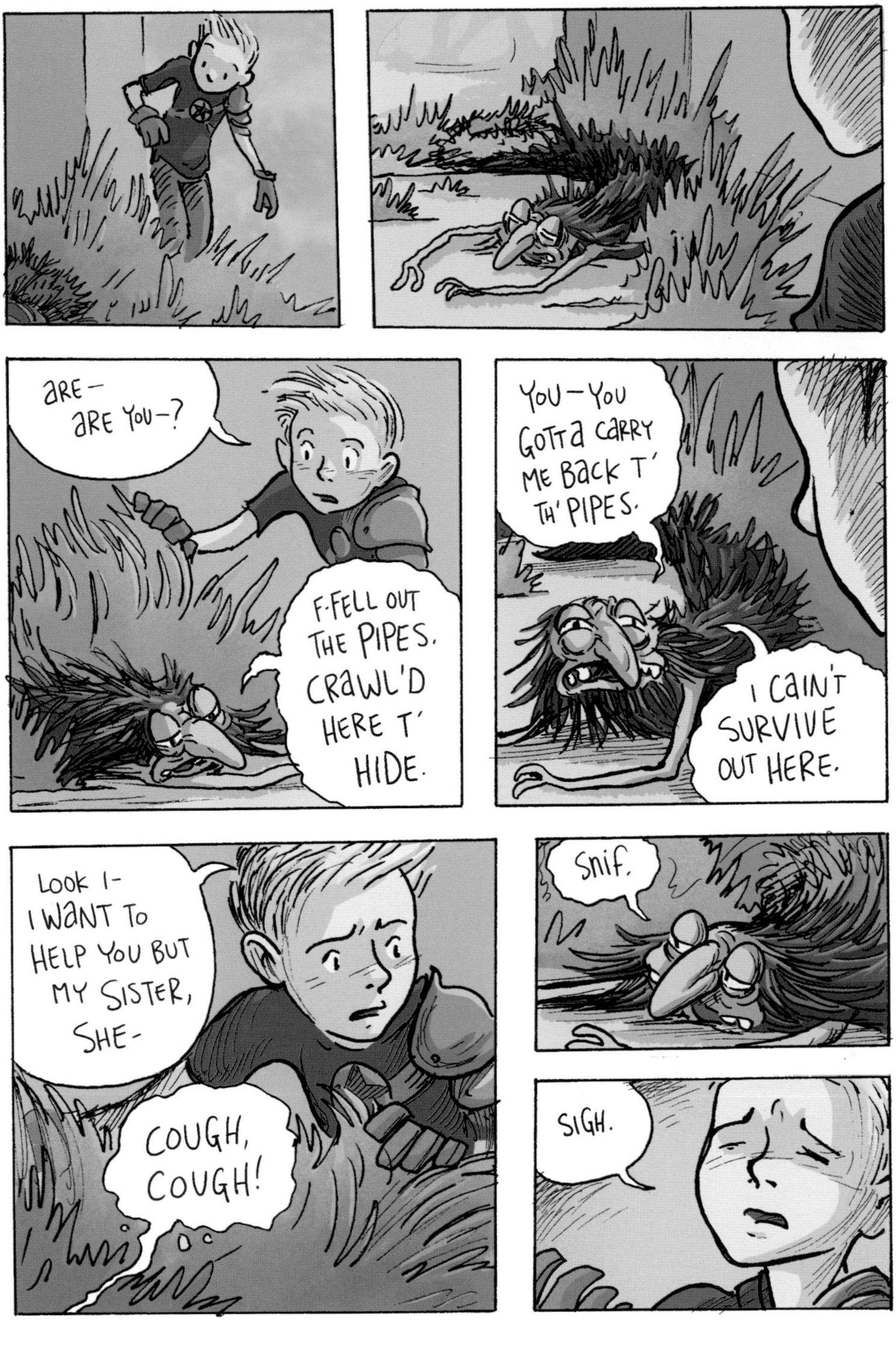
are— are YOU—?
F-FELL OUT THE PIPES. CRAWL'D HERE T' HIDE.
YOU—YOU GOTTA CARRY ME BACK T' TH' PIPES.
I CAIN'T SURVIVE OUT HERE.
LOOK I- I WANT TO HELP YOU BUT MY SISTER, SHE-
COUGH, COUGH!
Snif.
SIGH.

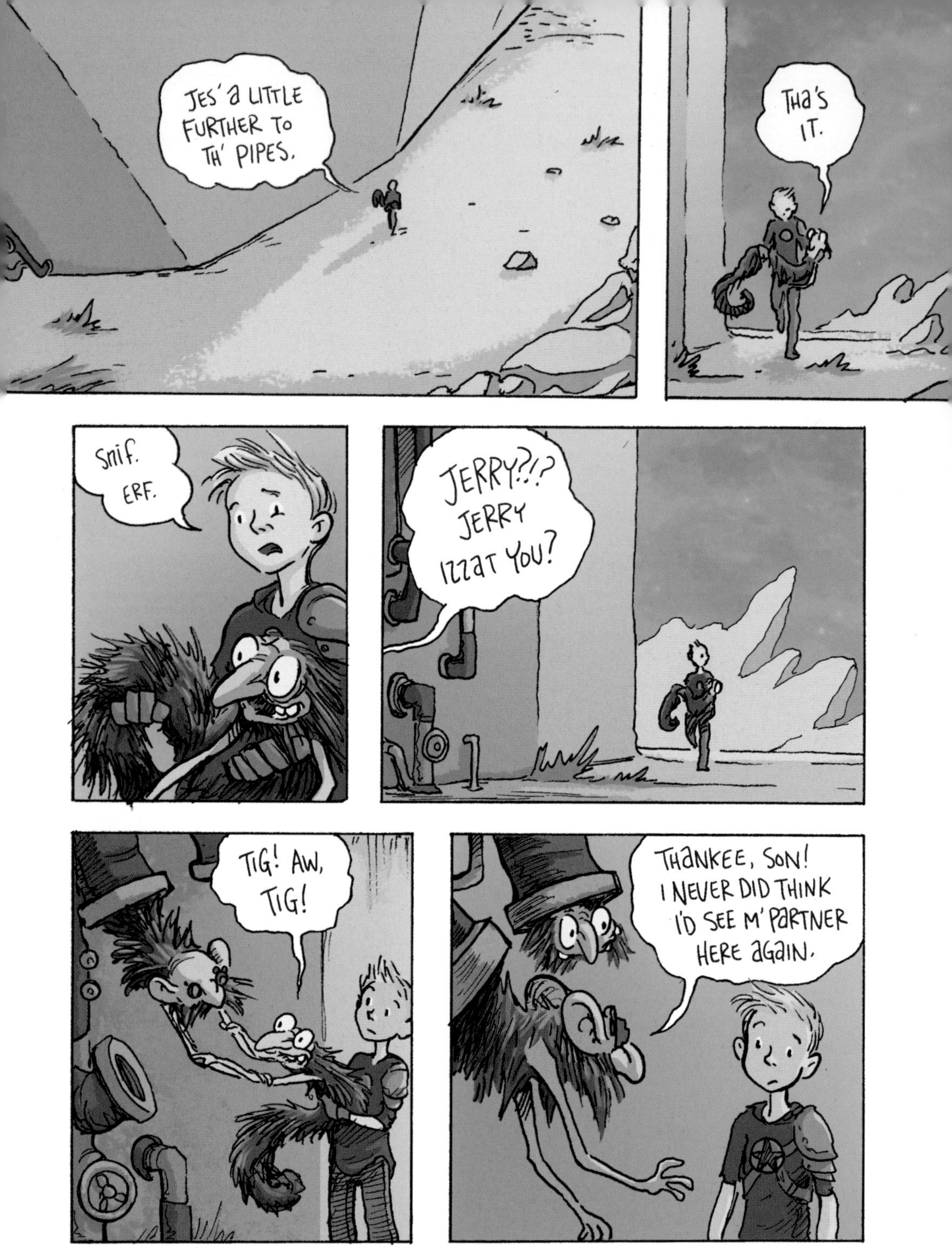
JES' a LITTLE FURTHER TO TH' PIPES.
THa's IT.
Snif. ERF.
JERRY?!? JERRY IZZaT YOU?
TIG! AW, TIG!
THaNKEE, SON! I NEVER DID THINK I'D SEE M' PaRTNER HERE aGaIN.

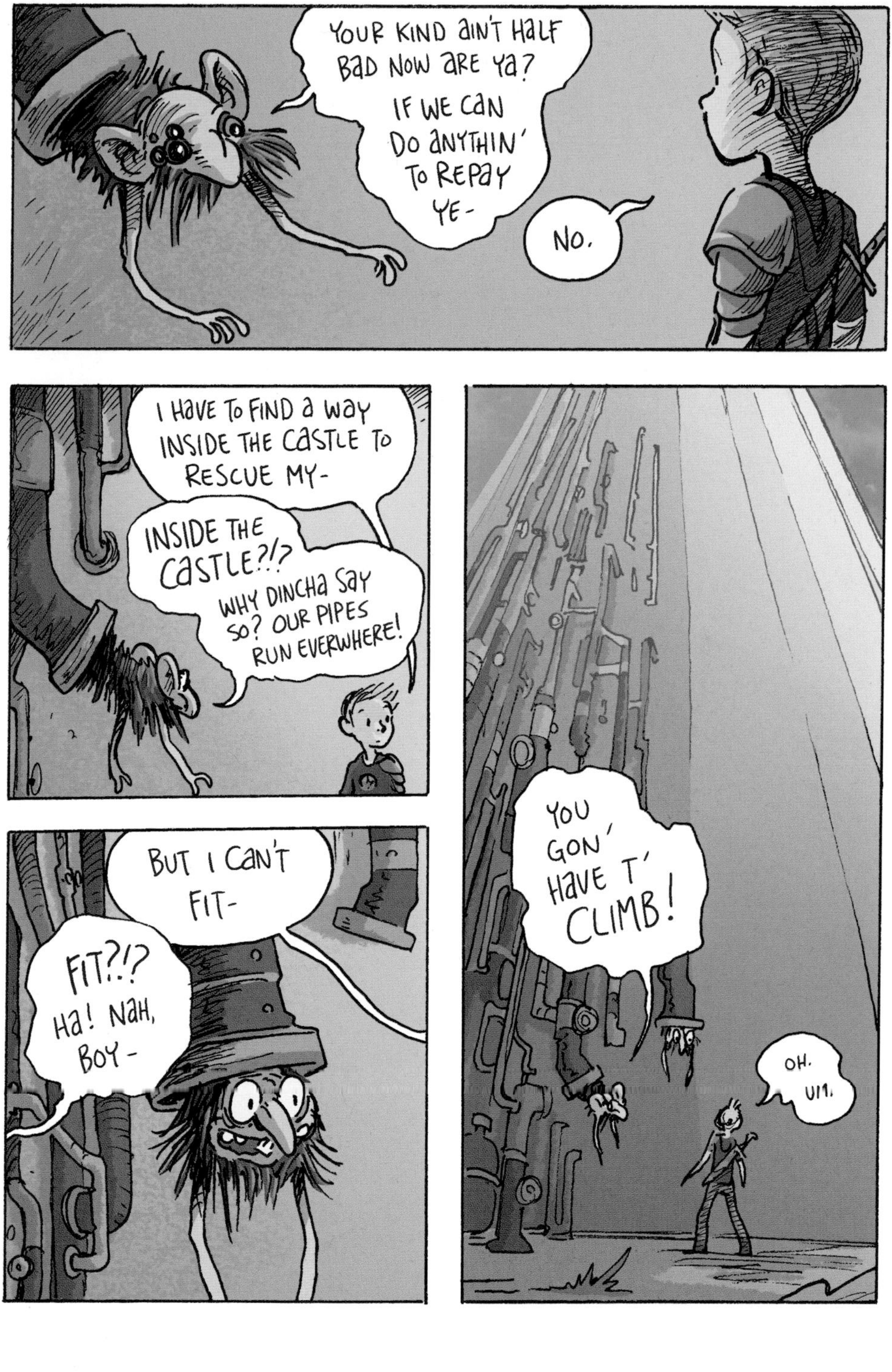
YOUR KIND AIN'T HALF BAD NOW ARE YA? IF WE CAN DO ANYTHIN' TO REPAY YE-
NO.
I HAVE TO FIND A WAY INSIDE THE CASTLE TO RESCUE MY-
INSIDE THE CASTLE?!? WHY DINCHA SAY SO? OUR PIPES RUN EVERWHERE!
BUT I CAN'T FIT-
FIT?!? HA! NAH, BOY-
YOU GON' HAVE T' CLIMB!
OH. UM.

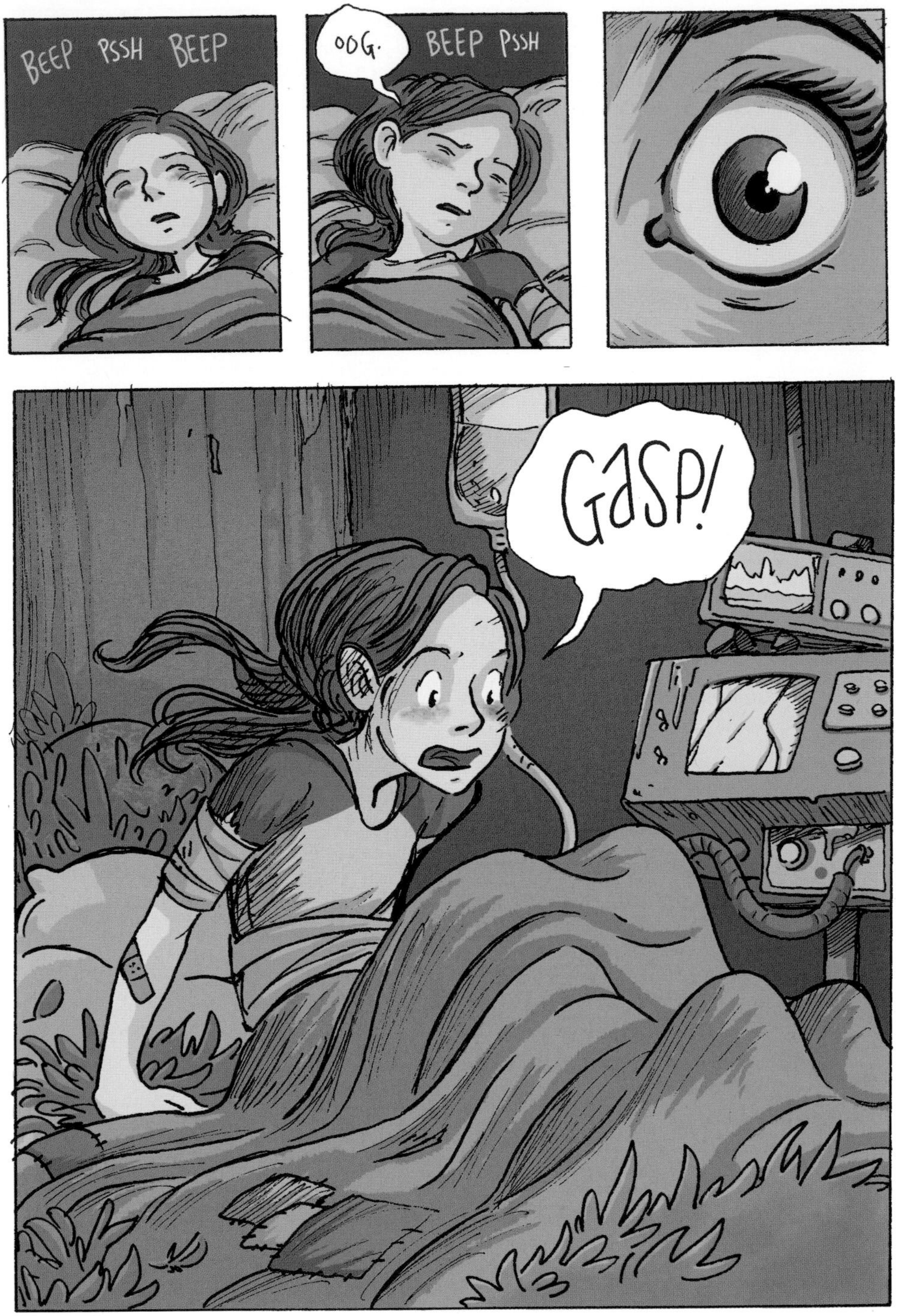
BEEP PSSH BEEP
OOG.
BEEP PSSH
GASP!

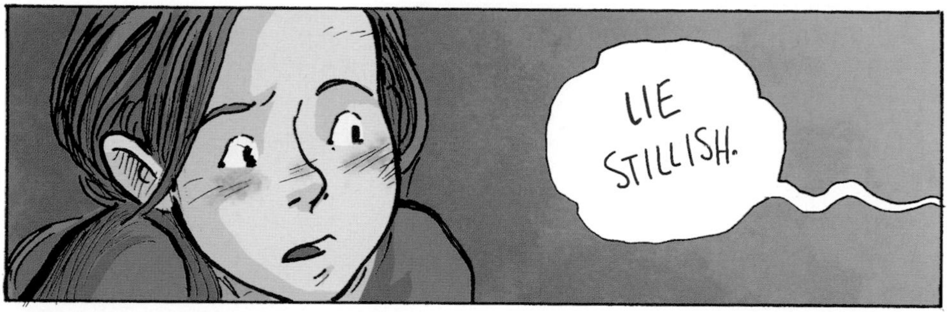
LIE STILLISH.

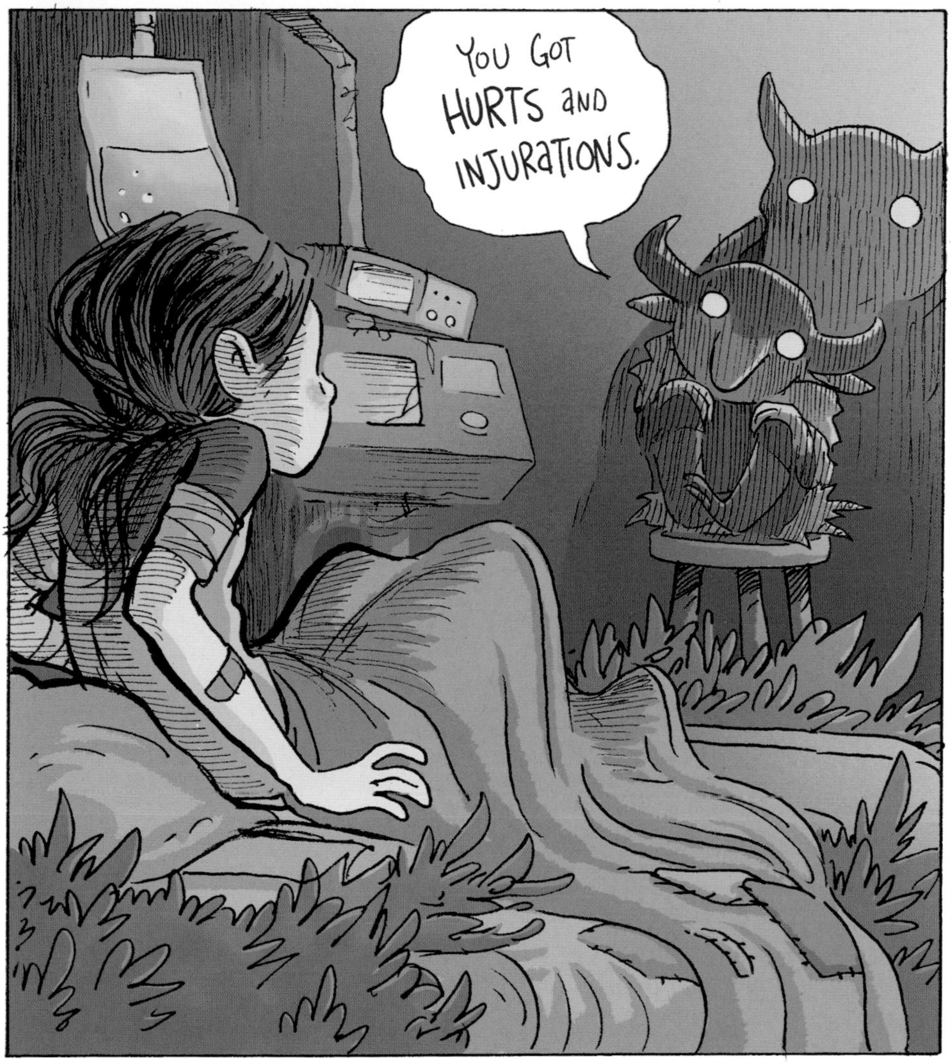
YOU GOT HURTS AND INJURATIONS.

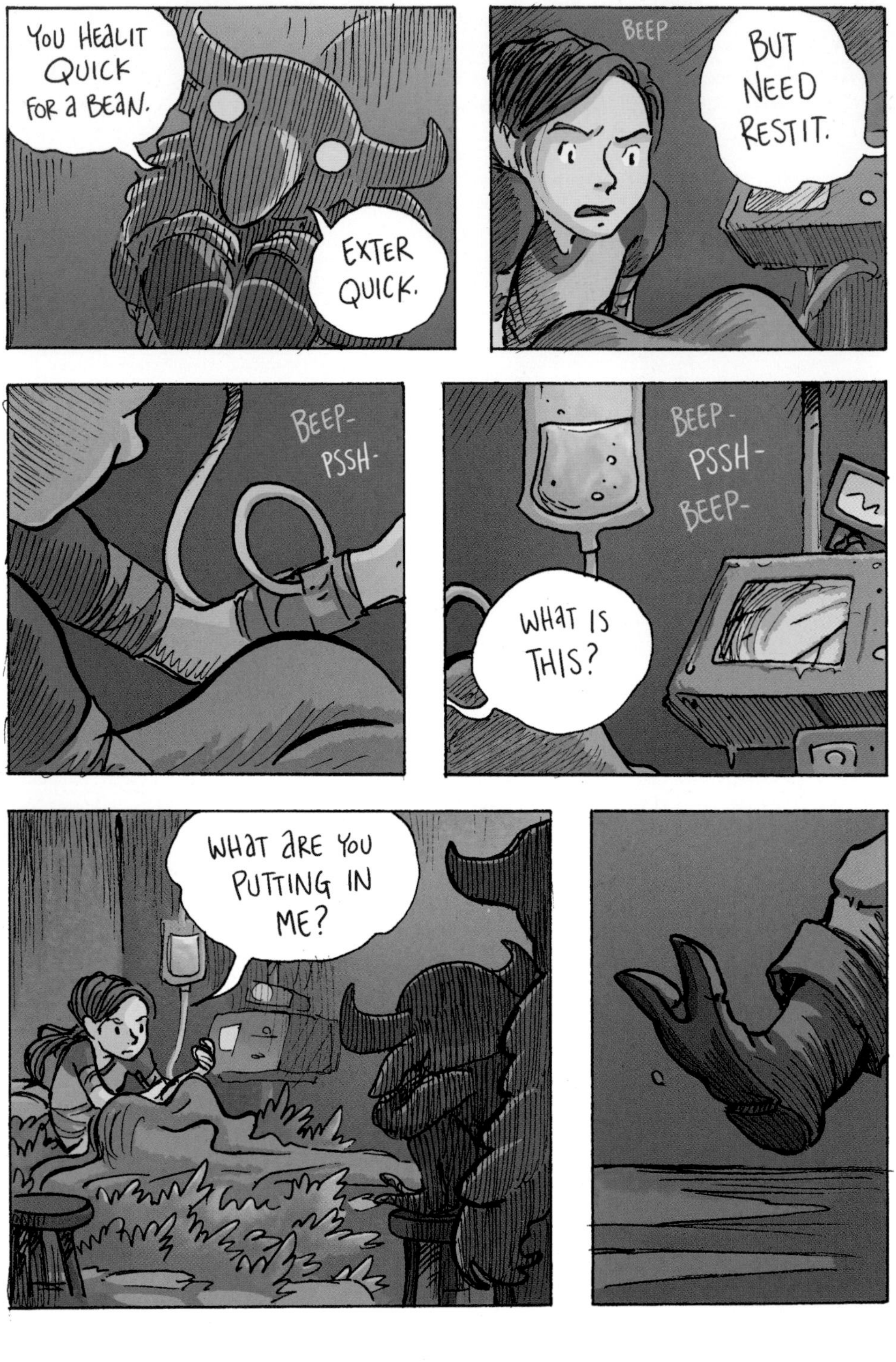
YOU HEALIT QUICK FOR A BEAN.
EXTER QUICK.
BEEP
BUT NEED RESTIT.
BEEP-
PSSH-
BEEP-
PSSH-
BEEP-
WHAT IS THIS?
WHAT ARE YOU PUTTING IN ME?

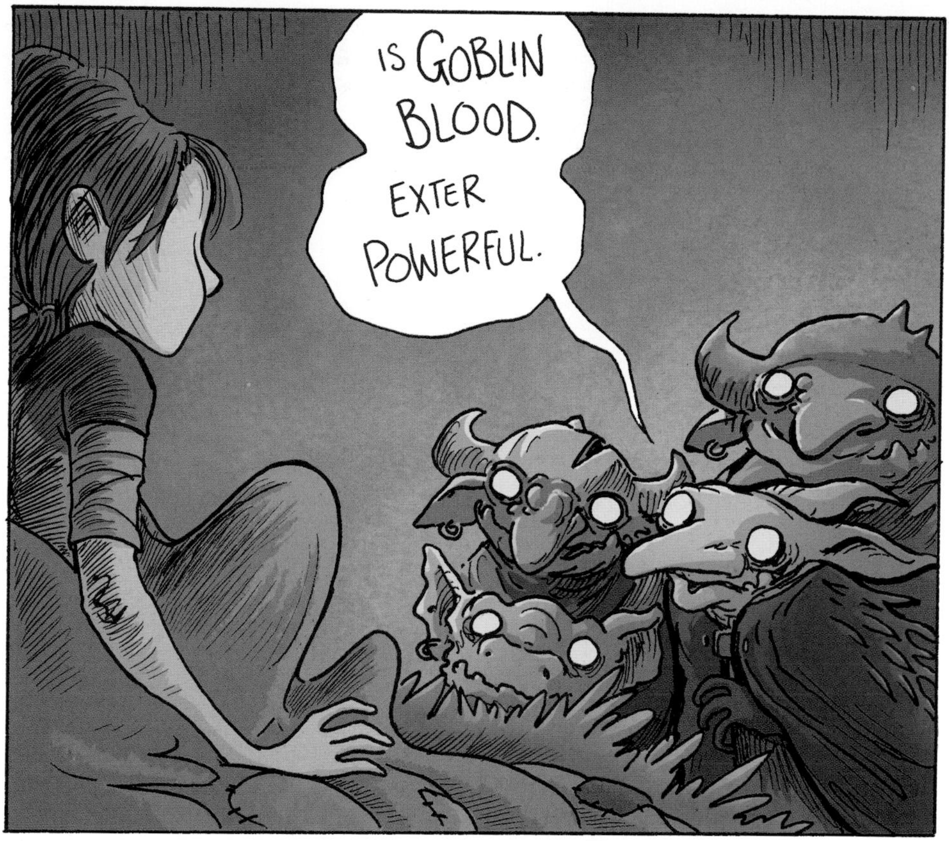
IS GOBLIN BLOOD.
EXTER POWERFUL.

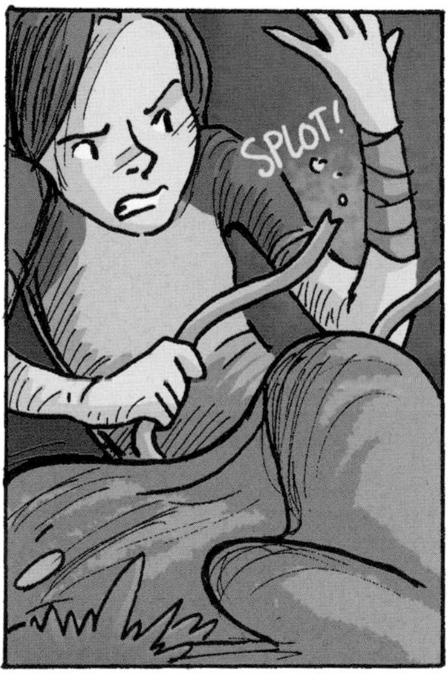
SPLOT!

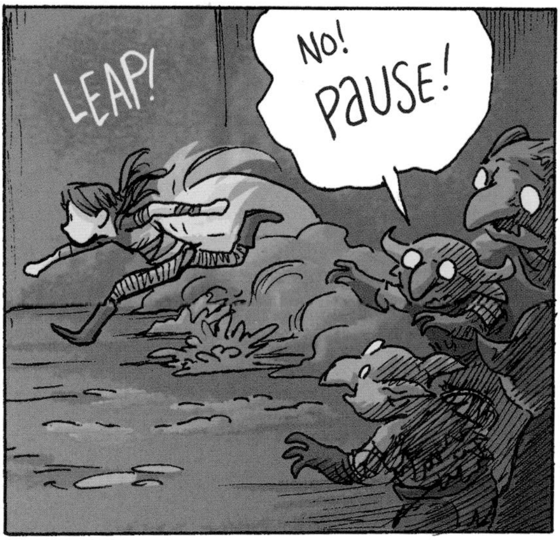
LEAP!
NO! PAUSE!

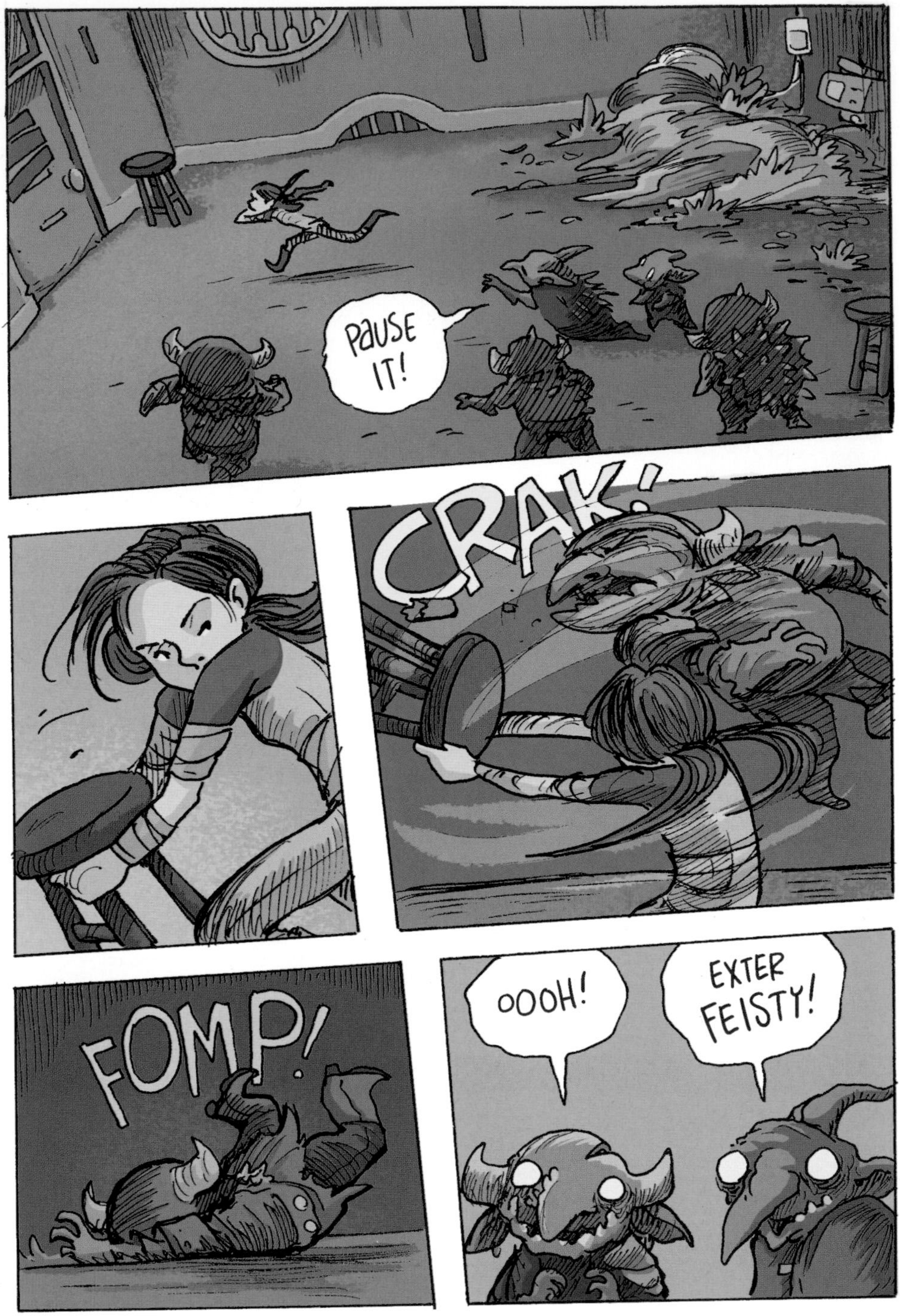
PAUSE IT!
CRAK!
FOMP!
OOOH!
EXTER FEISTY!

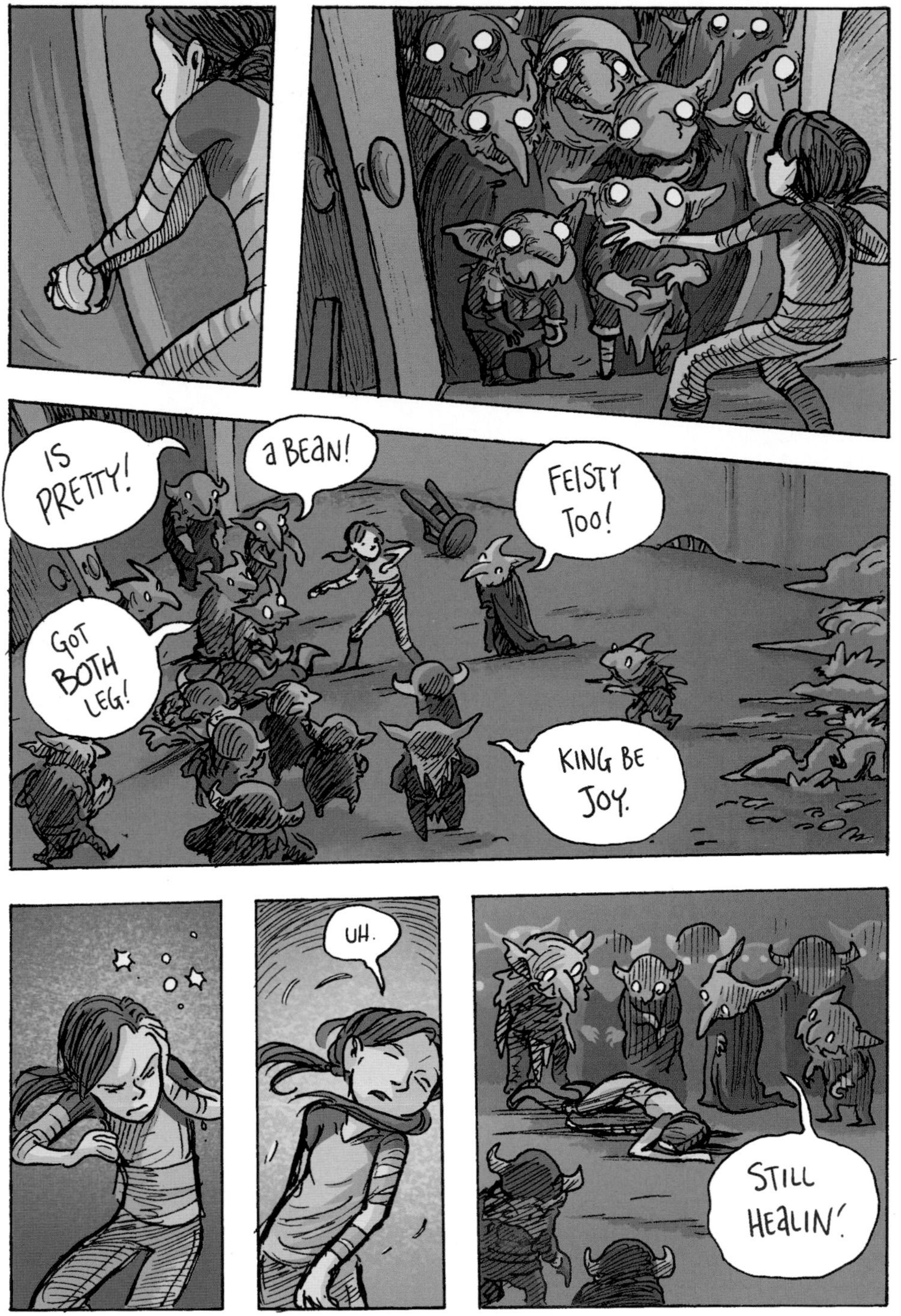
IS PRETTY!
a BEAN!
FEISTY TOO!
GOT BOTH LEG!
KING BE JOY.
UH.
STILL HEALIN'.

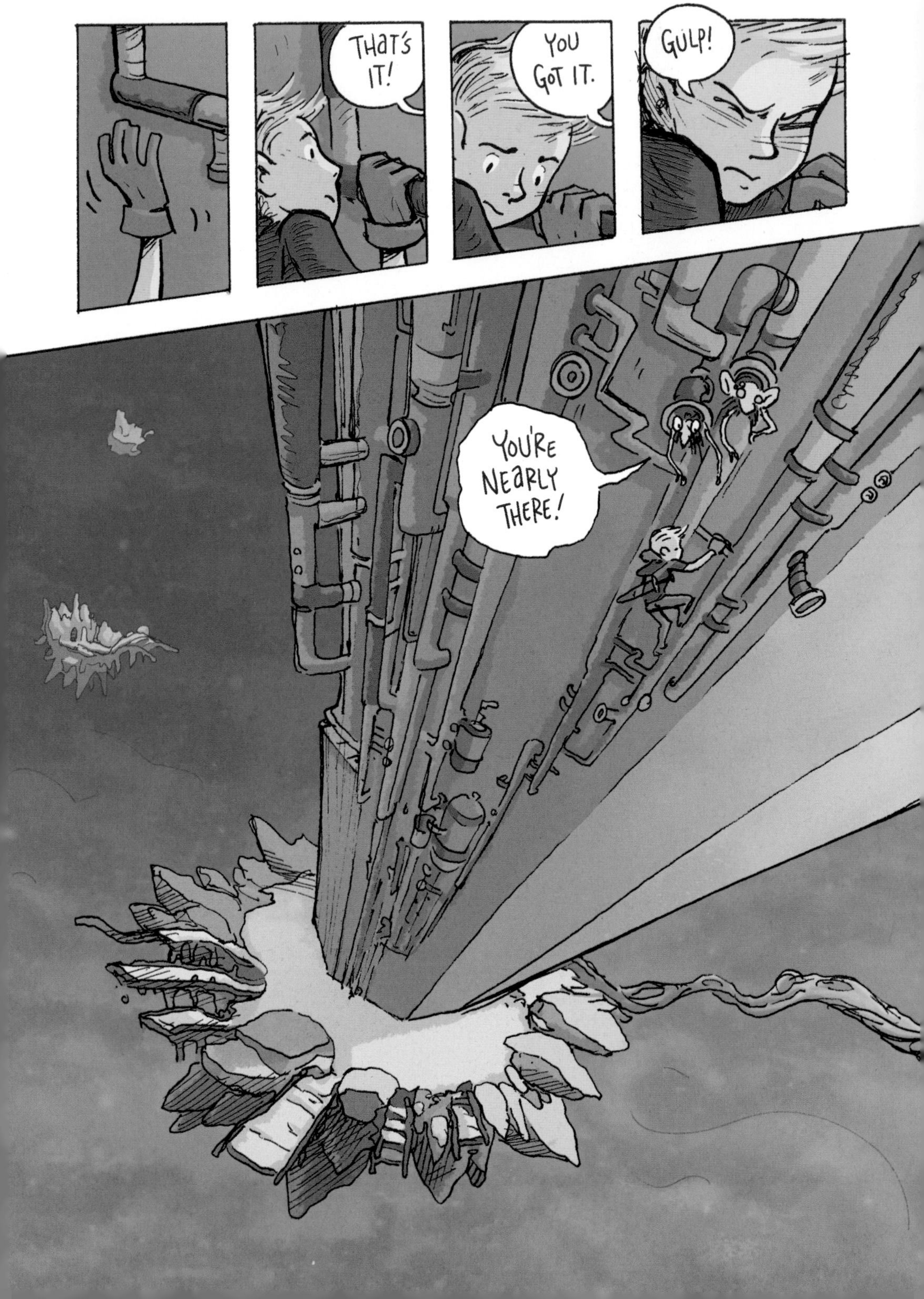
THAT'S IT!
YOU GOT IT.
GULP!
YOU'RE NEARLY THERE!

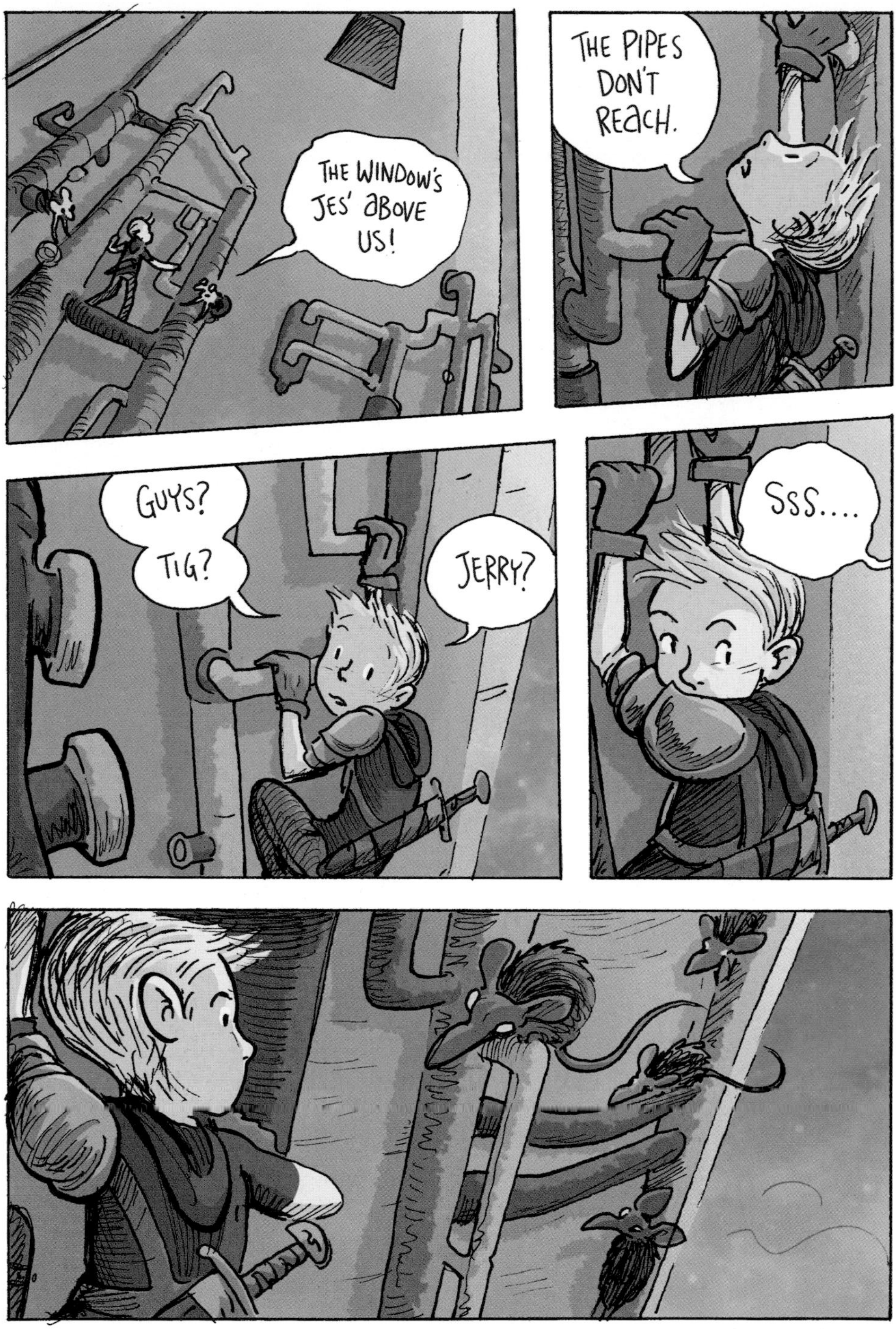
THE WINDOW'S JES' ABOVE US!
THE PIPES DON'T REACH.
GUYS?
TIG?
JERRY?
SSS....

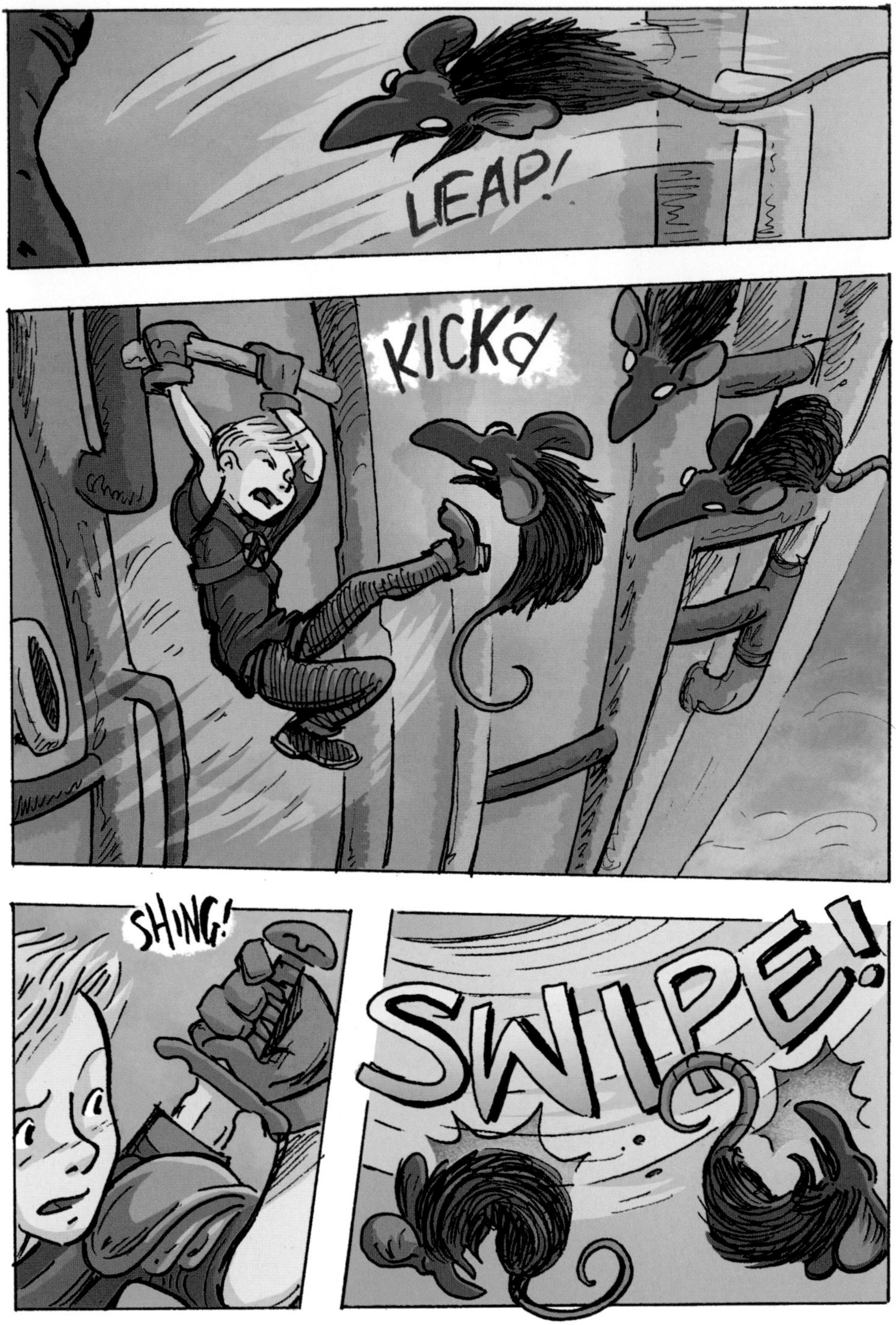
LEAP!
KICK'd
SHING!
SWIPE!

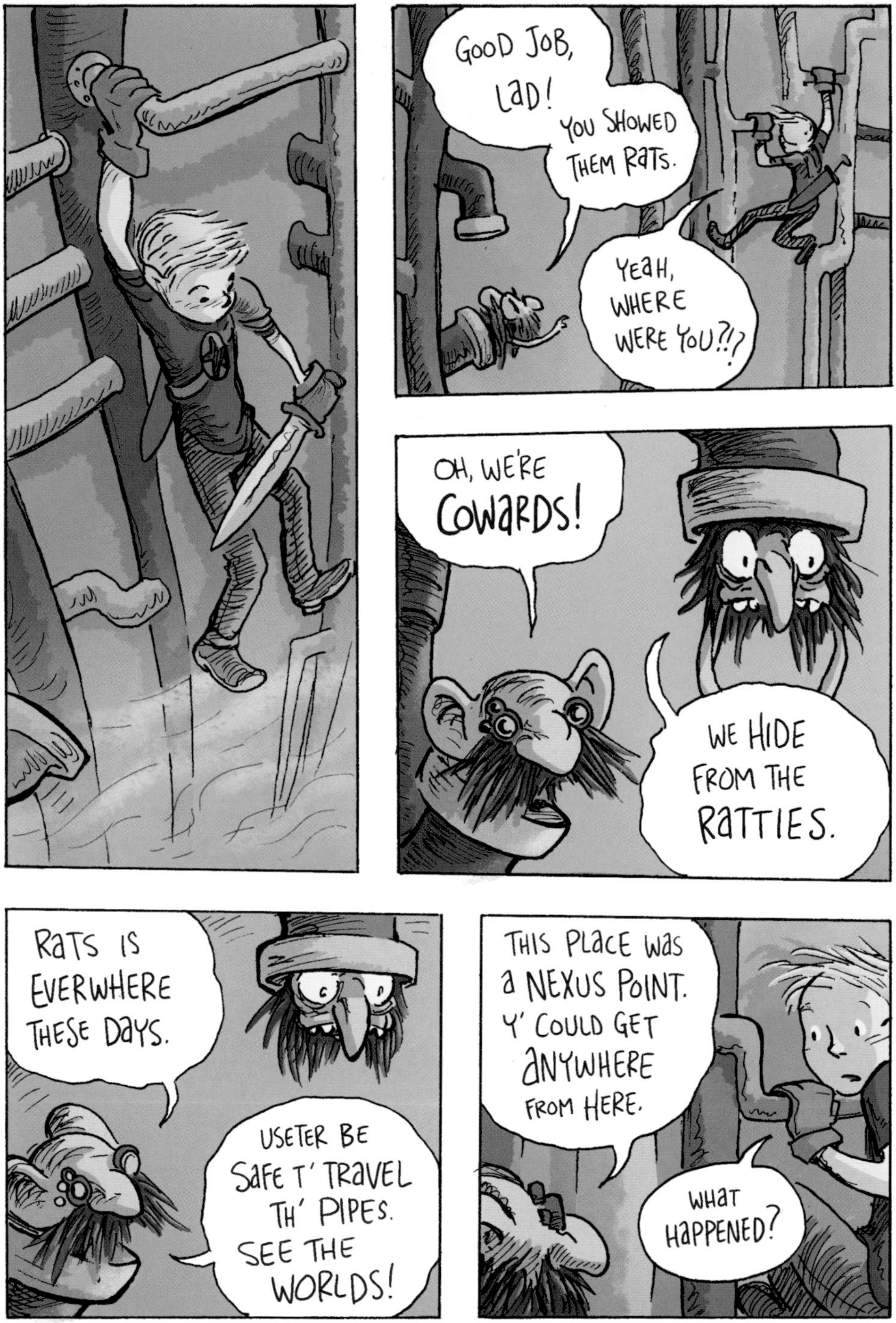
GOOD JOB, LAD!
YOU SHOWED THEM RATS.
YEAH, WHERE WERE YOU?!?
OH, WE'RE COWARDS!
WE HIDE FROM THE RATTIES.
RATS IS EVERWHERE THESE DAYS.
USETER BE SAFE T' TRAVEL TH' PIPES. SEE THE WORLDS!
THIS PLACE WAS A NEXUS POINT. Y' COULD GET ANYWHERE FROM HERE.
WHAT HAPPENED?

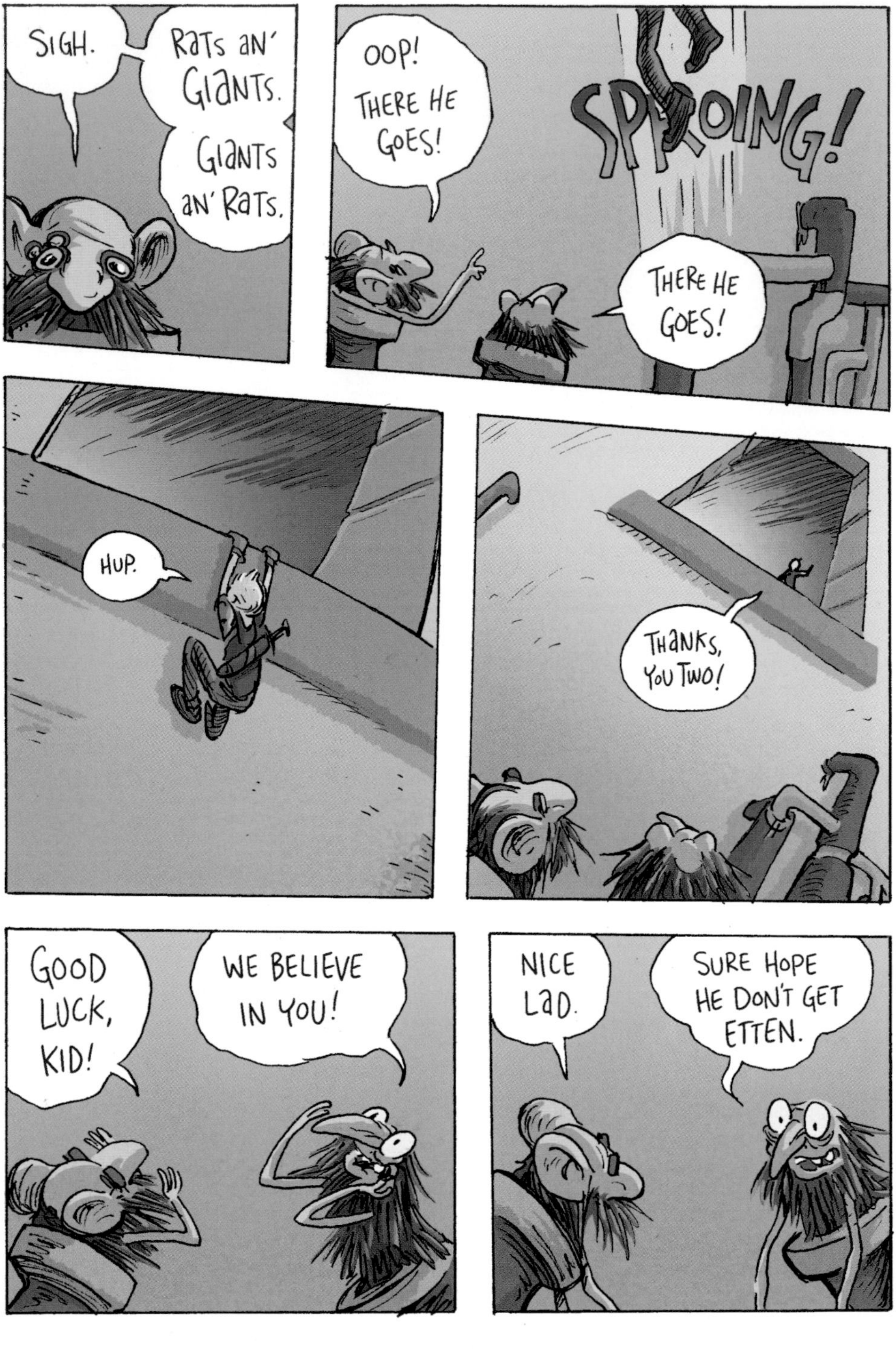
SIGH.
RATS AN' GIANTS.
GIANTS AN' RATS.
OOP! THERE HE GOES!
SPROING!
THERE HE GOES!
HUP.
THANKS, YOU TWO!
GOOD LUCK, KID!
WE BELIEVE IN YOU!
NICE LAD.
SURE HOPE HE DON'T GET ETTEN.

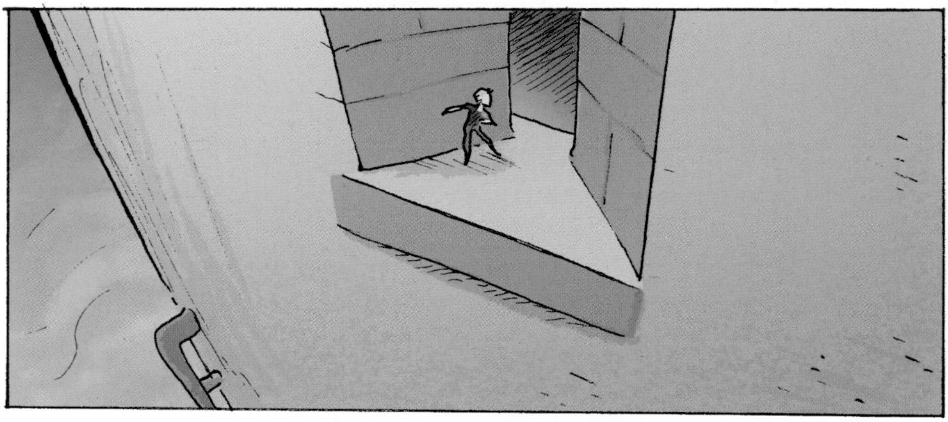
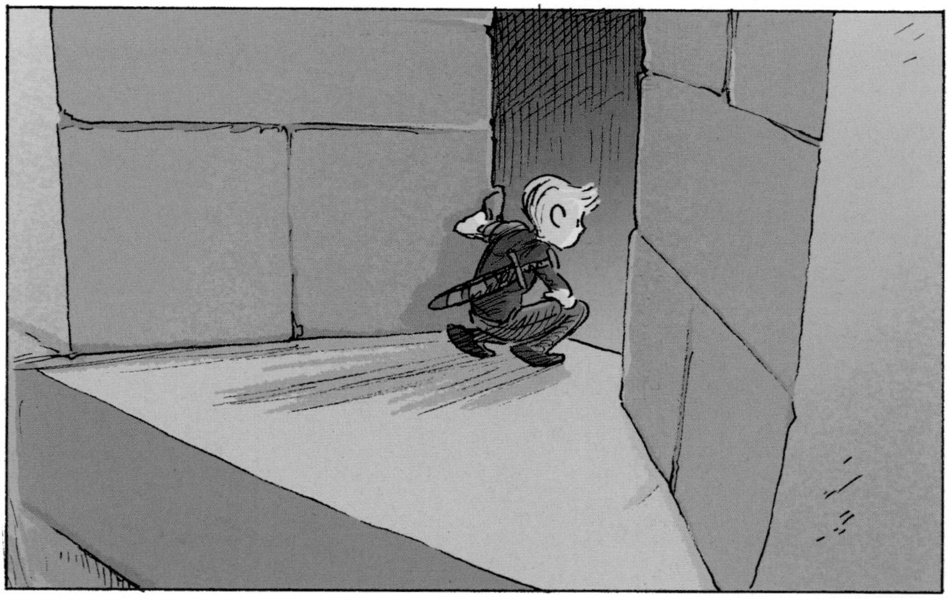
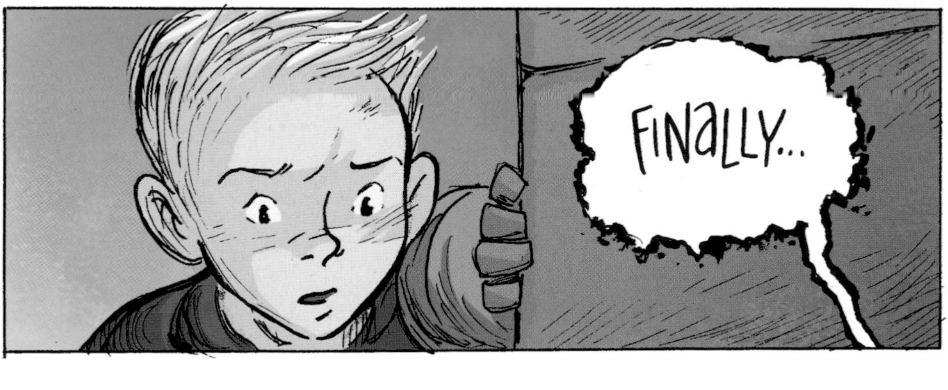
FINALLY...

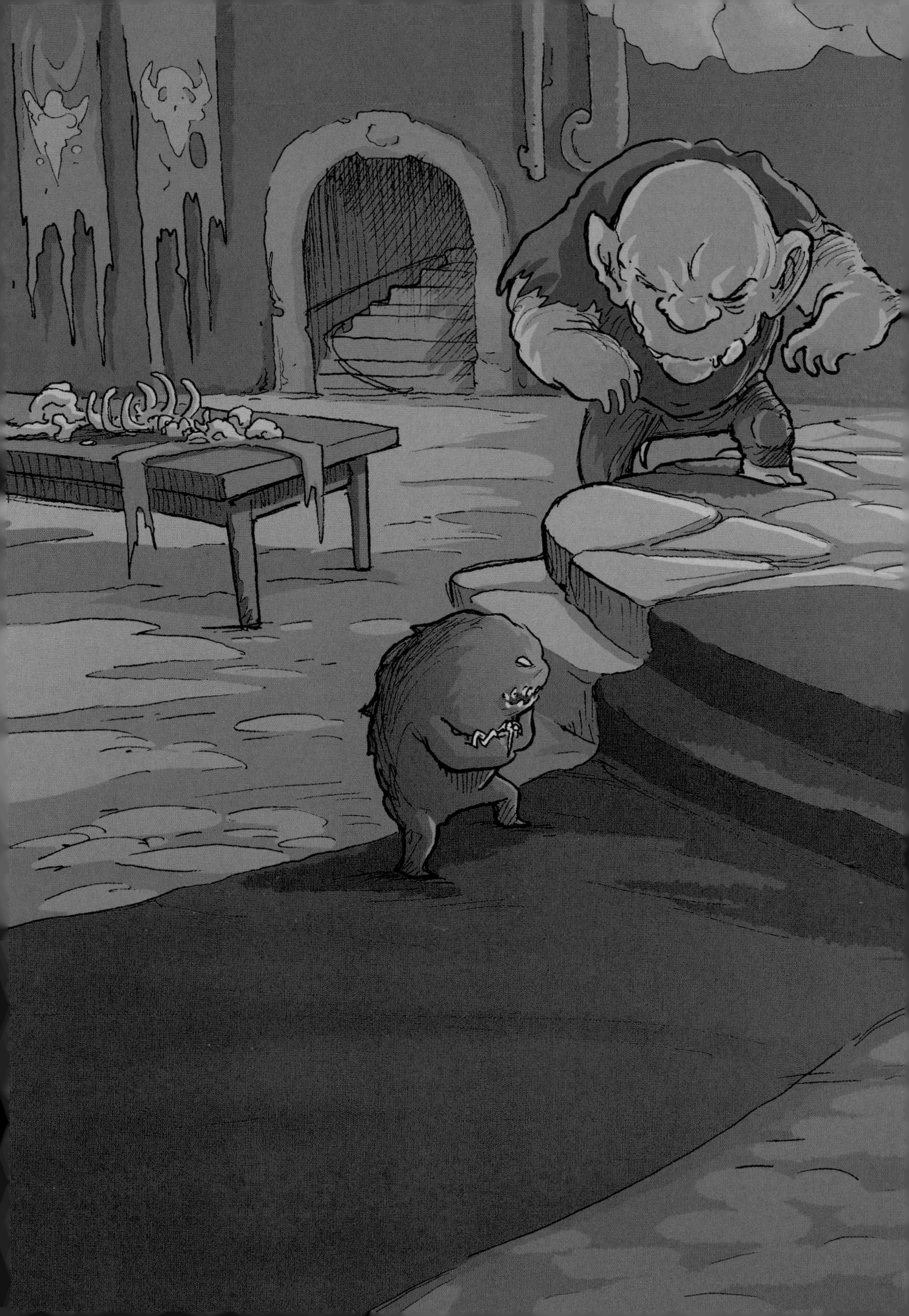

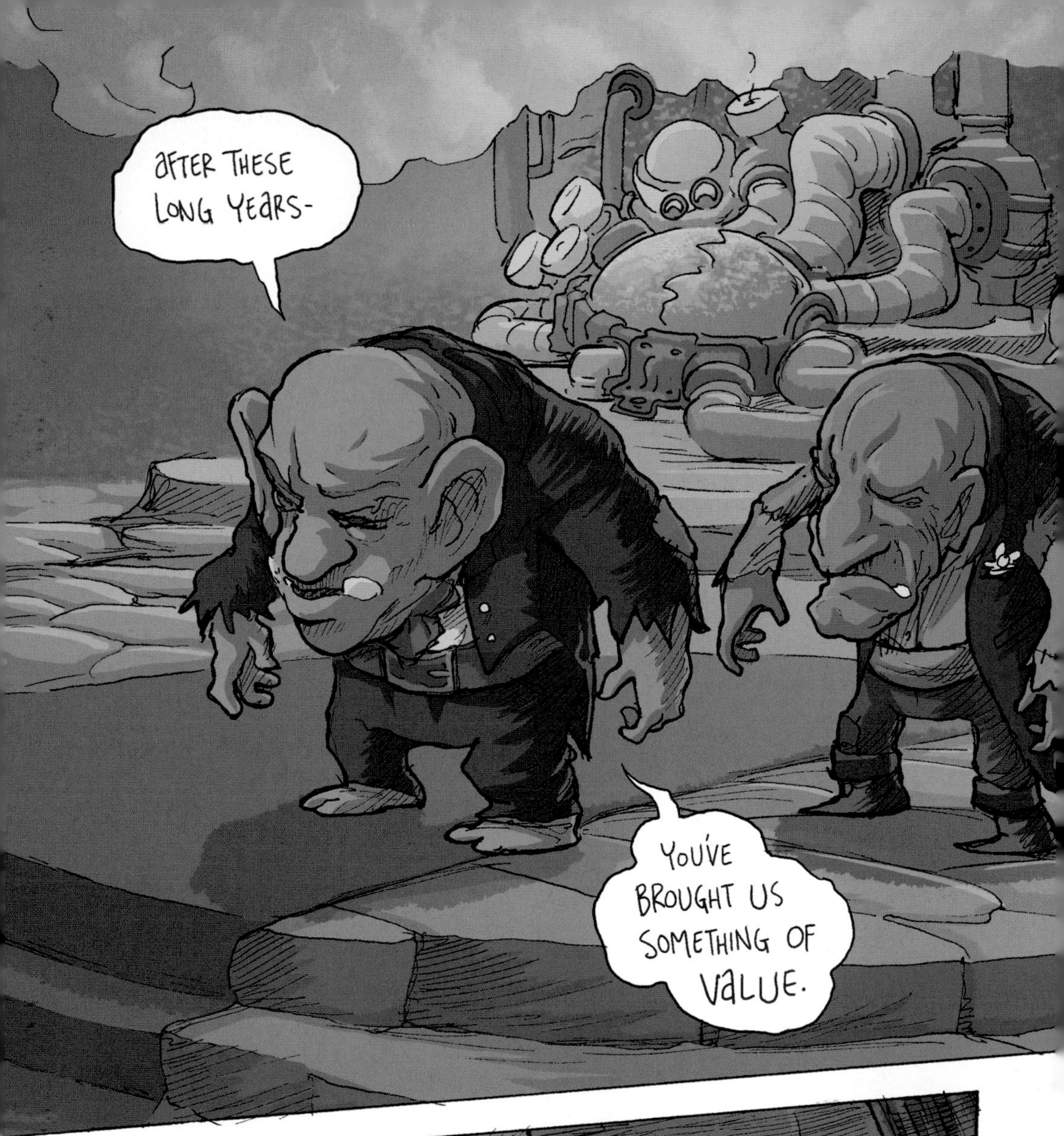
AFTER THESE LONG YEARS-
YOU'VE BROUGHT US SOMETHING OF VALUE.

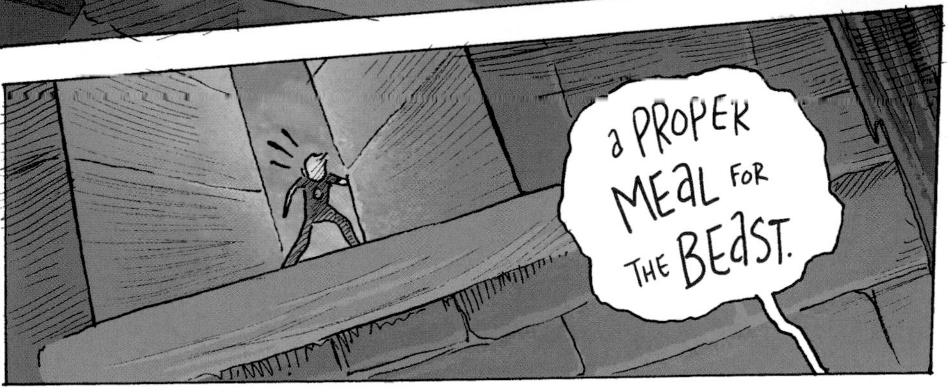
A PROPER MEAL FOR THE BEAST.

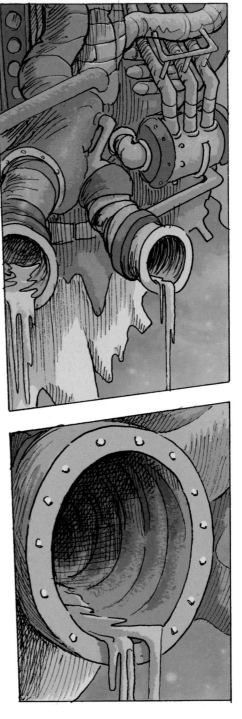

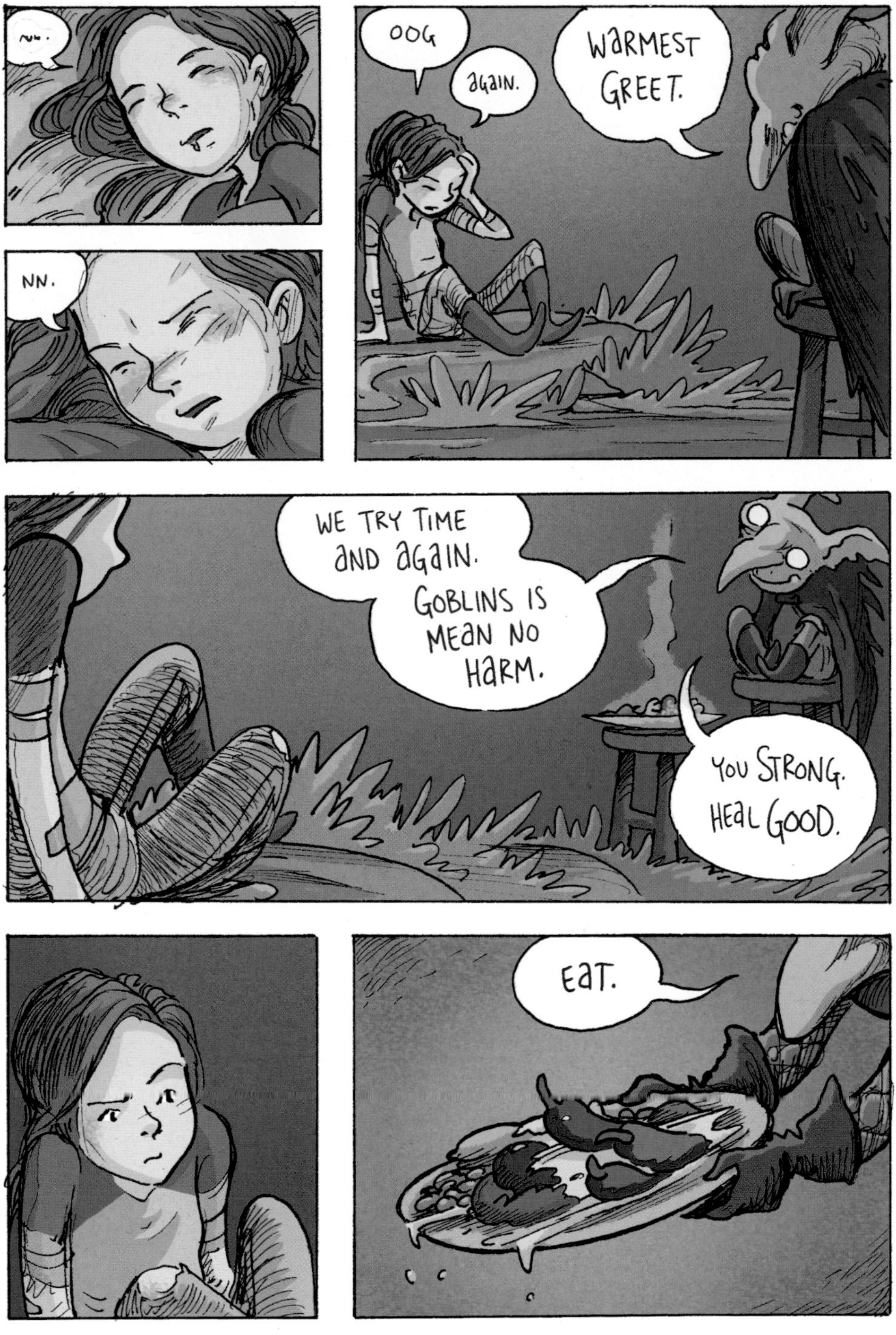
NN.
OOG
AGAIN.
WARMEST GREET.
WE TRY TIME AND AGAIN.
GOBLINS IS MEAN NO HARM.
YOU STRONG. HEAL GOOD.
EAT.

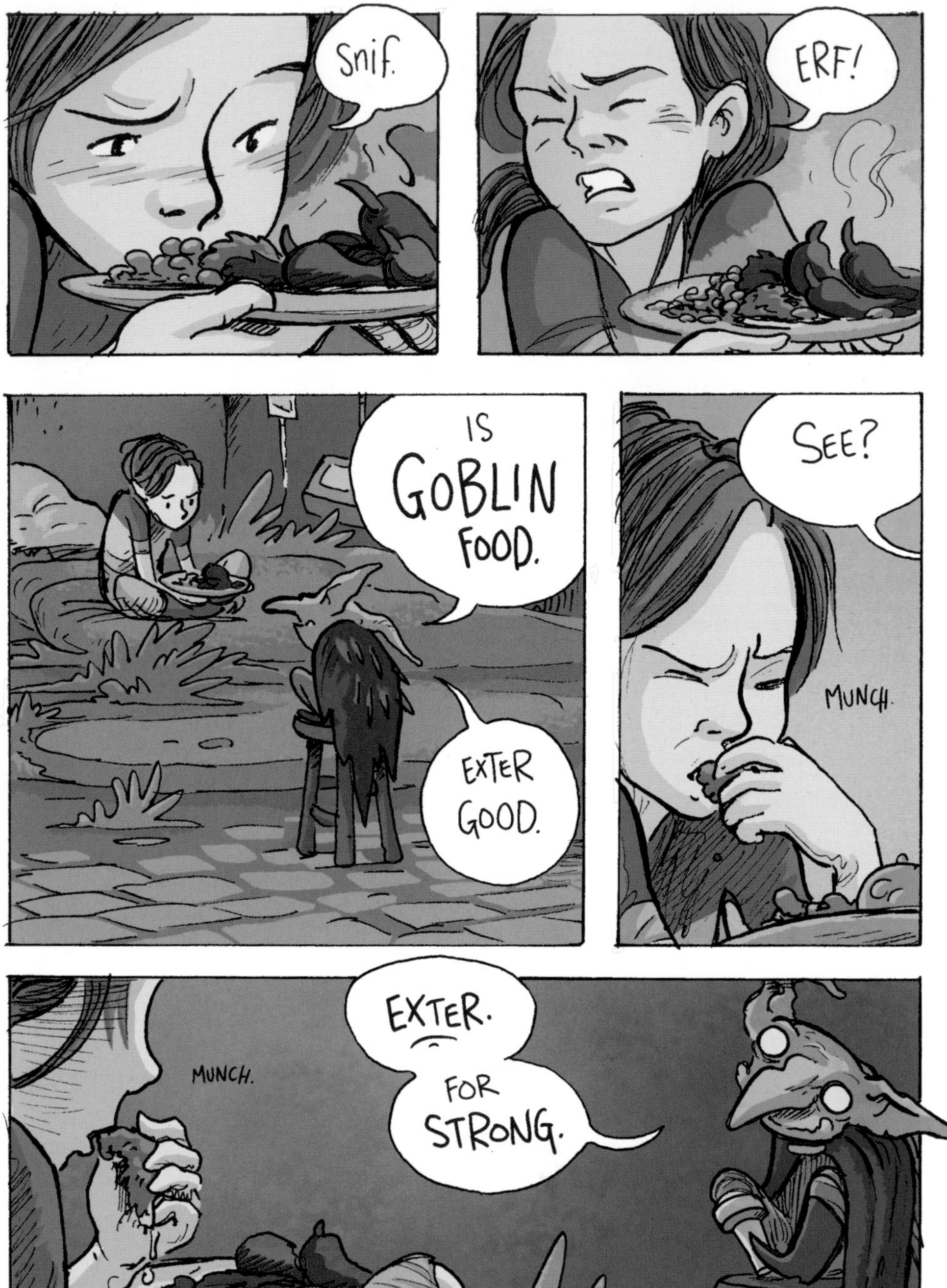
Snif.
ERF!
IS GOBLIN FOOD.
EXTER GOOD.
SEE?
MUNCH.
MUNCH.
EXTER.
FOR STRONG.

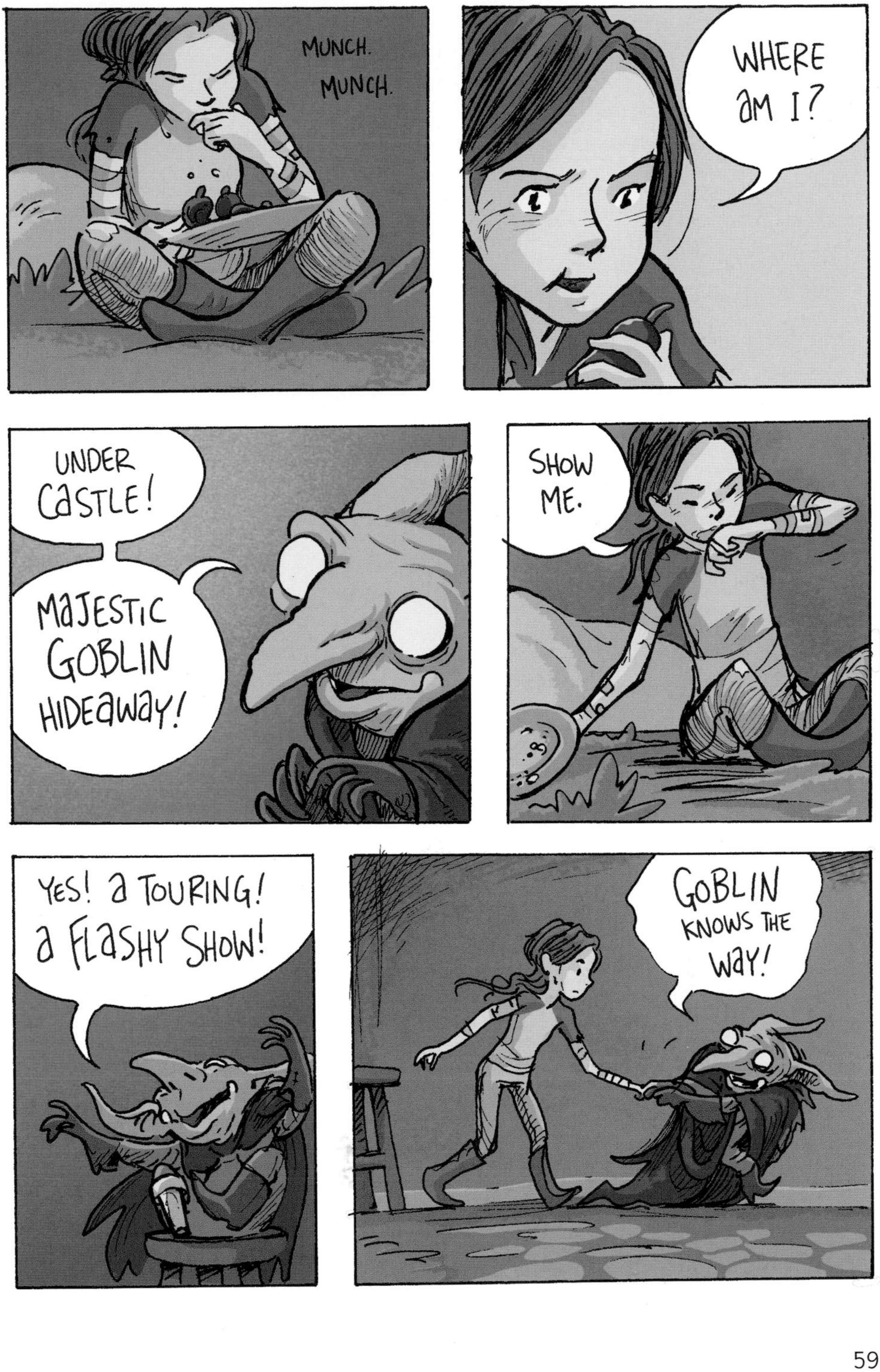
MUNCH.
MUNCH.
WHERE am I?
UNDER CASTLE!
MaJESTIC GOBLIN HIDEaway!
SHOW ME.
YES! a TOURING! a FLaSHY SHOW!
GOBLIN KNOWS THE Way!

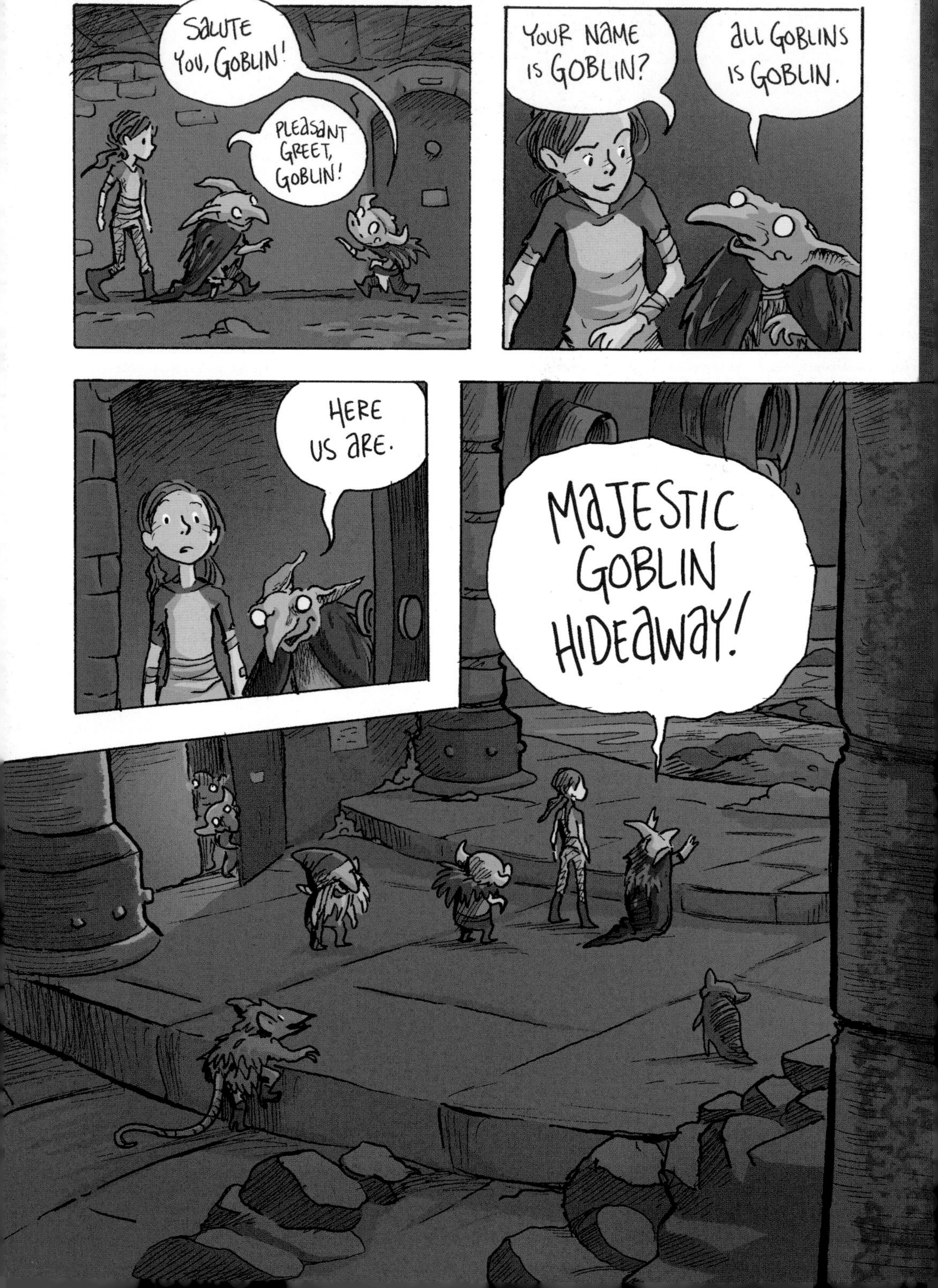

SALUTE YOU, GOBLIN!
PLEASANT GREET, GOBLIN!
YOUR NAME IS GOBLIN?
ALL GOBLINS IS GOBLIN.
HERE US ARE.
MAJESTIC GOBLIN HIDEAWAY!

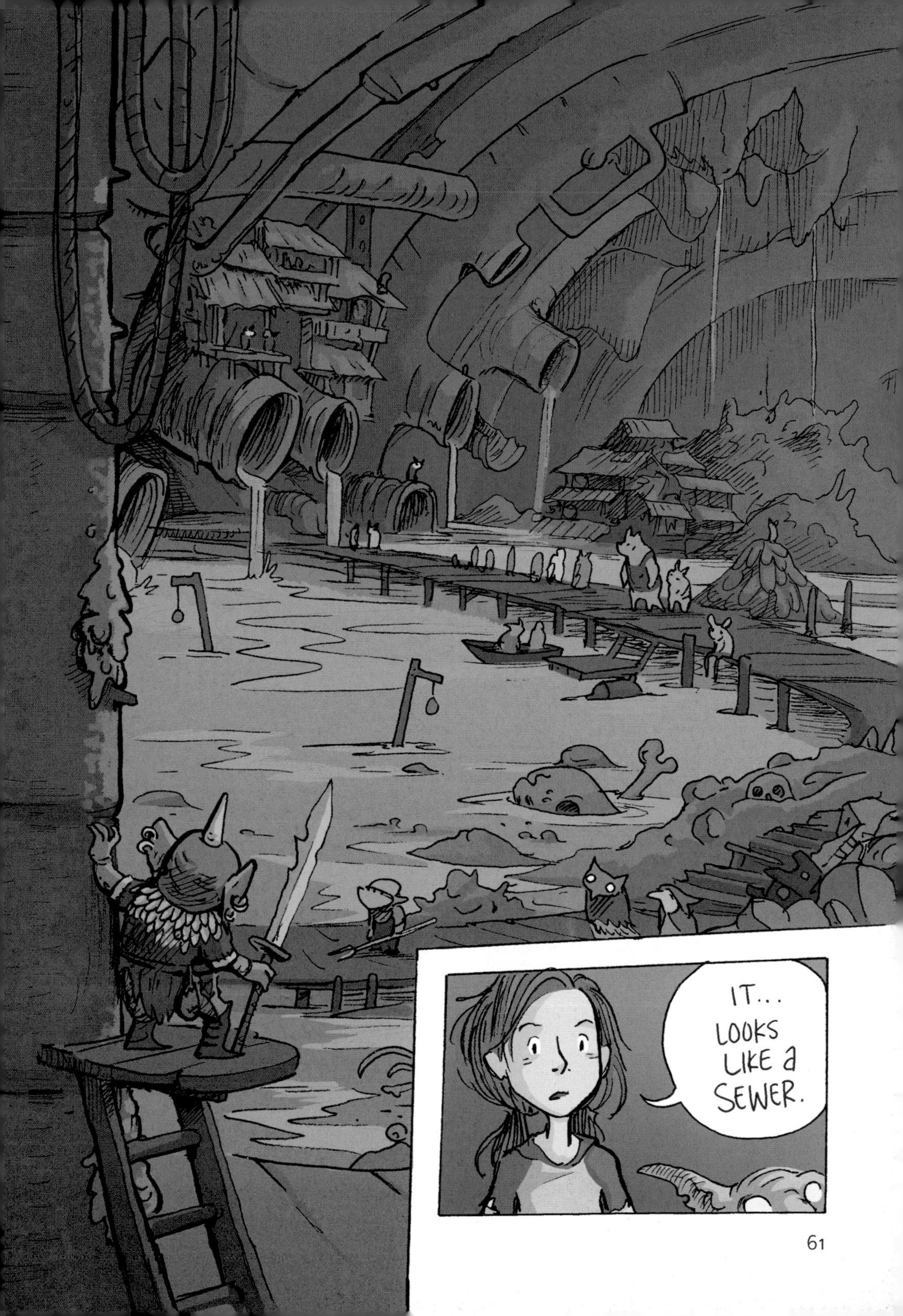
IT... LOOKS LIKE a SEWER.

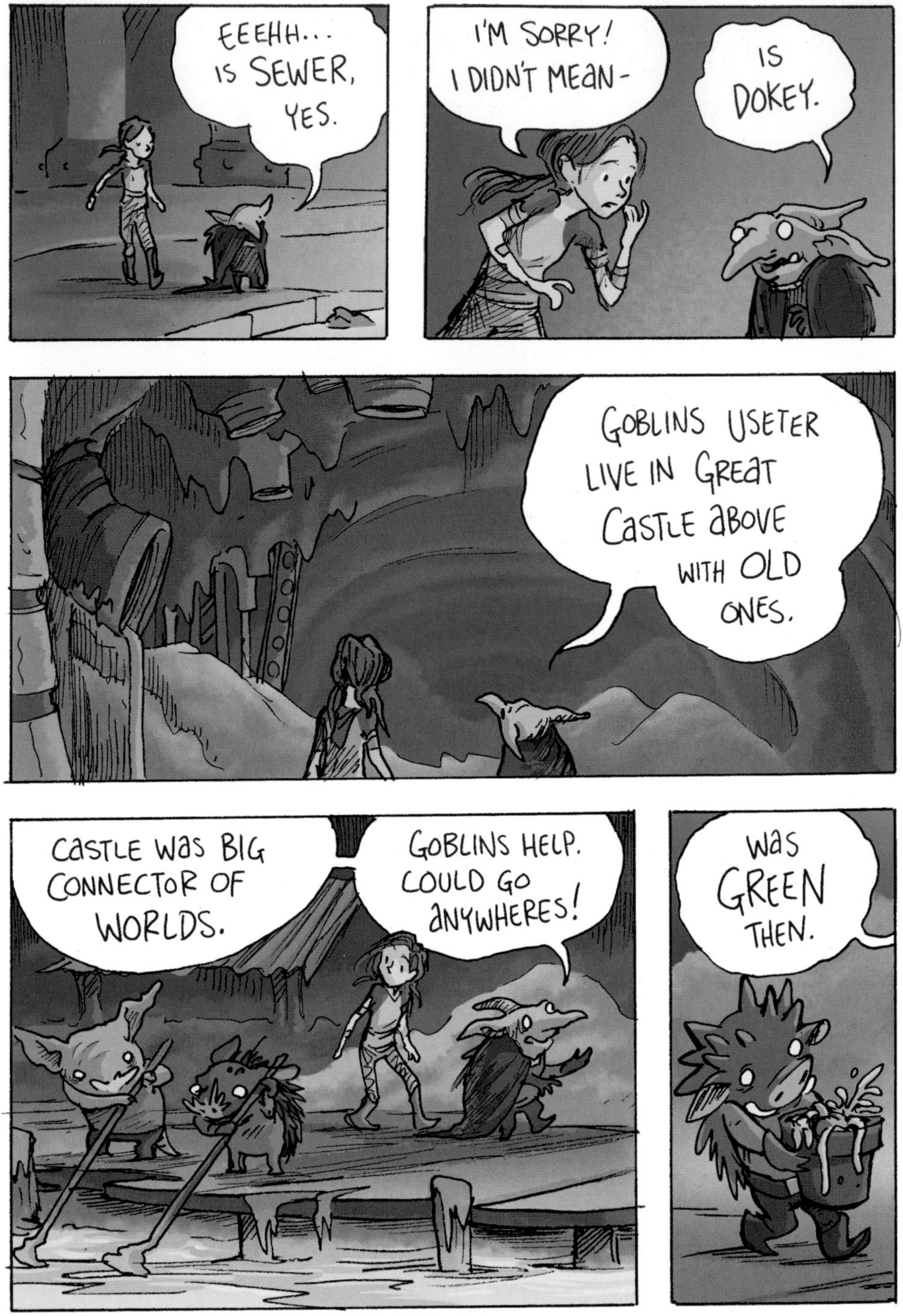
EEEHH... IS SEWER, YES.
I'M SORRY! I DIDN'T MEAN-
IS DOKEY.
GOBLINS USETER LIVE IN GREAT CASTLE ABOVE WITH OLD ONES.
CASTLE WAS BIG CONNECTOR OF WORLDS.
GOBLINS HELP. COULD GO ANYWHERES!
WAS GREEN THEN.

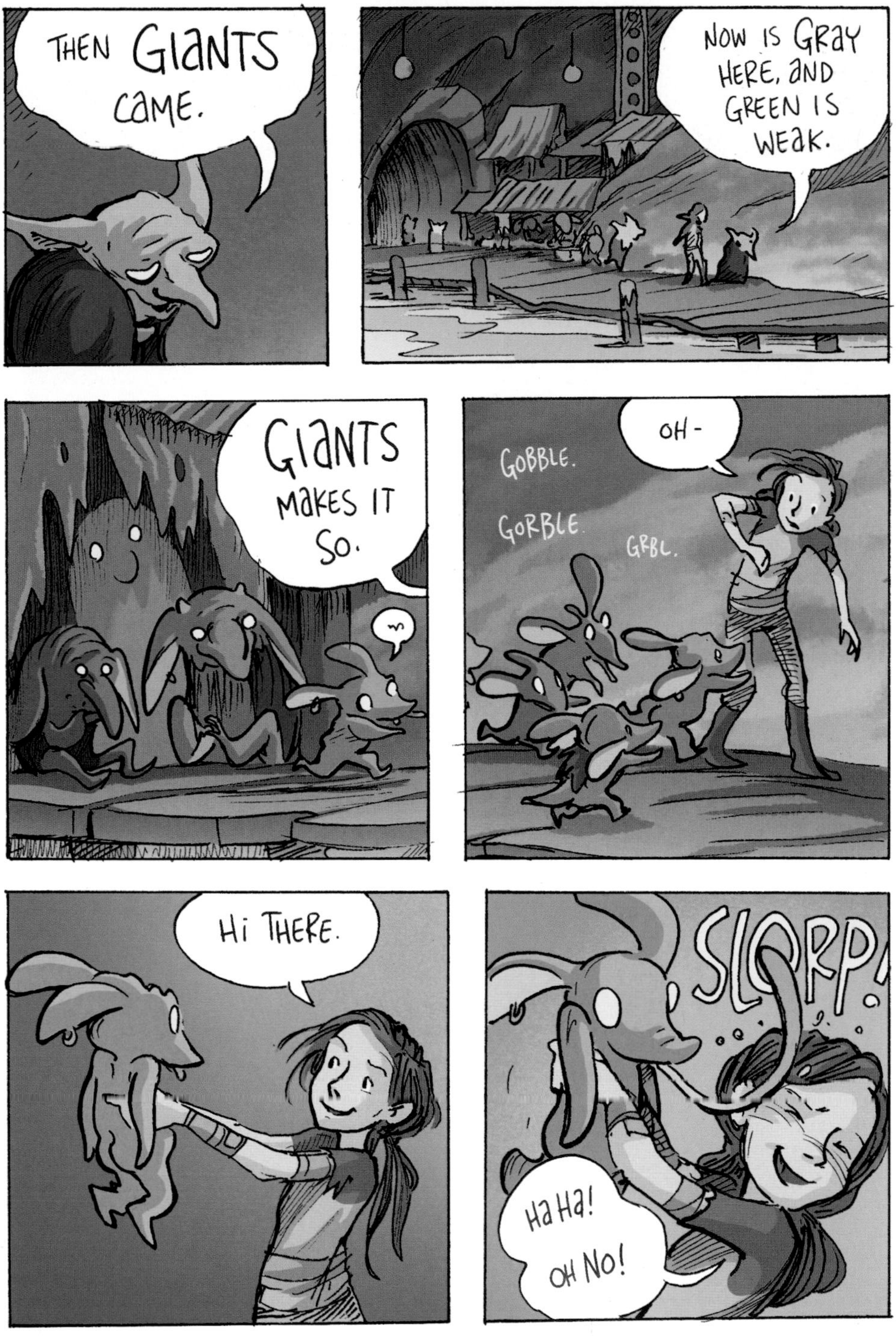
THEN GIANTS CAME.
NOW IS GRAY HERE, AND GREEN IS WEAK.
GIANTS MAKES IT SO.
GOBBLE.
GORBLE.
GRBL.
OH -
HI THERE.
SLORP!
HA HA!
OH NO!

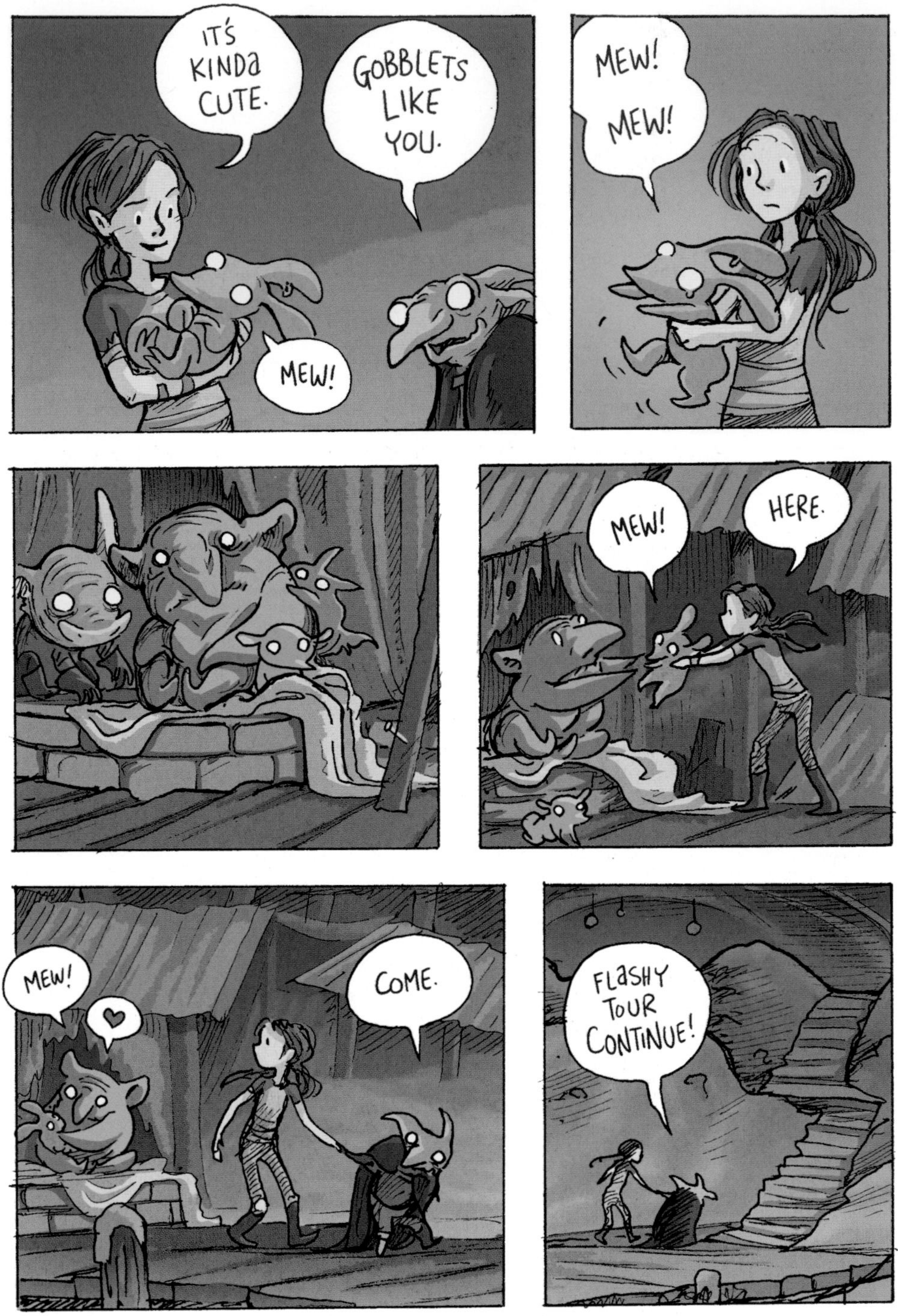
IT'S KINDA CUTE.
GOBBLETS LIKE YOU.
MEW!
MEW!
MEW!
MEW!
HERE.
MEW!
COME.
FLASHY TOUR CONTINUE!

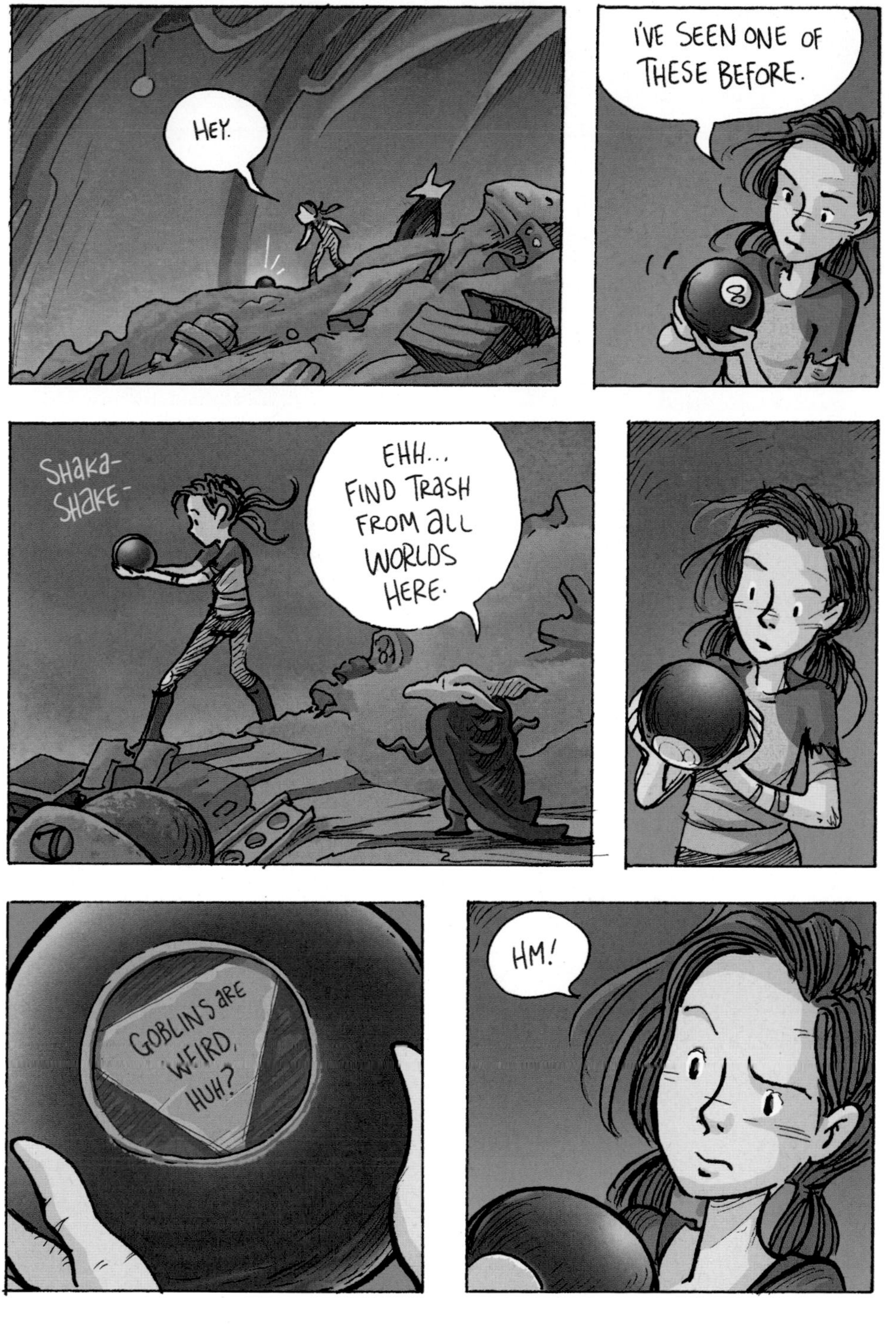
HEY.
I'VE SEEN ONE OF THESE BEFORE.
SHAKA-SHAKE-
EHH... FIND TRASH FROM ALL WORLDS HERE.
GOBLINS ARE WEIRD, HUH?
HM!

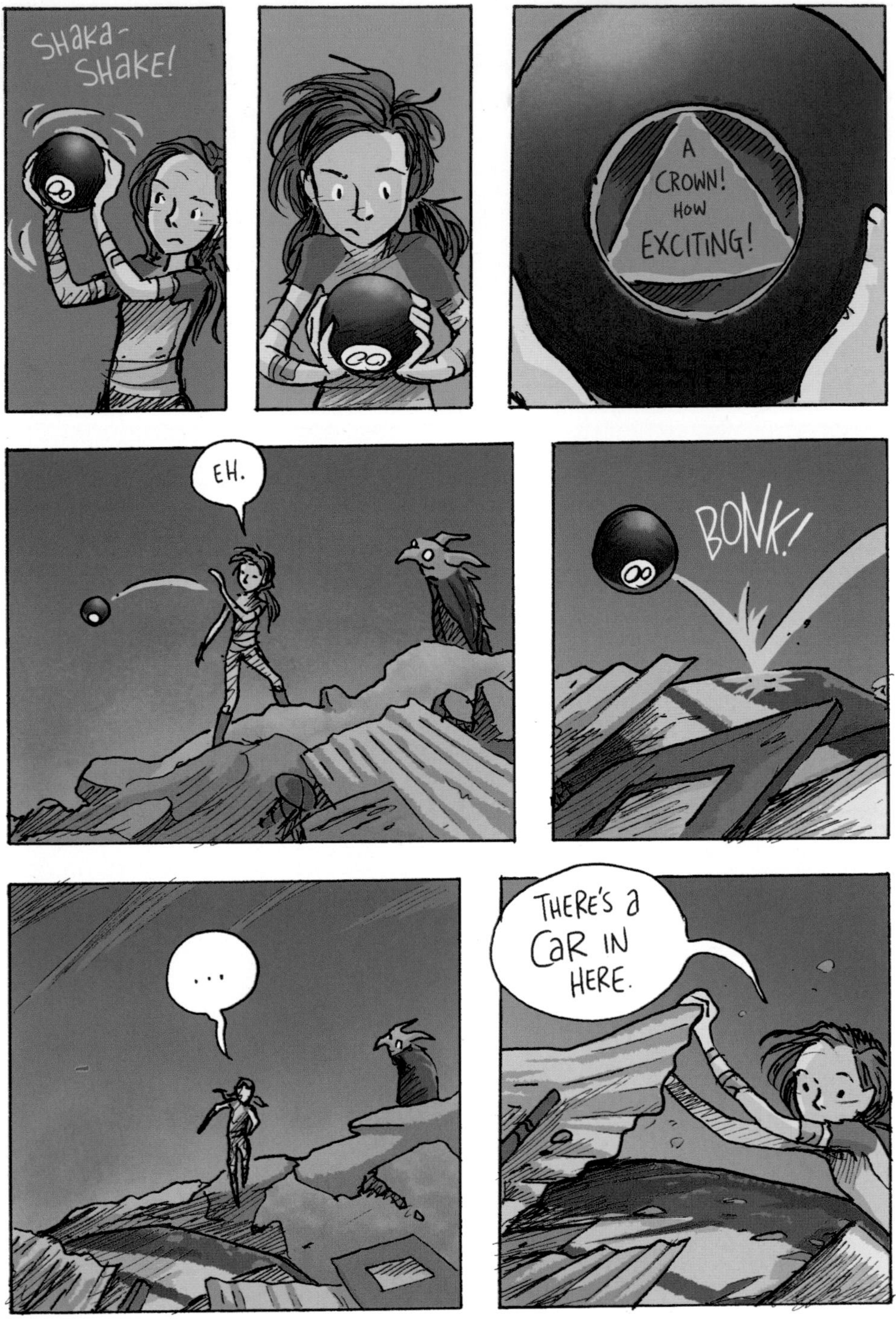
SHAKA-
SHAKE!
A CROWN! HOW EXCITING!
EH.
BONK!
...
THERE'S a CaR IN HERE.

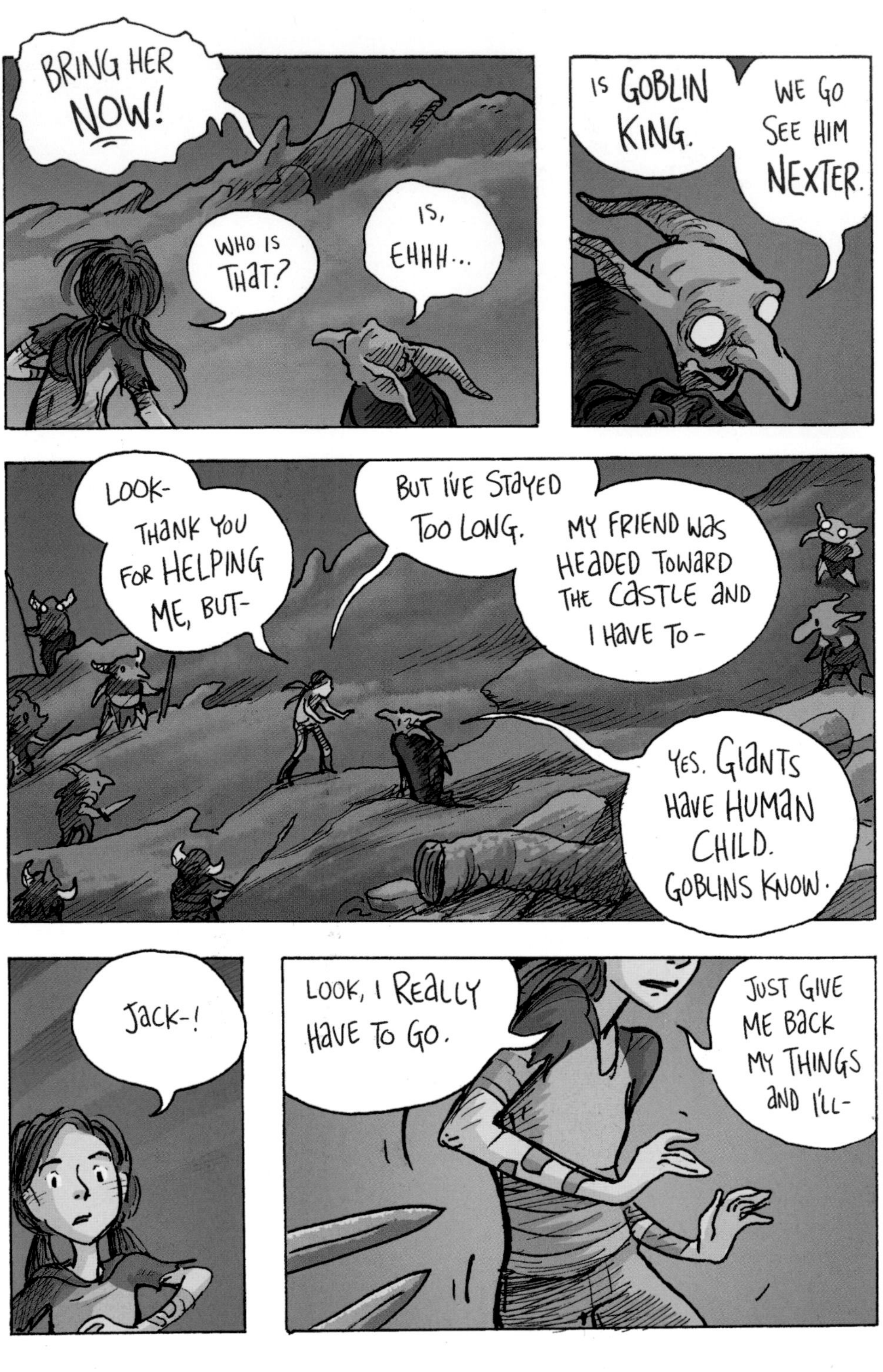
BRING HER NOW!
WHO IS THAT?
IS, EHHH...
IS GOBLIN KING.
WE GO SEE HIM NEXTER.
LOOK- THANK YOU FOR HELPING ME, BUT-
BUT I'VE STAYED TOO LONG.
MY FRIEND WAS HEADED TOWARD THE CASTLE AND I HAVE TO-
YES. GIANTS HAVE HUMAN CHILD. GOBLINS KNOW.
JACK-!
LOOK, I REALLY HAVE TO GO.
JUST GIVE ME BACK MY THINGS AND I'LL-

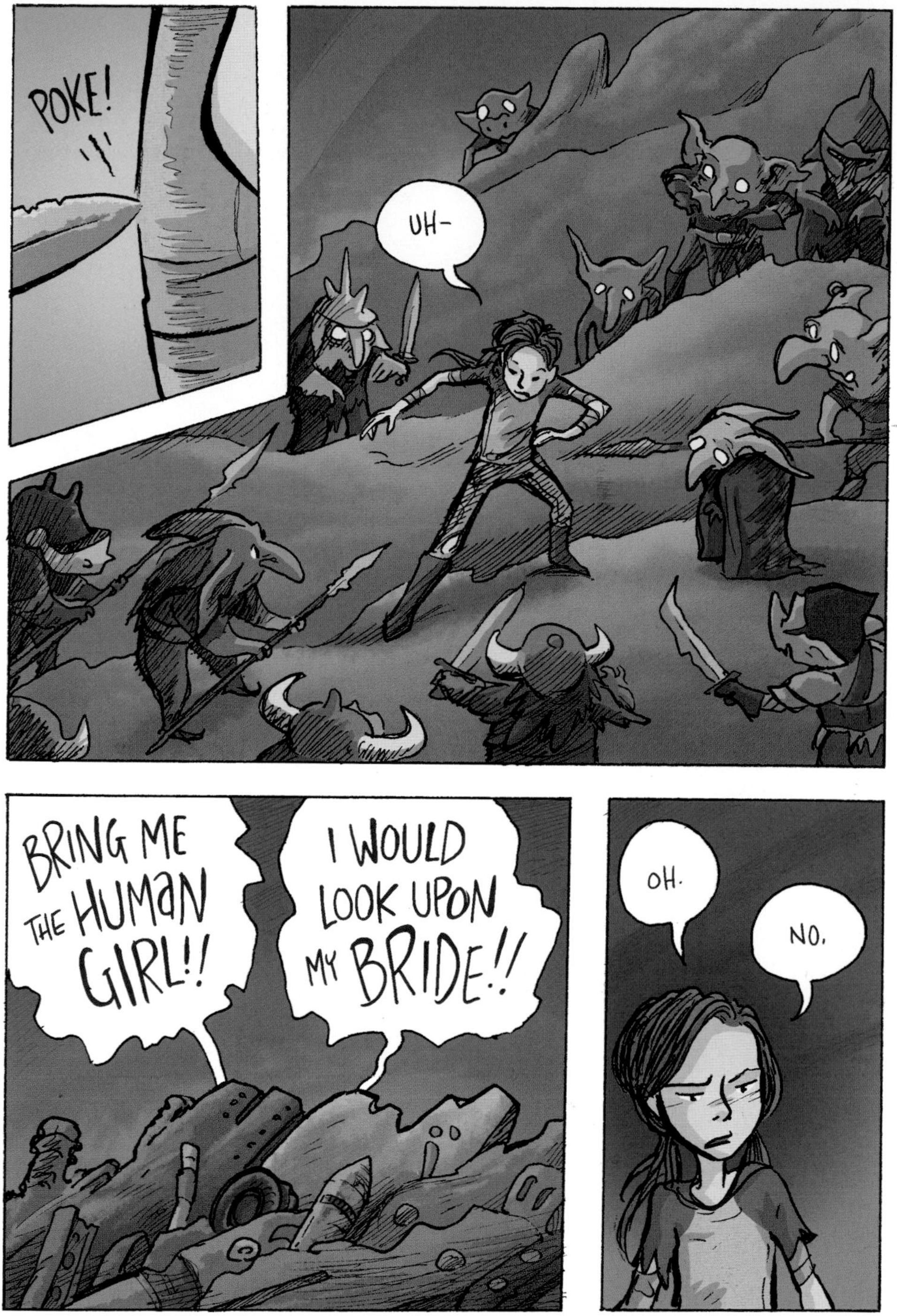
POKE!
UH-
BRING ME THE HUMAN GIRL!!
I WOULD LOOK UPON MY BRIDE!!
OH.
NO.

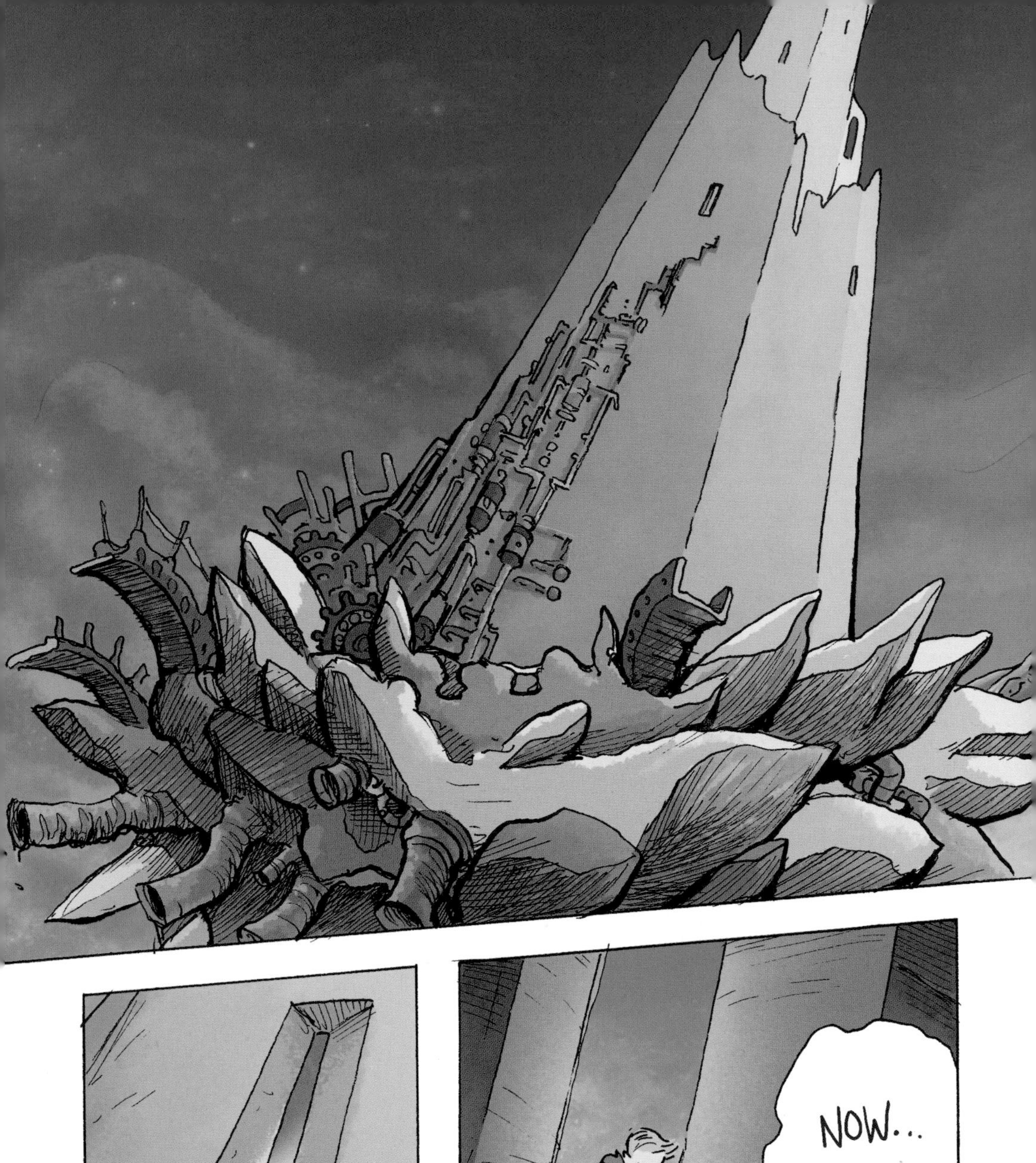

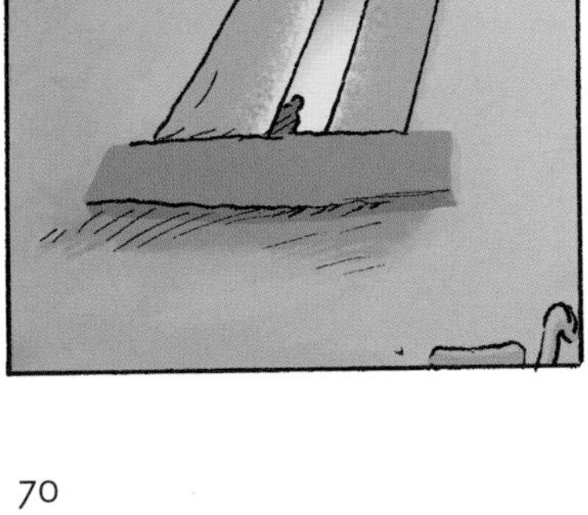

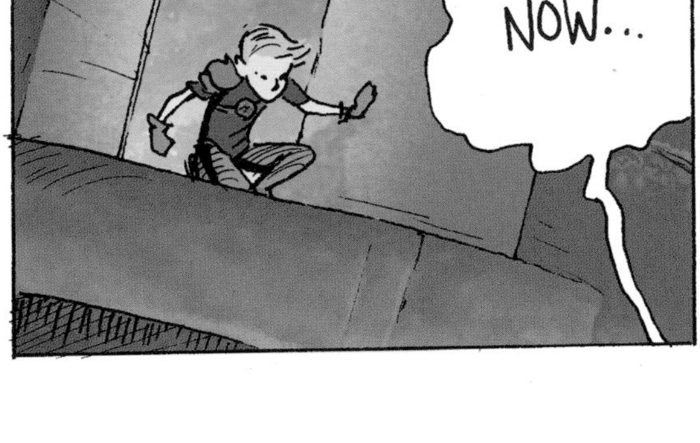
NOW...

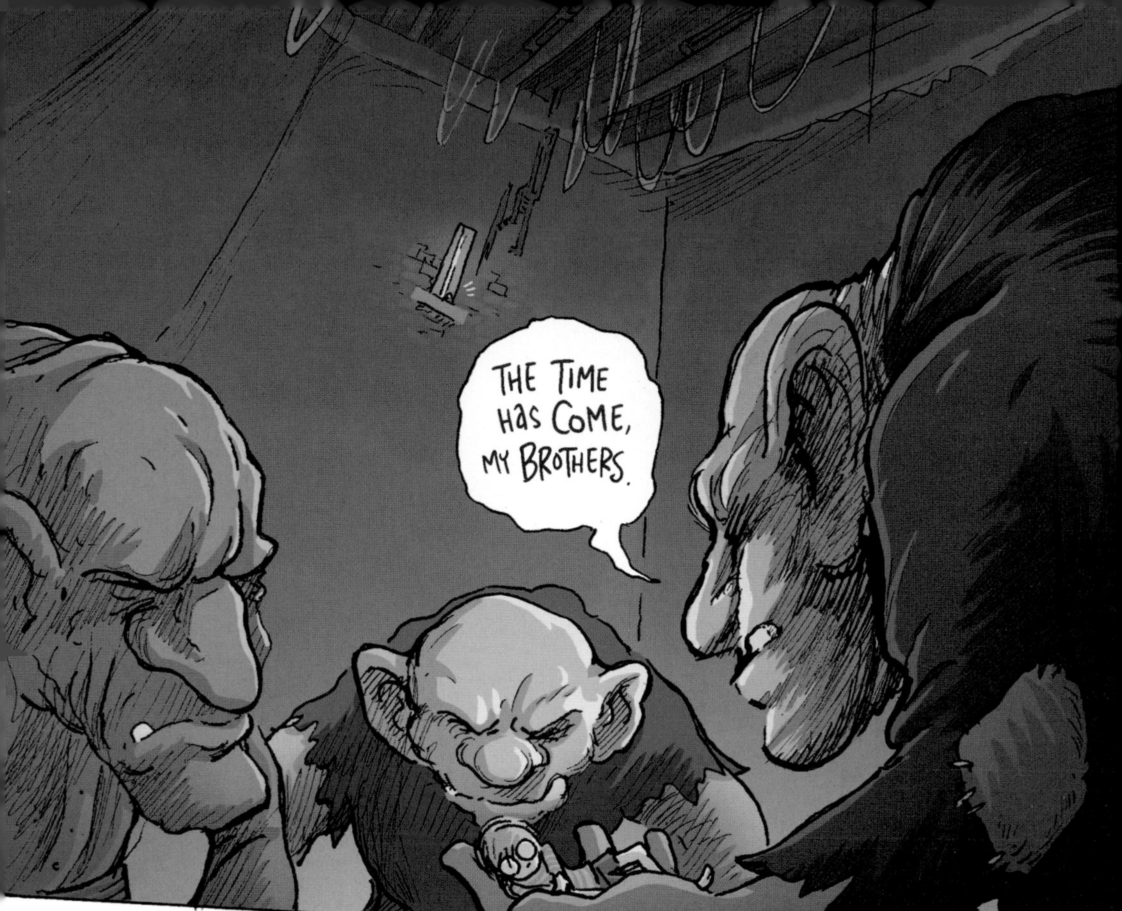
THE TIME HAS COME, MY BROTHERS.

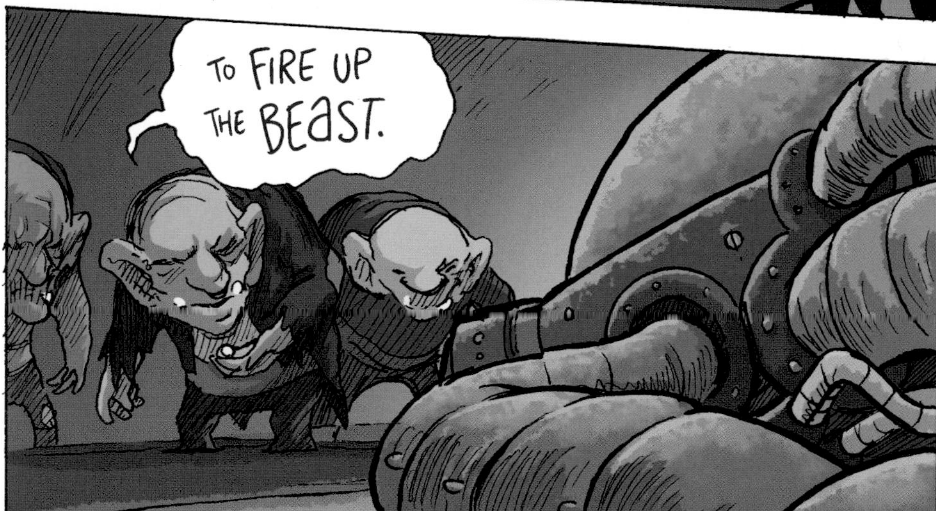
TO FIRE UP THE BEAST.

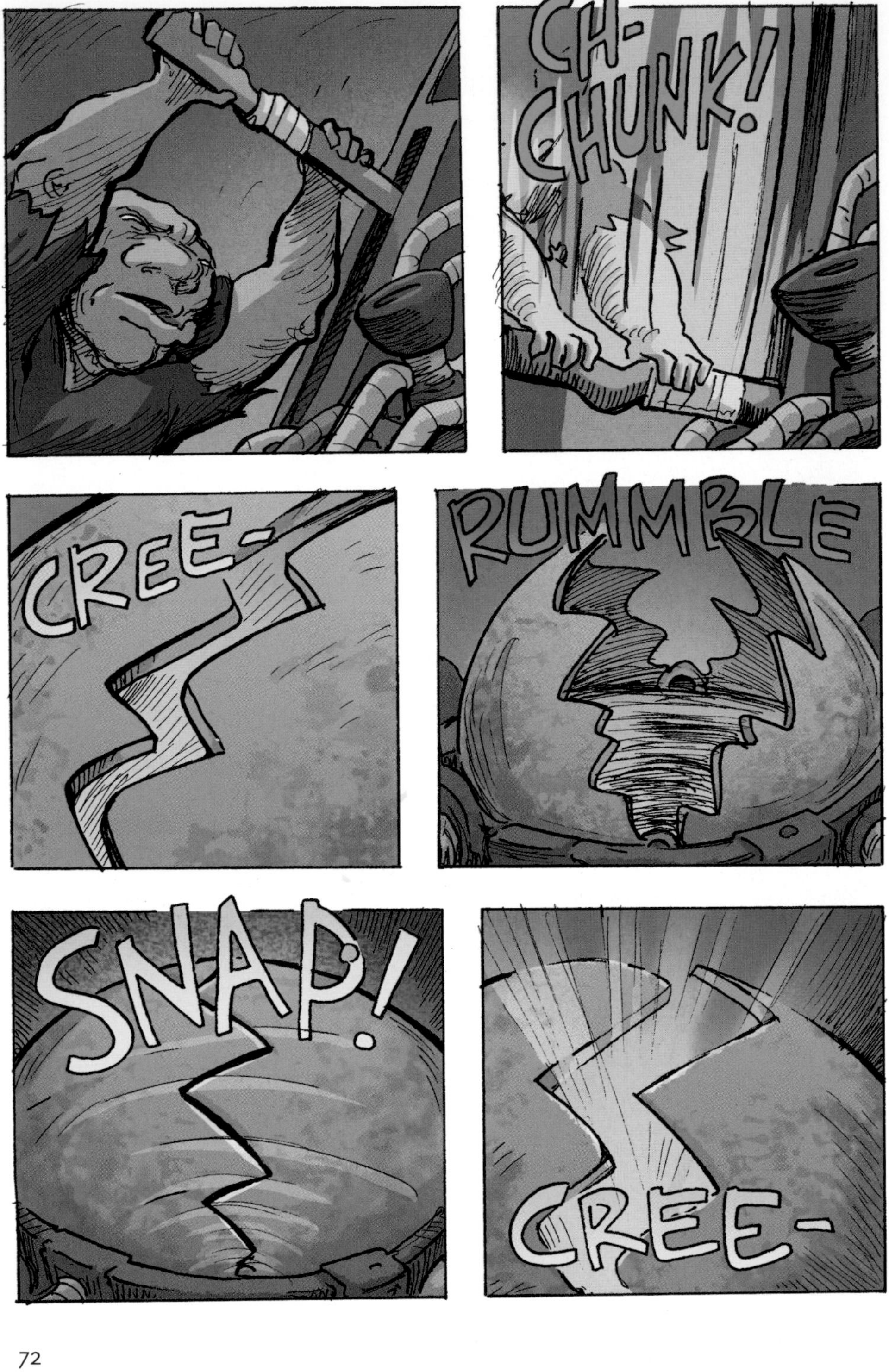
CH-
CHUNK!
CREE-
RUMMBLE
SNAP!
CREE-

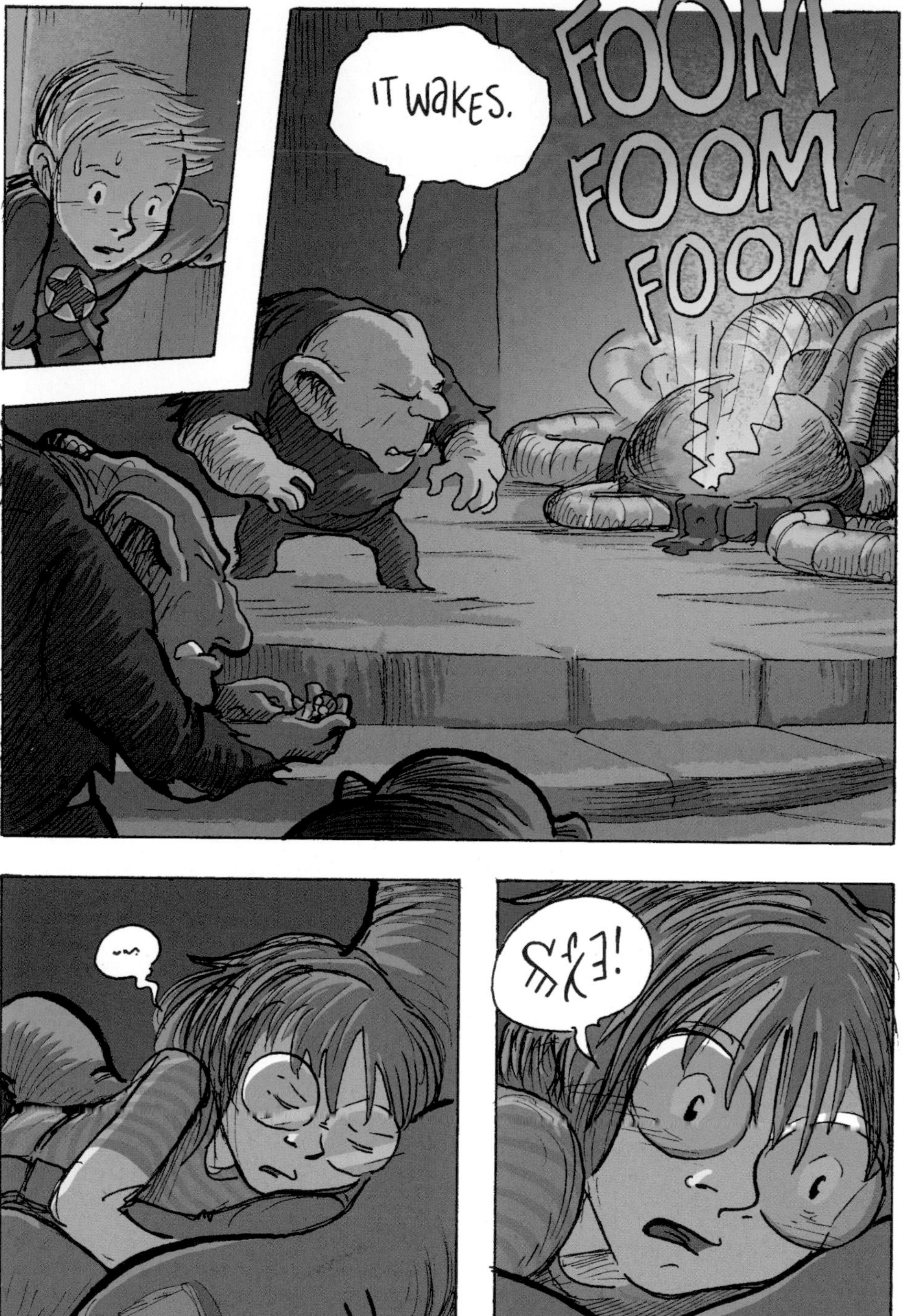
IT WAKES.
FOOM
FOOM
FOOM

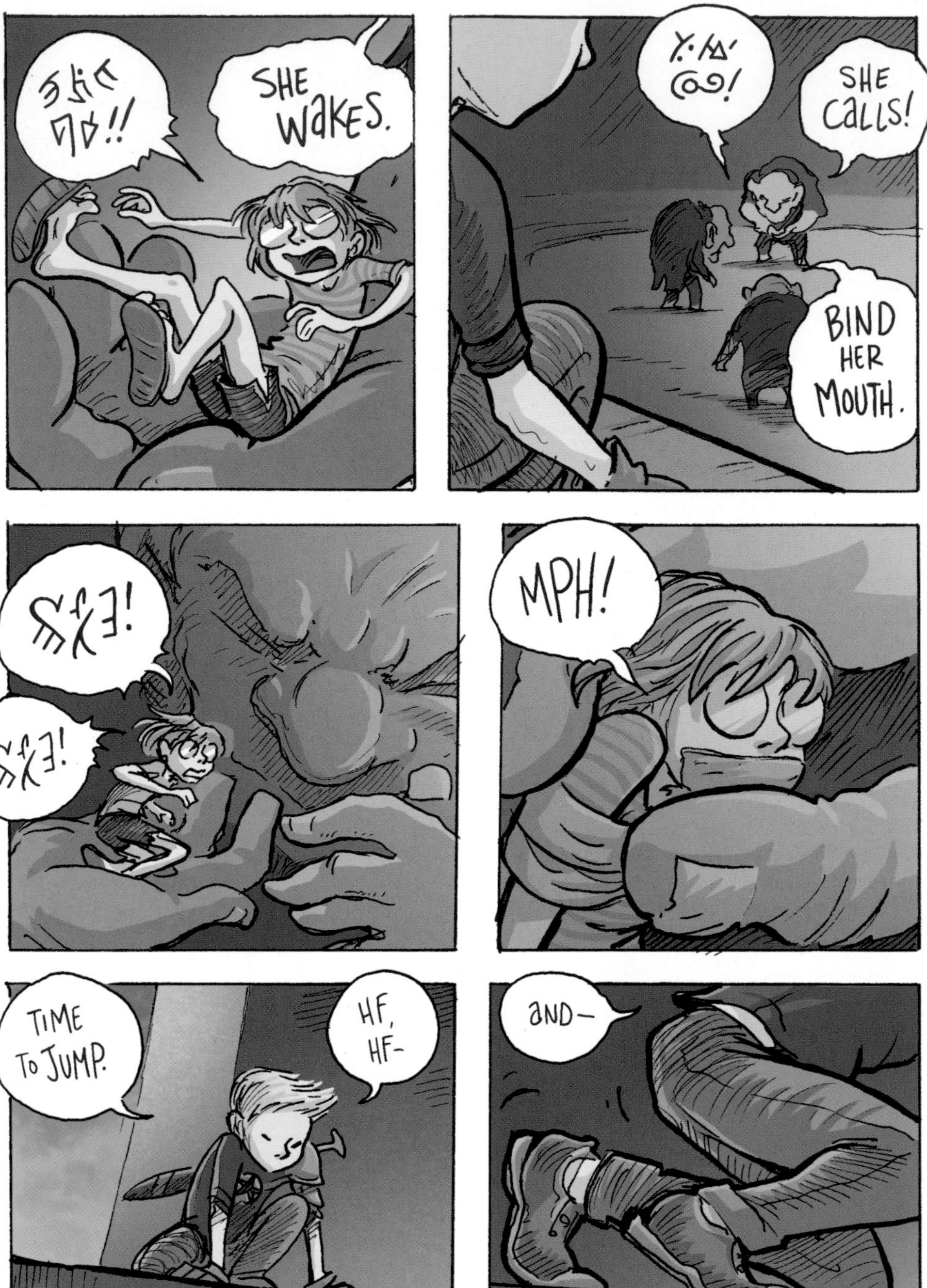
SHE WAKES.
SHE CALLS!
BIND HER MOUTH.
MPH!
TIME TO JUMP.
HF, HF-
and-

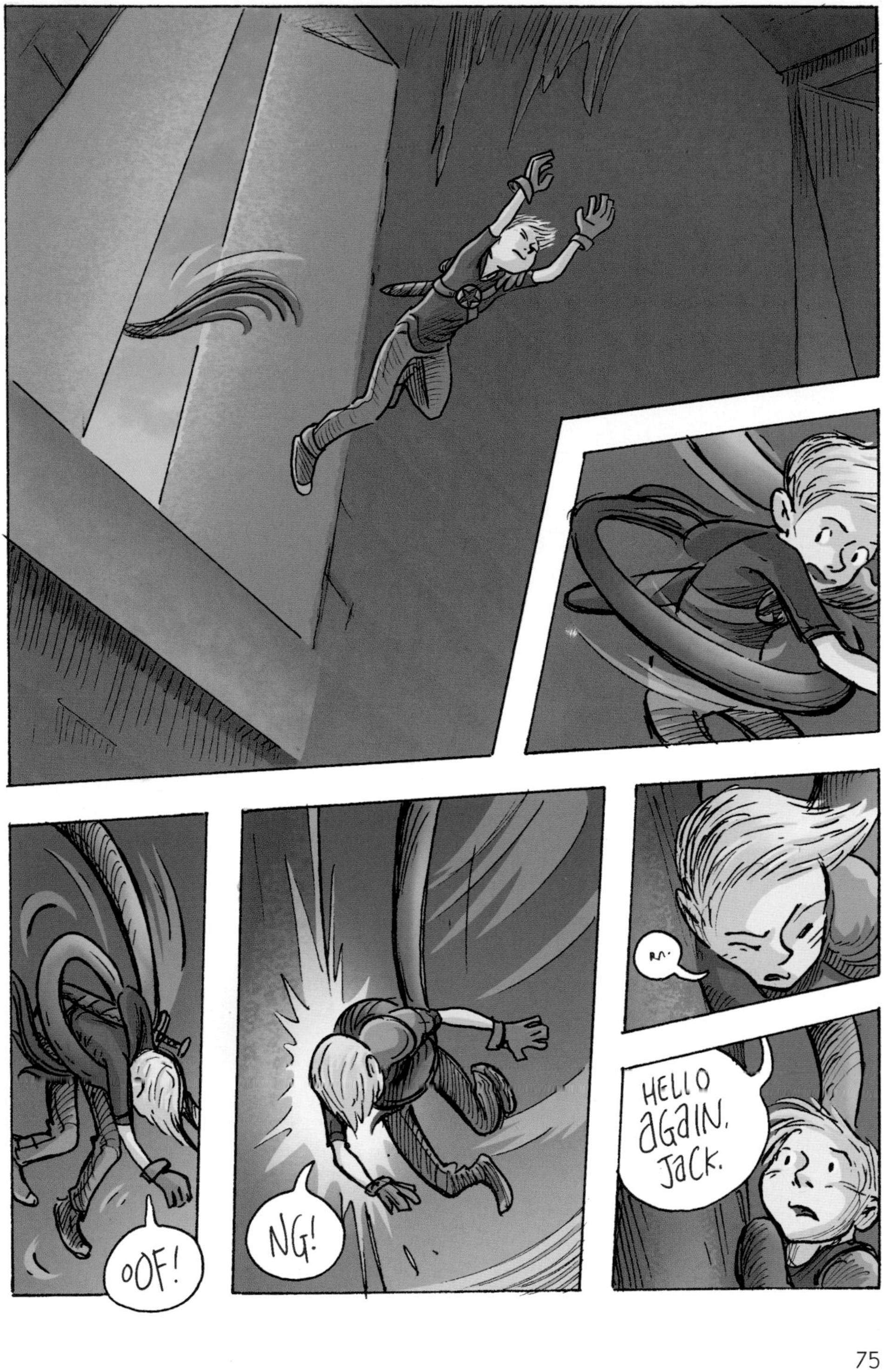
OOF!
NG!
HELLO again, Jack.

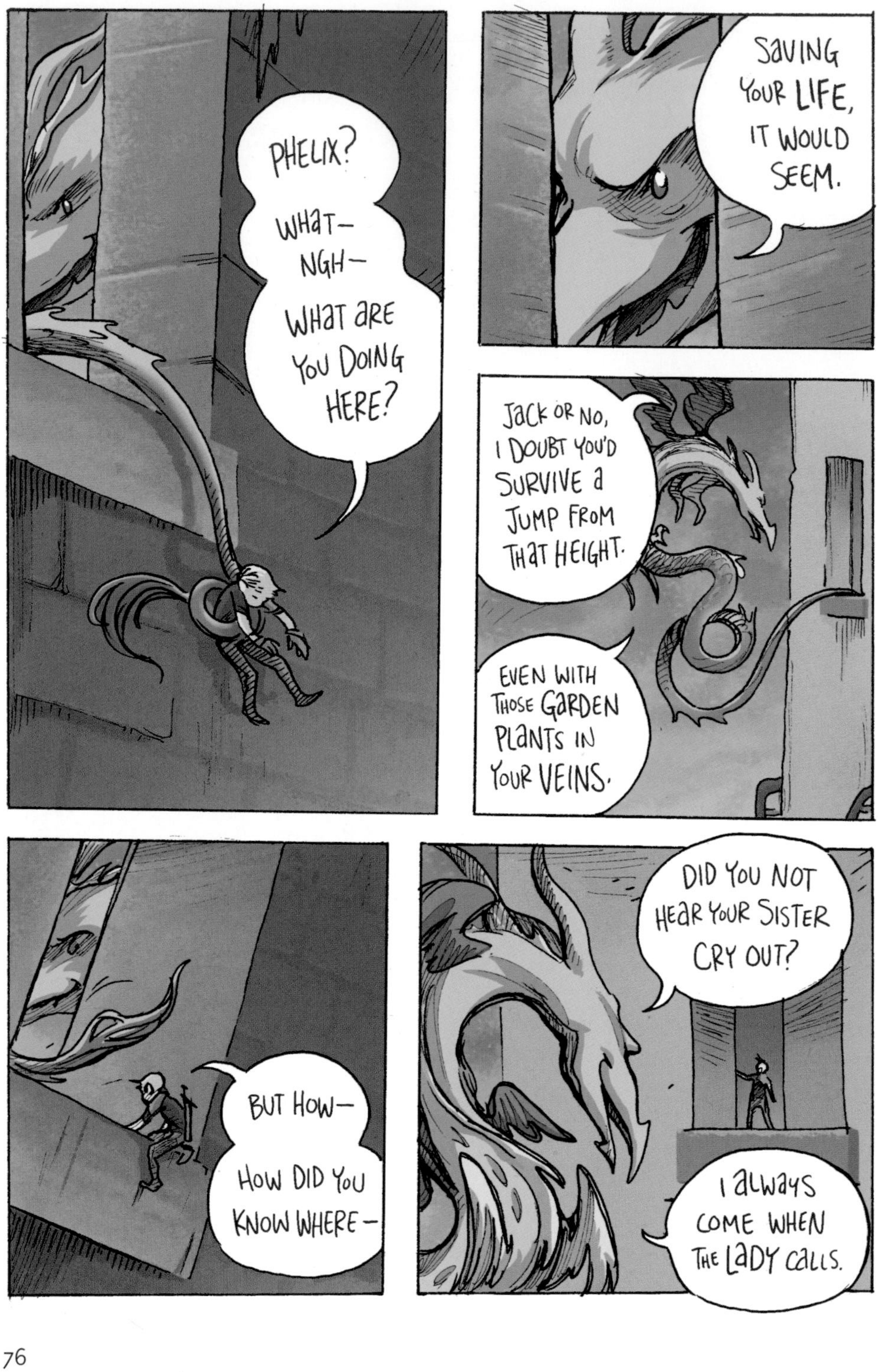
PHELIX?
WHAT— NGH— WHAT ARE YOU DOING HERE?
SAVING YOUR LIFE, IT WOULD SEEM.
JACK OR NO, I DOUBT YOU'D SURVIVE A JUMP FROM THAT HEIGHT.
EVEN WITH THOSE GARDEN PLANTS IN YOUR VEINS.
BUT HOW—
HOW DID YOU KNOW WHERE—
DID YOU NOT HEAR YOUR SISTER CRY OUT?
I ALWAYS COME WHEN THE LADY CALLS.

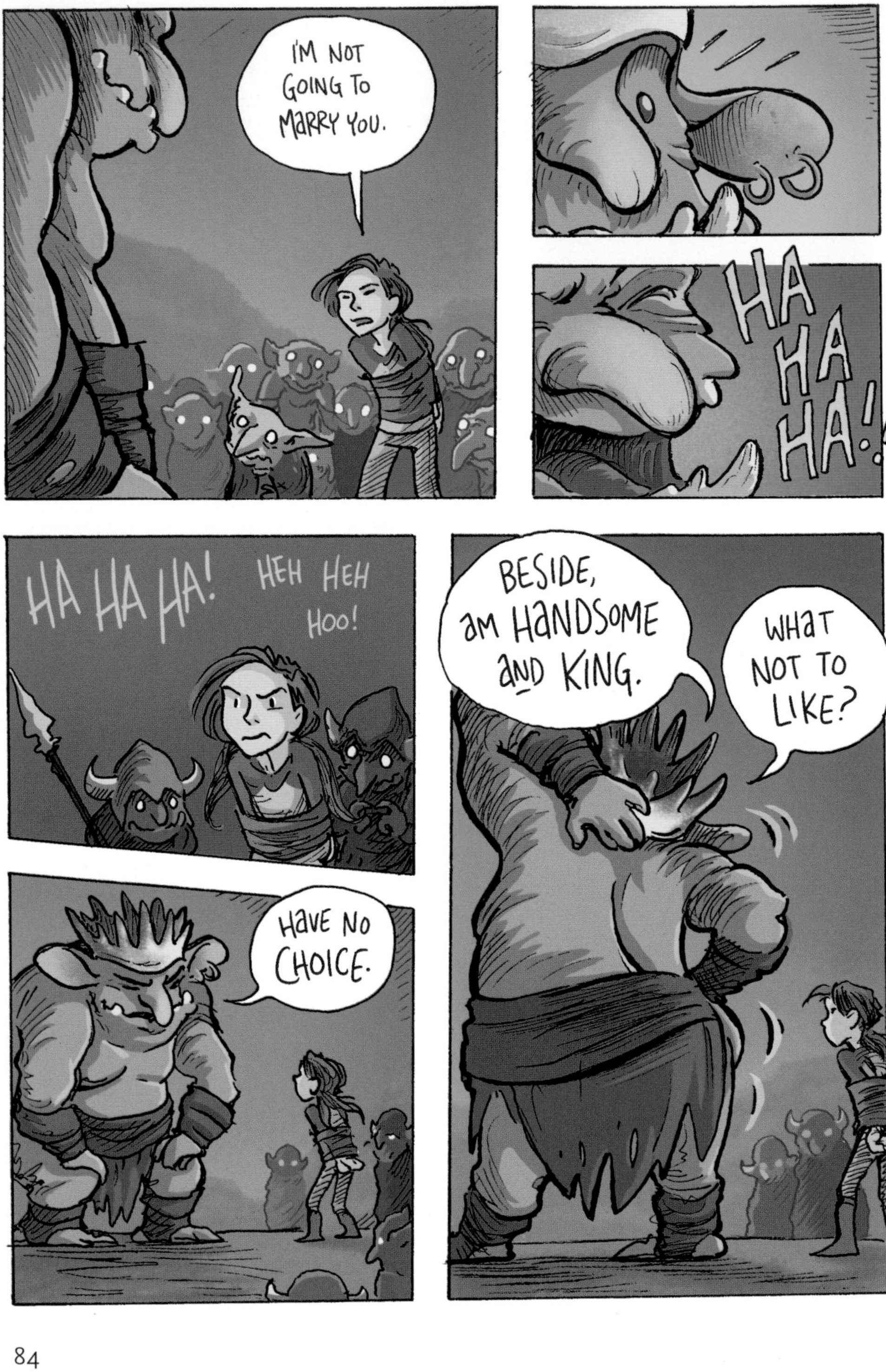
I'M NOT GOING TO MARRY YOU.
HA HA HA!!
HA HA HA!
HEH HEH HOO!
HAVE NO CHOICE.
BESIDE, AM HANDSOME AND KING.
WHAT NOT TO LIKE?

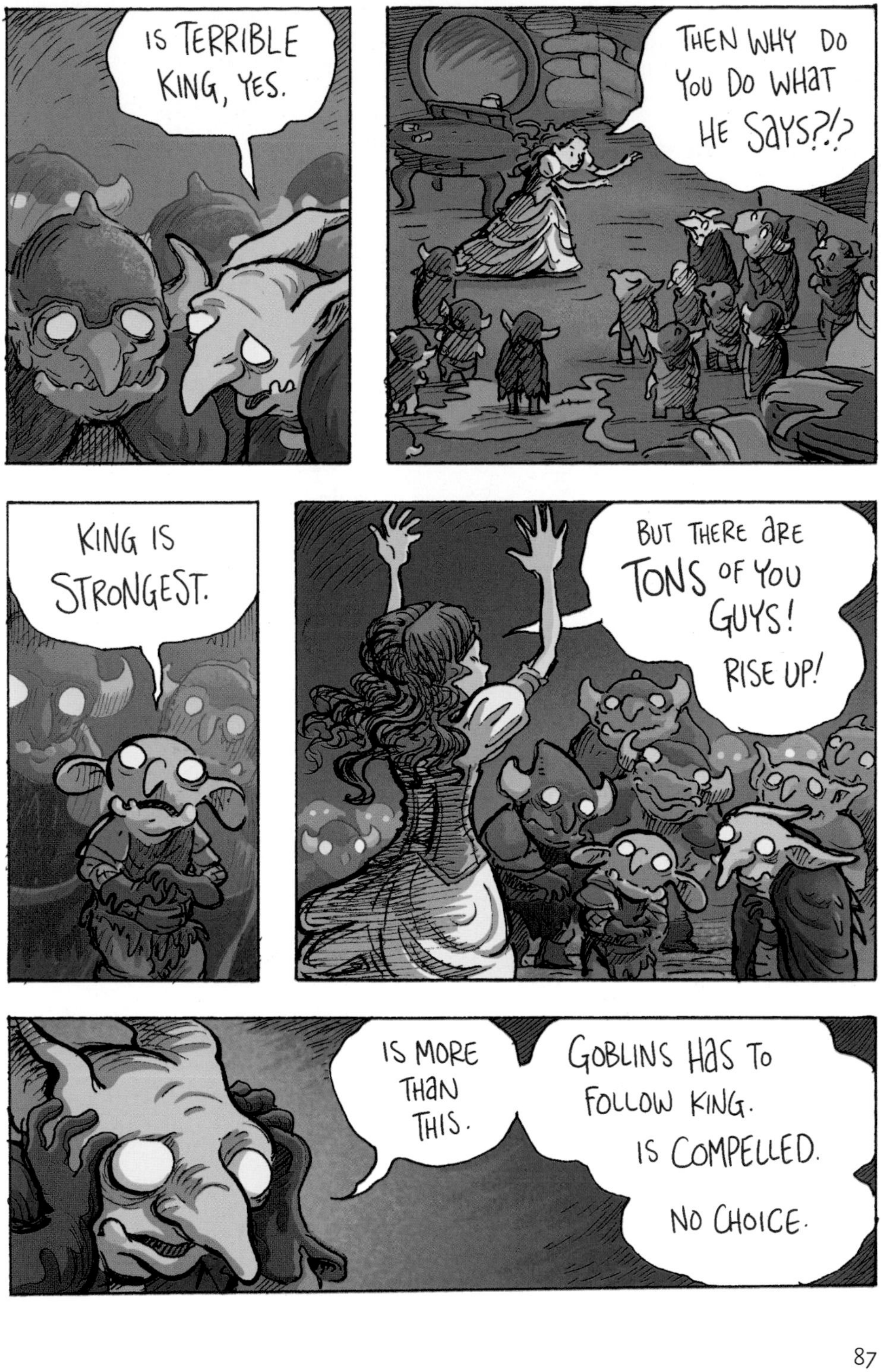
IS TERRIBLE KING, YES.
THEN WHY DO YOU DO WHAT HE SAYS?!?
KING IS STRONGEST.
BUT THERE ARE TONS OF YOU GUYS!
RISE UP!
IS MORE THAN THIS.
GOBLINS HAS TO FOLLOW KING.
IS COMPELLED.
NO CHOICE.

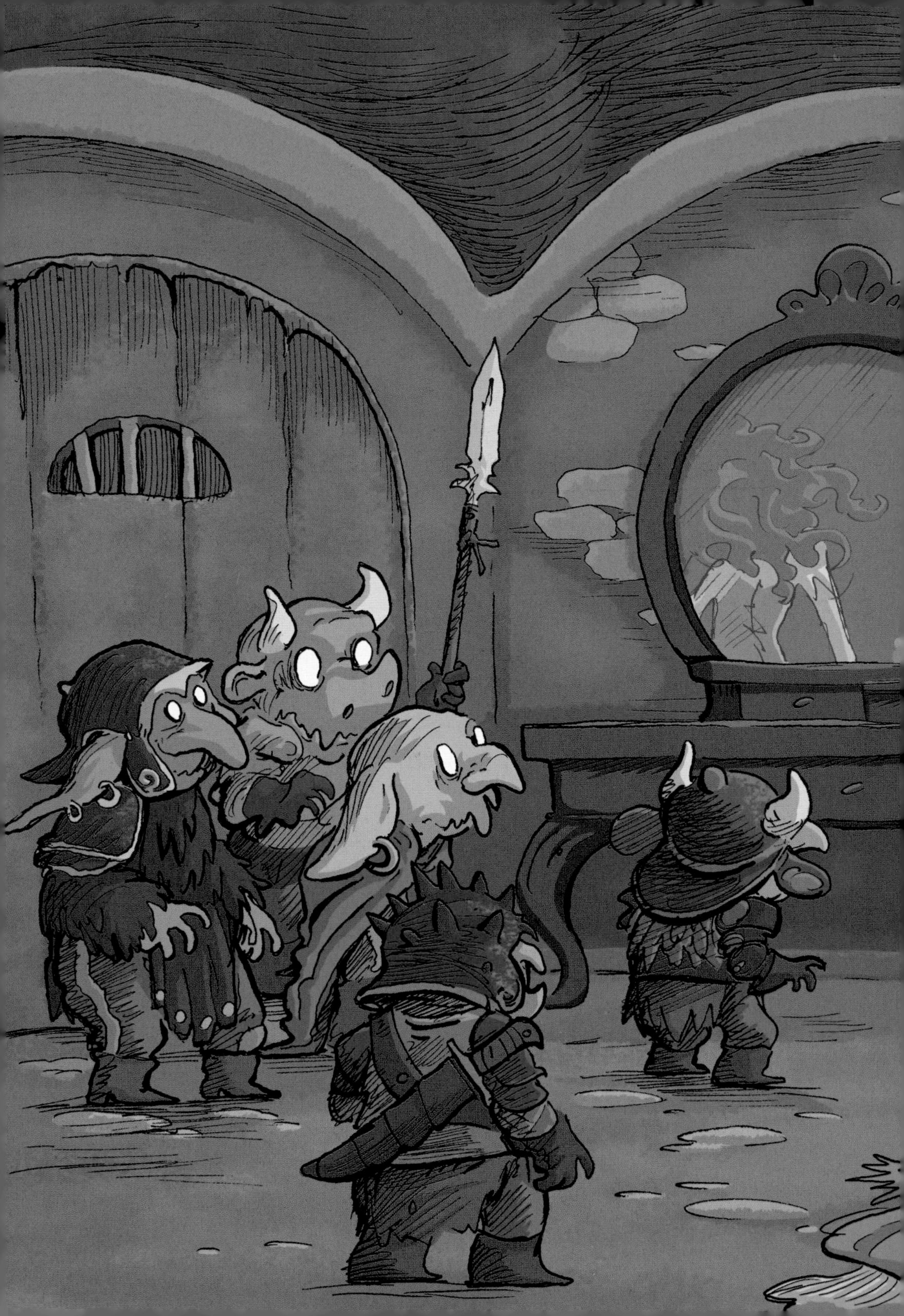

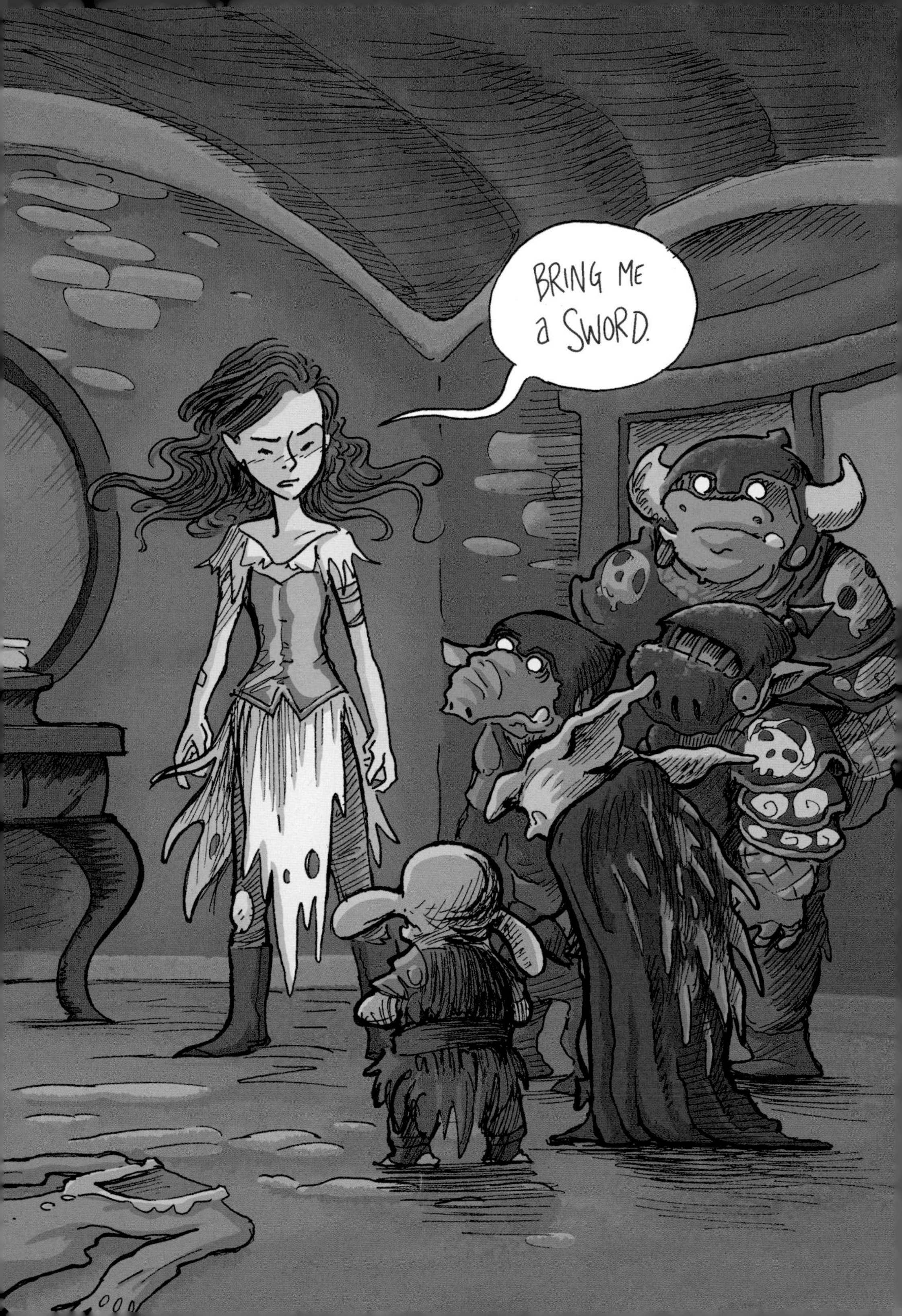
BRING ME a SWORD.

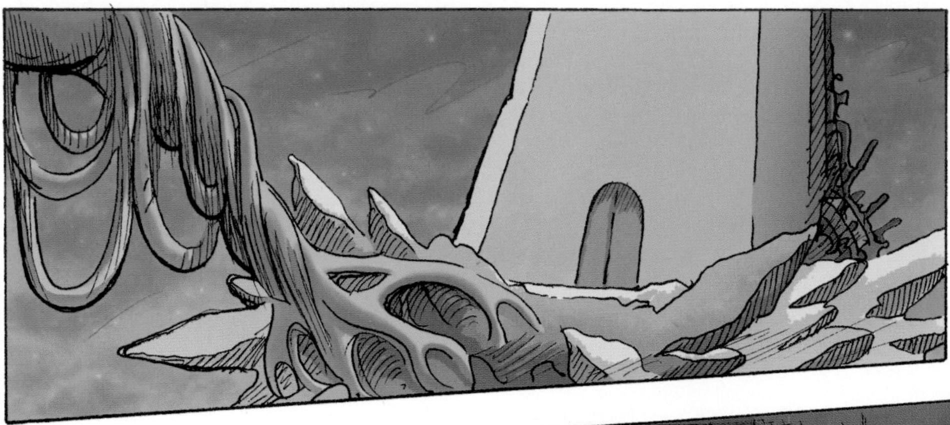

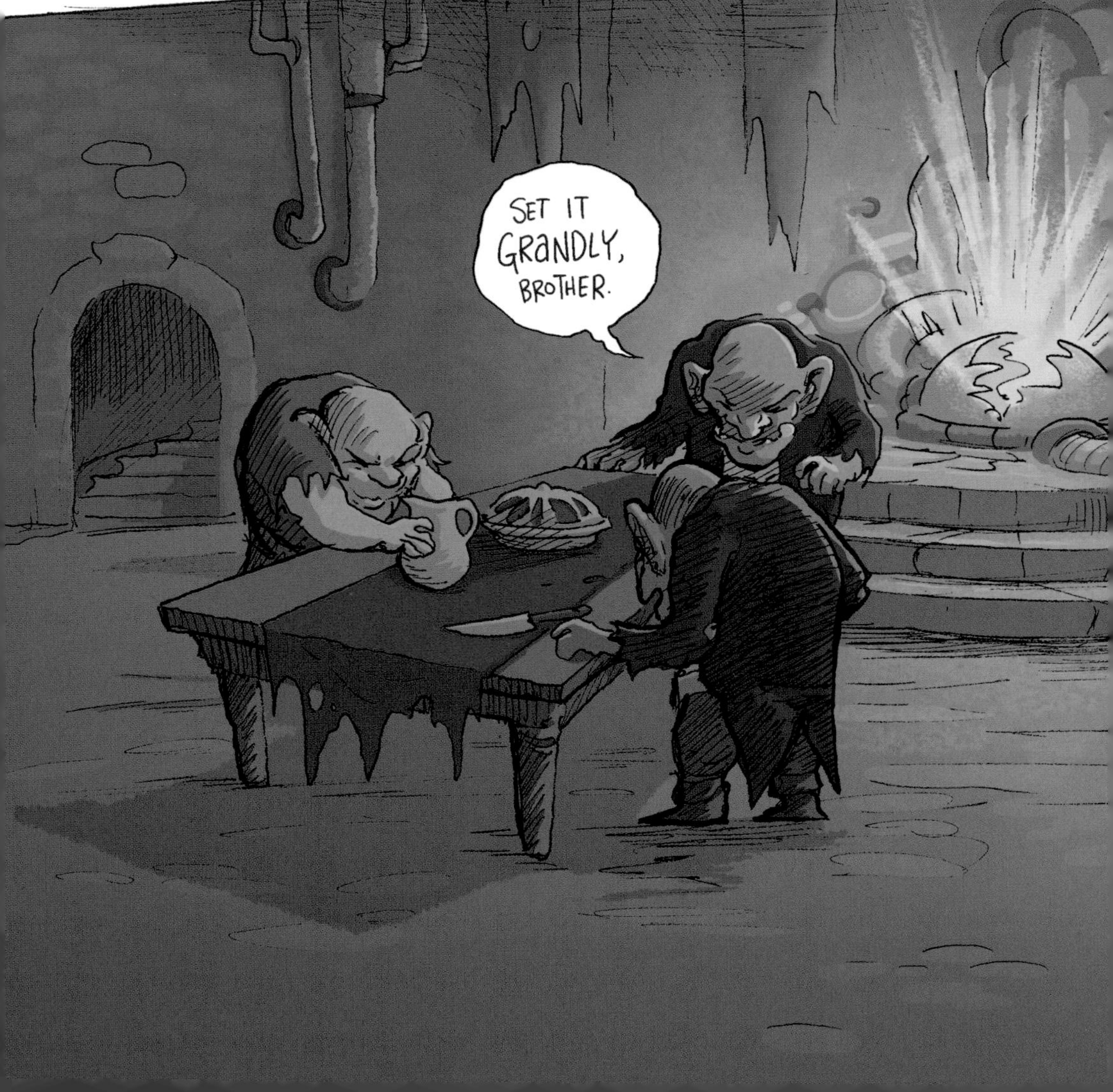
SET IT GRANDLY, BROTHER.

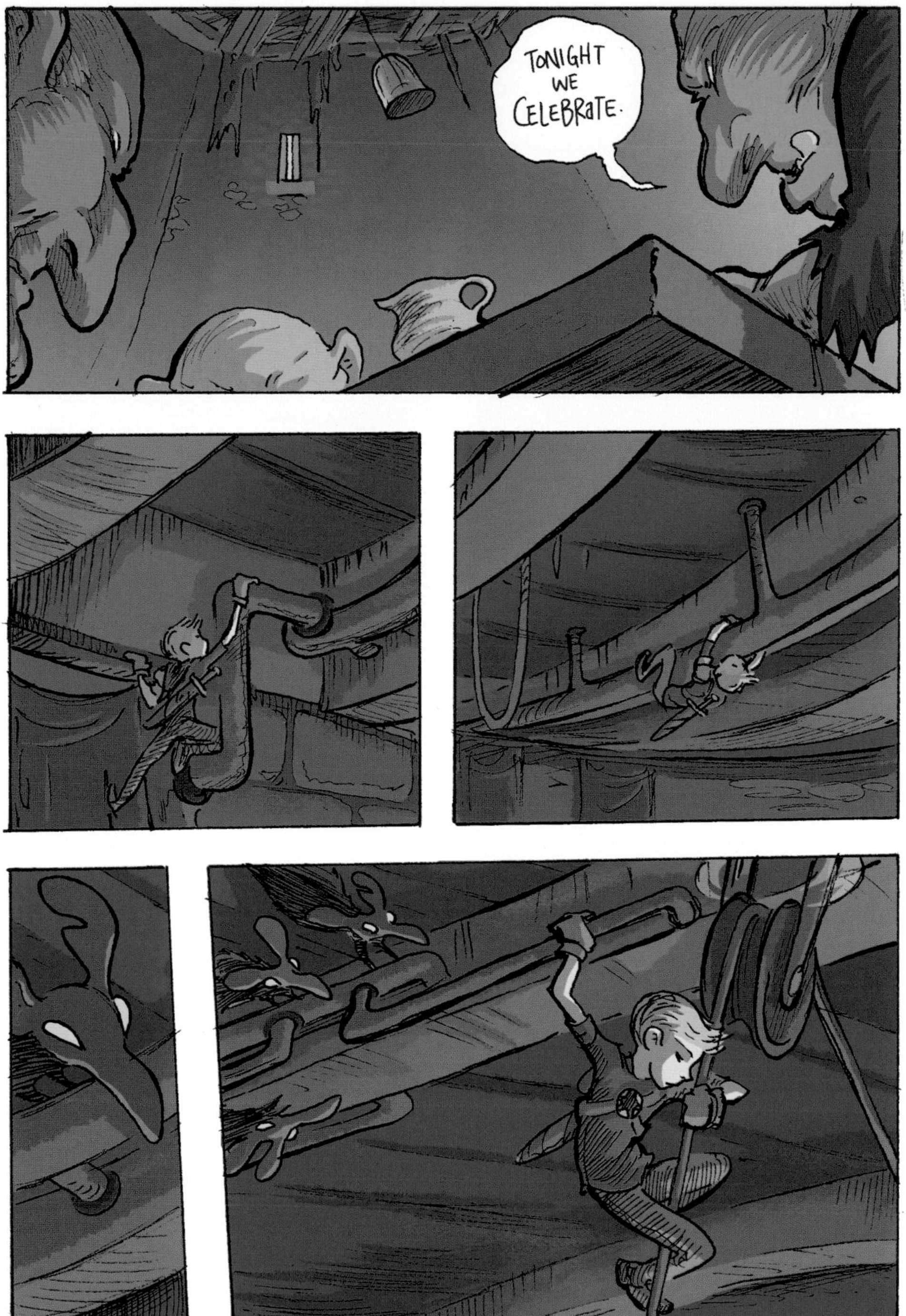
TONIGHT WE CELEBRATE.

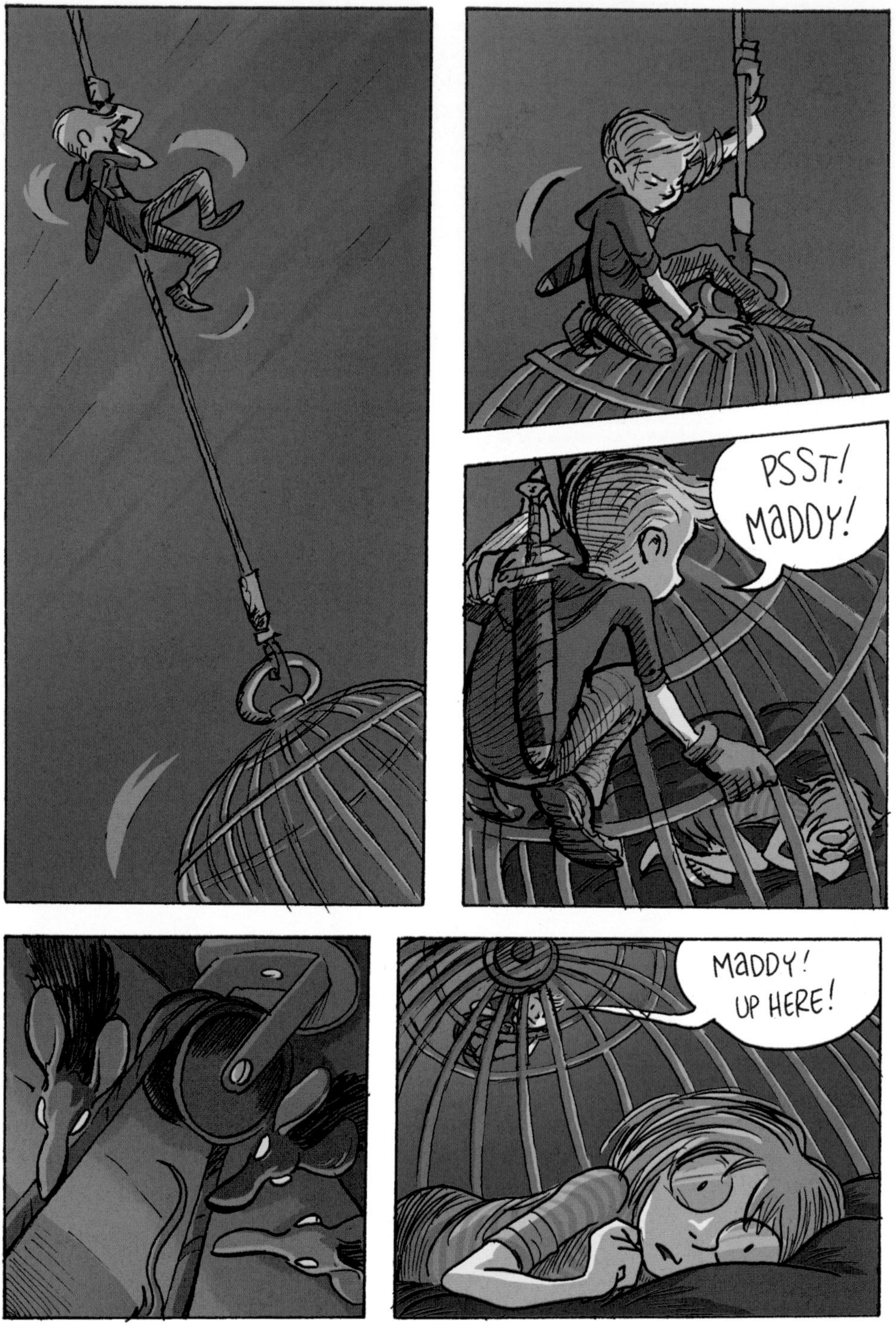
PSST! MADDY!
MADDY! UP HERE!

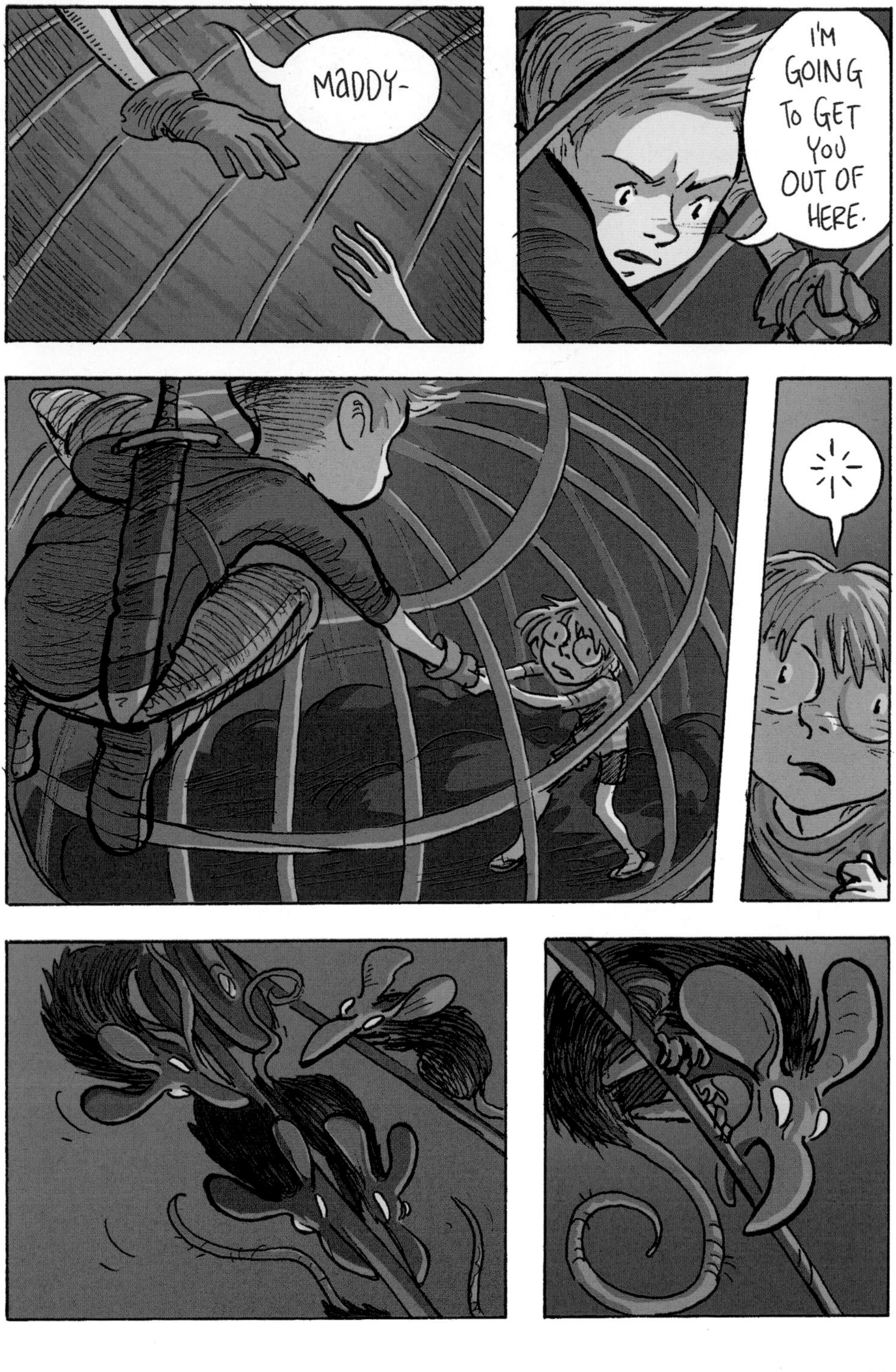
MADDY-
I'M GOING TO GET YOU OUT OF HERE.

98

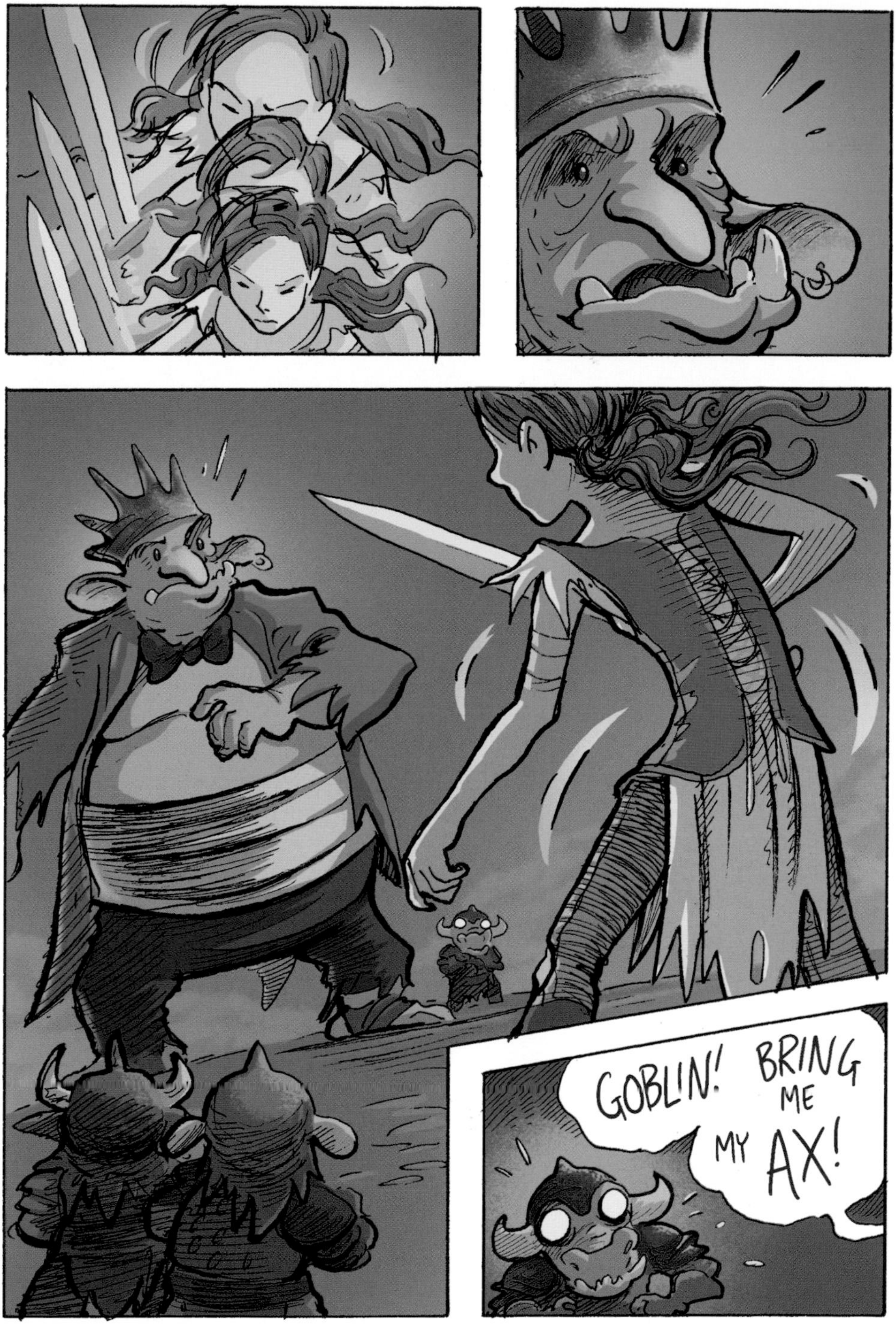
GOBLIN! BRING ME MY AX!

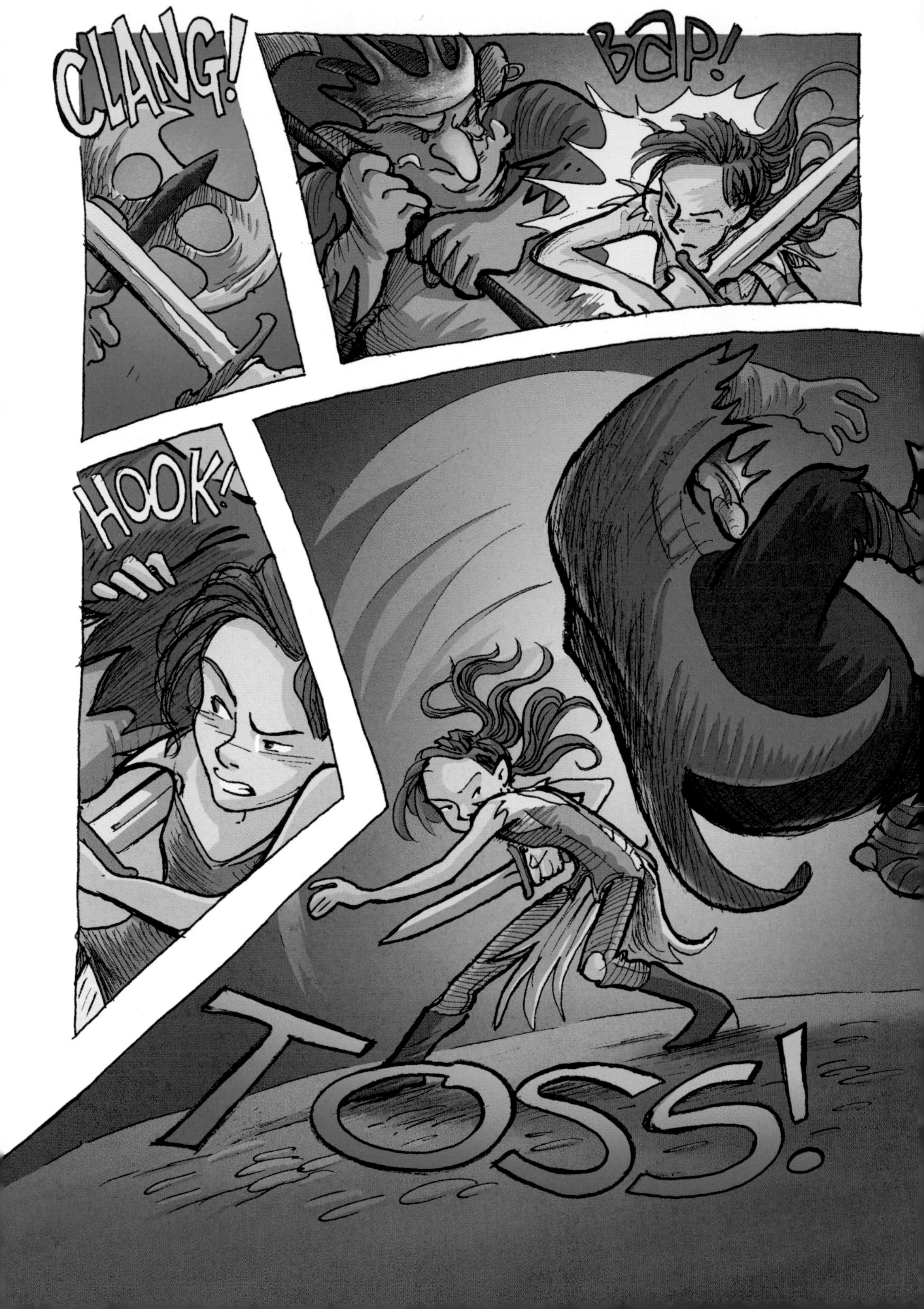
CLANG!
BAP!
HOOK!
TOSS!

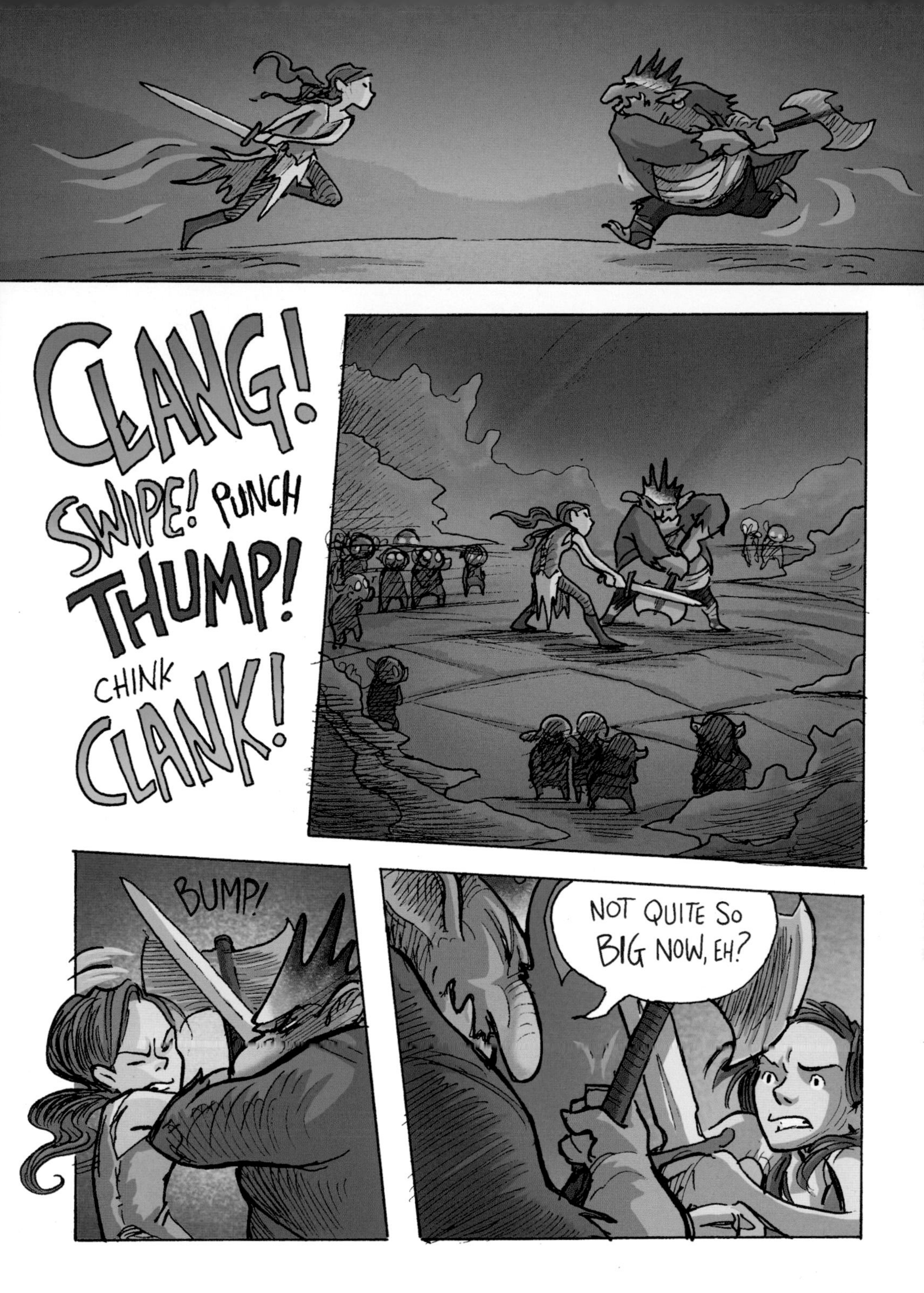
CLANG!
SWIPE! PUNCH
THUMP!
CHINK
CLANK!
BUMP!
NOT QUITE SO BIG NOW, EH?

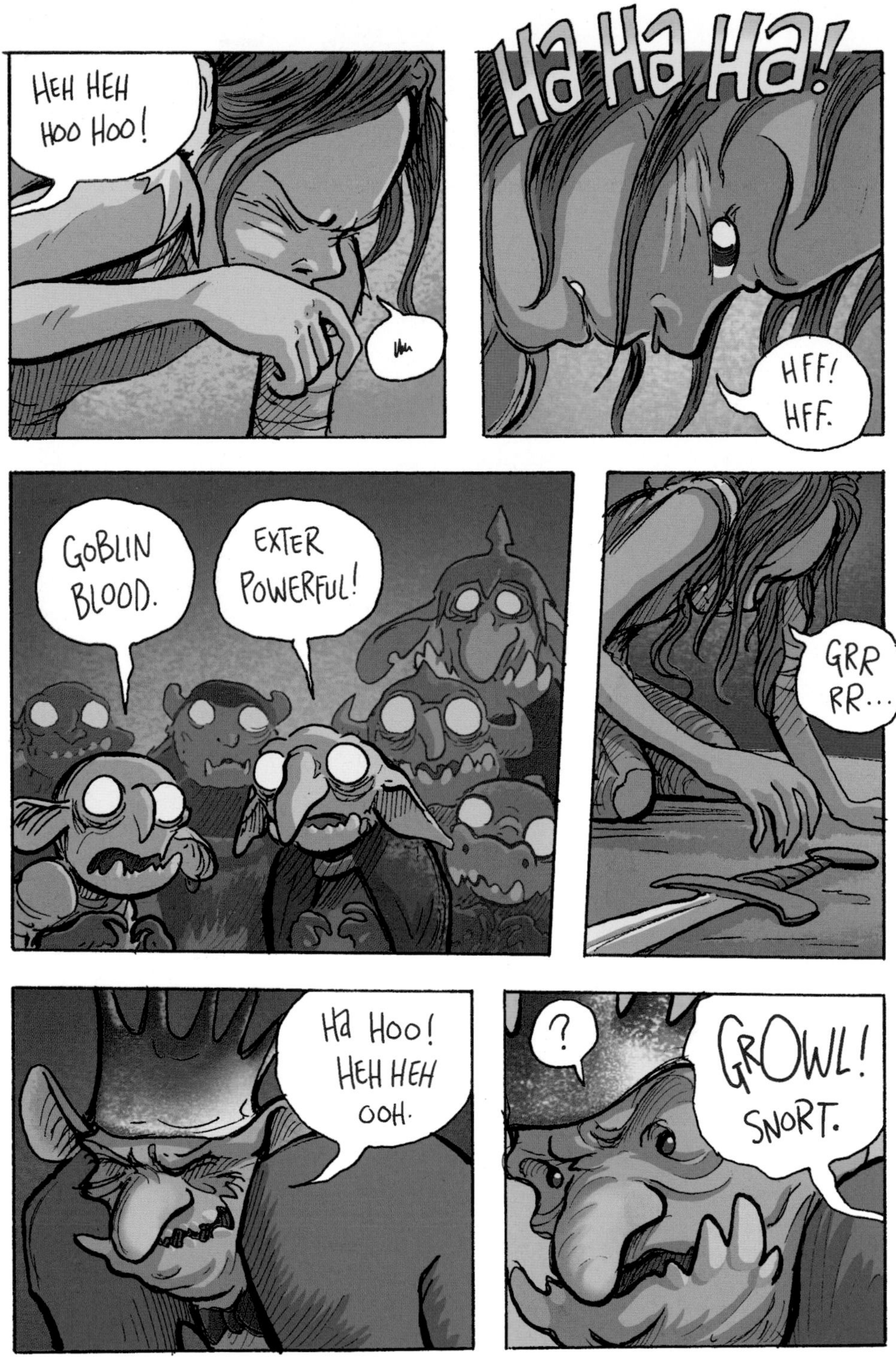
HEH HEH HOO HOO!
HA HA HA!
HFF! HFF.
GOBLIN BLOOD.
EXTER POWERFUL!
GRR RR...
HA HOO! HEH HEH OOH.
?
GROWL! SNORT.

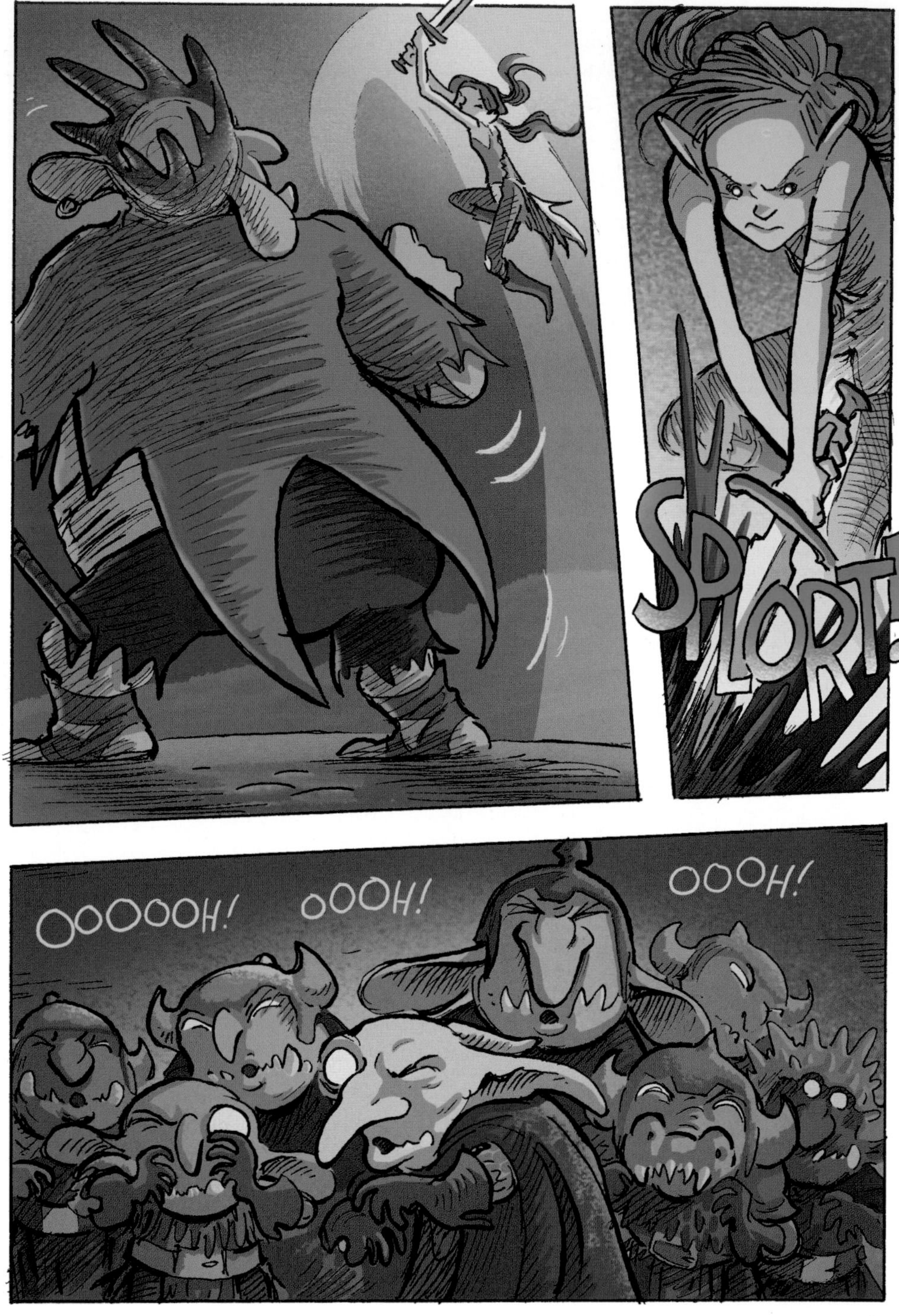
SPLORT!
OOOOOH!
OOOH!
OOOH!

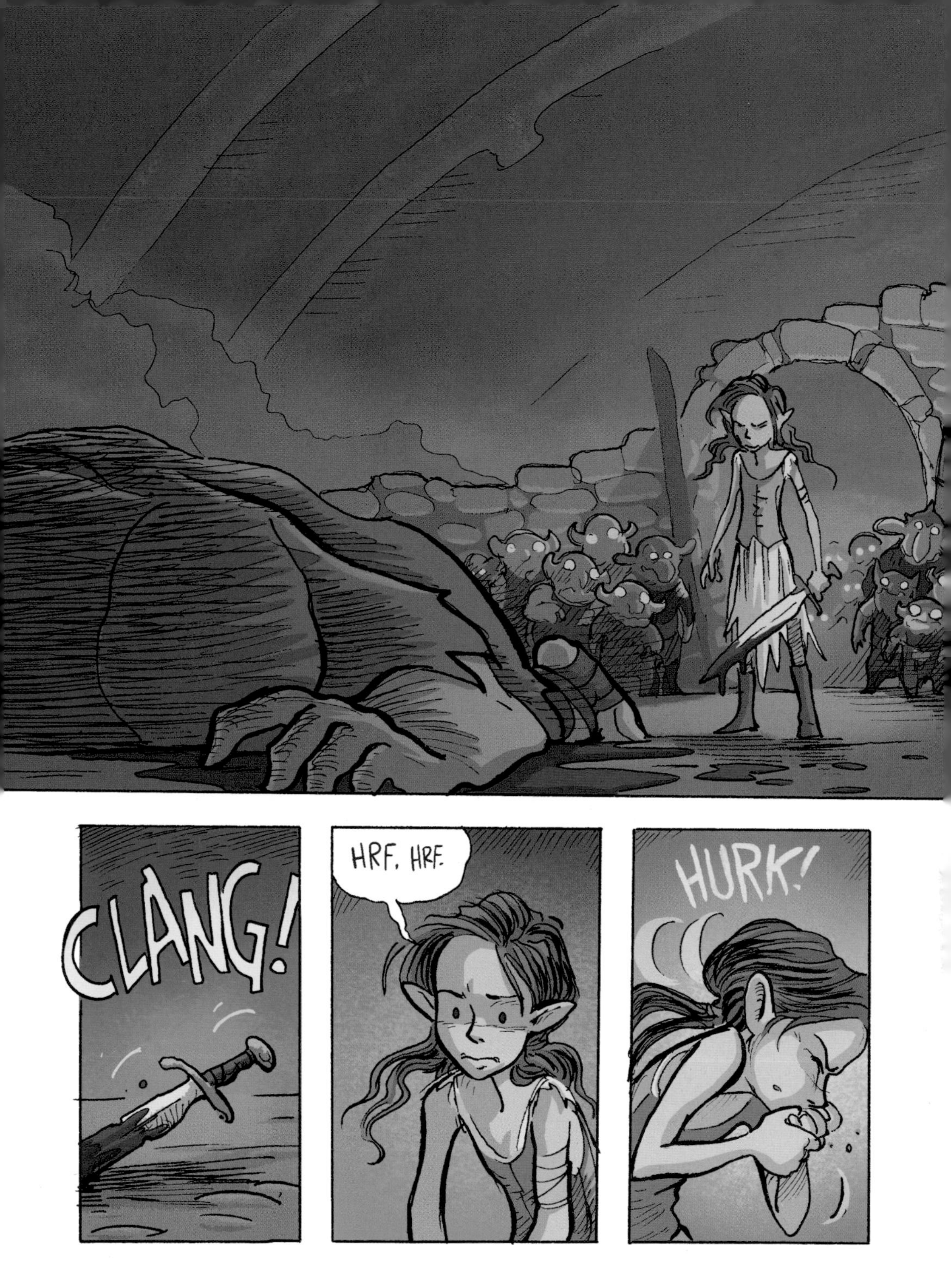
CLANG!
HRF. HRF.
HURK!

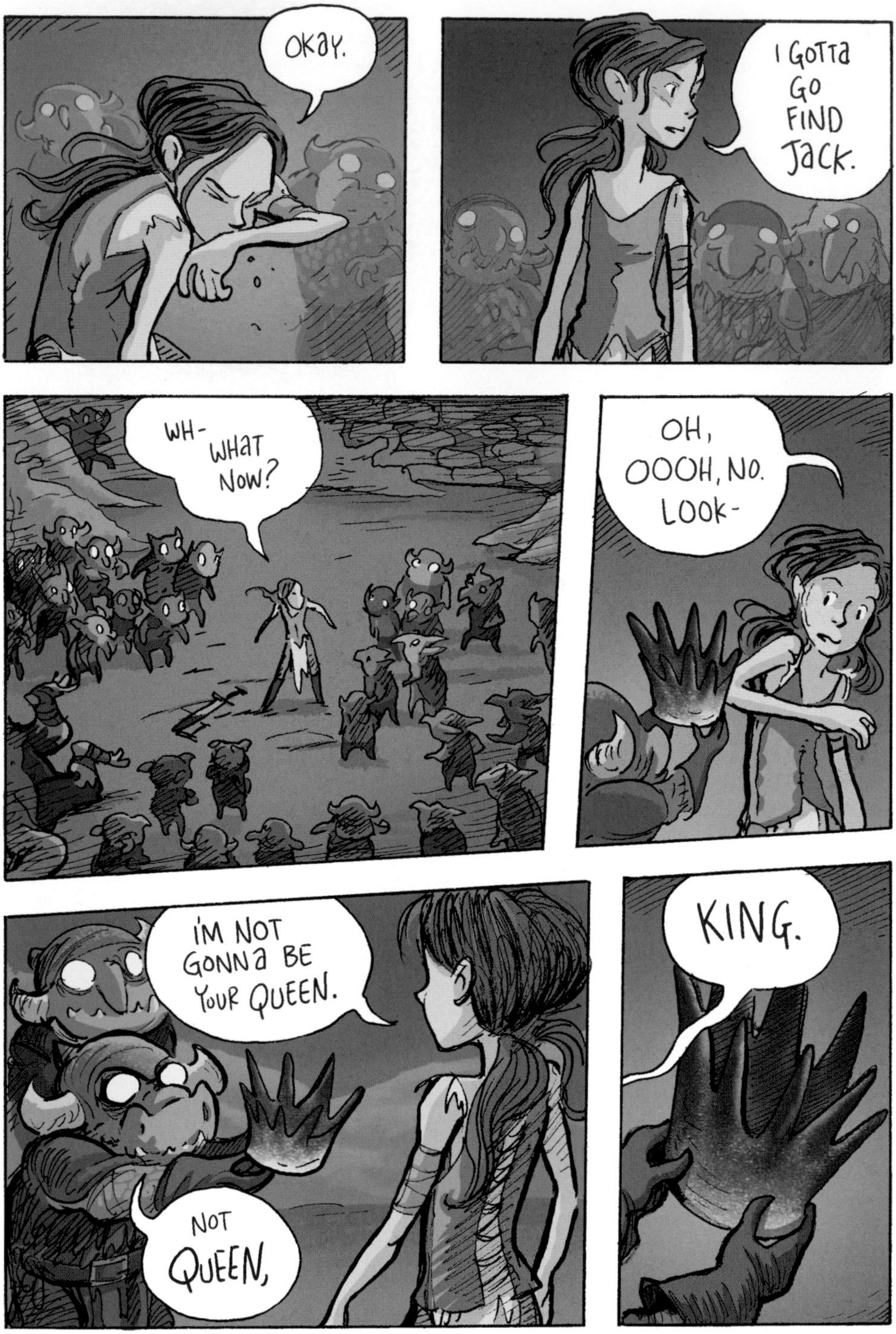
OKAY.
I GOTTA GO FIND JACK.
WH- WHAT NOW?
OH, OOOH, NO. LOOK-
I'M NOT GONNA BE YOUR QUEEN.
NOT QUEEN,
KING.

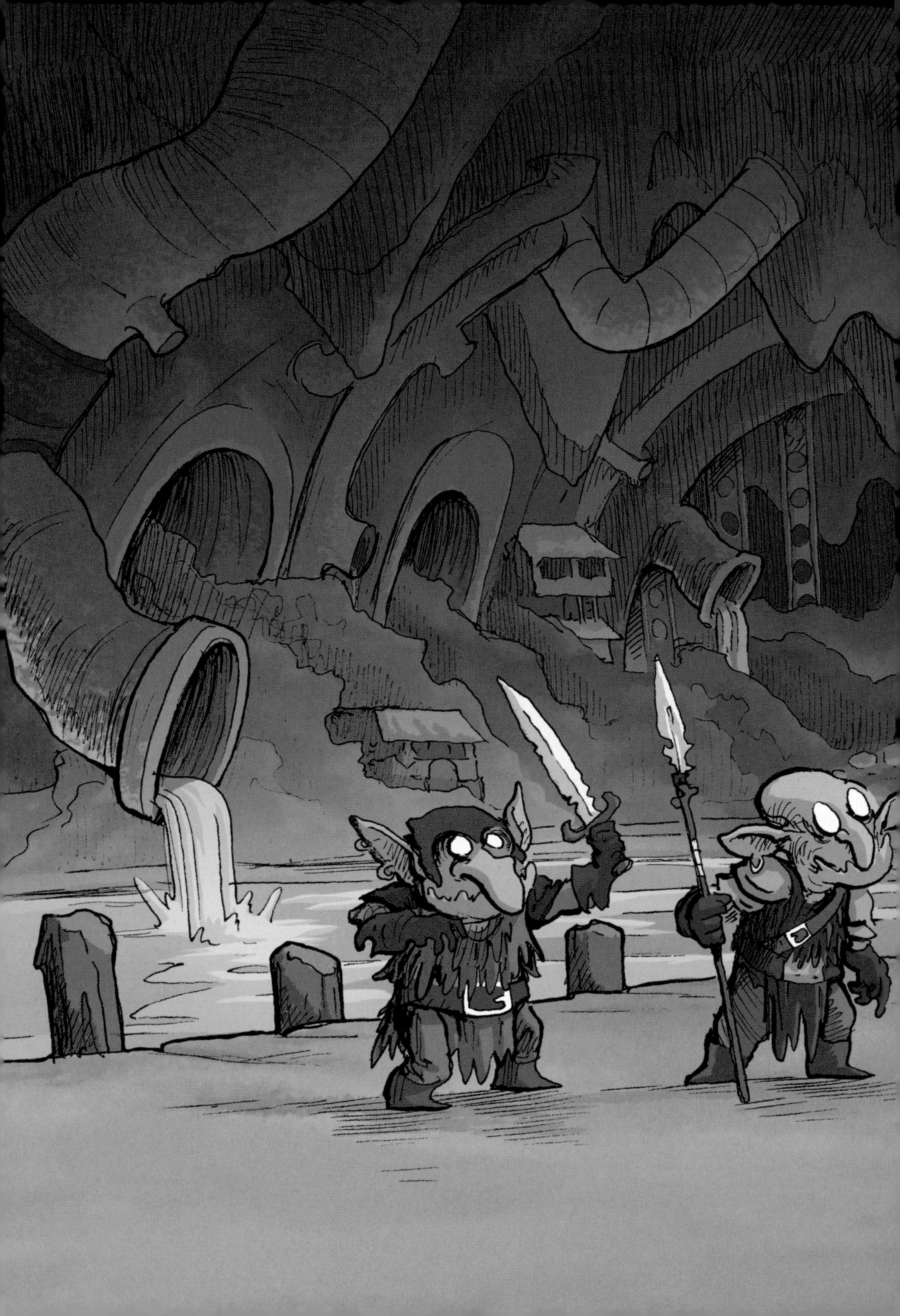

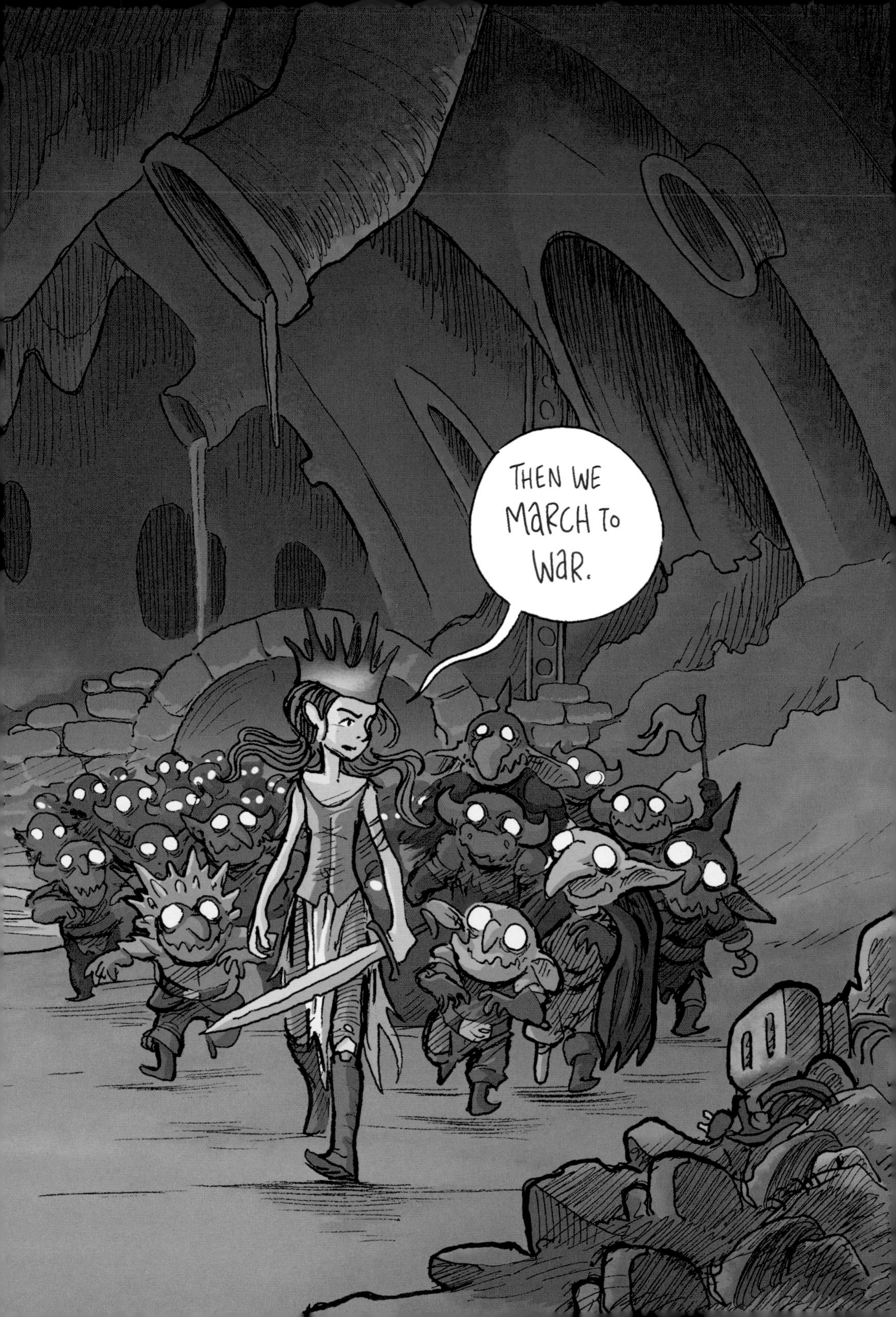
THEN WE MARCH TO WAR.

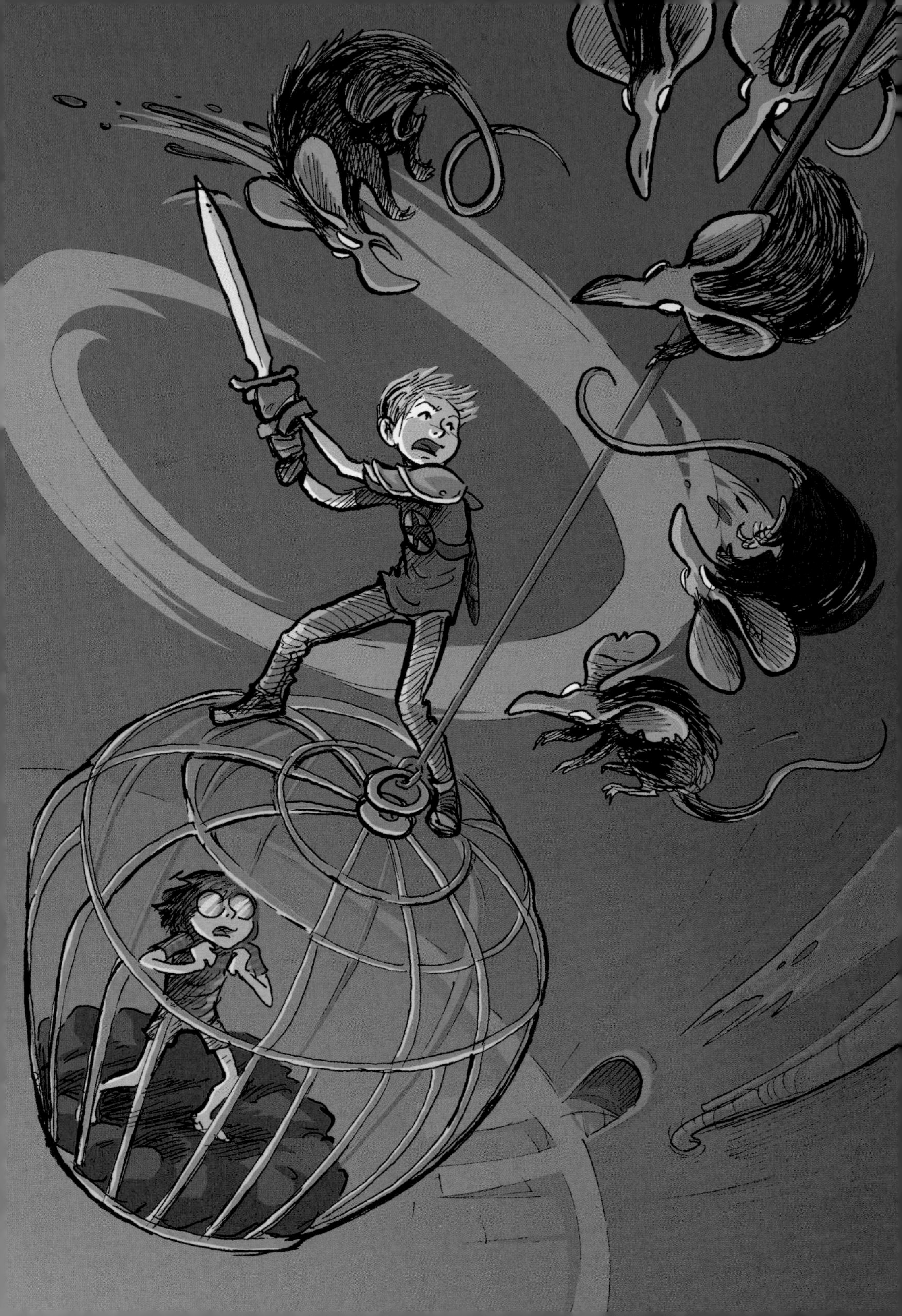

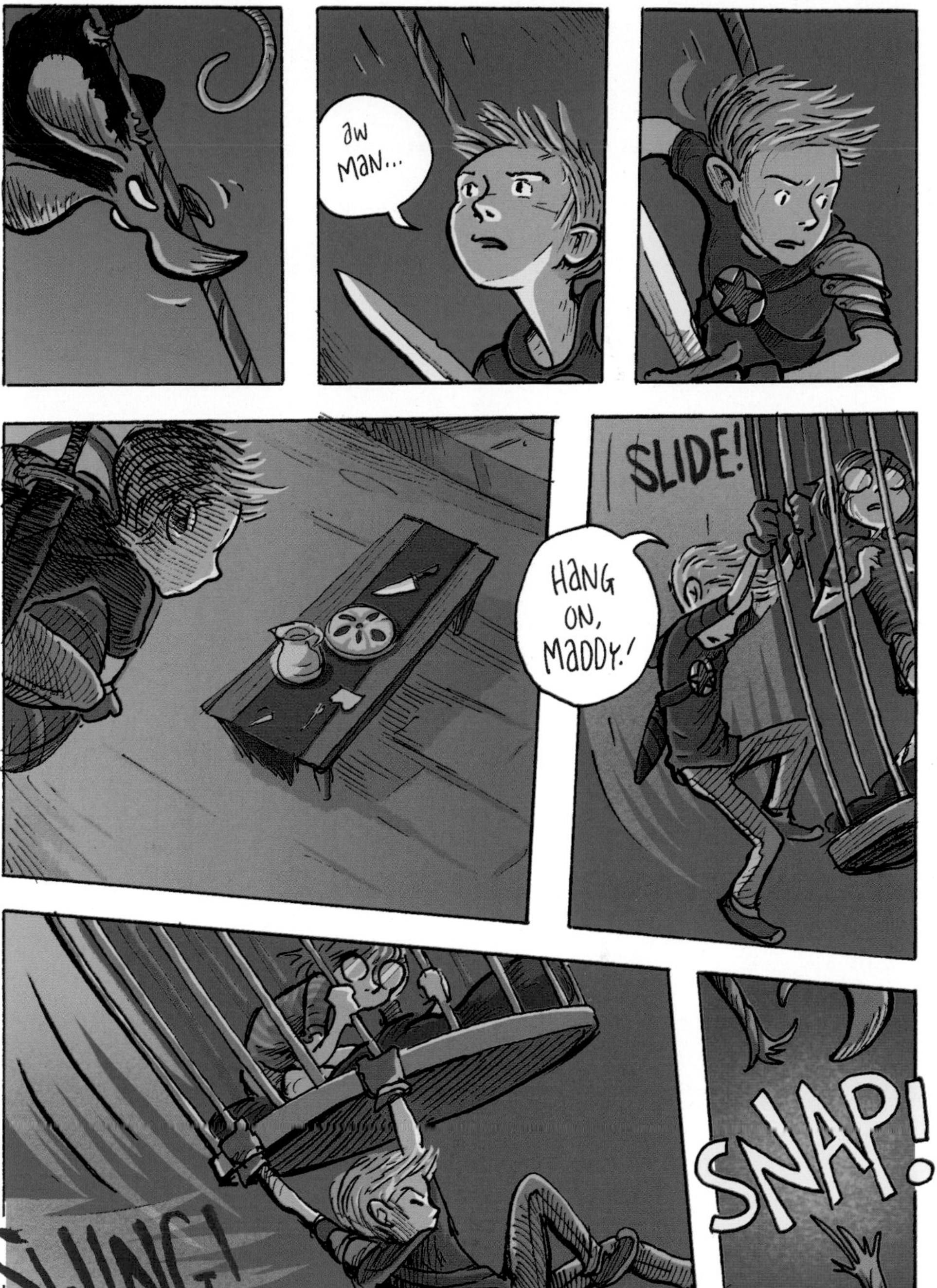
aw man...
SLIDE!
HANG ON, MADDY!
SWING!
SNAP!

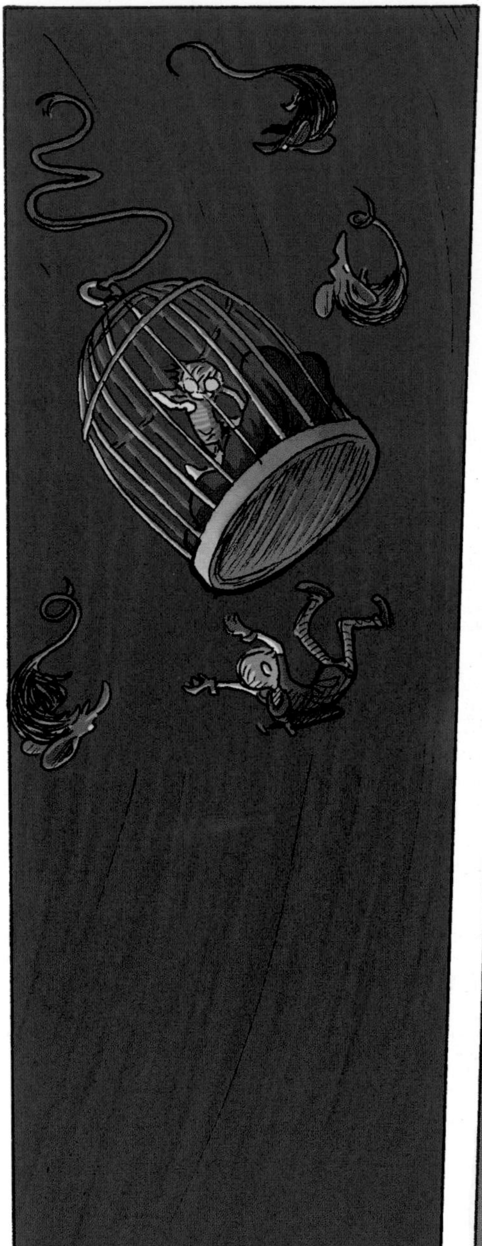
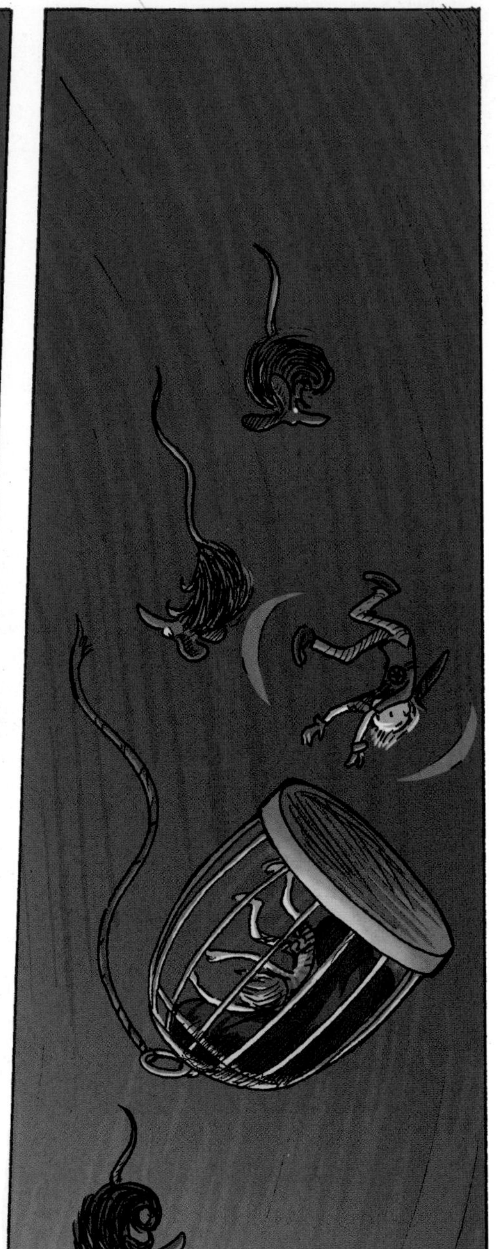

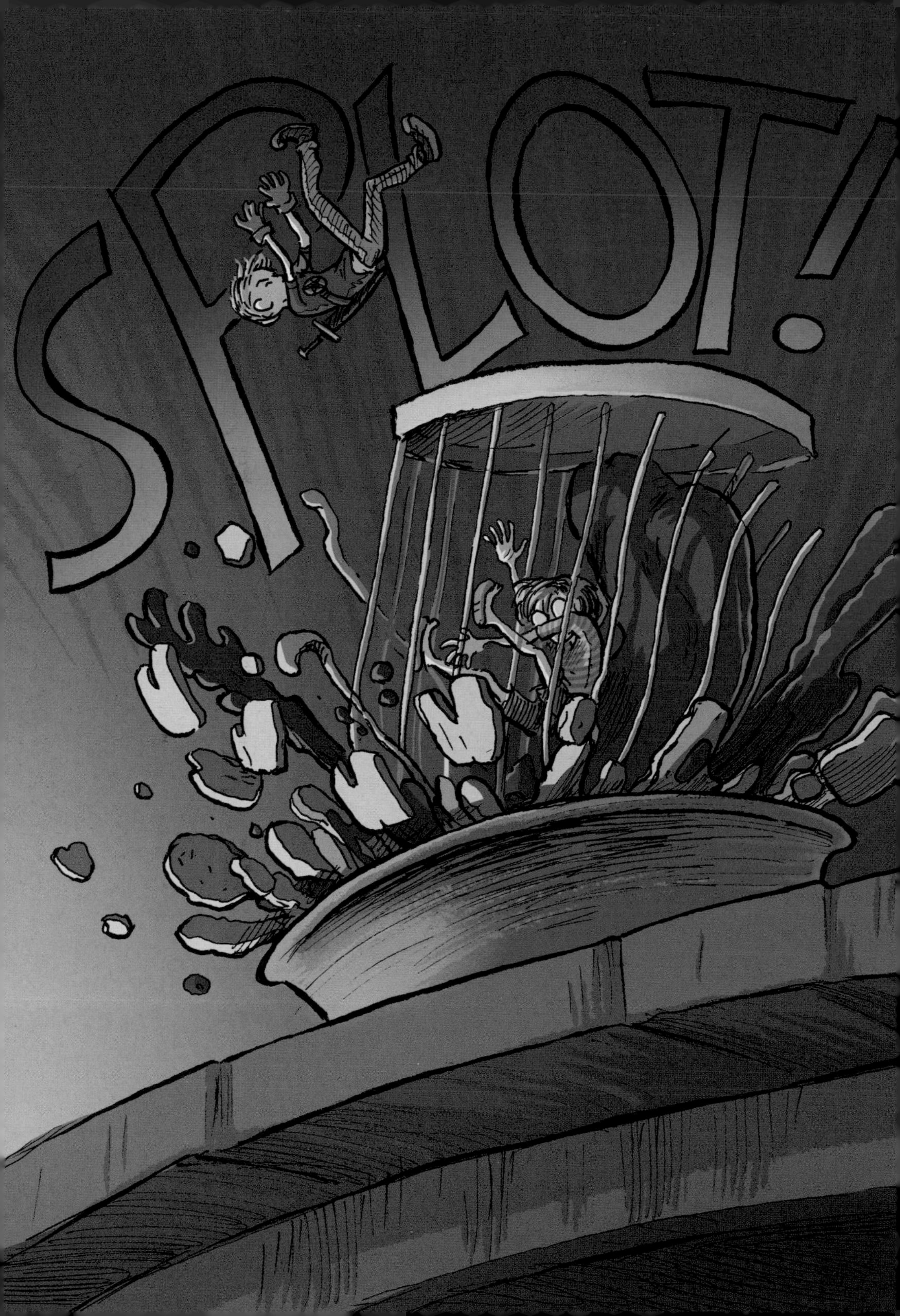
SPLOT!

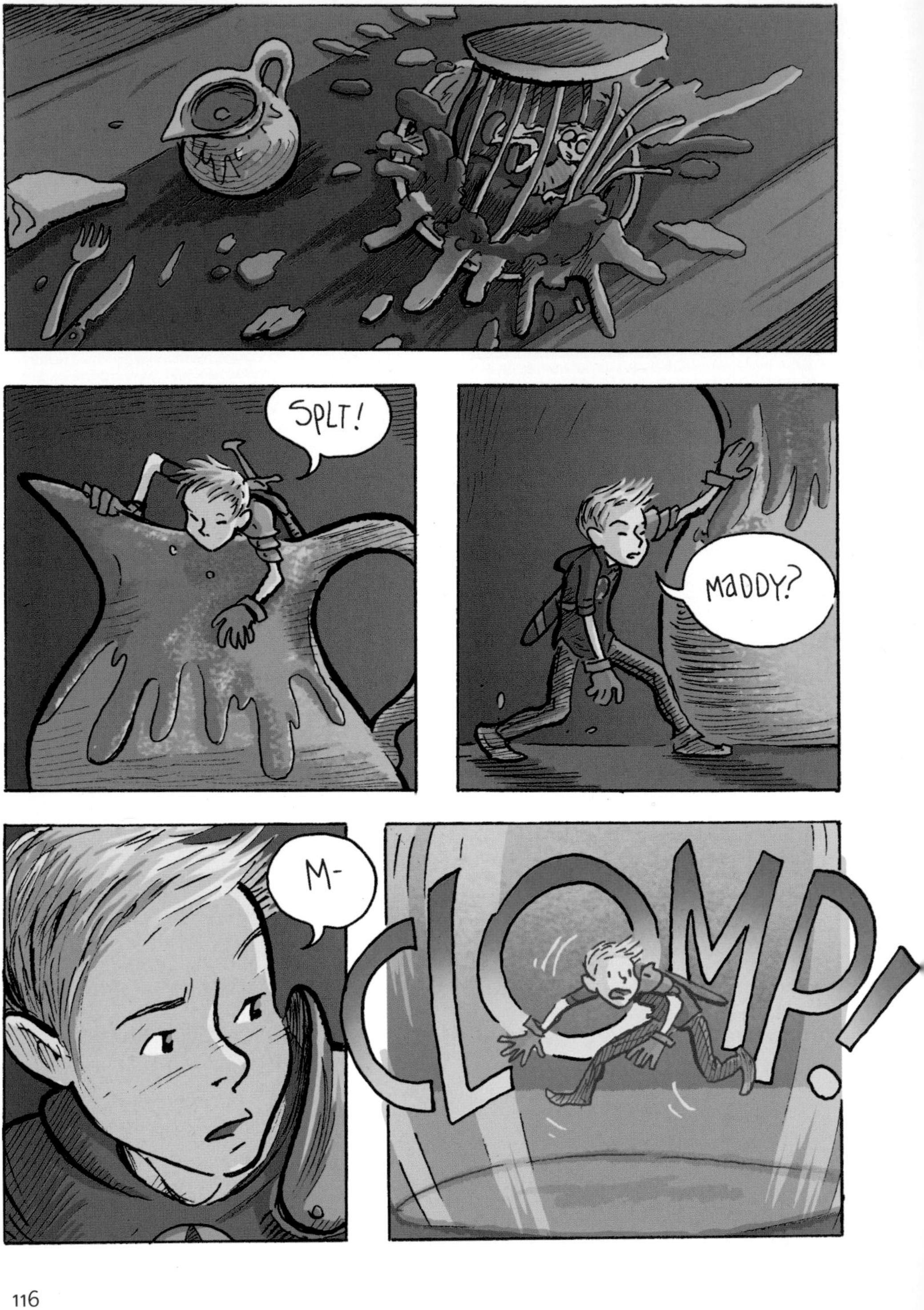
SPLT!
MADDY?
M-
CLOMP!

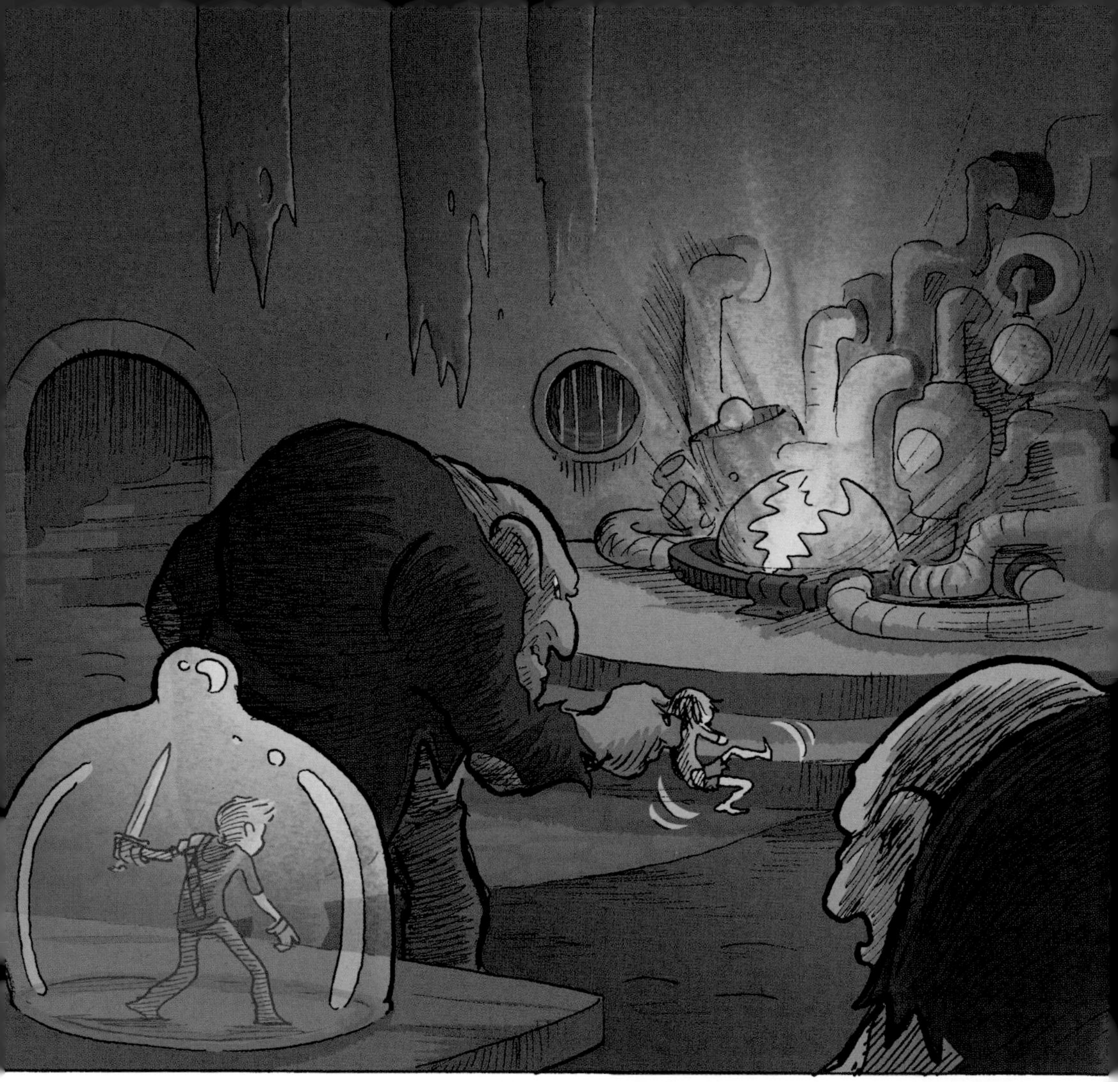

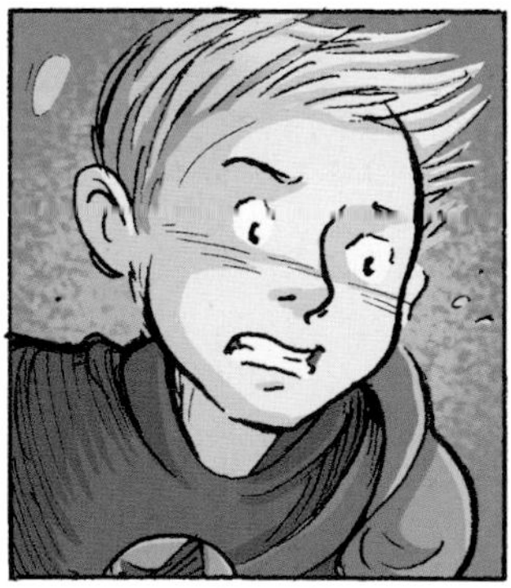

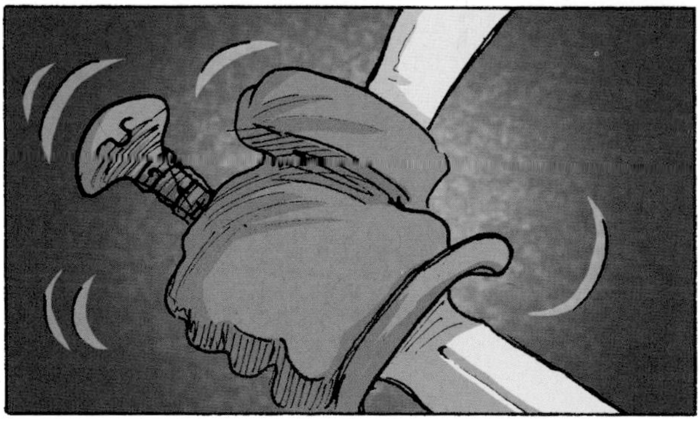

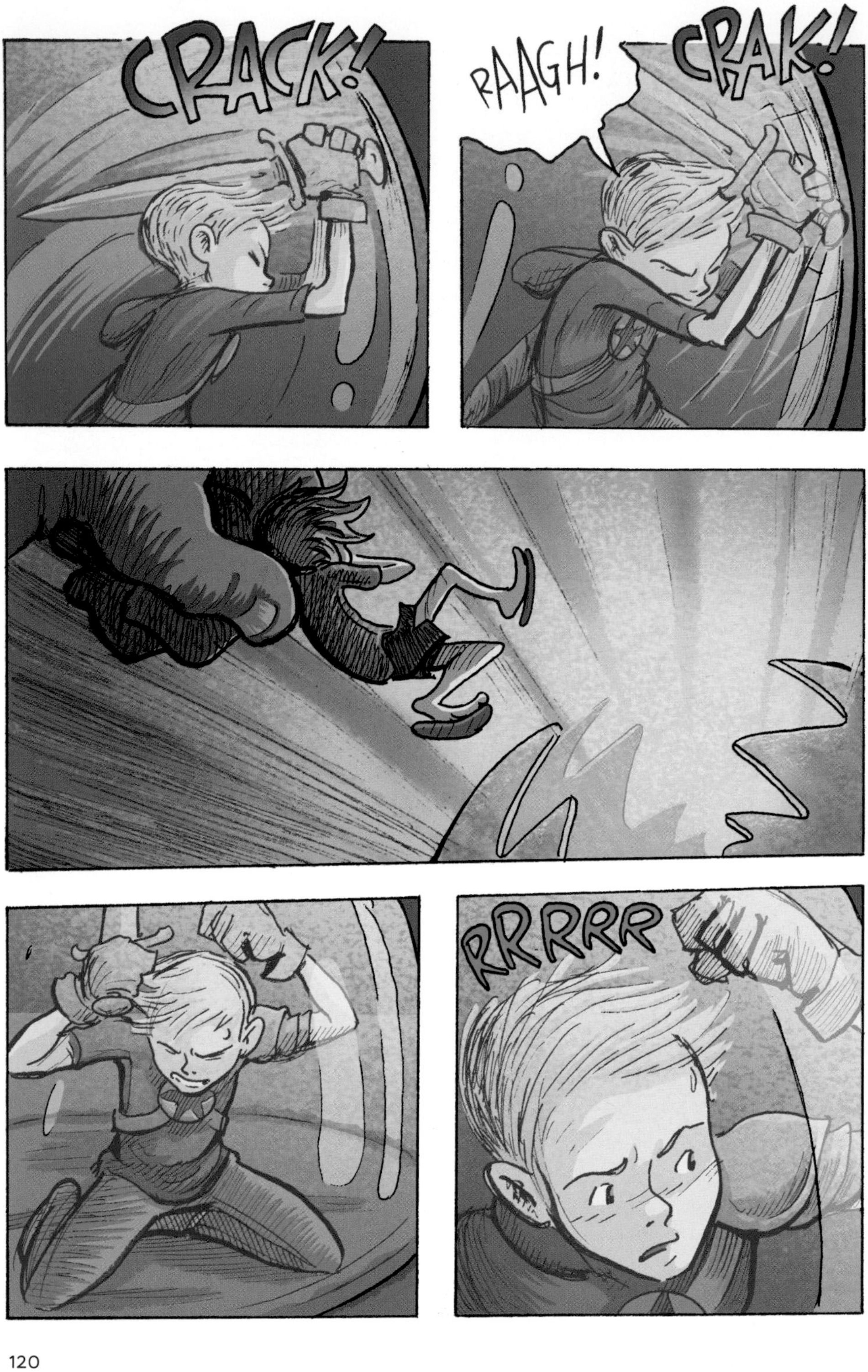
CRACK!
RAAGH!
CRAK!
RRRRR

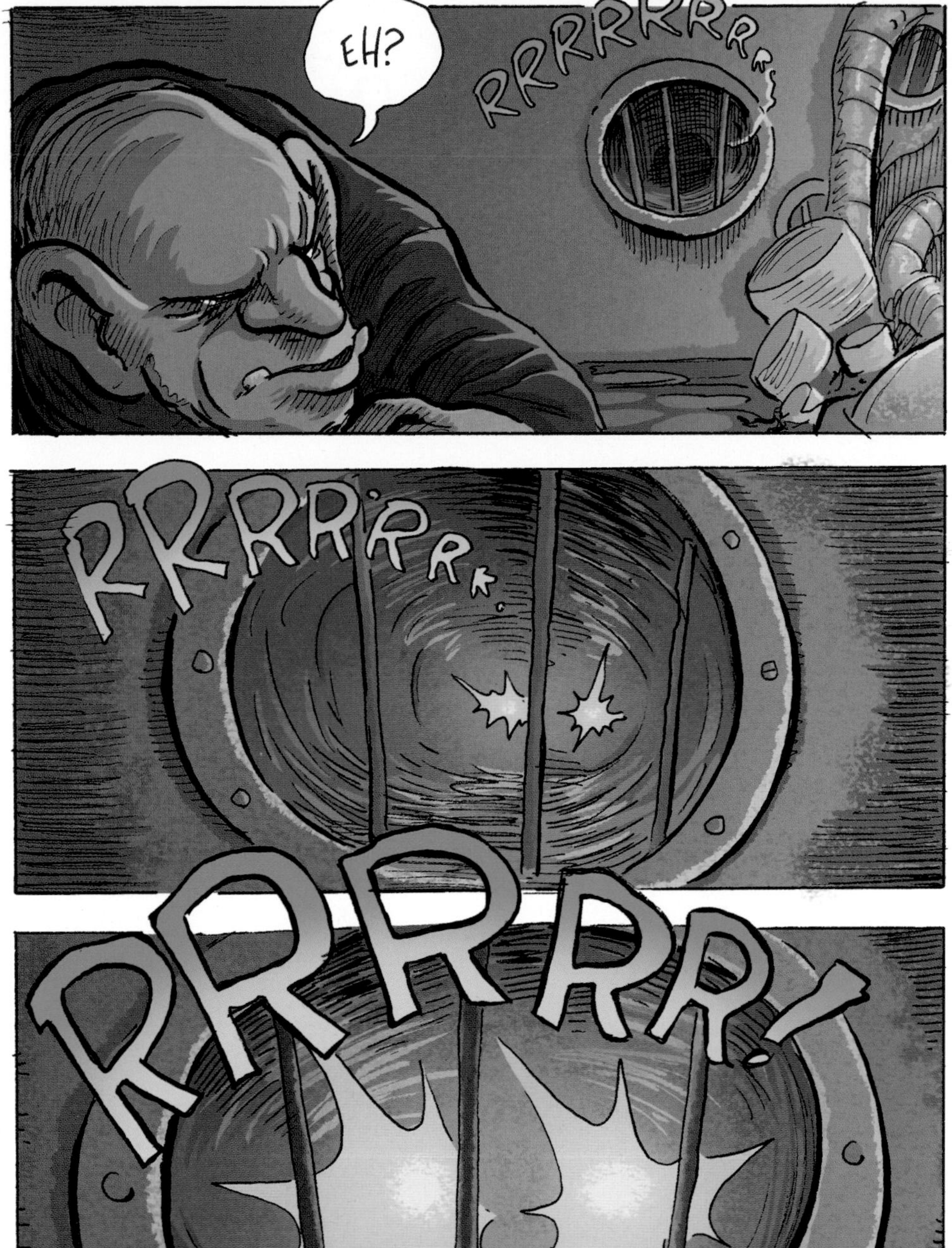
EH?
RRRRRRRR
RRRRRRR
RRRRRR!

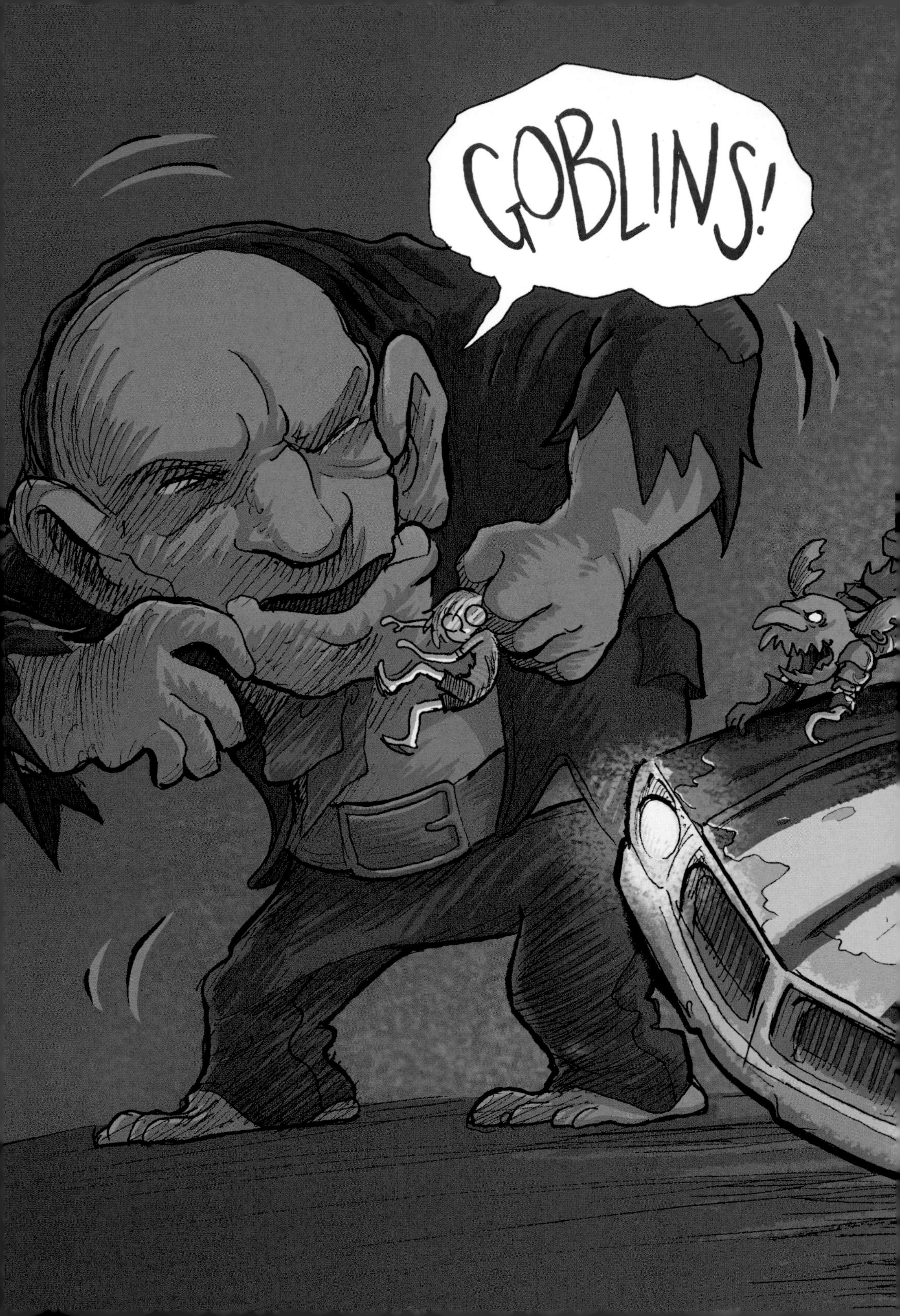
GOBLINS!

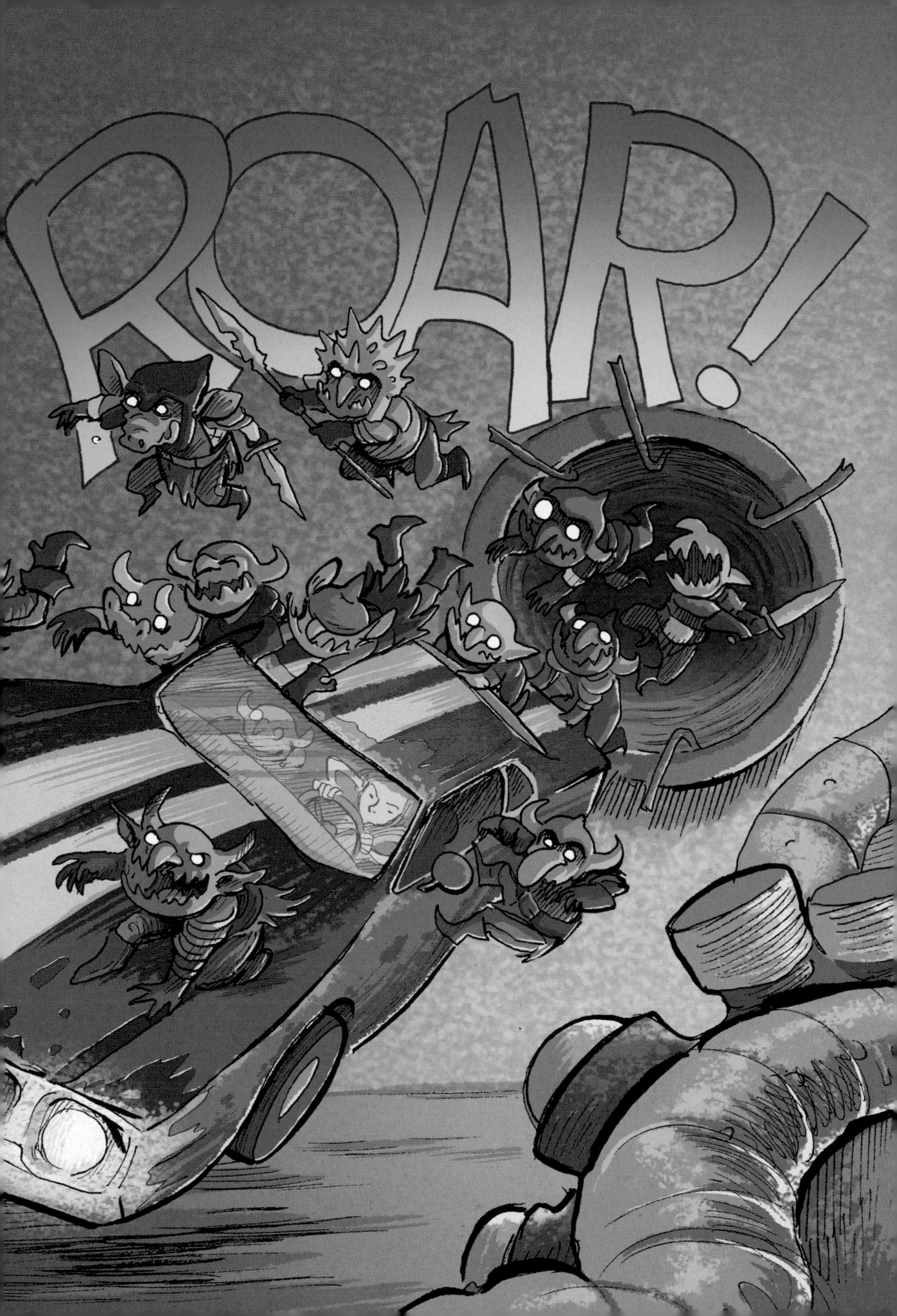
ROAR!

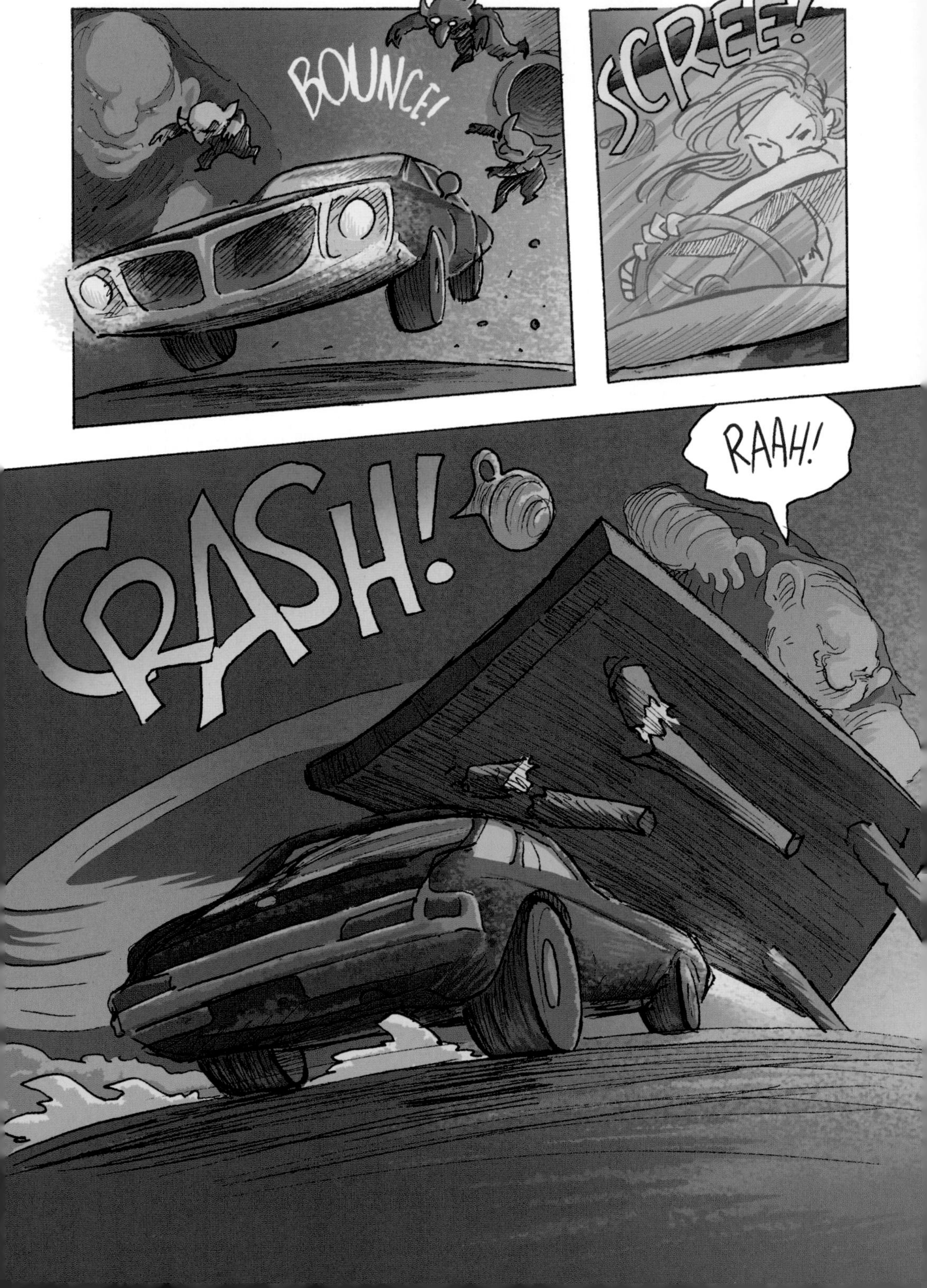
BOUNCE!
SCREE!
CRASH!
RAAH!

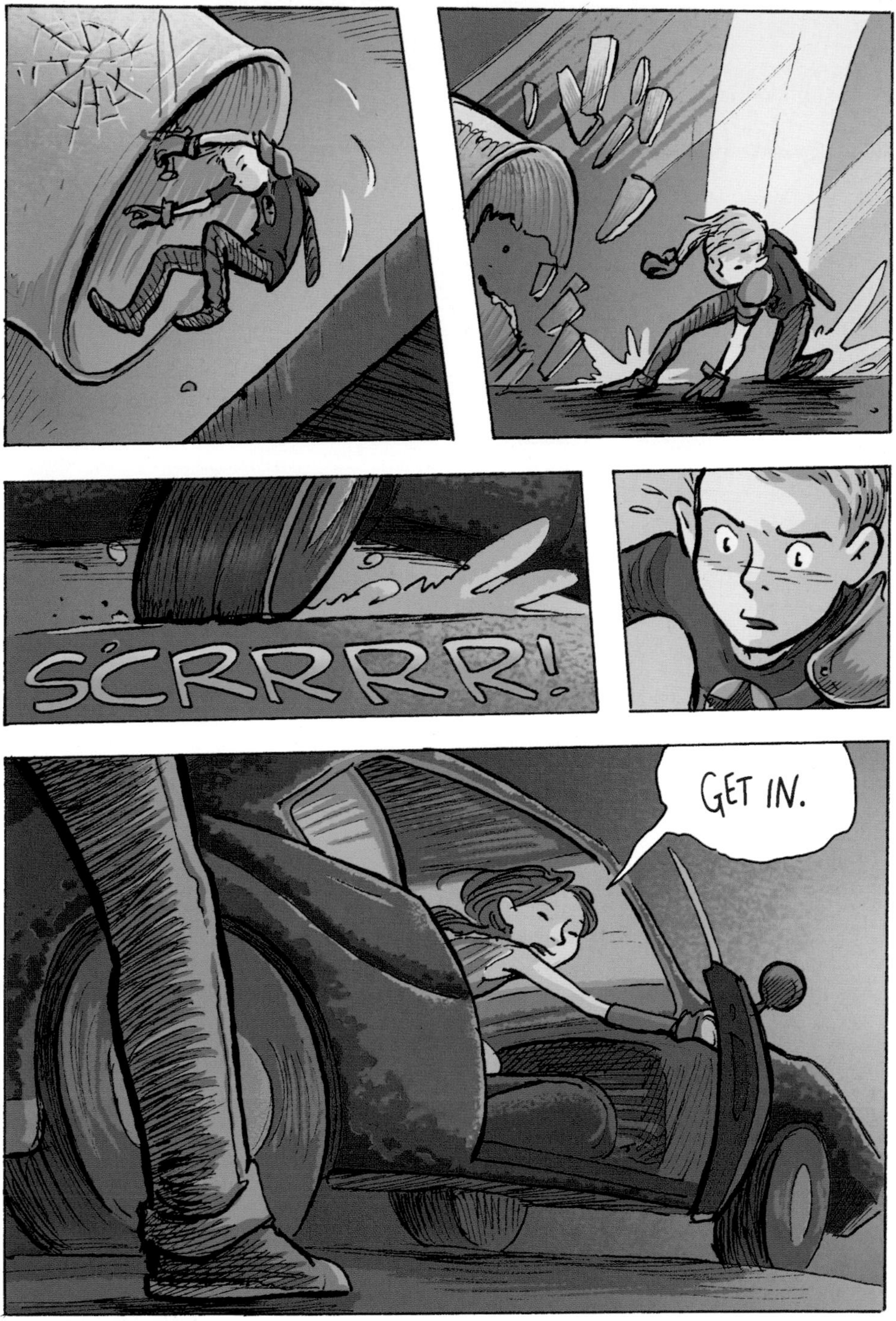
SCRRRR!
GET IN.

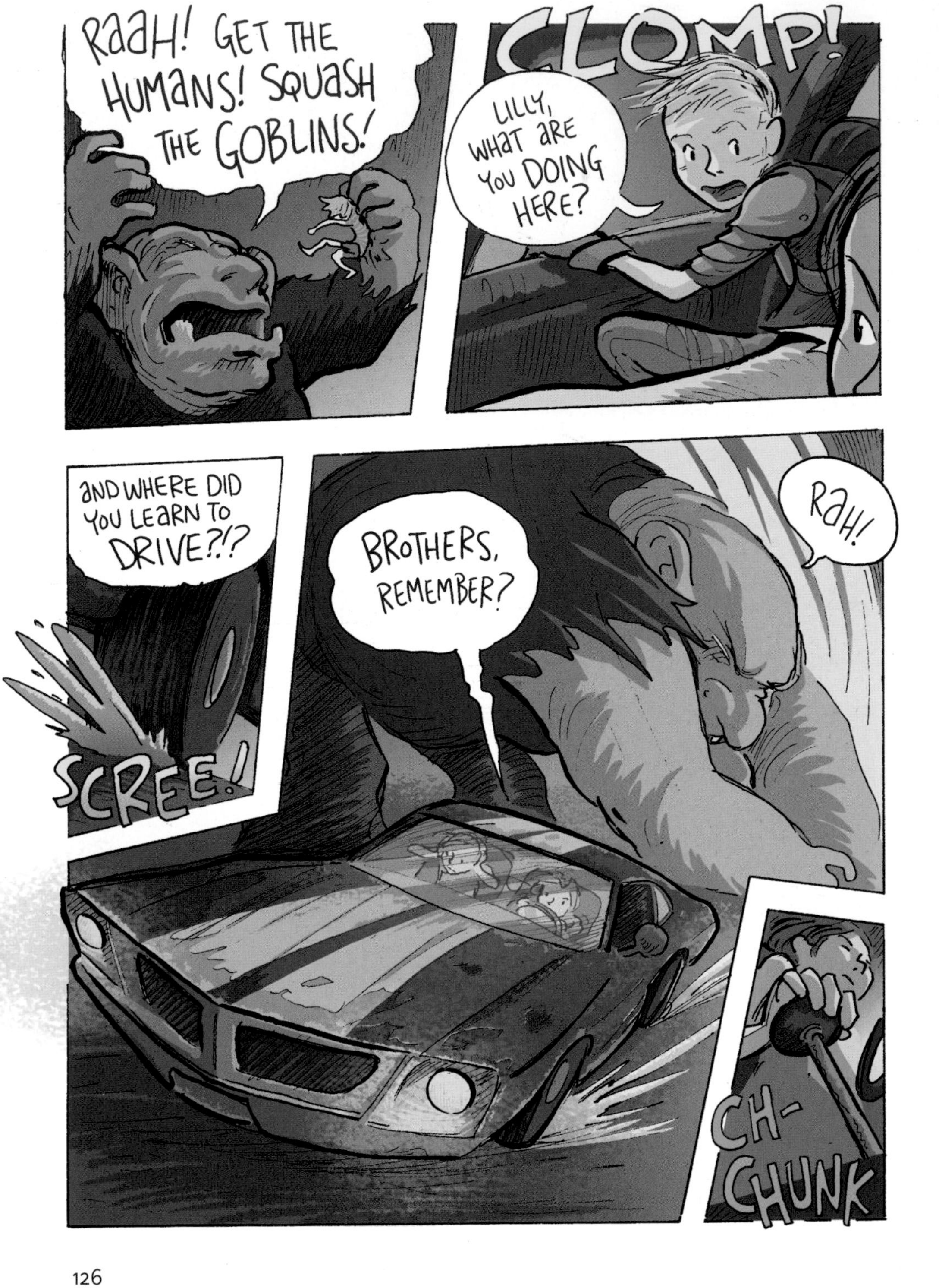
RAAH! GET THE HUMANS! SQUASH THE GOBLINS!
CLOMP!
LILLY, WHAT ARE YOU DOING HERE?
AND WHERE DID YOU LEARN TO DRIVE?!?
BROTHERS, REMEMBER?
RAH!
SCREE!
CH-CHUNK

AND THE LITTLE—

GOBLINS, YEAH.

THEY'RE ON OUR SIDE.

I'M SORT OF THEIR KING.

AX.

GOT IT.

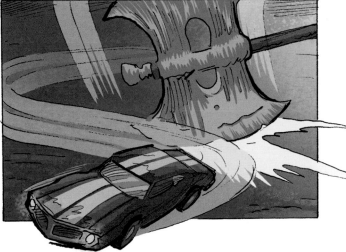

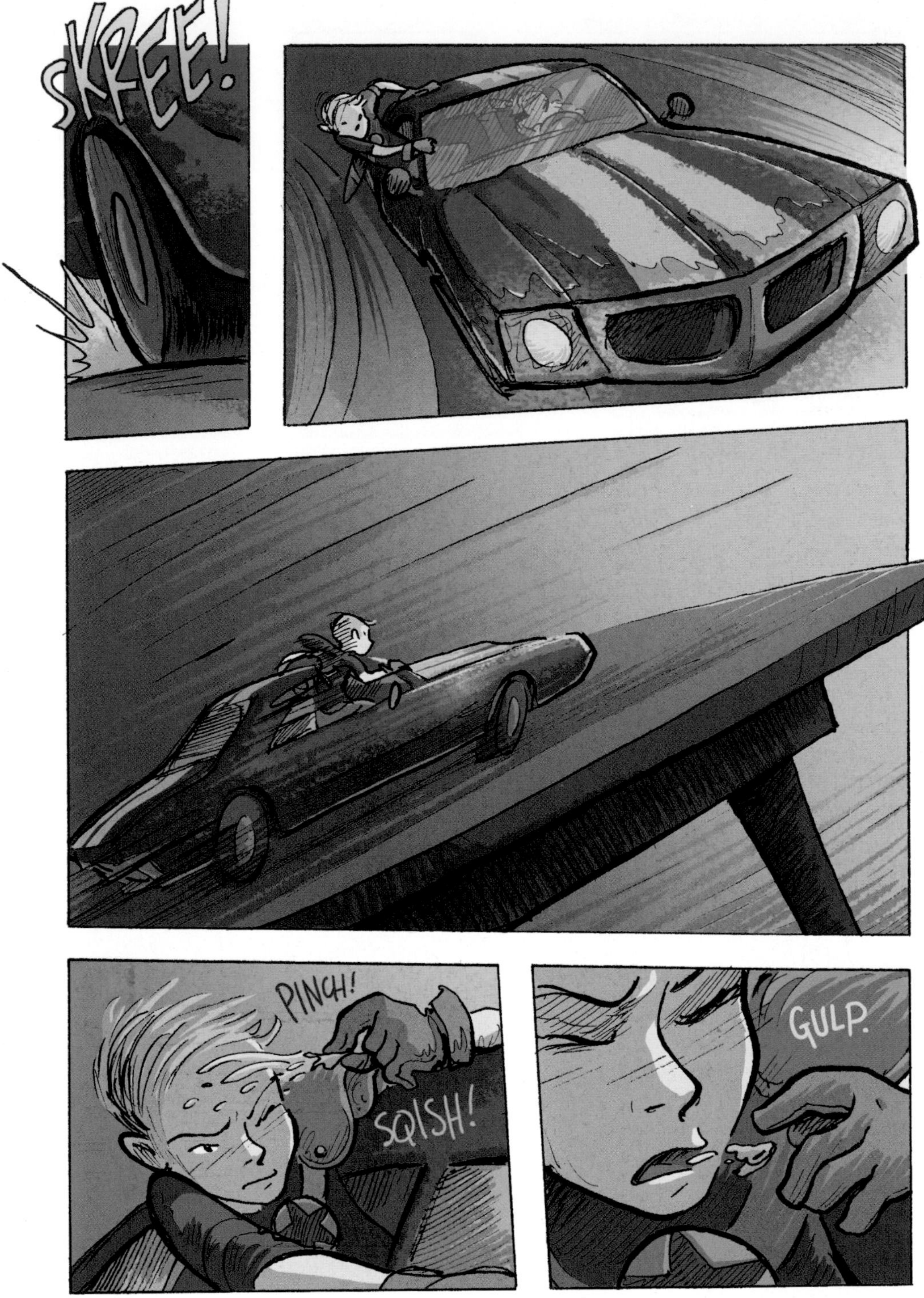
SKREE!
PINCH!
SQISH!
GULP.

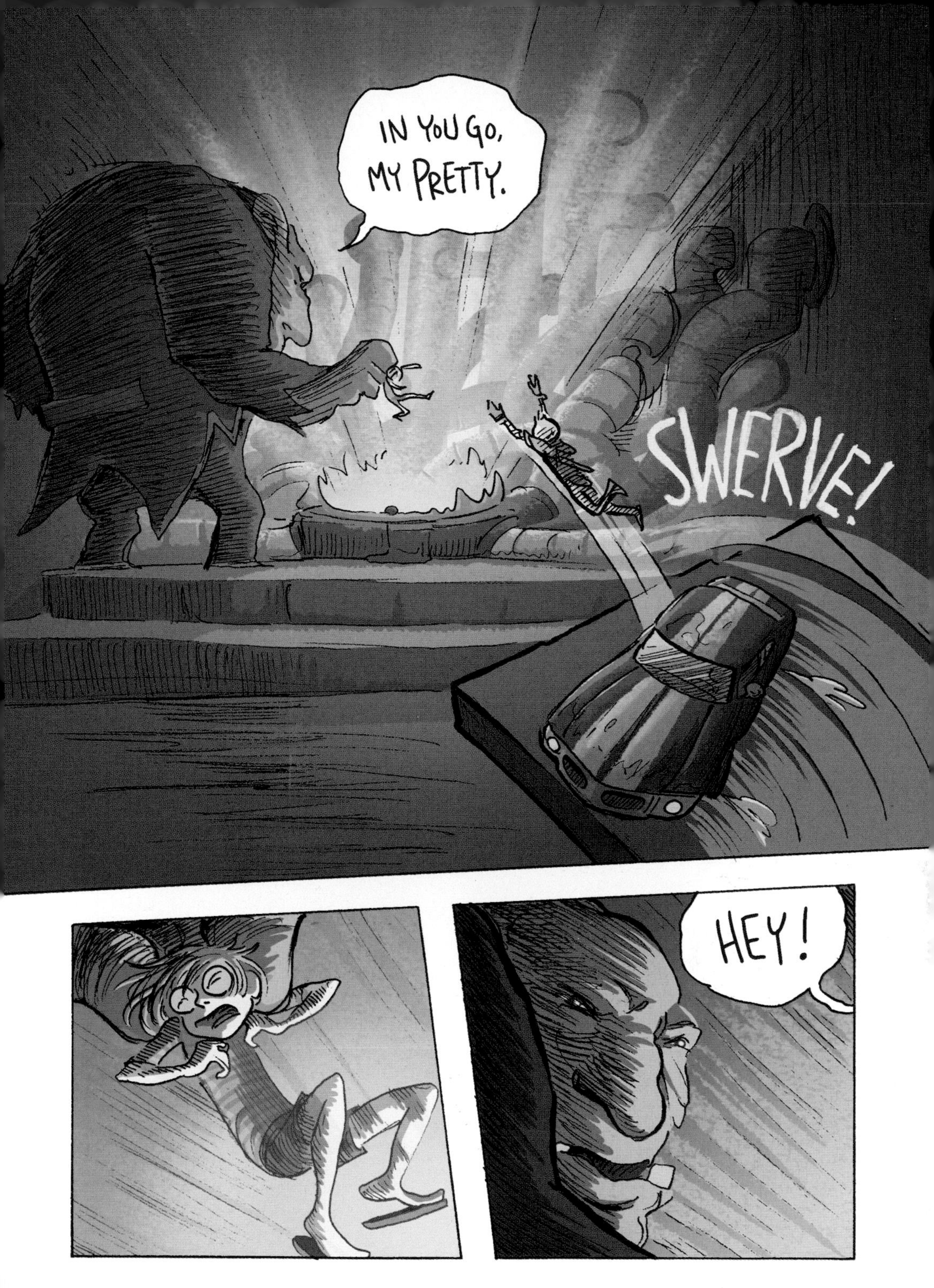
IN YOU GO, MY PRETTY.
SWERVE!
HEY!

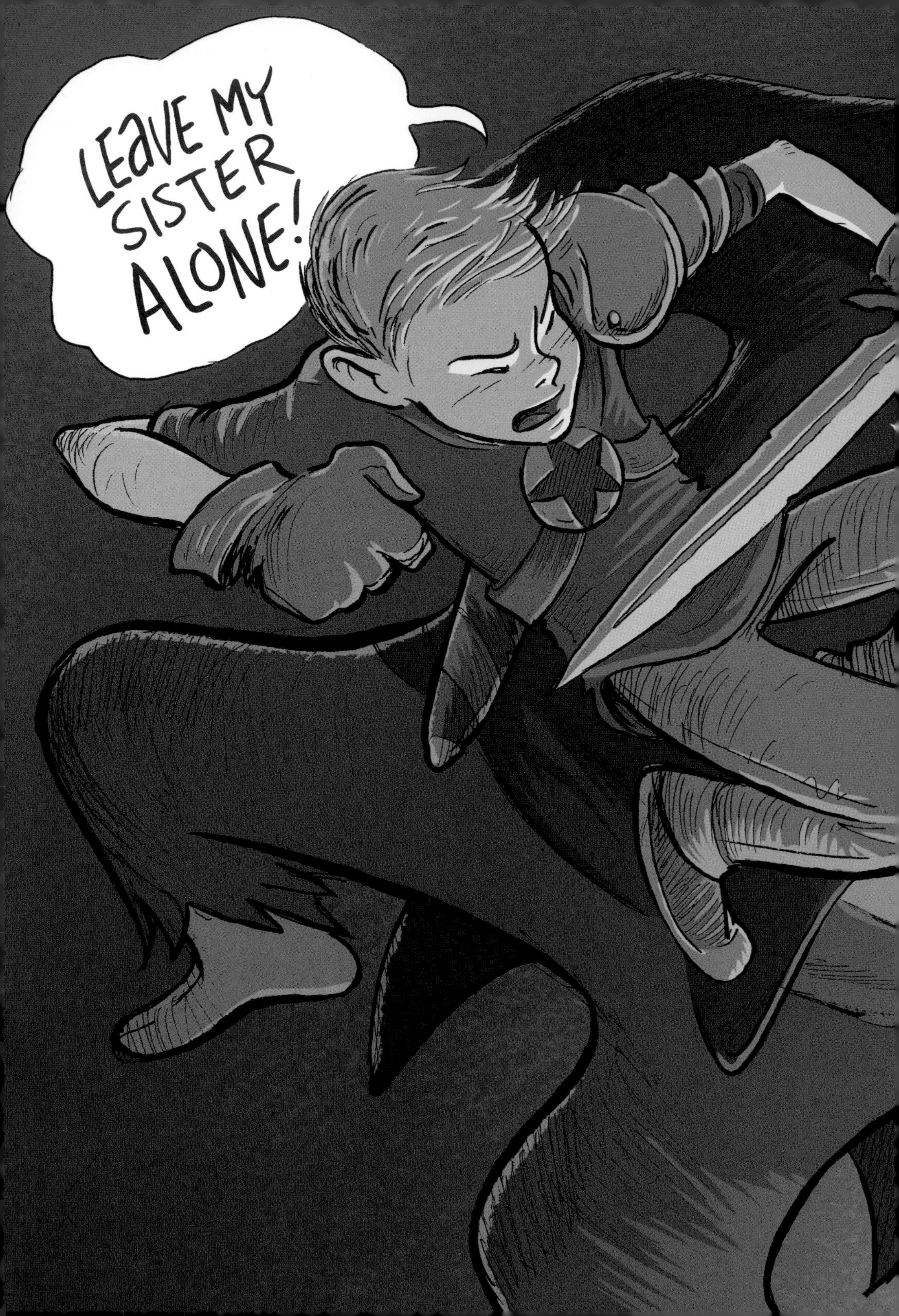
LEAVE MY SISTER ALONE!

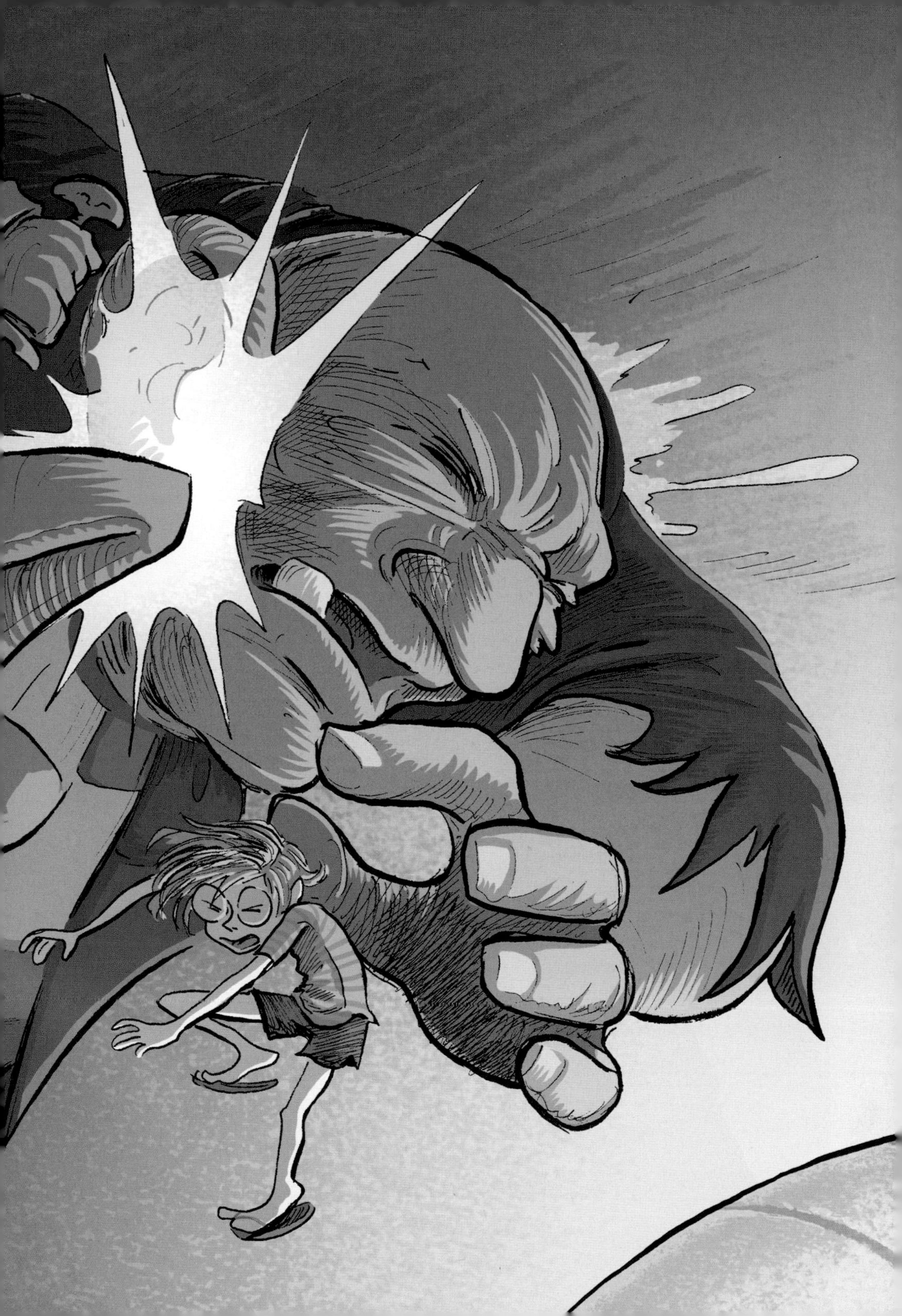

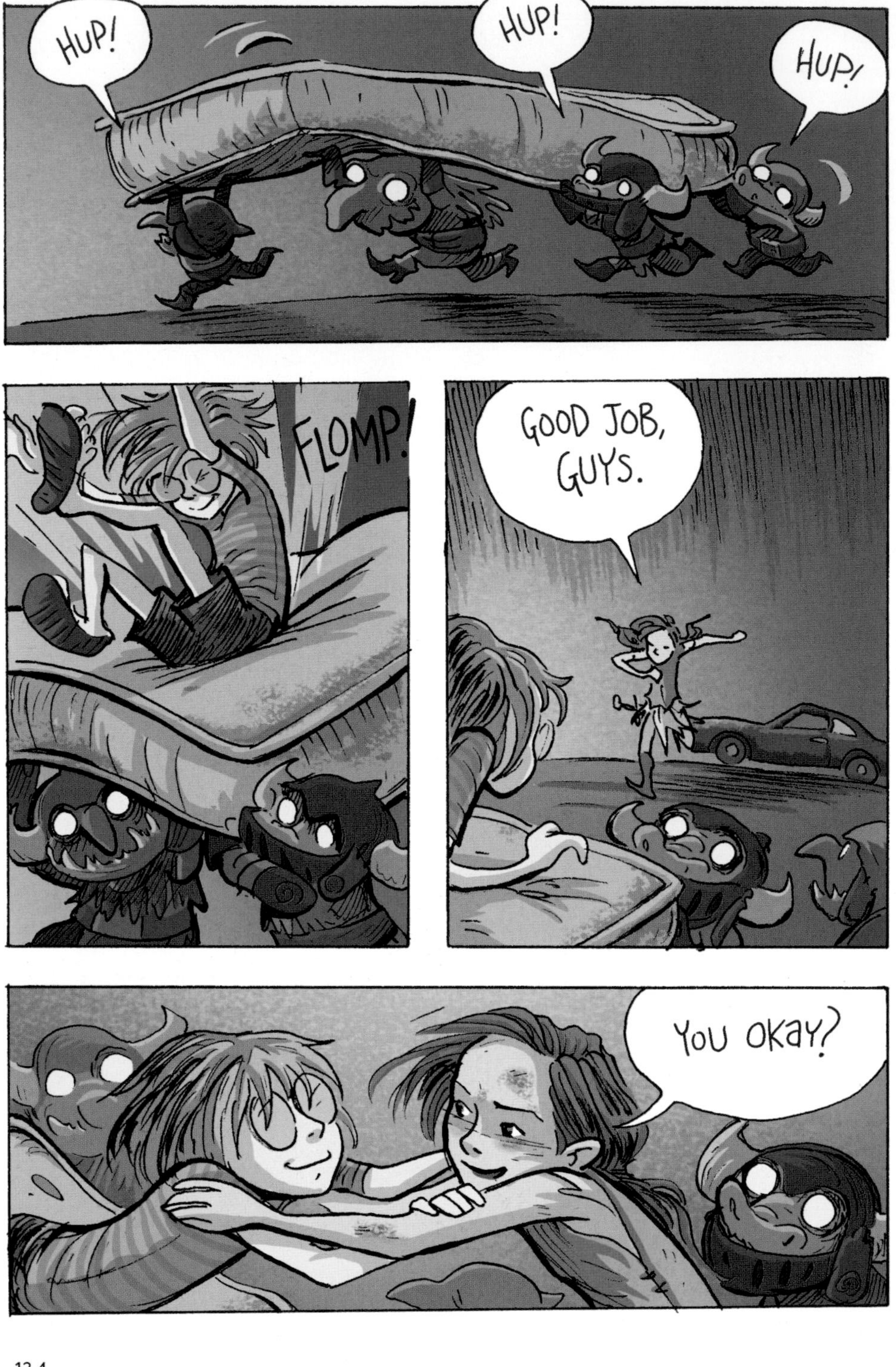
HUP!
HUP!
HUP!
FLOMP!
GOOD JOB, GUYS.
YOU OKAY?

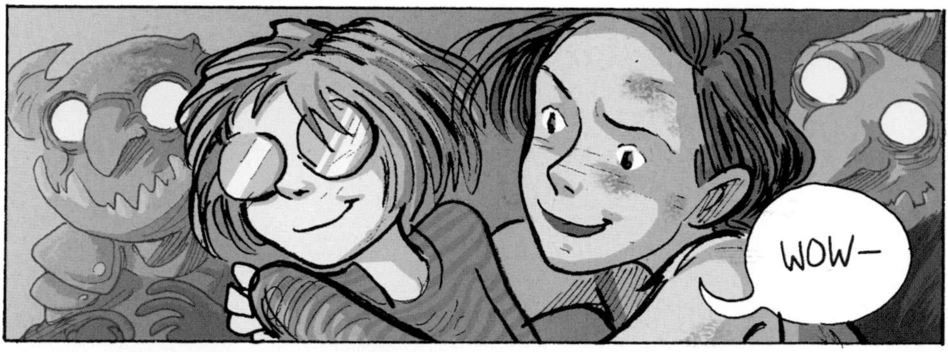
WOW-

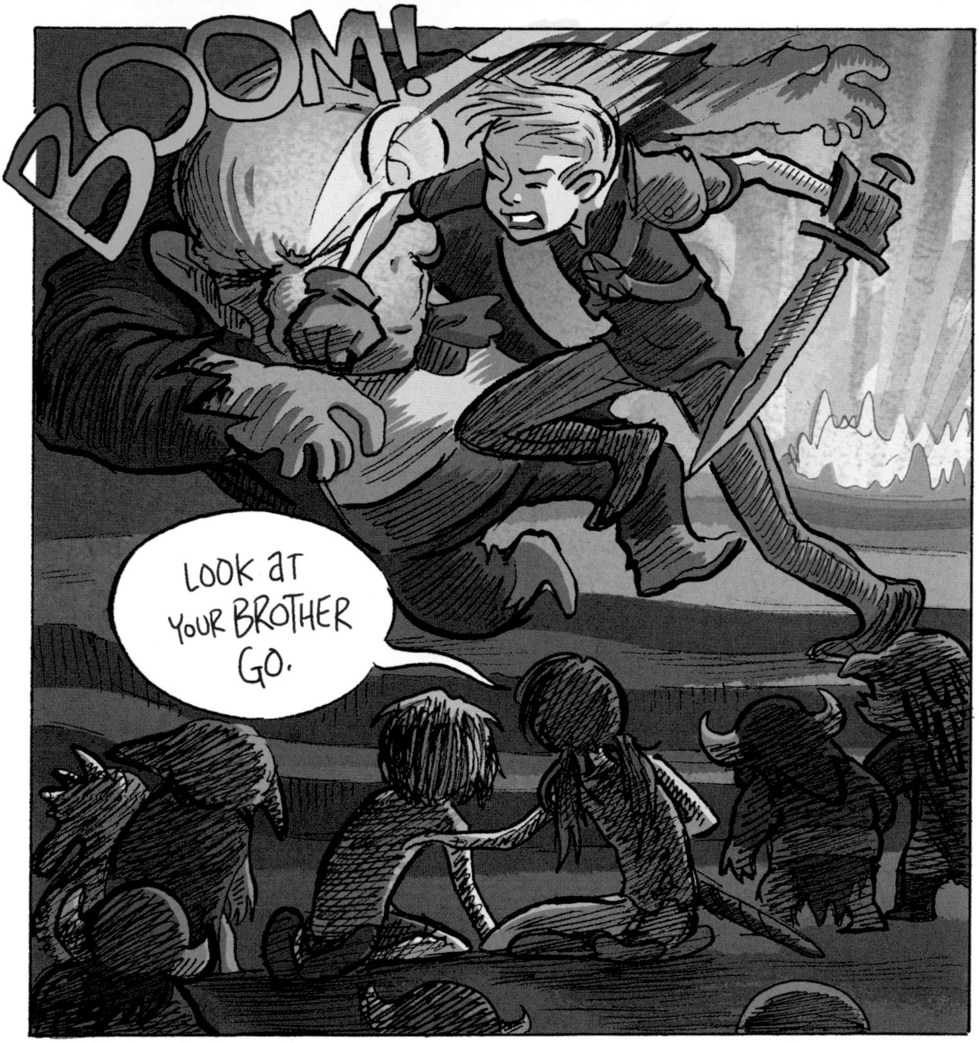
BOOM!
LOOK AT YOUR BROTHER GO.

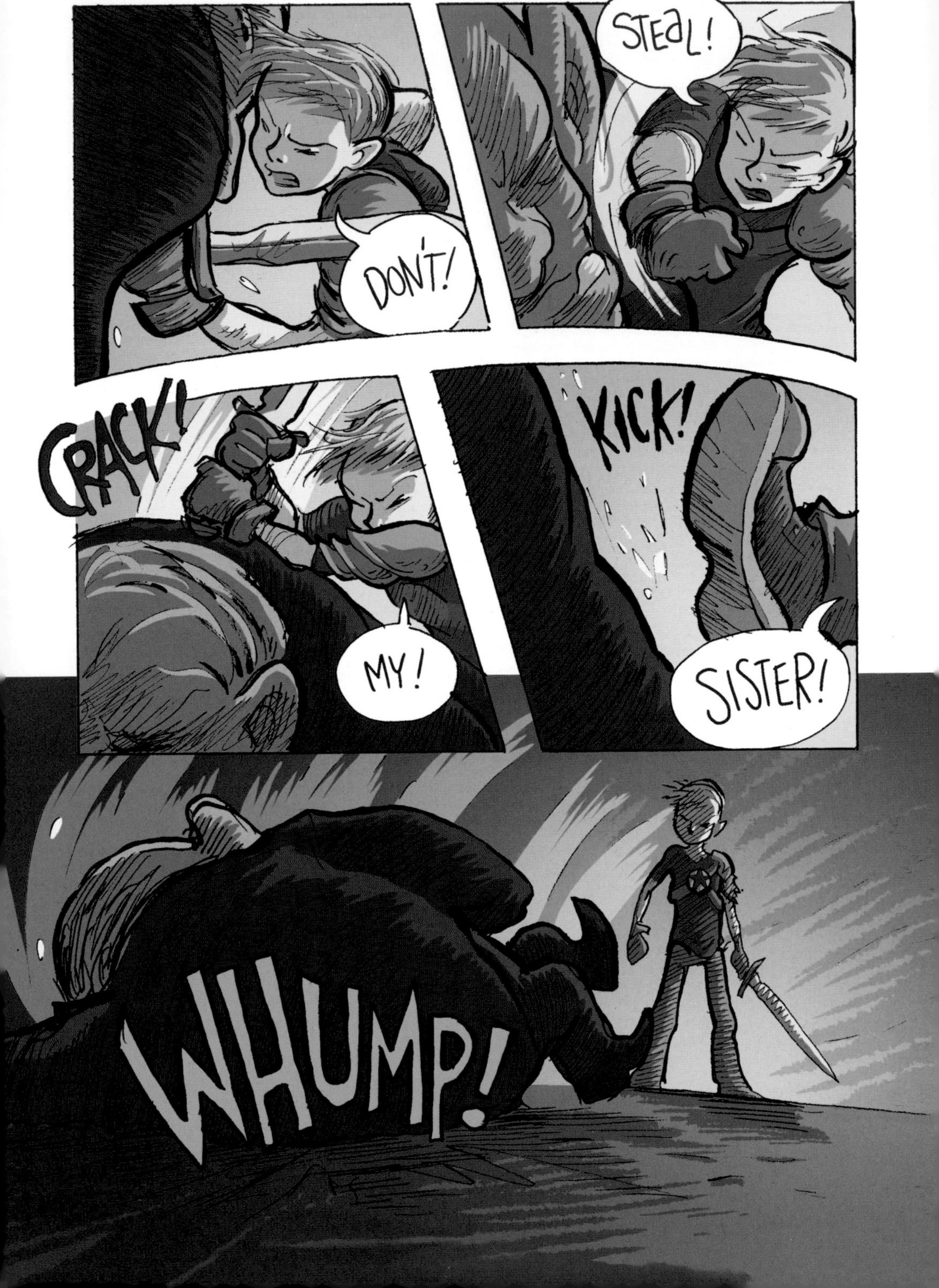
DON'T!
STEAL!
CRACK!
MY!
KICK!
SISTER!
WHUMP!

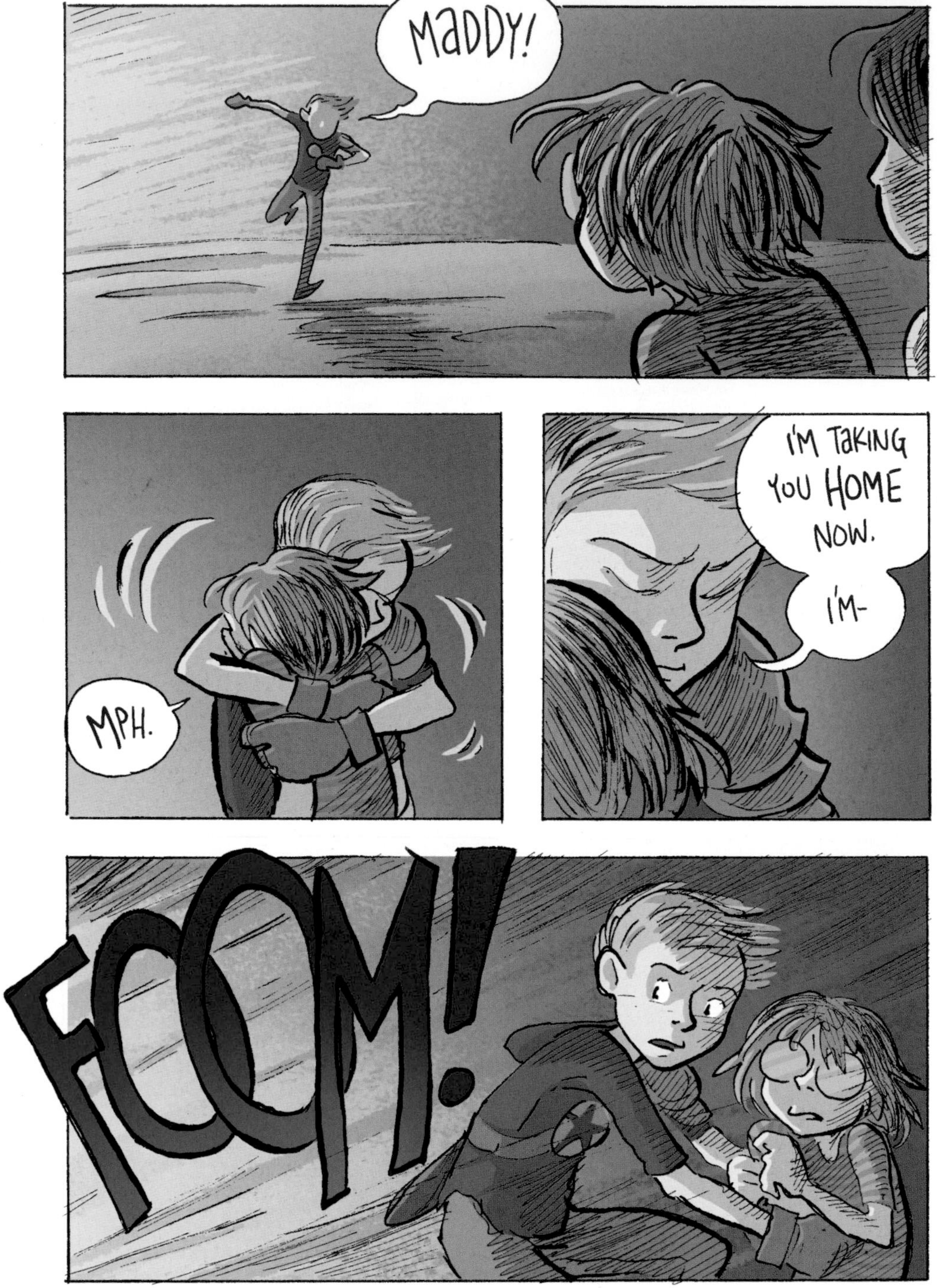
MADDY!
MPH.
I'M TAKING YOU HOME NOW.
I'M-
FOOM!

140

141

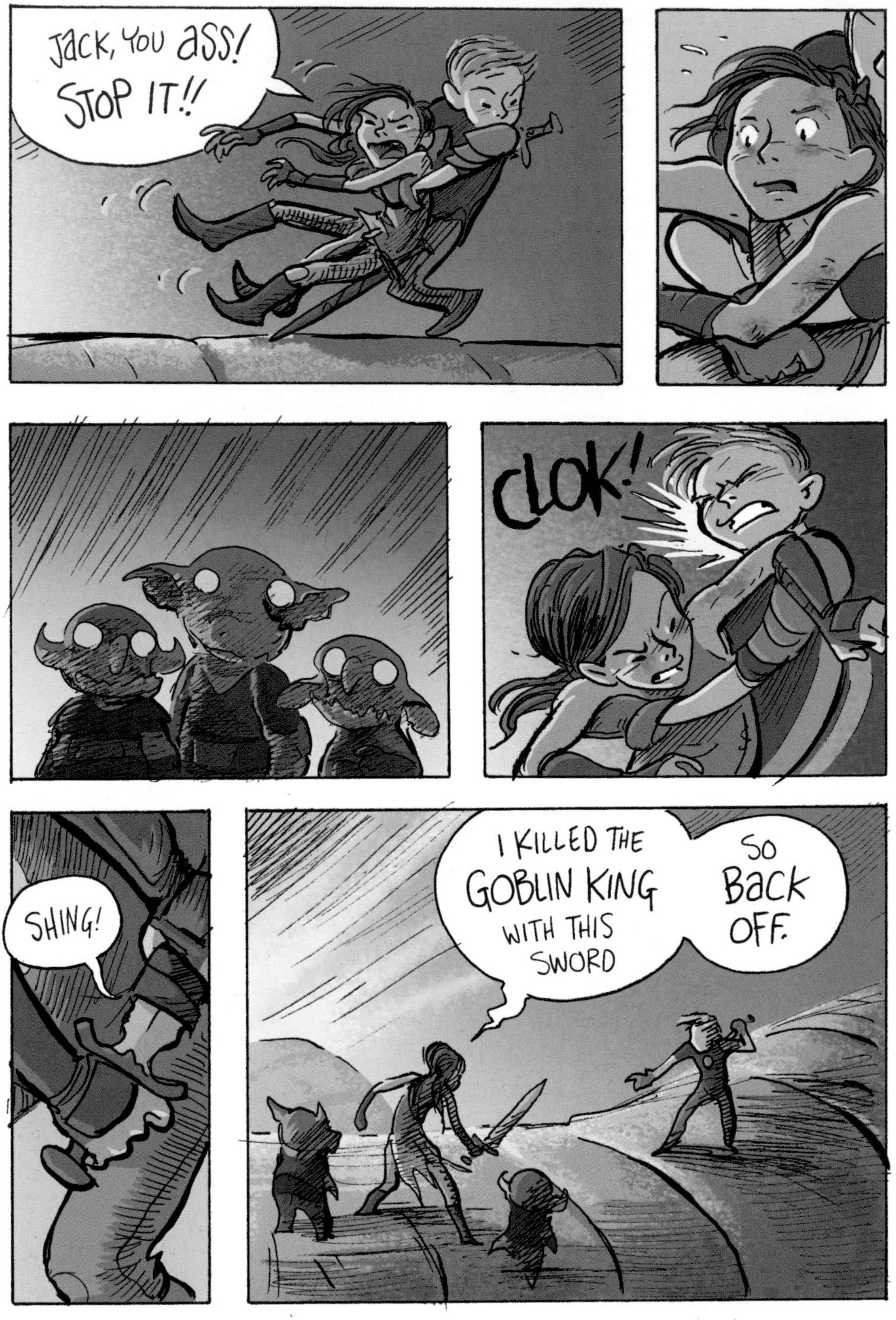
JACK, YOU ASS! STOP IT!!
CLOK!
SHING!
I KILLED THE GOBLIN KING WITH THIS SWORD
SO BACK OFF.

143

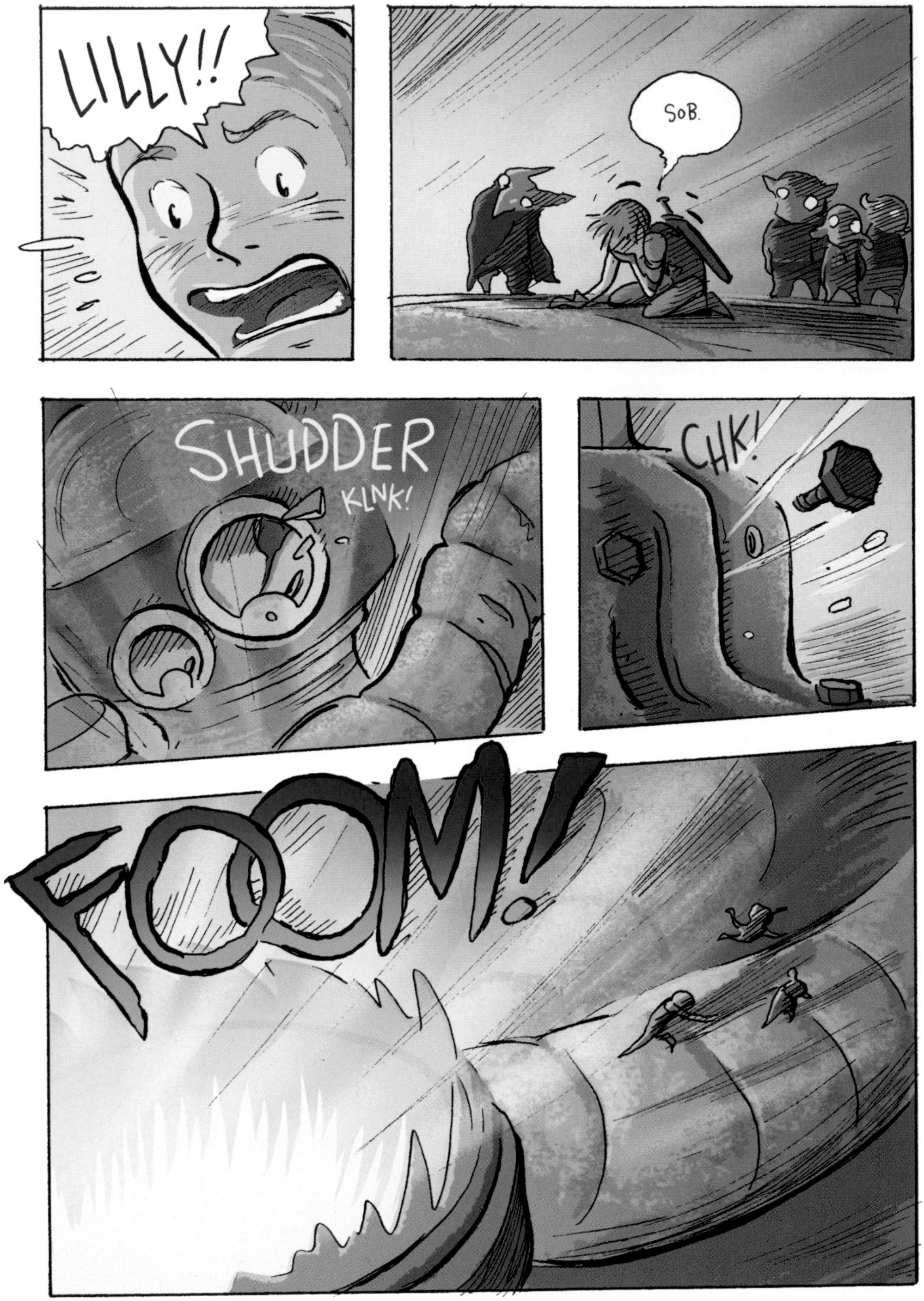
LILLY!!
SOB.
SHUDDER
KLNK!
CHK!
FOOOM!

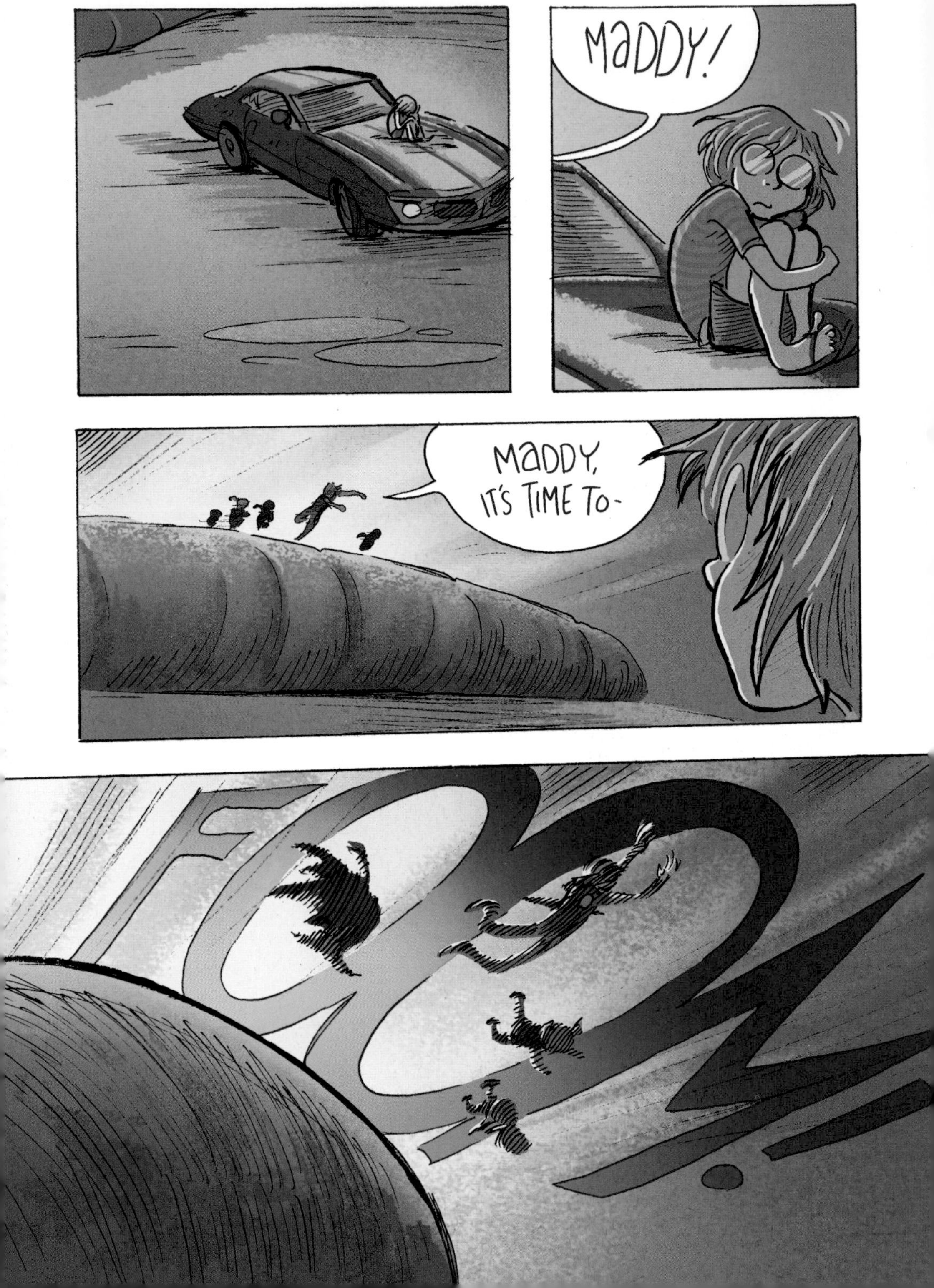
MADDY!
MADDY, IT'S TIME TO-
FOOM!

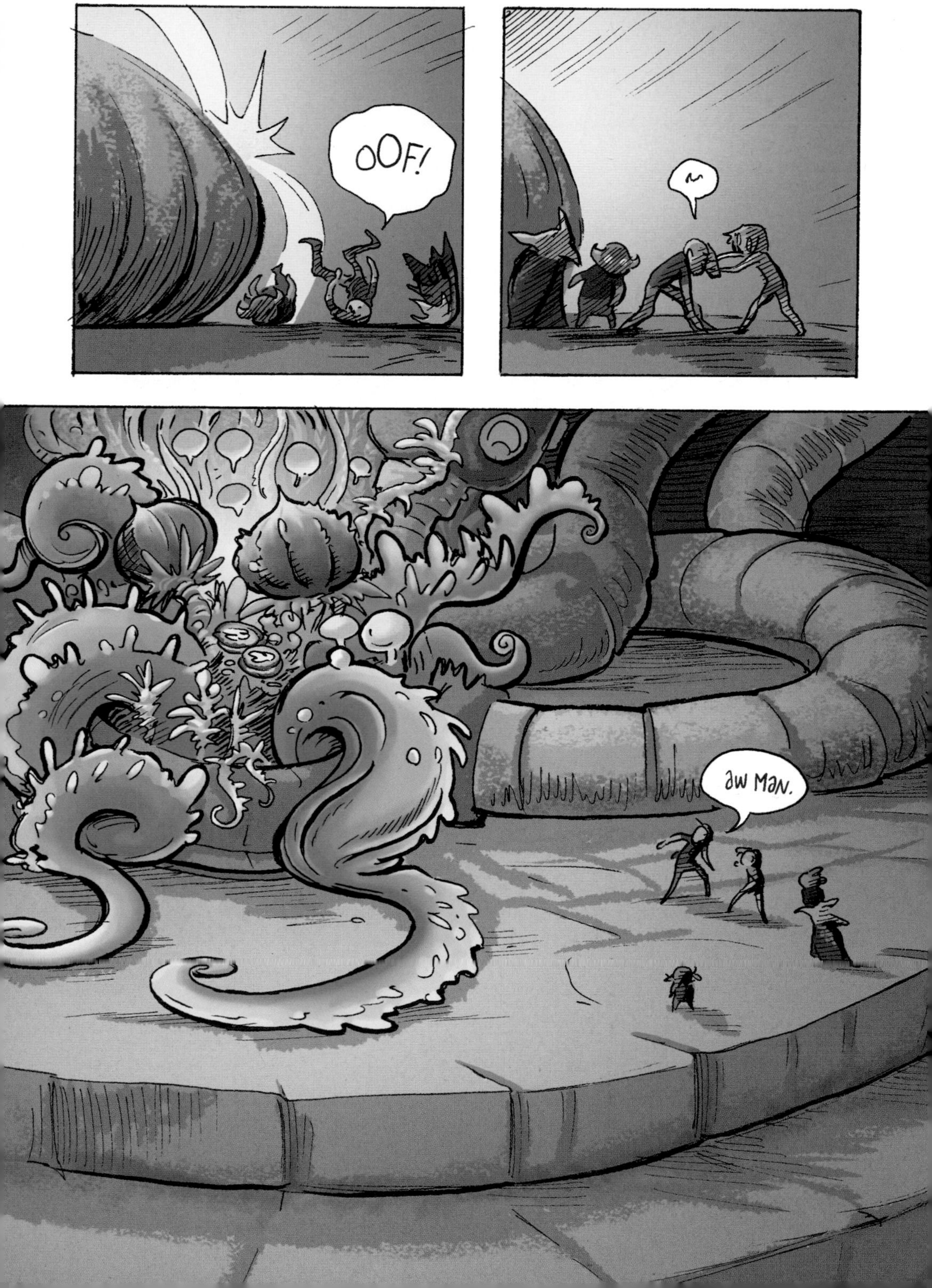
OOF!
aw man.

150

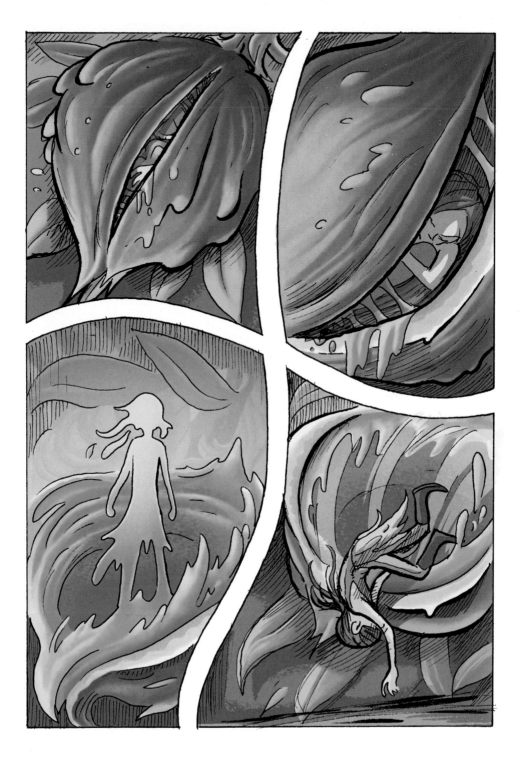

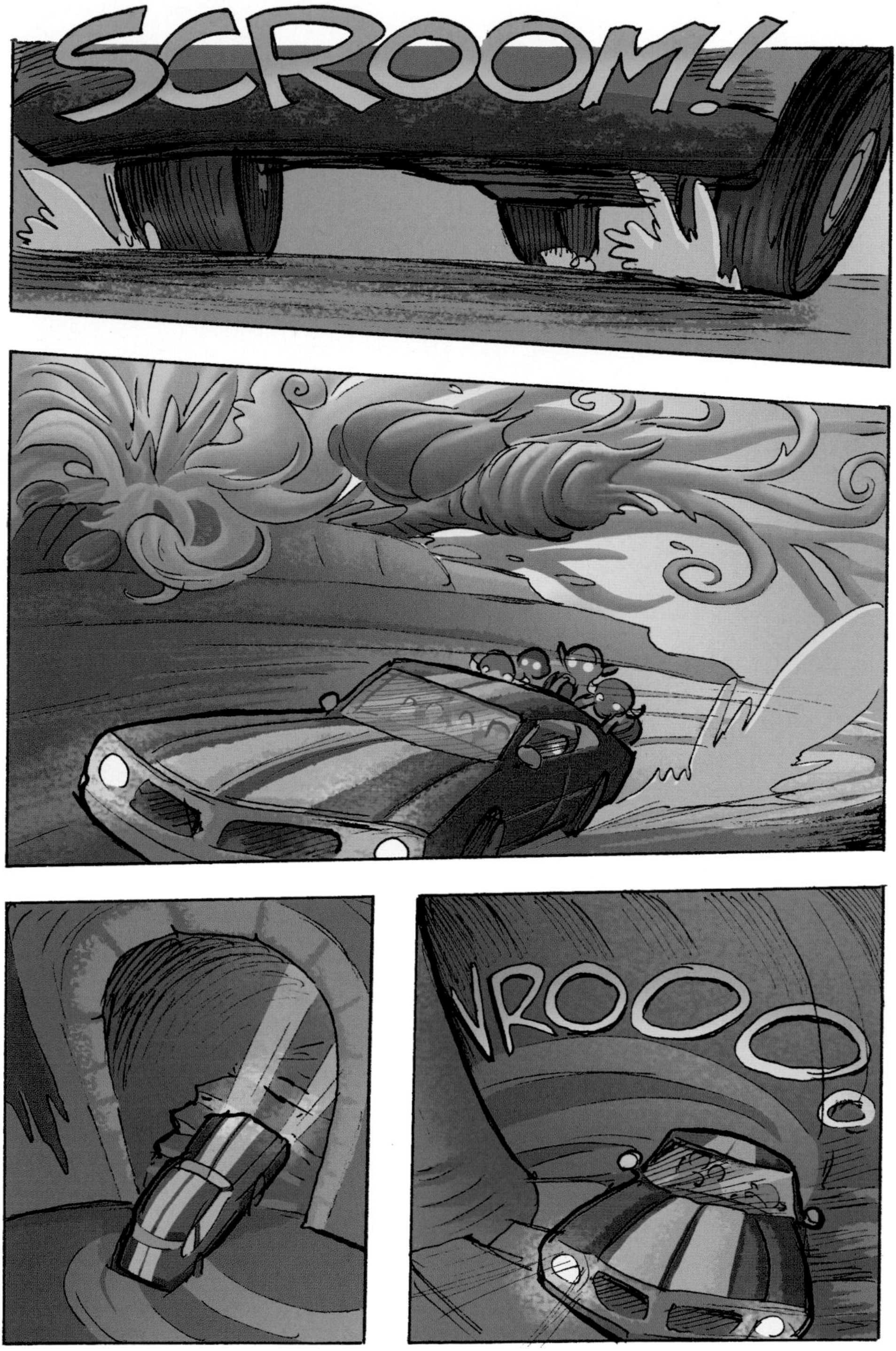
SCROOM!
VROOOOo

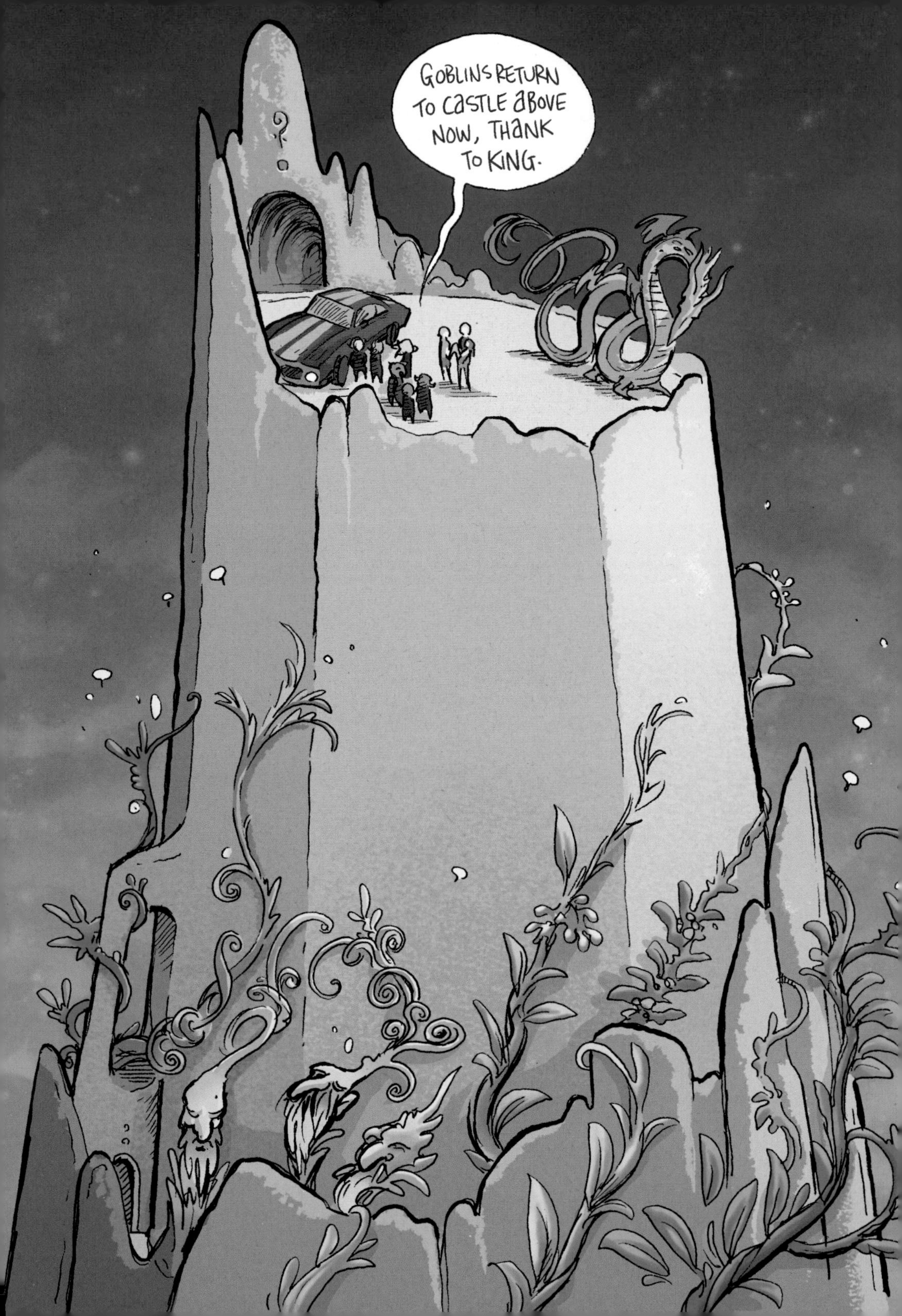
GOBLINS RETURN TO CASTLE ABOVE NOW, THANK TO KING.

155

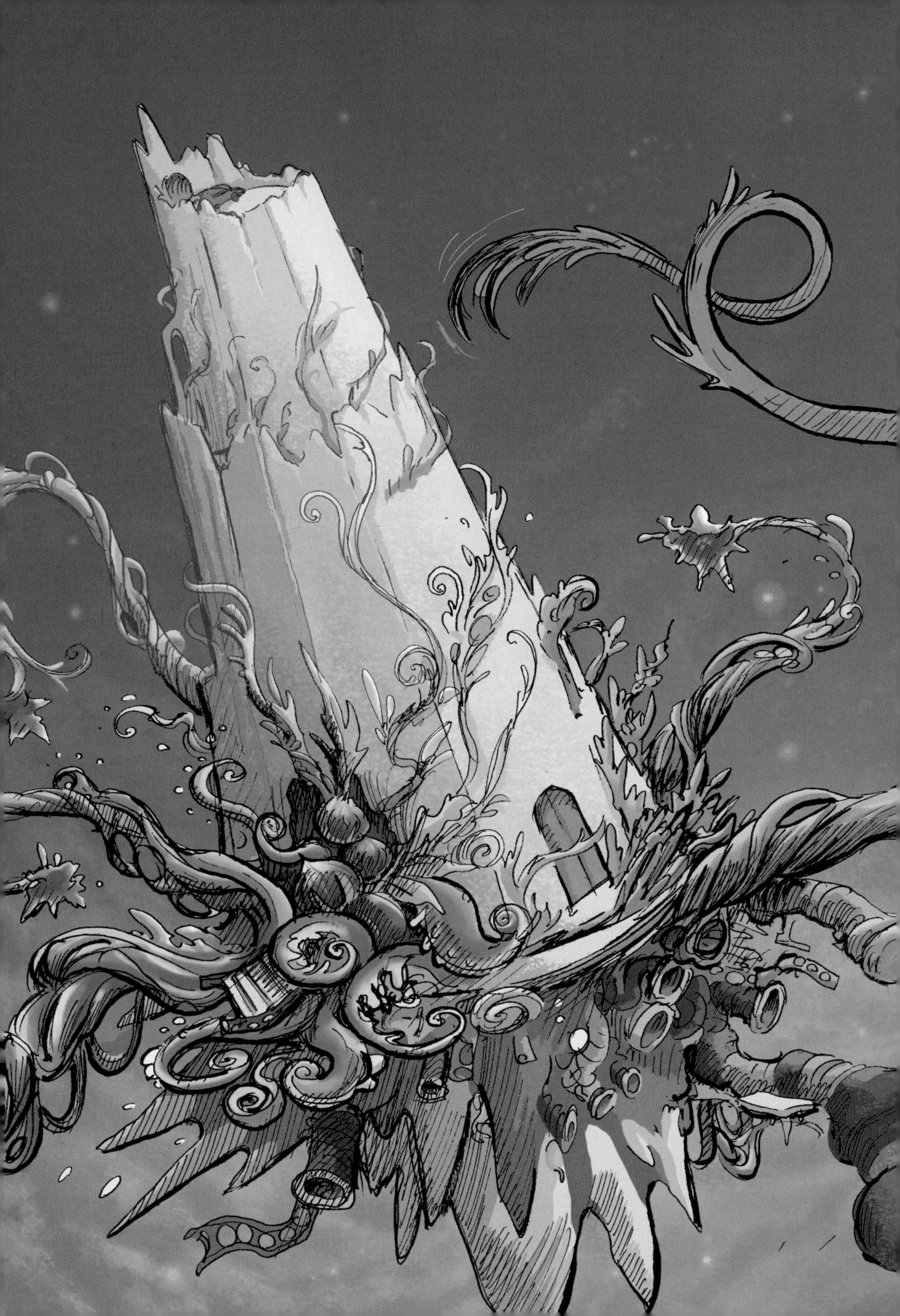

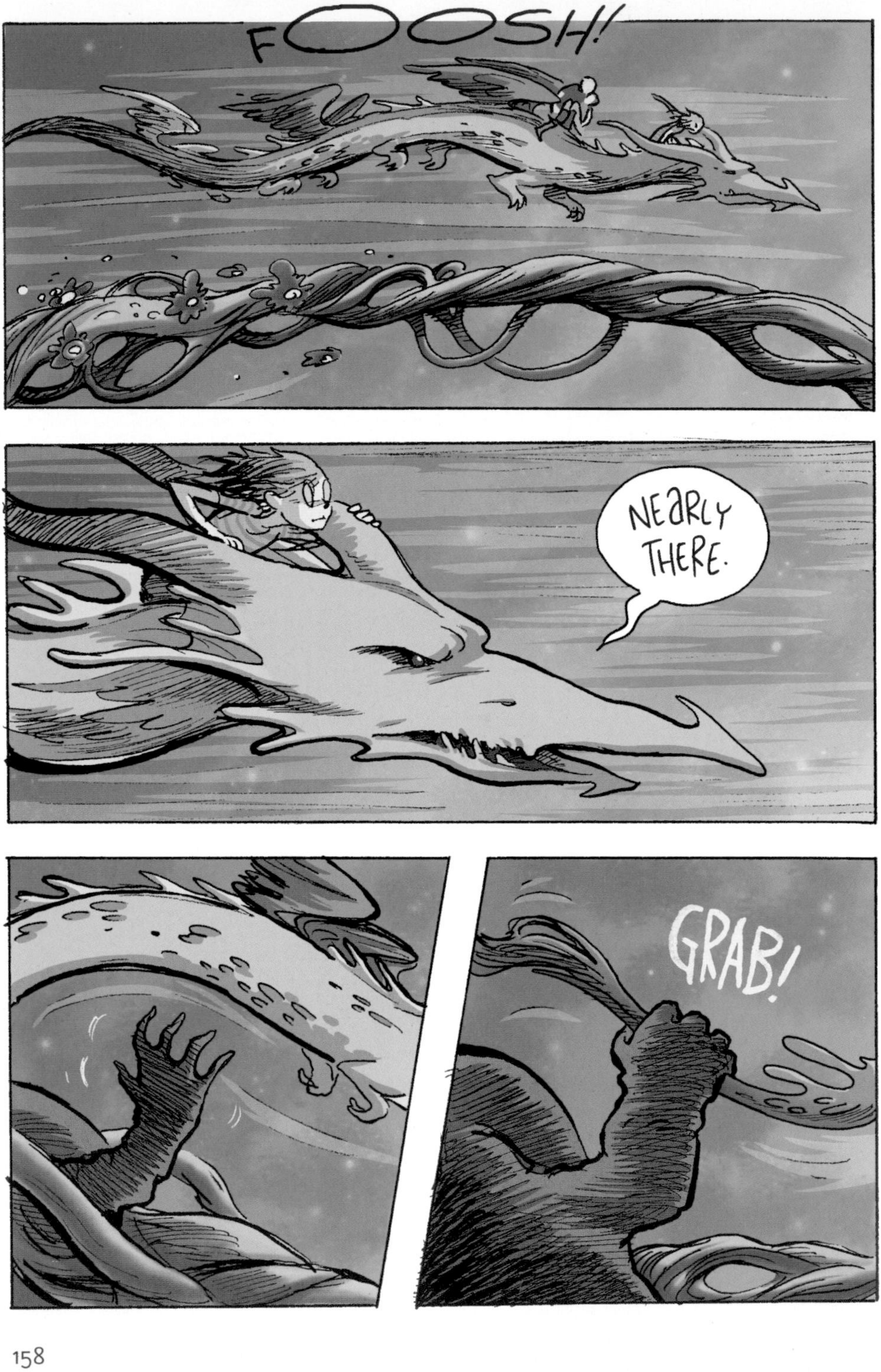
FOOSH!
NEARLY THERE.
GRAB!

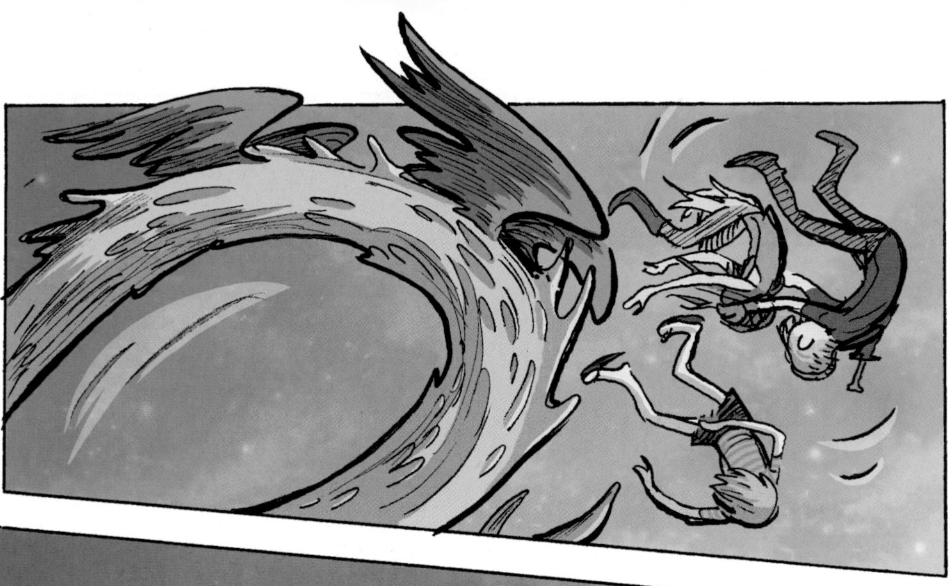

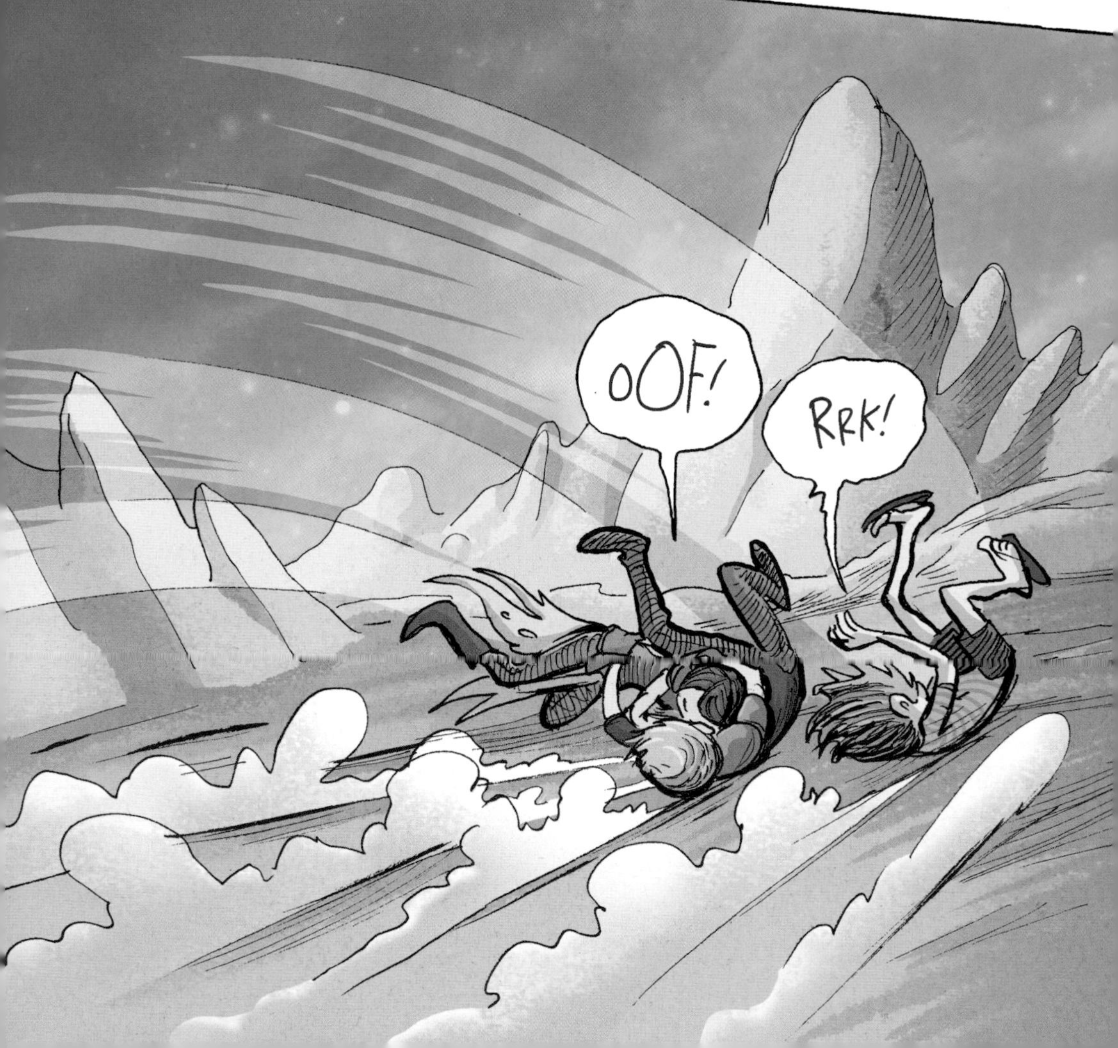
OOF!
RRK!

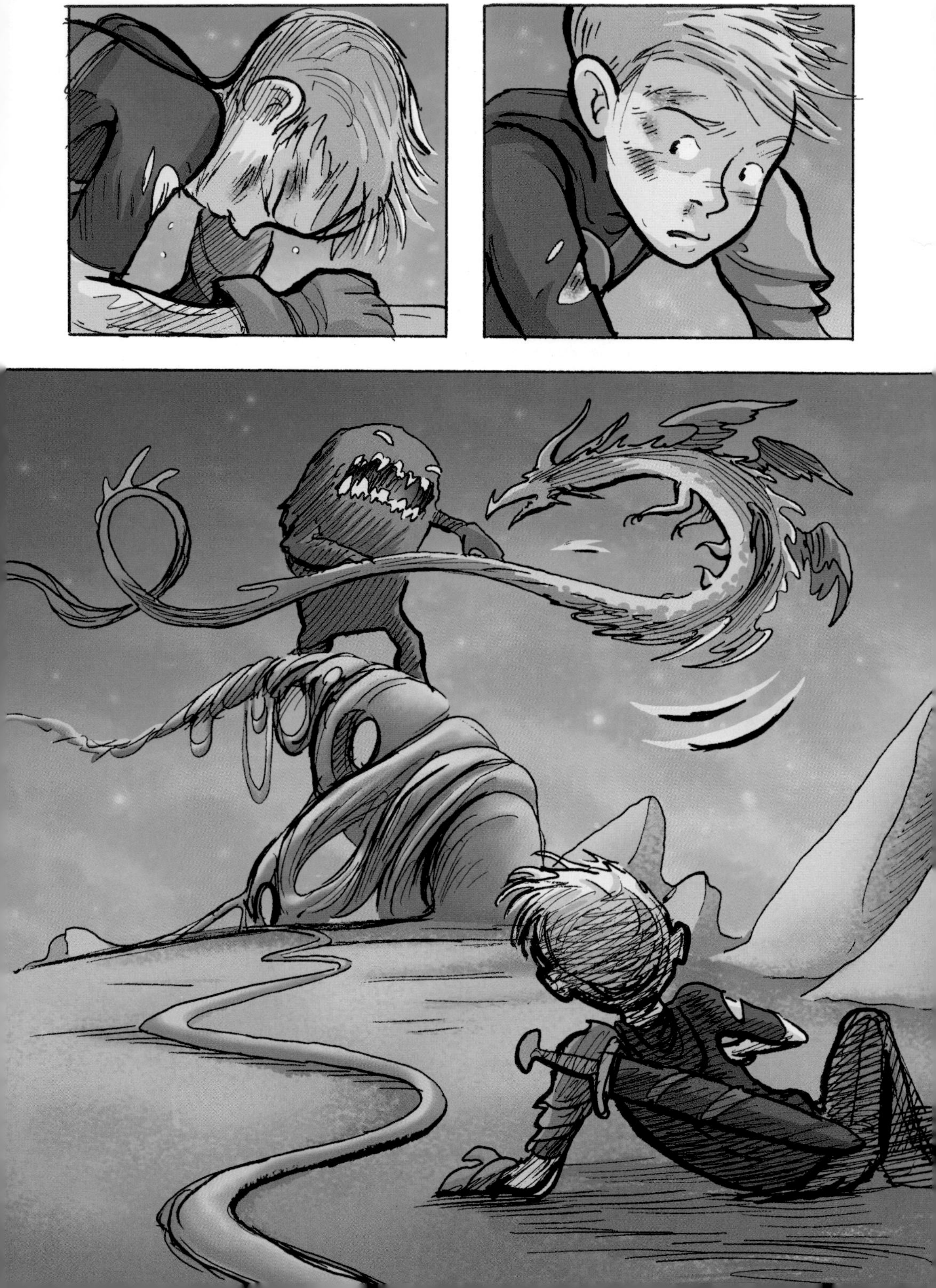

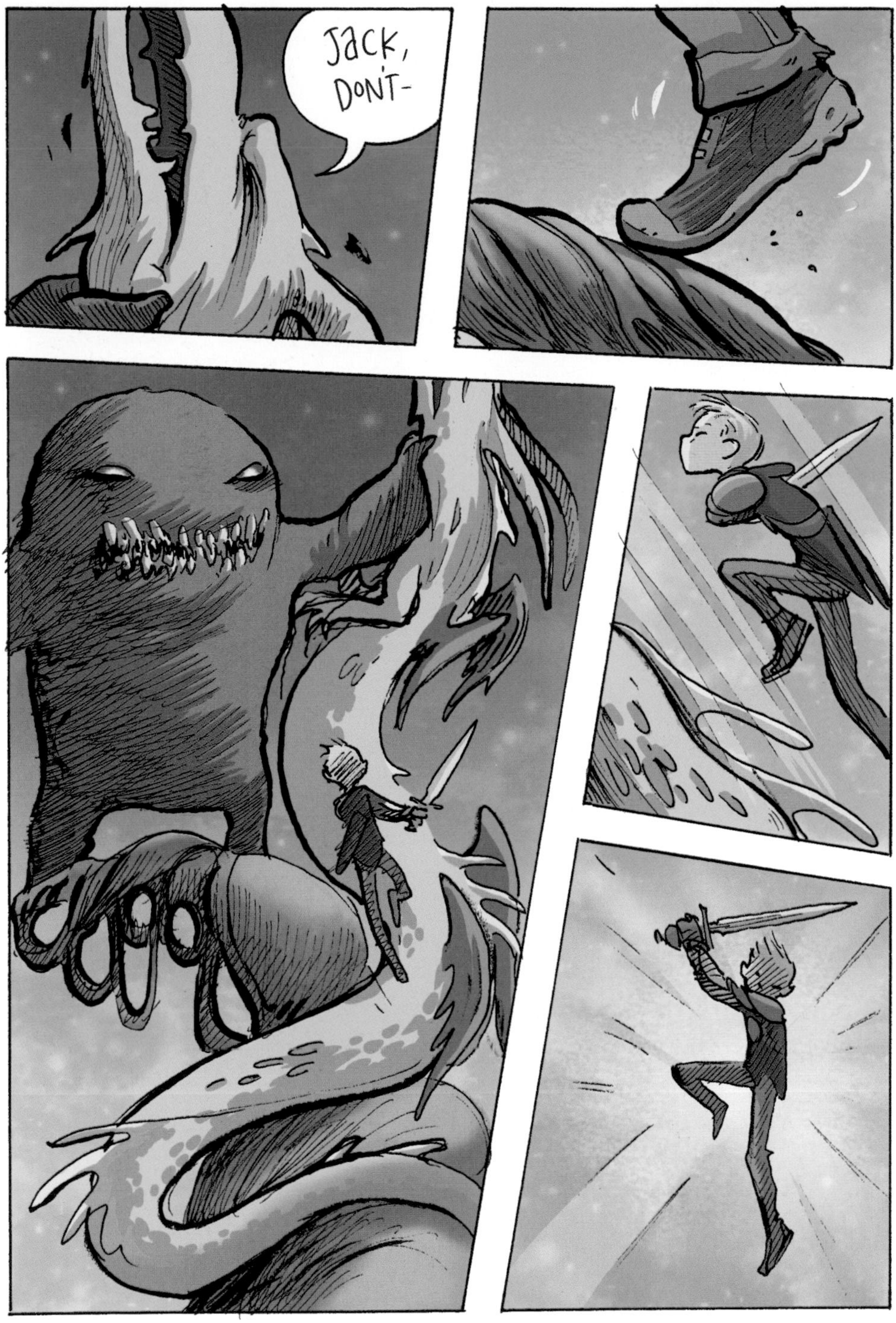
JACK, DON'T-

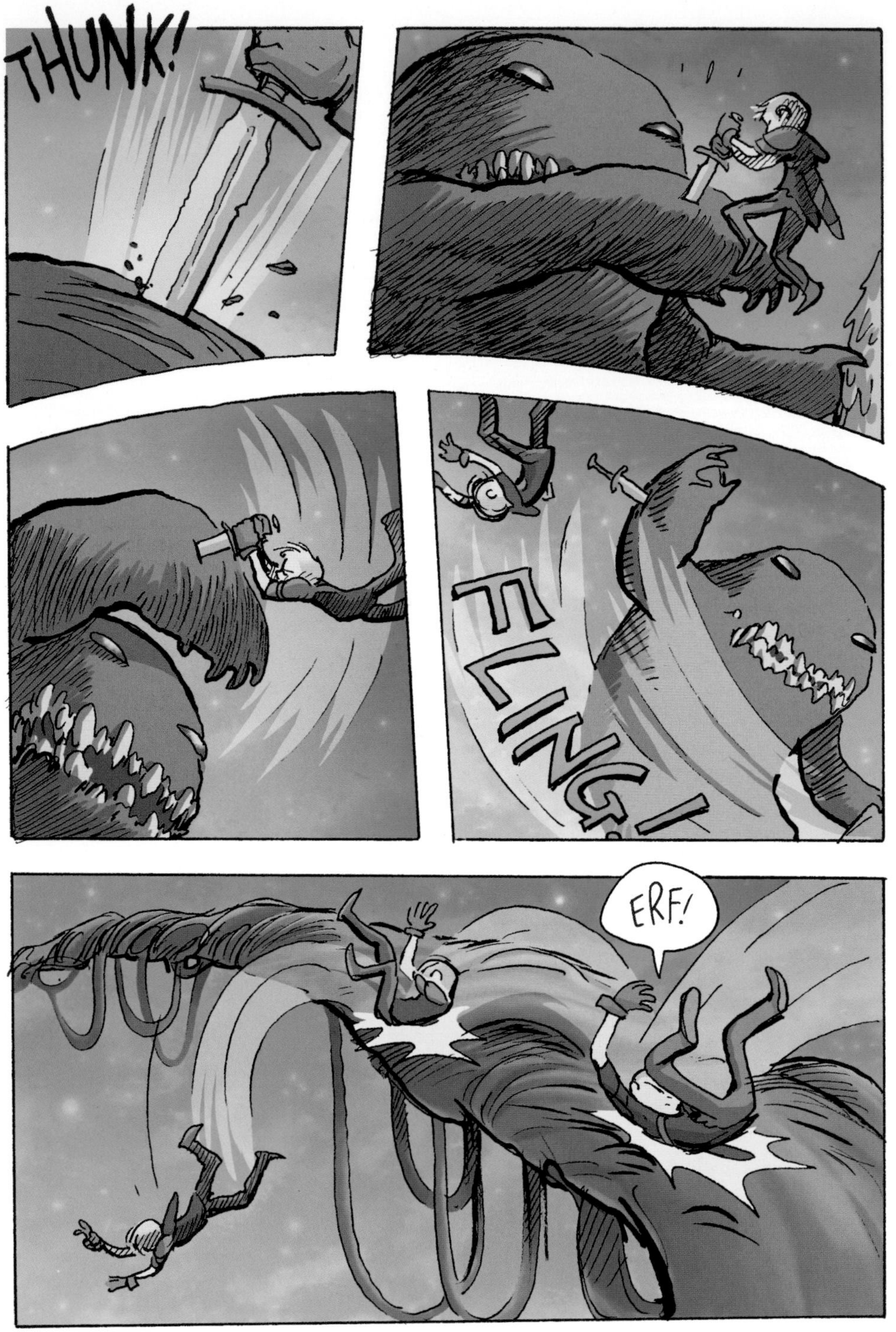
THUNK!
FLING!
ERF!

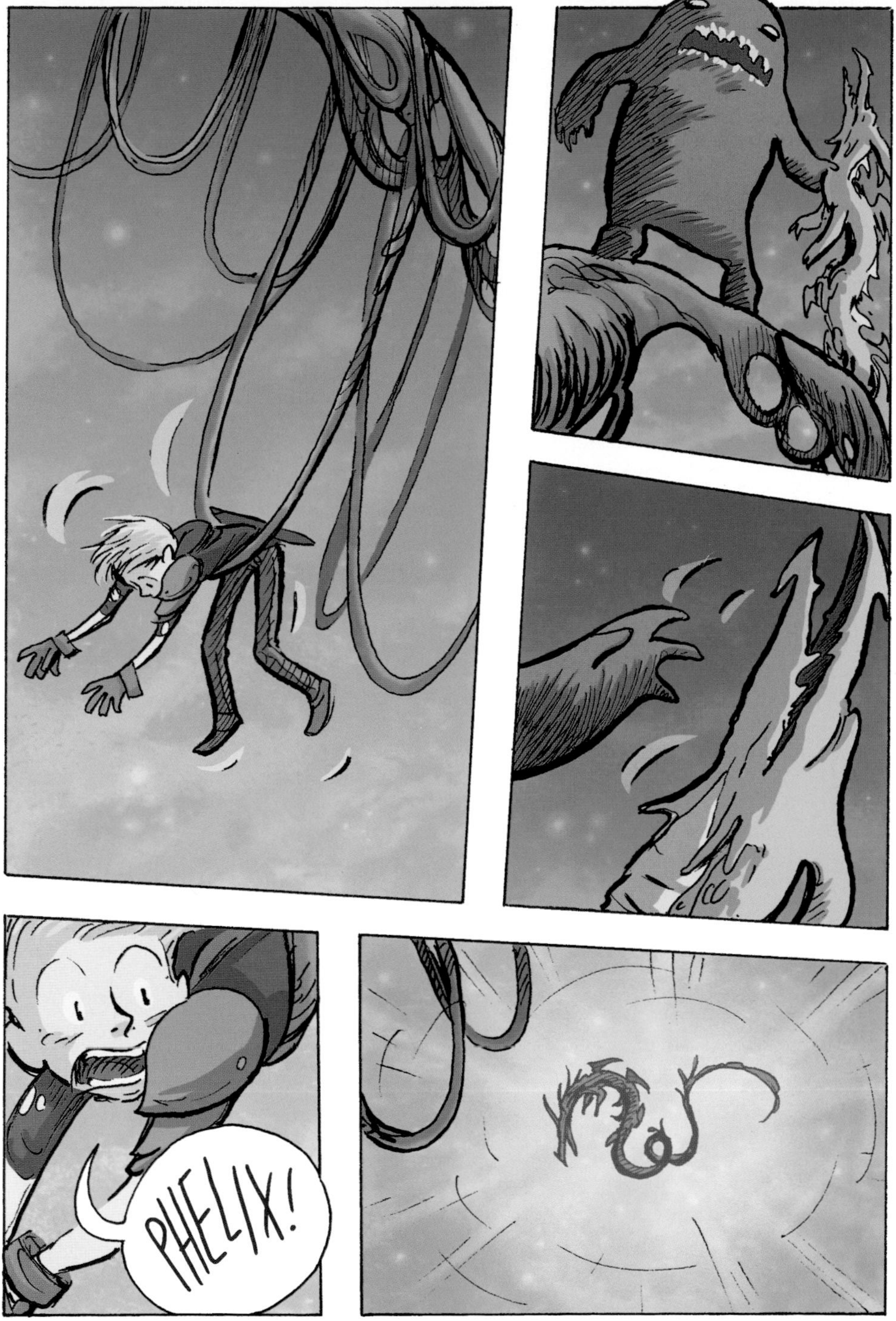
PHELIX!

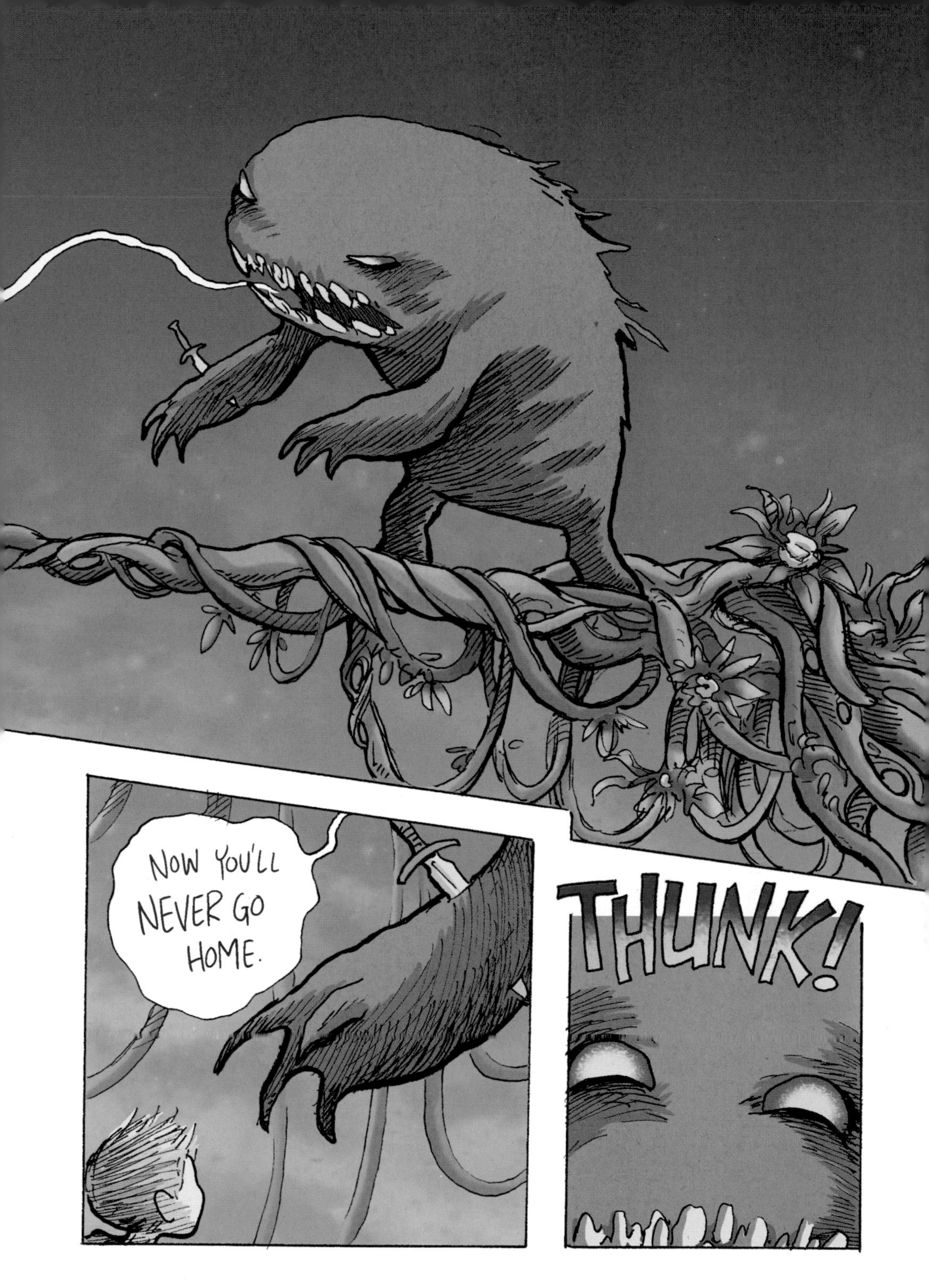
NOW YOU'LL NEVER GO HOME.
THUNK!

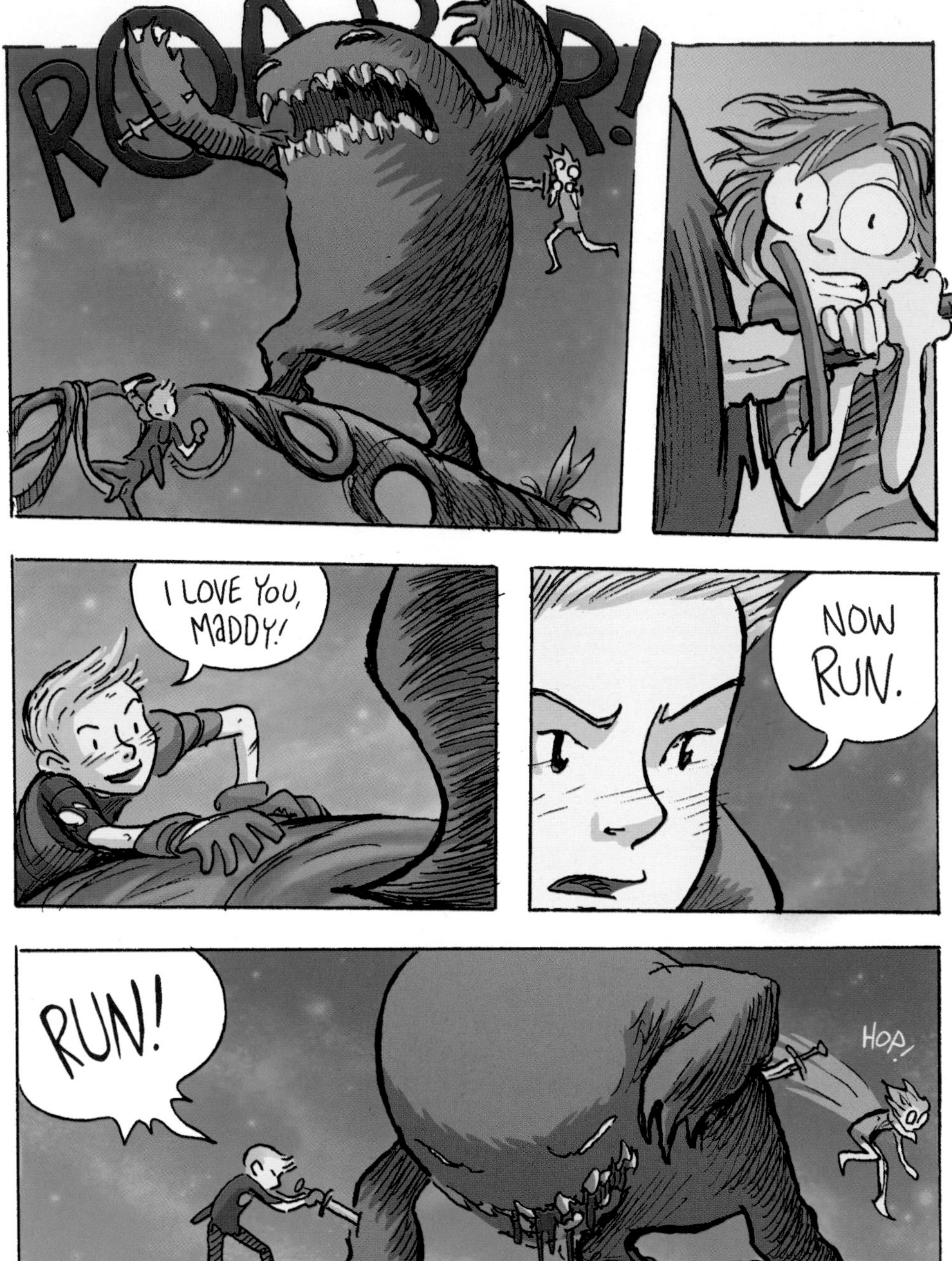

ROARR!
I LOVE YOU, MADDY!
NOW RUN.
RUN!
HOP!

169

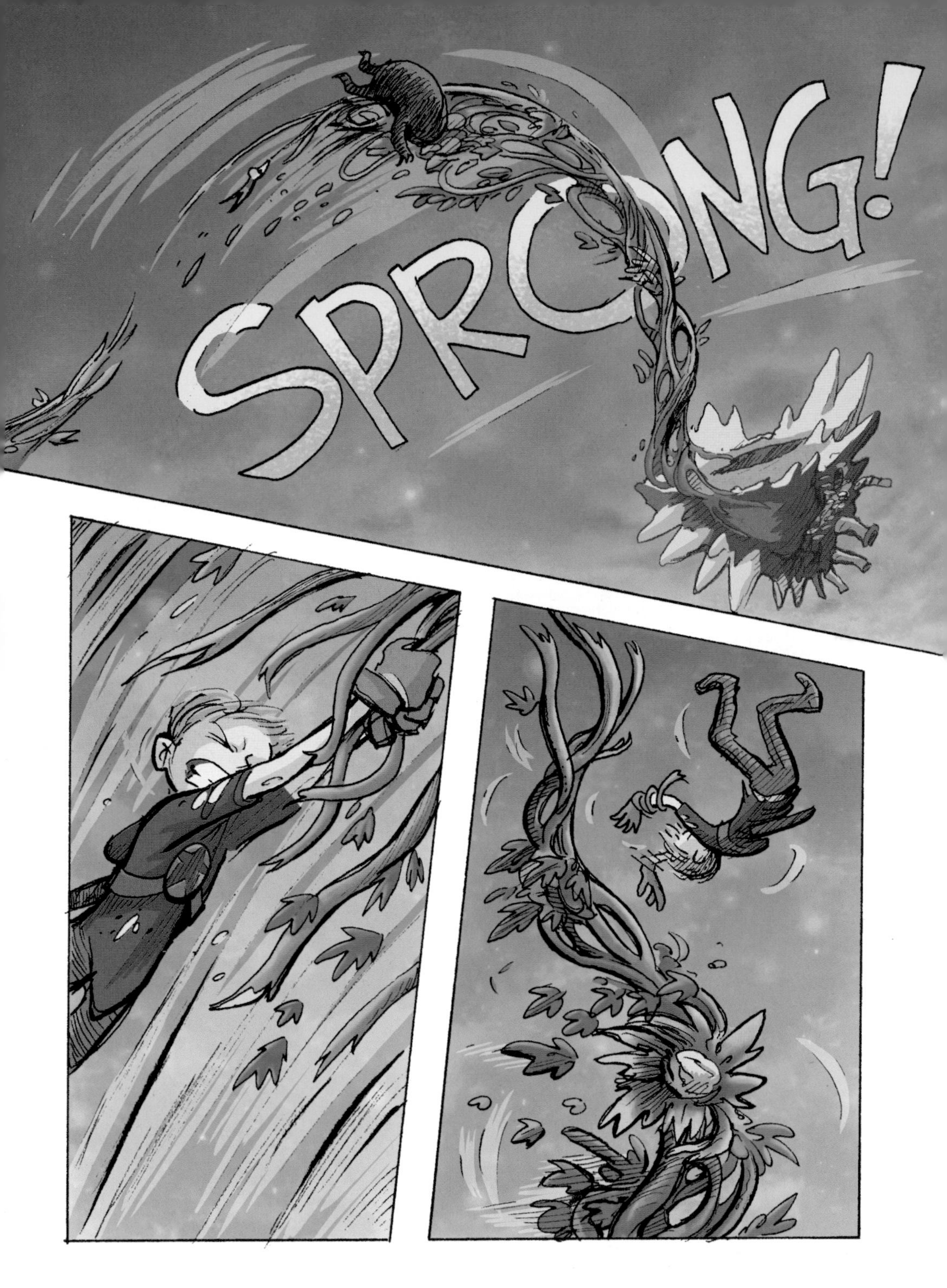
SPROONG!

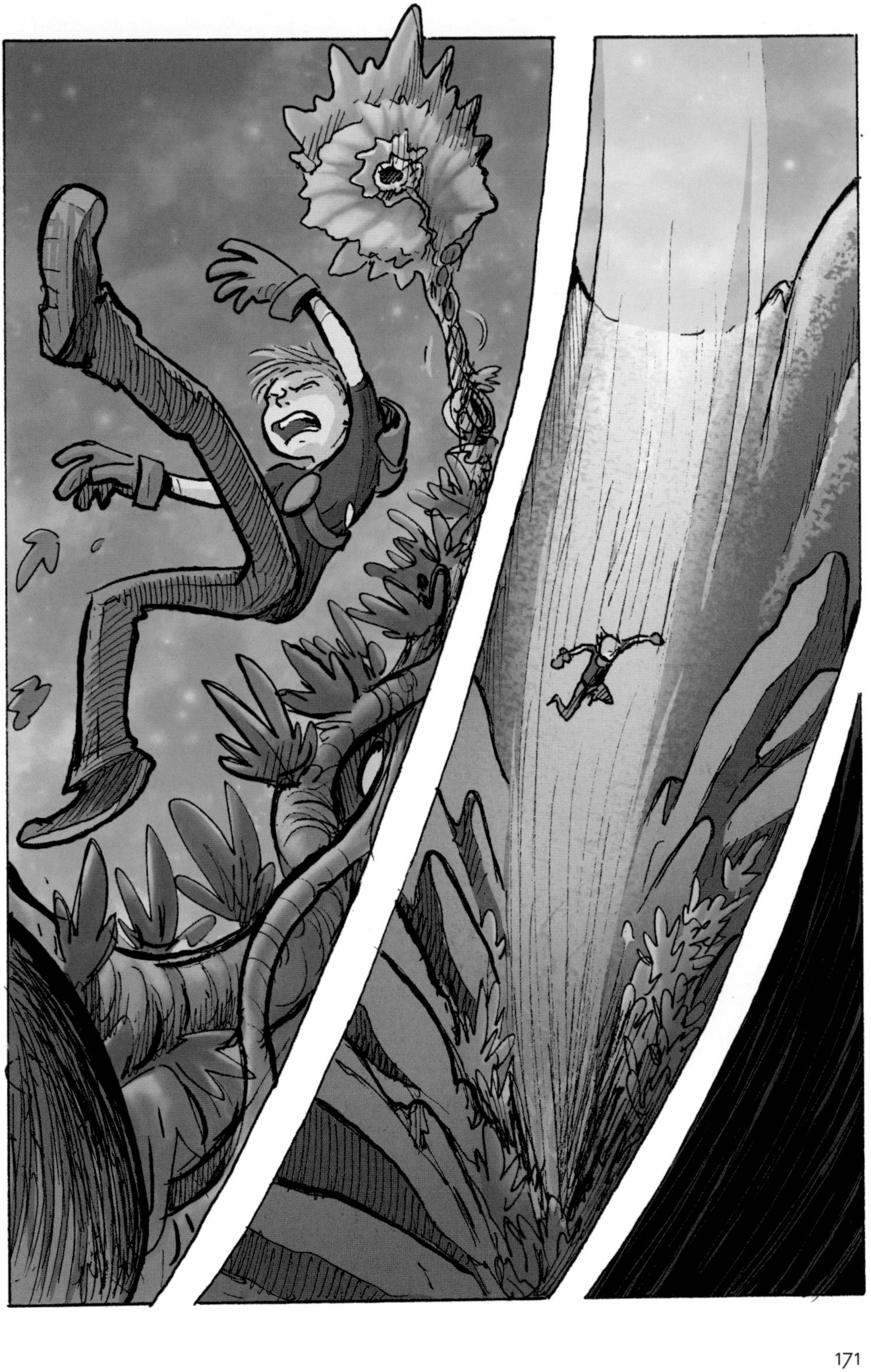

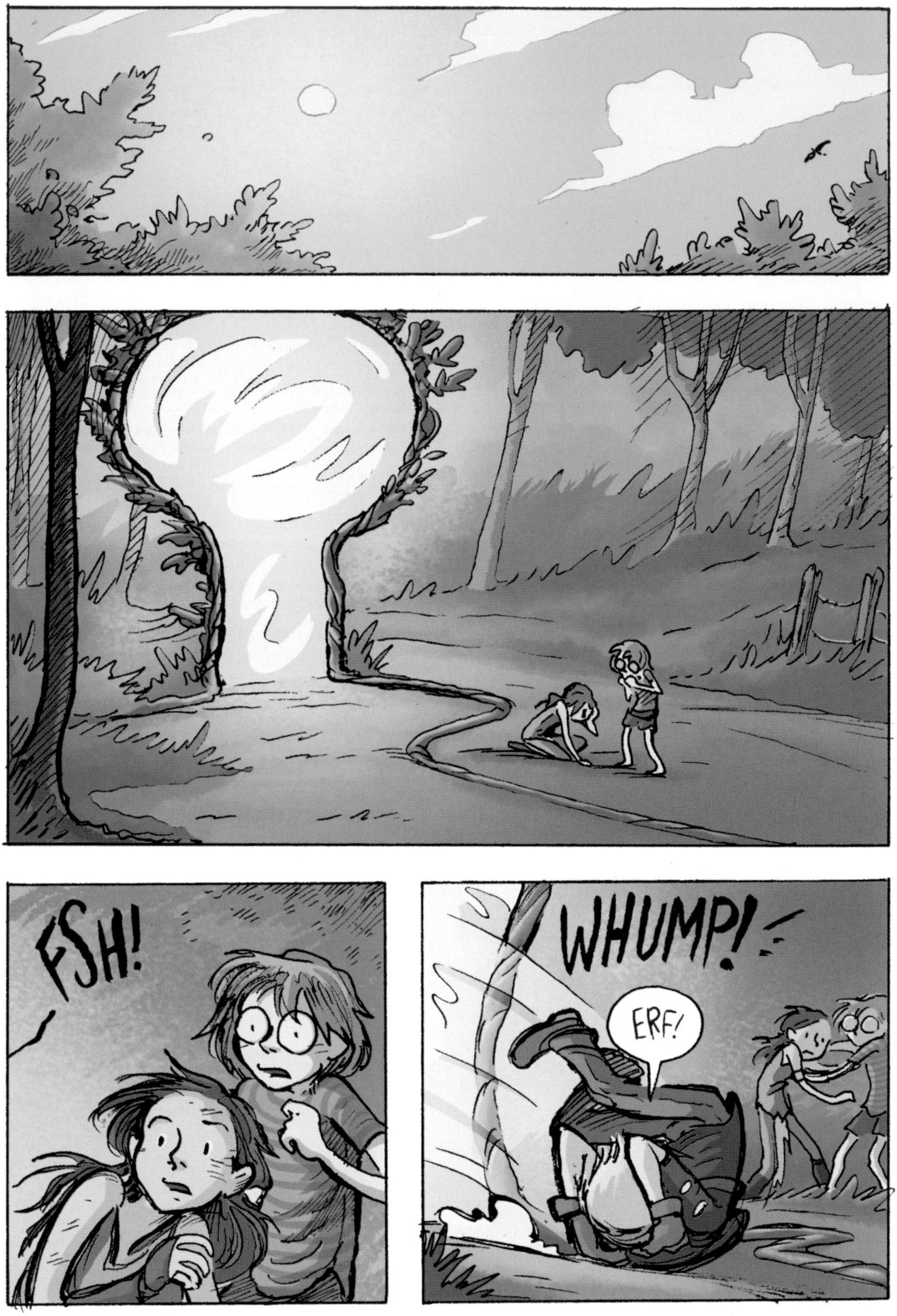
FSH!
WHUMP!
ERF!

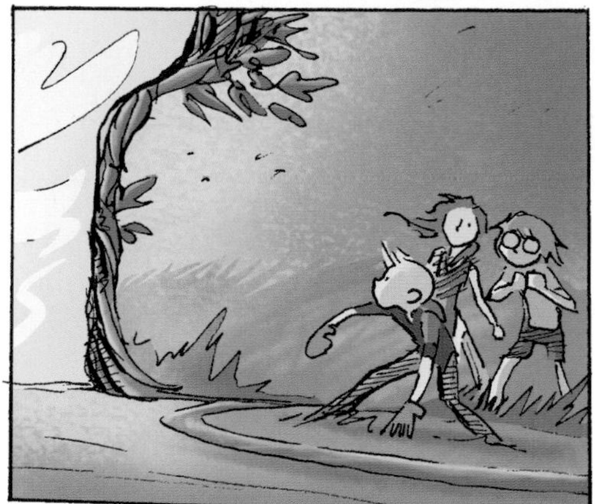

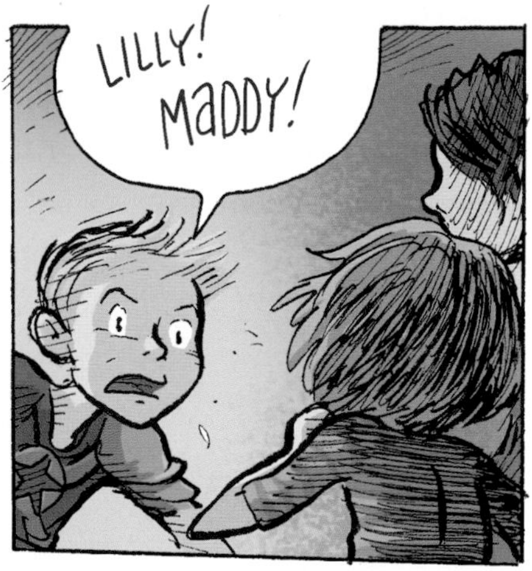
LILLY! MADDY!

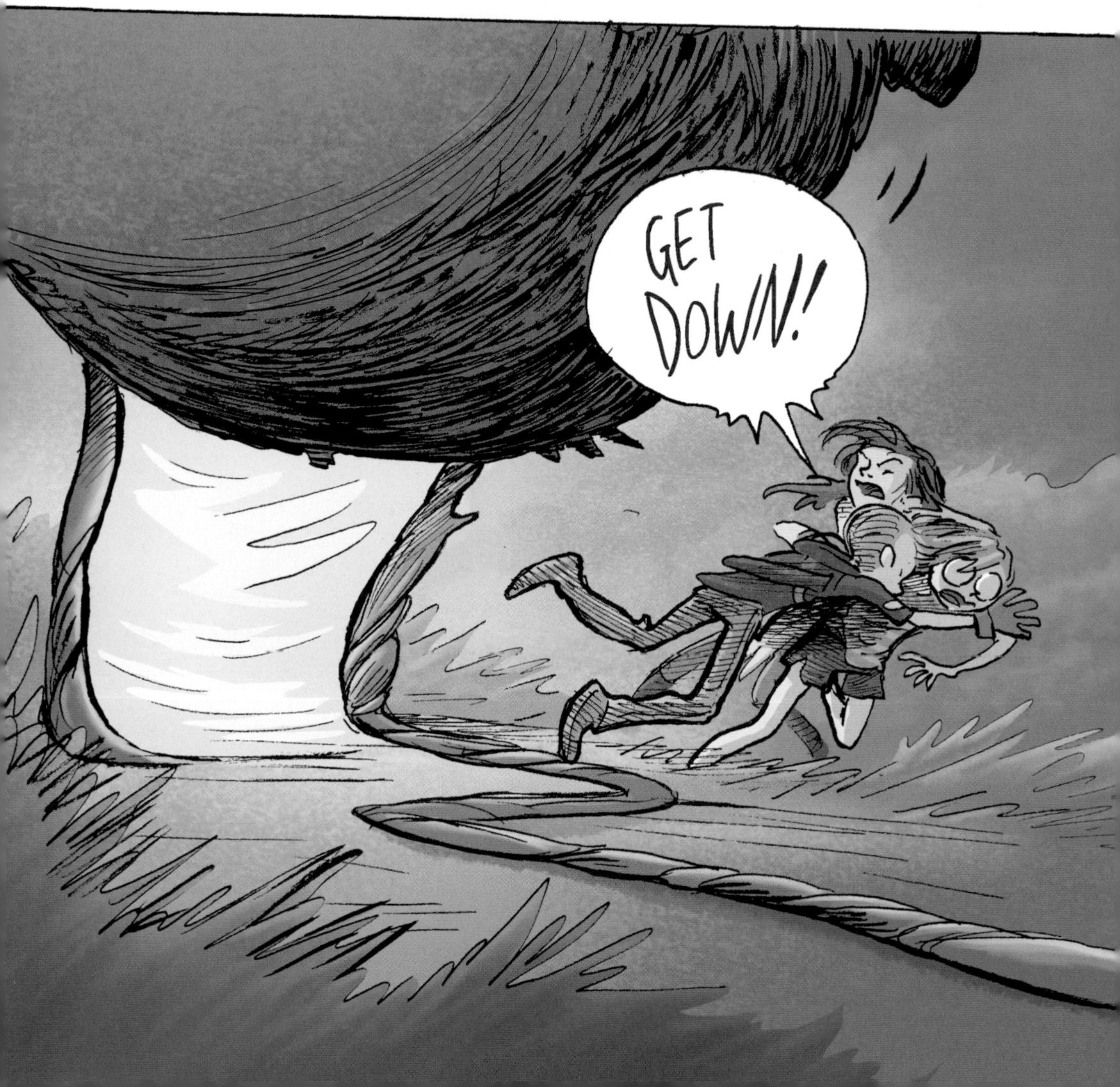
GET DOWN!

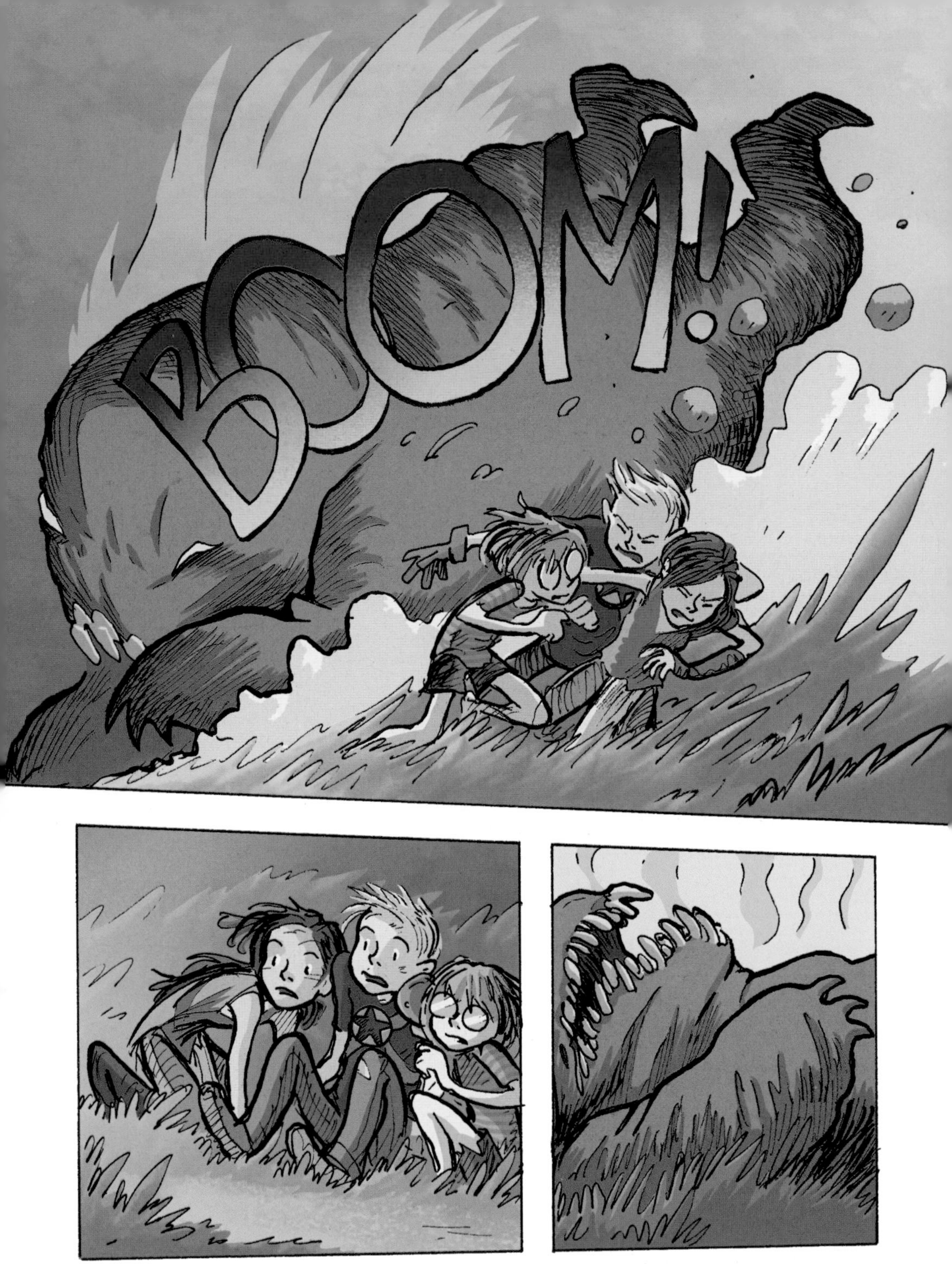
BOOM!

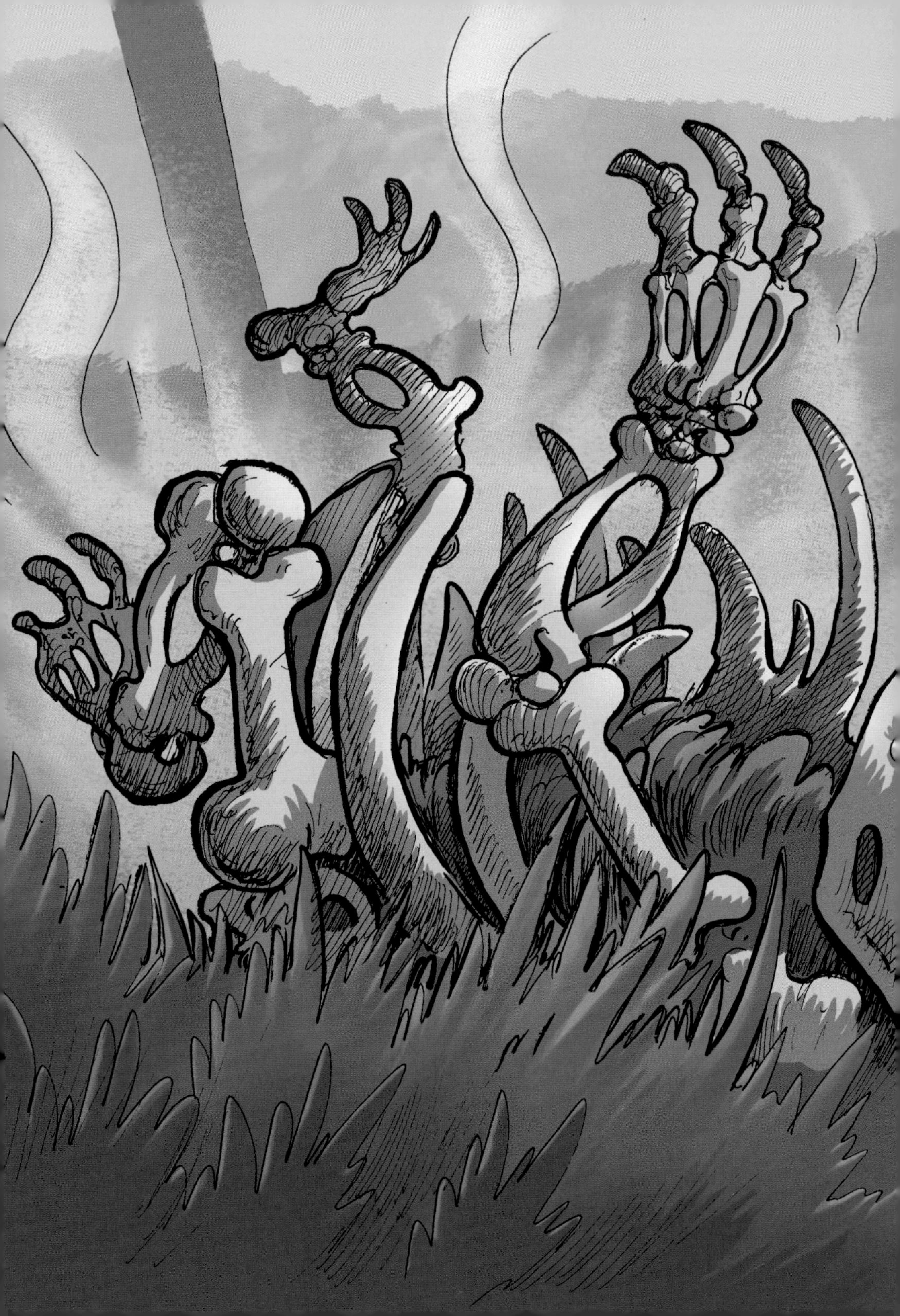

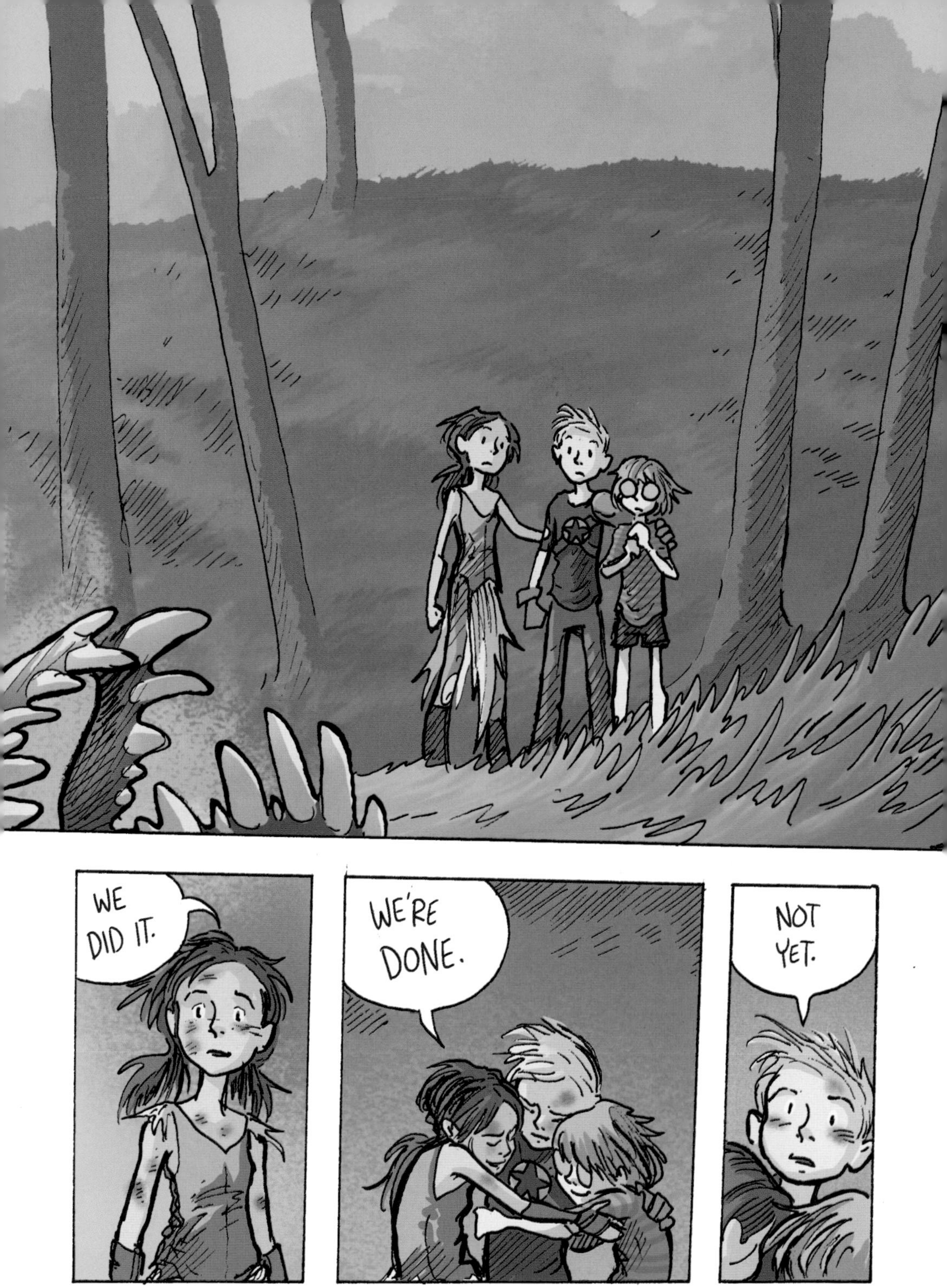
WE DID IT.
WE'RE DONE.
NOT YET.

MOM?

SHE'S STILL AT WORK.

THAT'S WEIRD.

HUH.

Regular and Certified Mail

NOTICE OF FORECLOSURE

YOU ARE IN DEFAULT UNDER A DEED OF TRUST DATED 5/25/2006. UNLESS YOU TAKE IMMEDIATE ACTION TO PROTECT YOUR PROPERTY, IT WILL BE SOLD AT A PUBLIC AUCTION.

YOU NEED AN EXPLANATION OF ... E PROCEEDINGS AGAINST YOU, YOU ...LD CONTACT A LAWYER.

...ntal amount of unpaid balance ...erest thereon of the obligation ...y the property to be sold ...nable estimated costs

C'MON MADDY, WE'VE STILL GOT A LOT OF WORK TO DO.

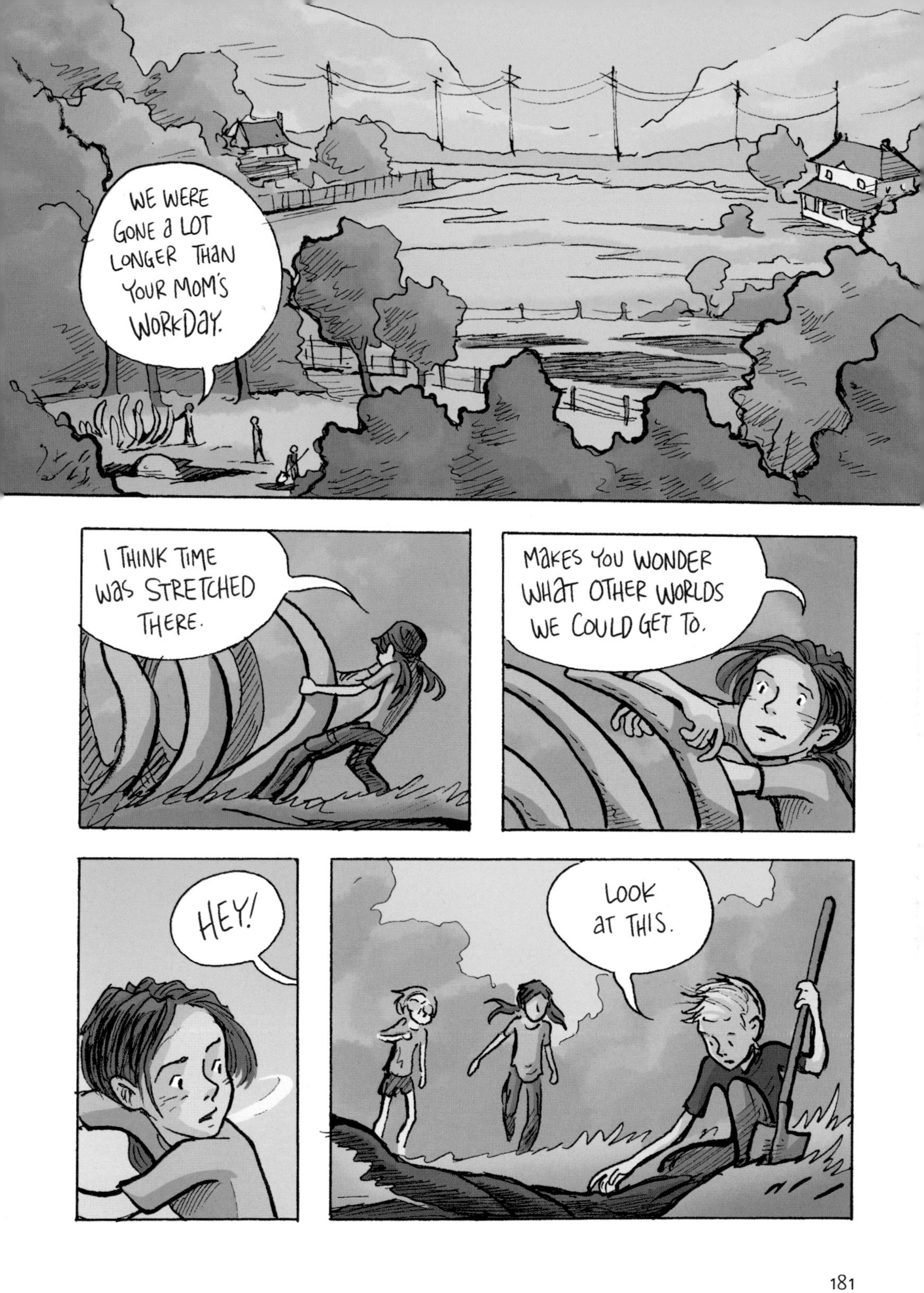
WE WERE GONE a LOT LONGER THAN YOUR MOM'S WORKDay.
I THINK TIME was STRETCHED THERE.
MaKES YOU WONDER WHaT OTHER WORLDS WE COULD GET TO.
HEY!
LOOK aT THIS.

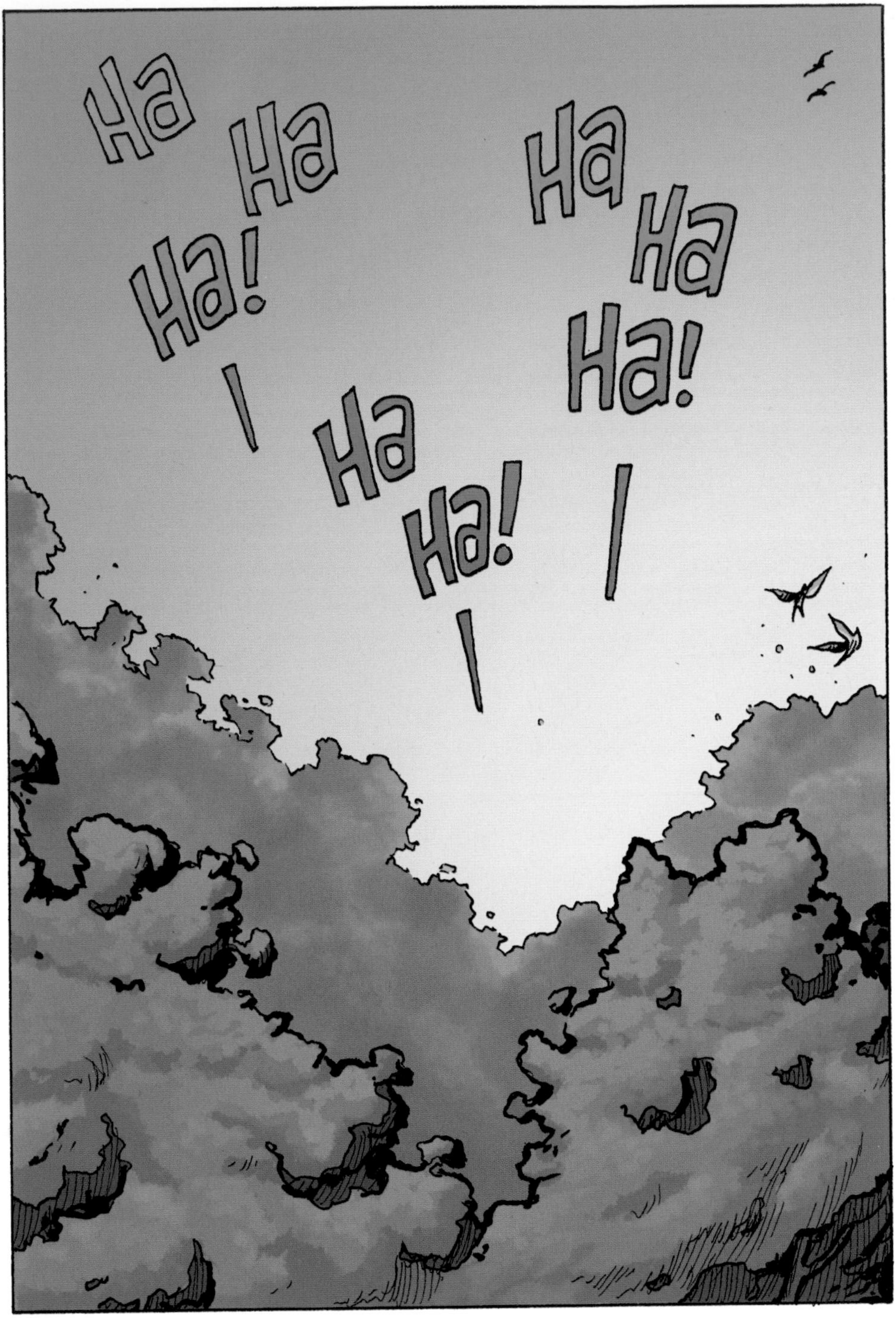
Ha Ha Ha!!
Ha Ha Ha!!
Ha Ha Ha!!

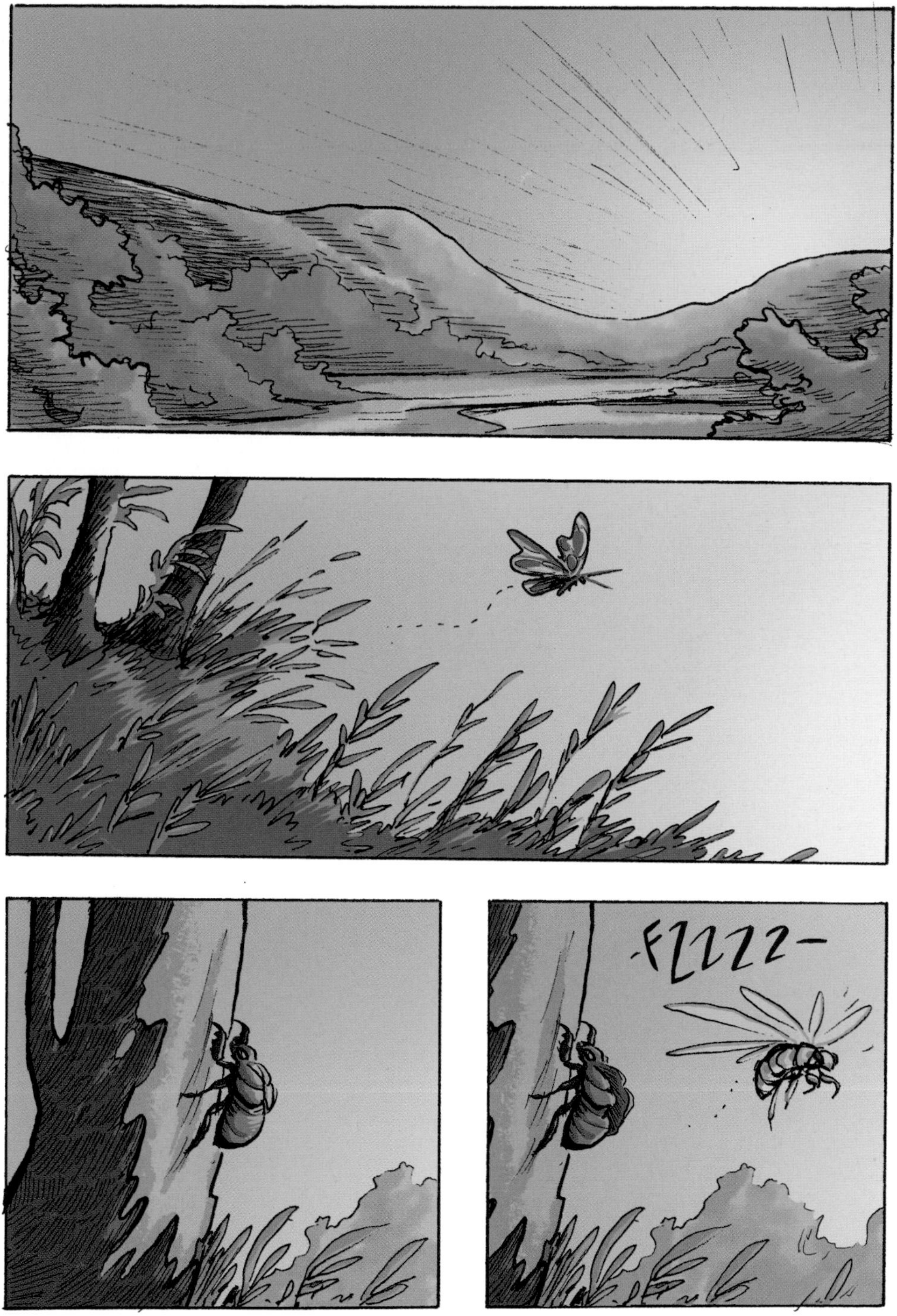
-FZZZZ-

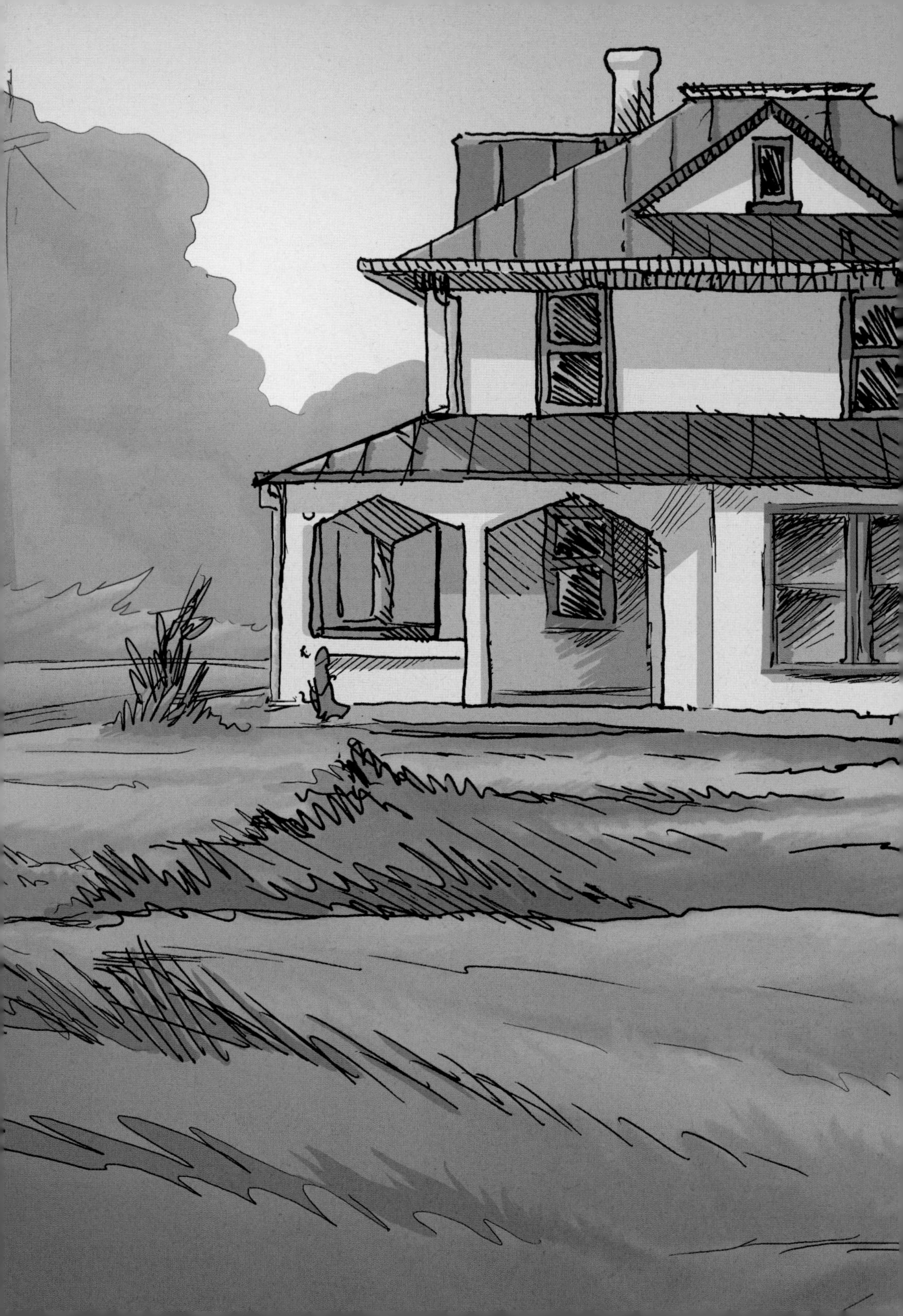

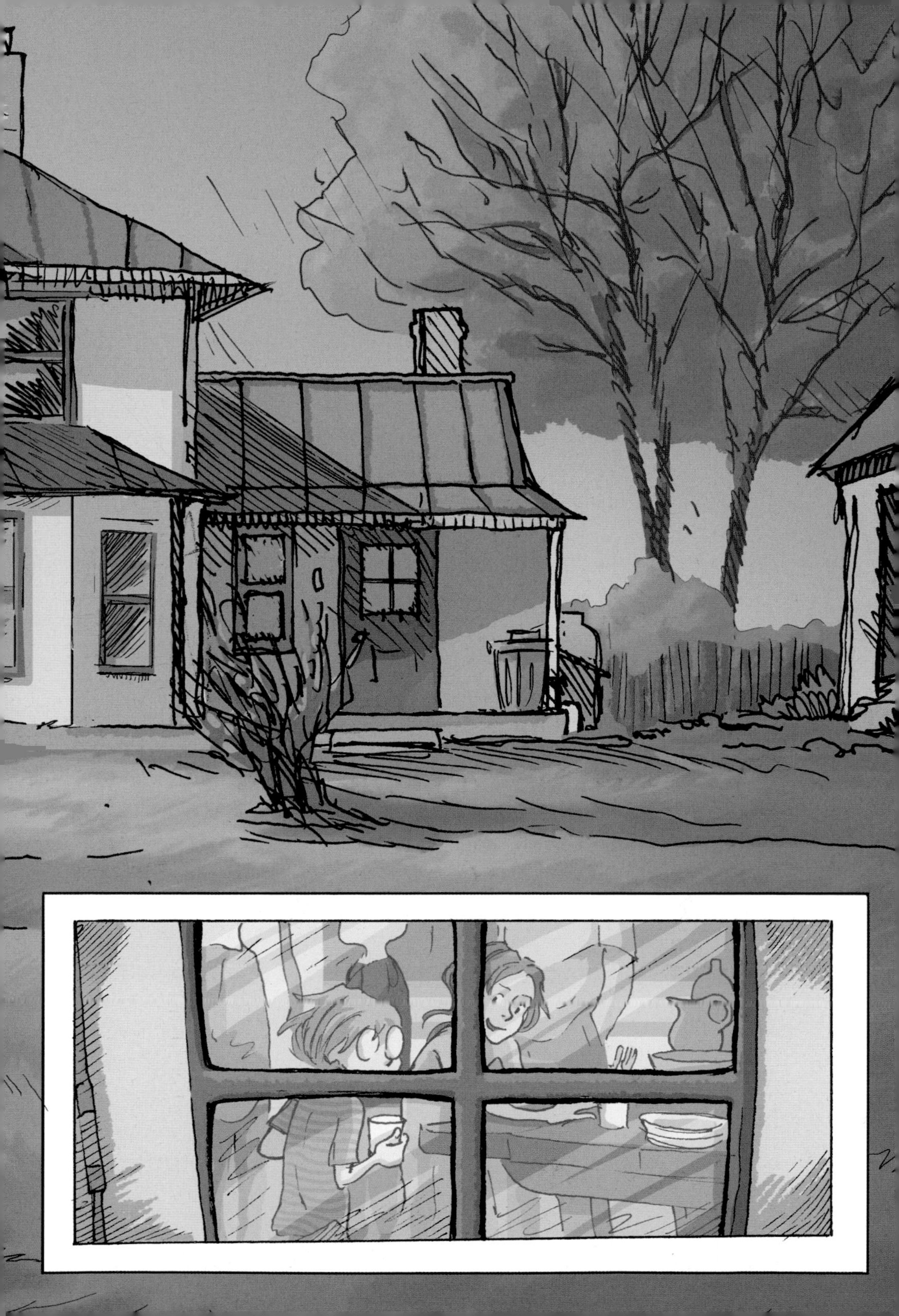

188

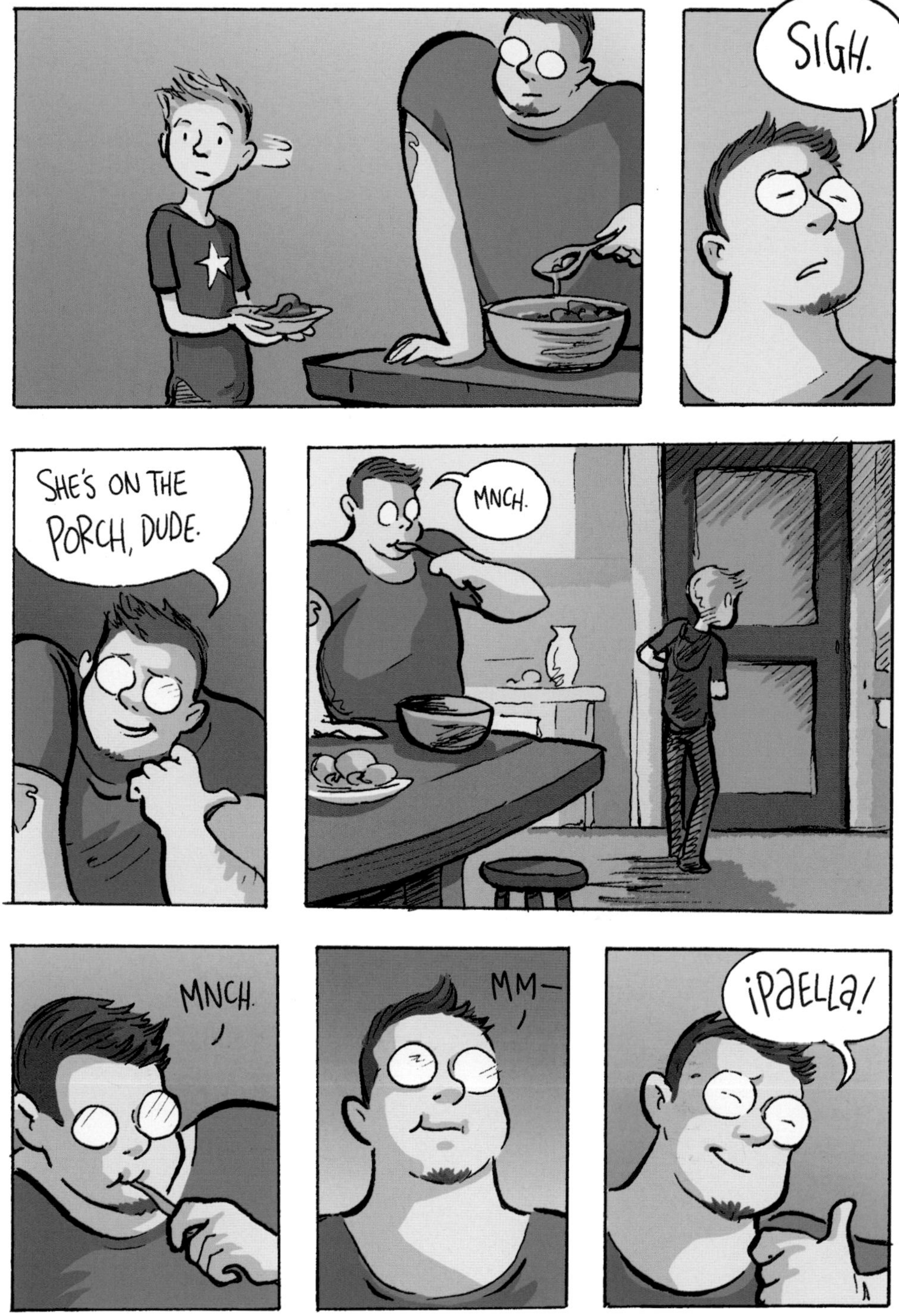
SIGH.
SHE'S ON THE PORCH, DUDE.
MNCH.
MNCH.
MM—
¡Paella!

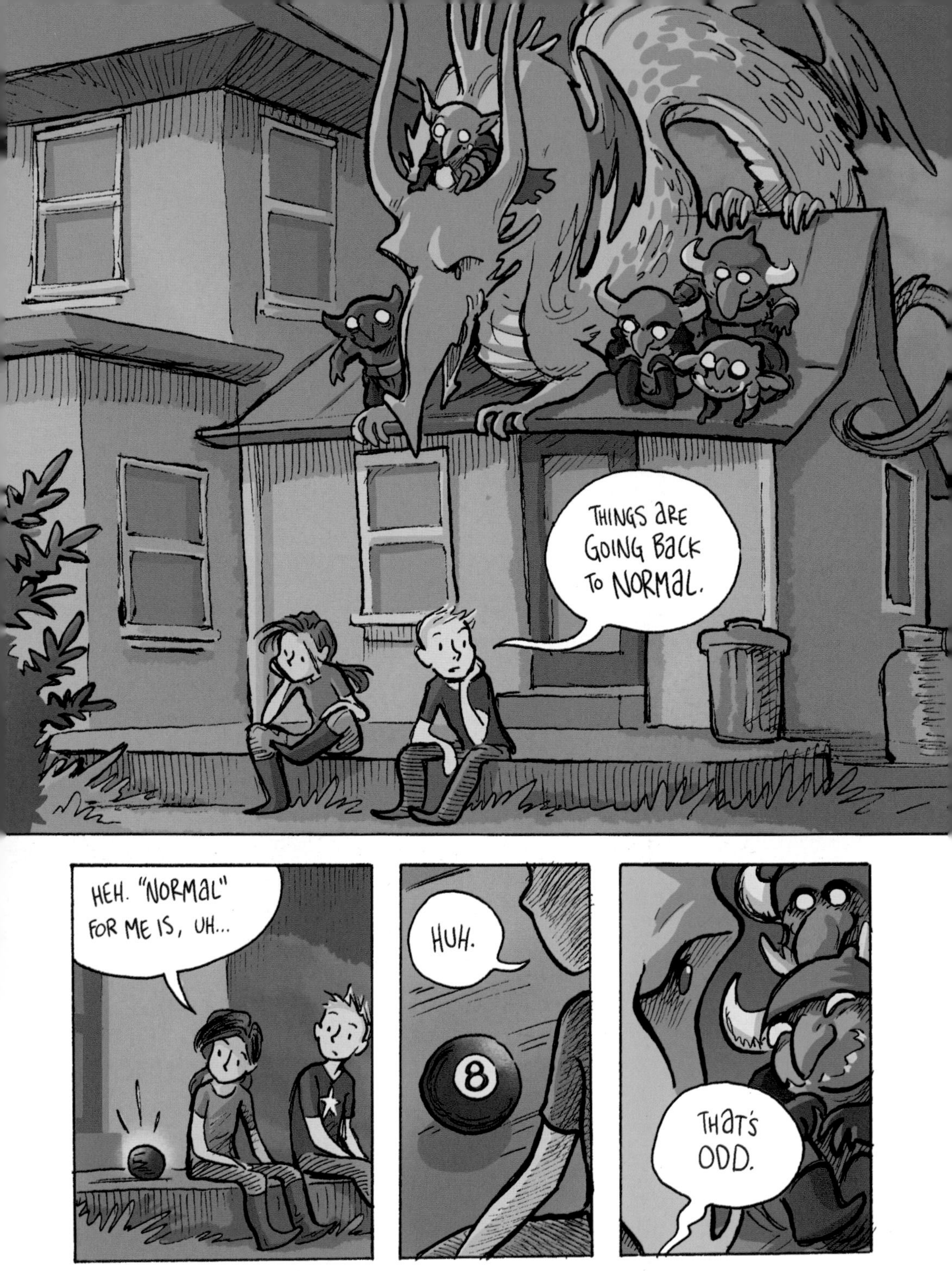
THINGS ARE GOING BACK TO NORMAL.
HEH. "NORMAL" FOR ME IS, UH...
HUH.
8
THAT'S ODD.

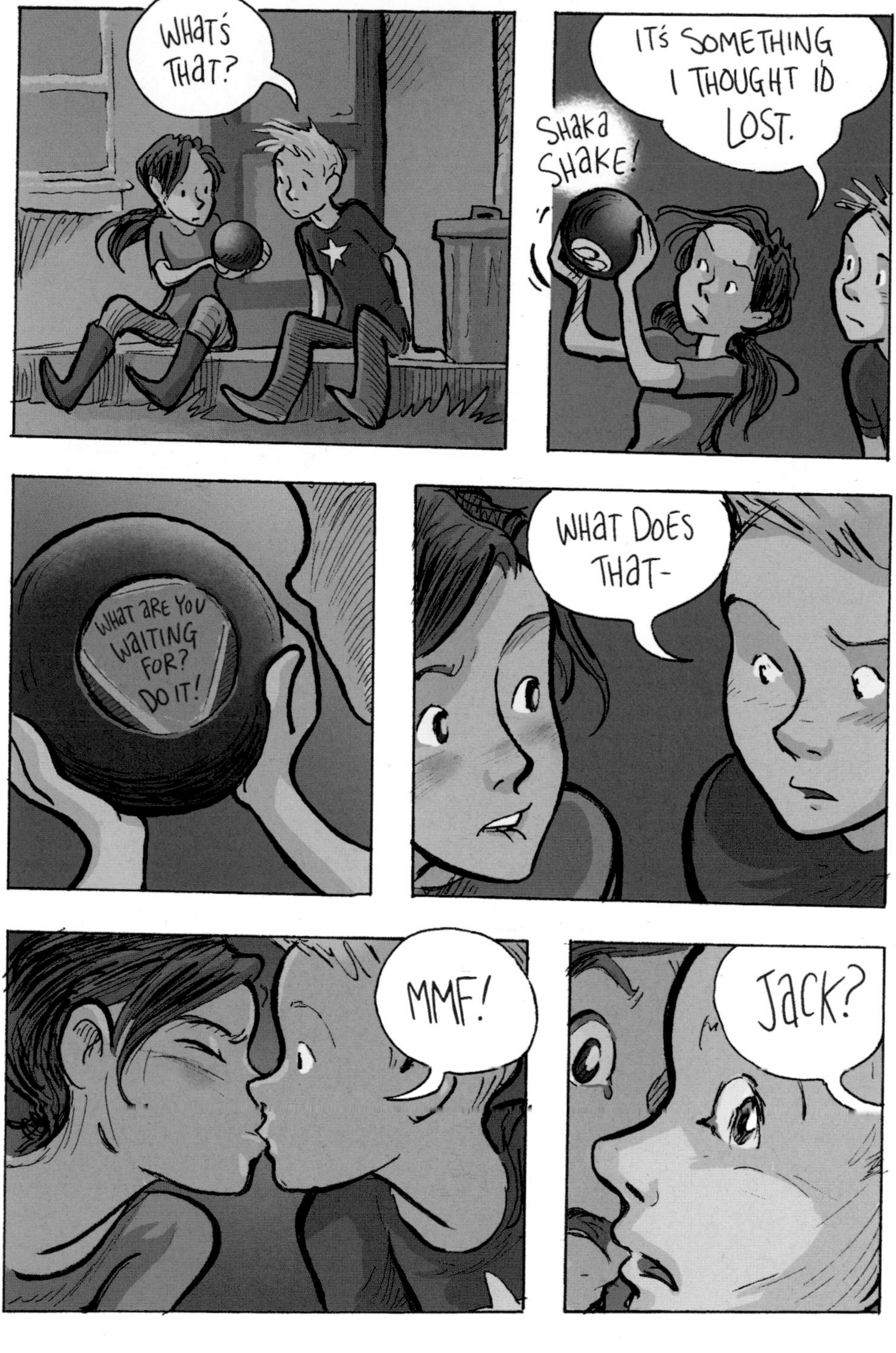
WHAT'S THAT?
SHAKA SHAKE!
IT'S SOMETHING I THOUGHT I'D LOST.
WHAT ARE YOU WAITING FOR? DO IT!
WHAT DOES THAT-
MMF!
JACK?

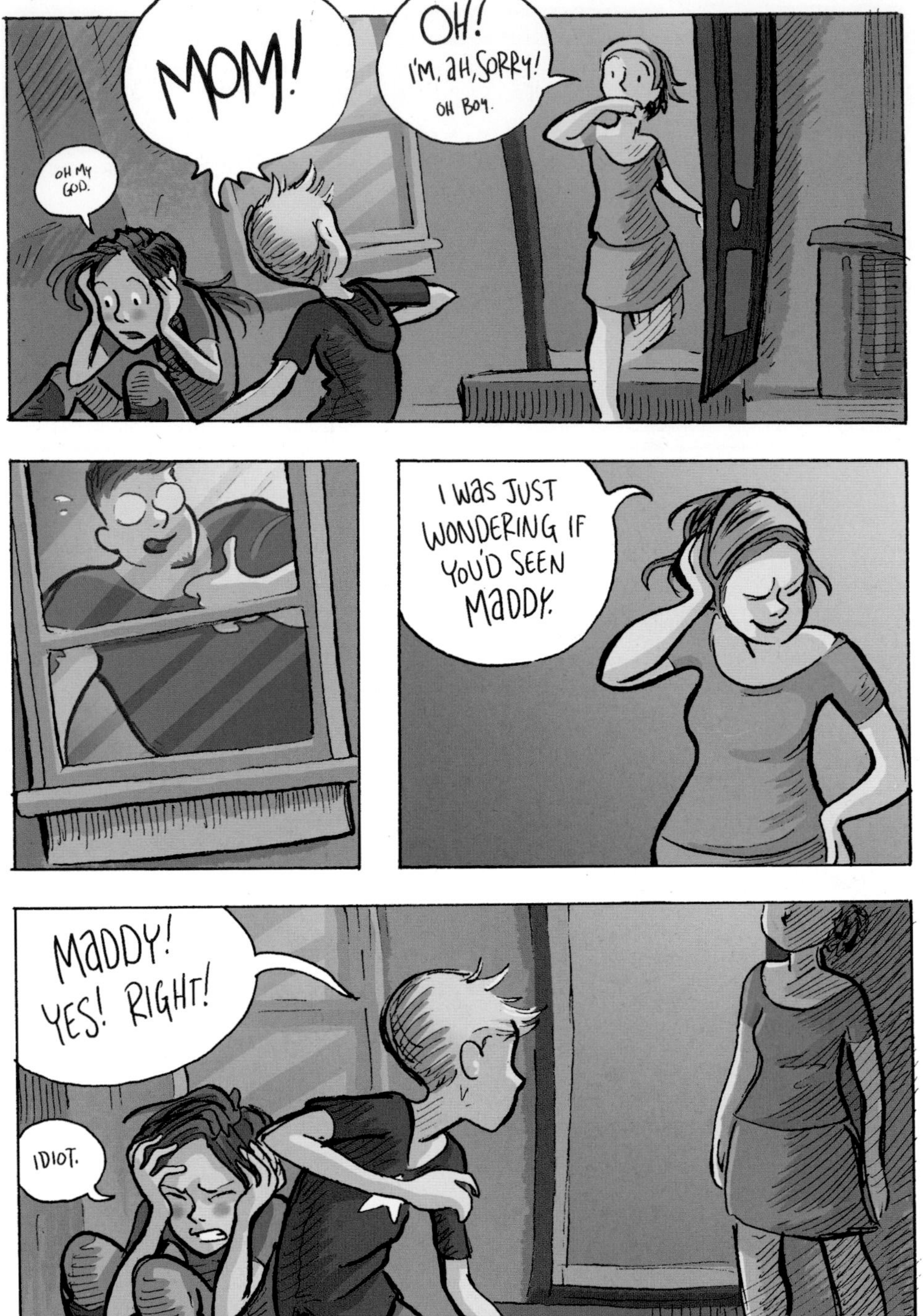
OH MY GOD.
MOM!
OH! I'M, AH, SORRY! OH BOY.
I WAS JUST WONDERING IF YOU'D SEEN MADDY.
MADDY! YES! RIGHT!
IDIOT.

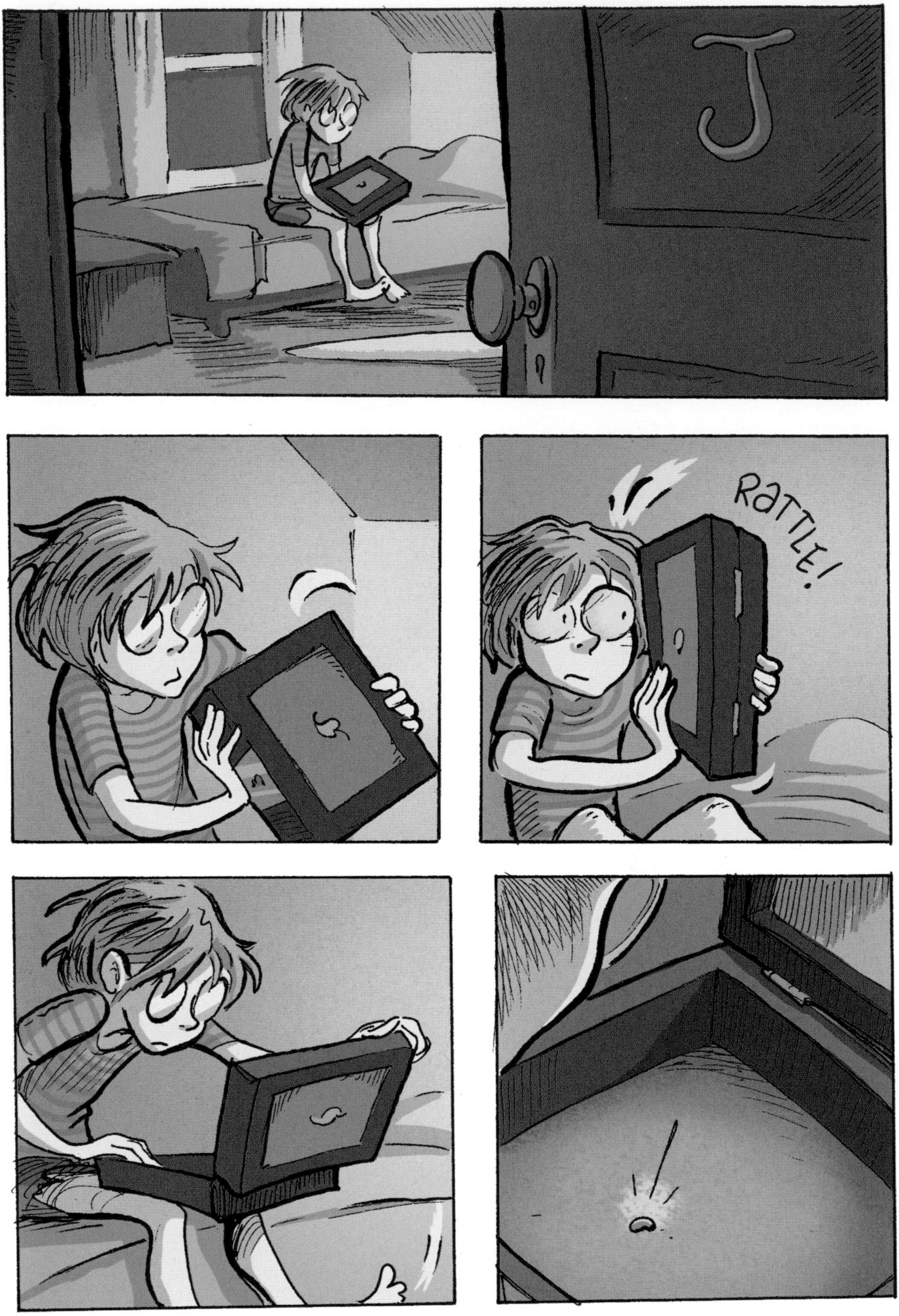
RATTLE!

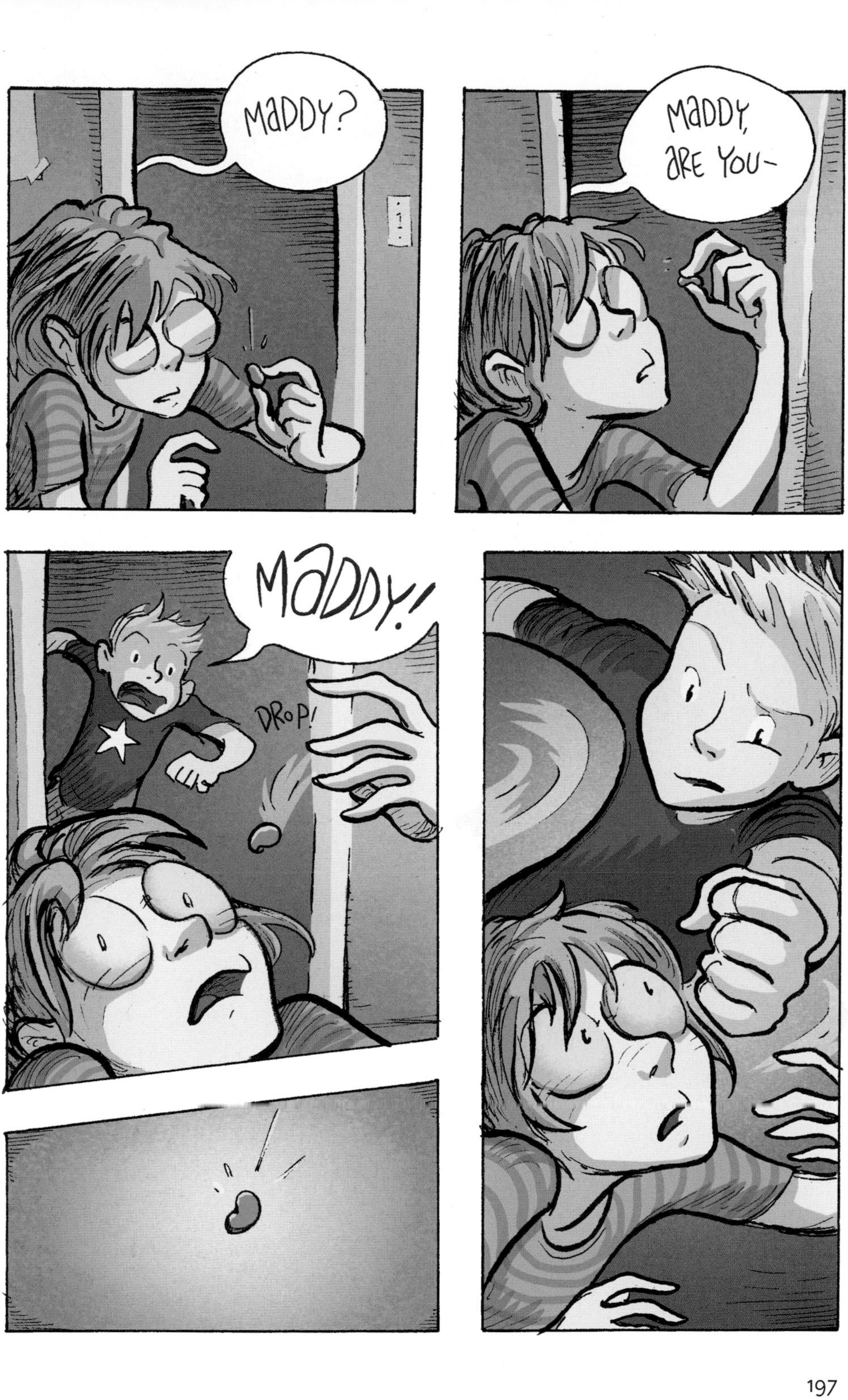
MADDY?
MADDY, ARE YOU-
MADDY!
DROP!

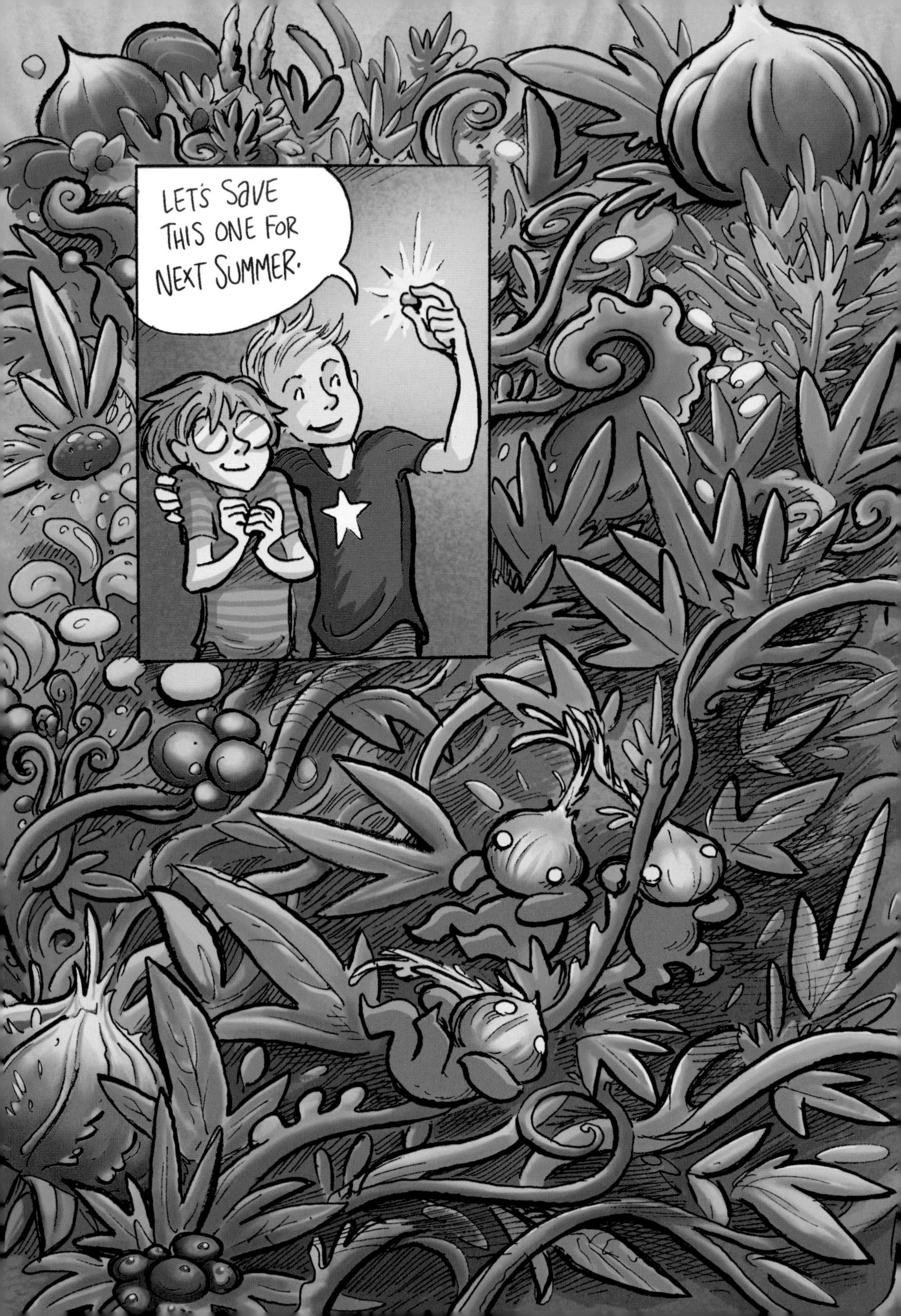
LET'S SAVE THIS ONE FOR NEXT SUMMER.

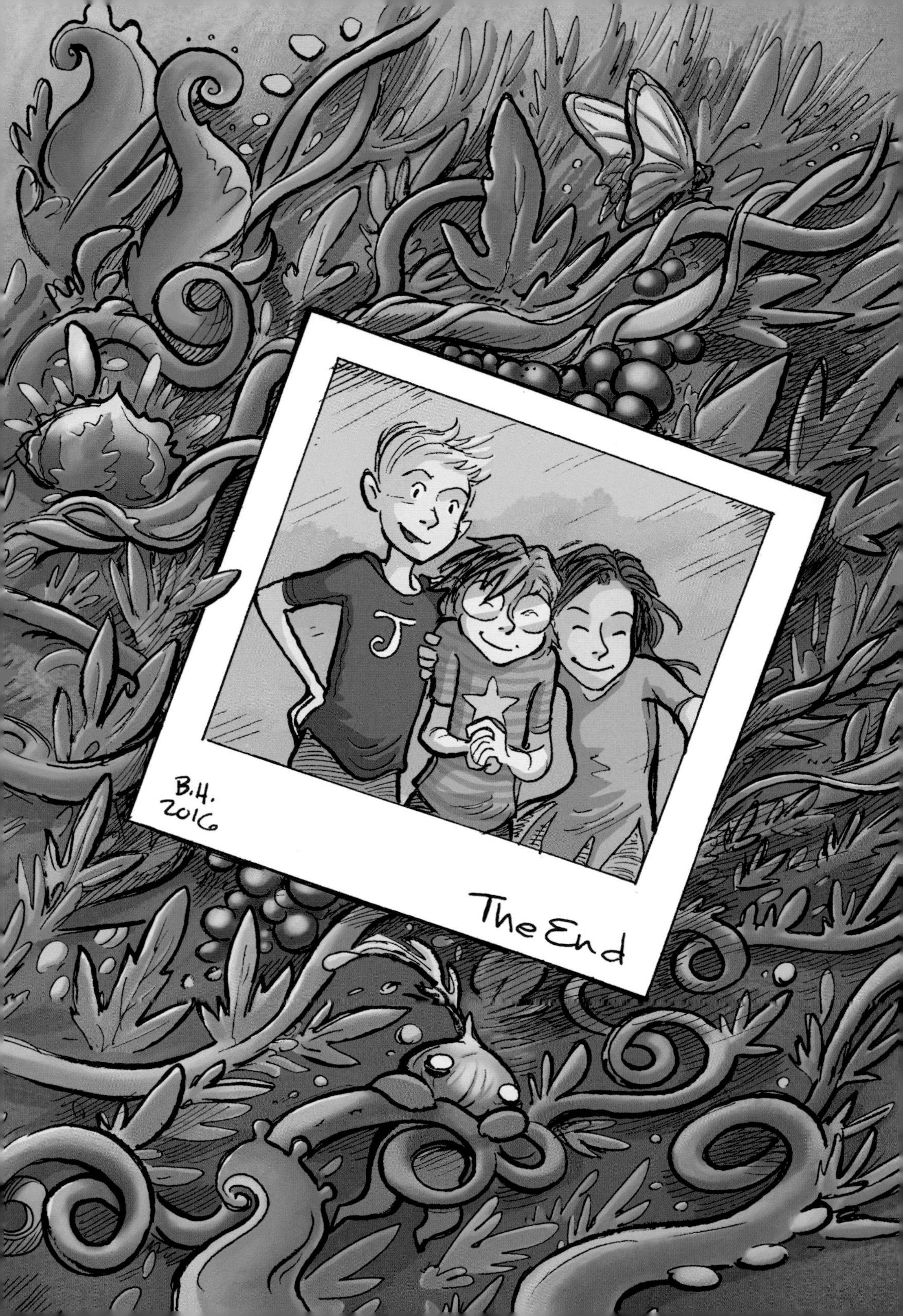
B.H.
2016
The End

EPILOGUE

THREE MONTHS LATER...

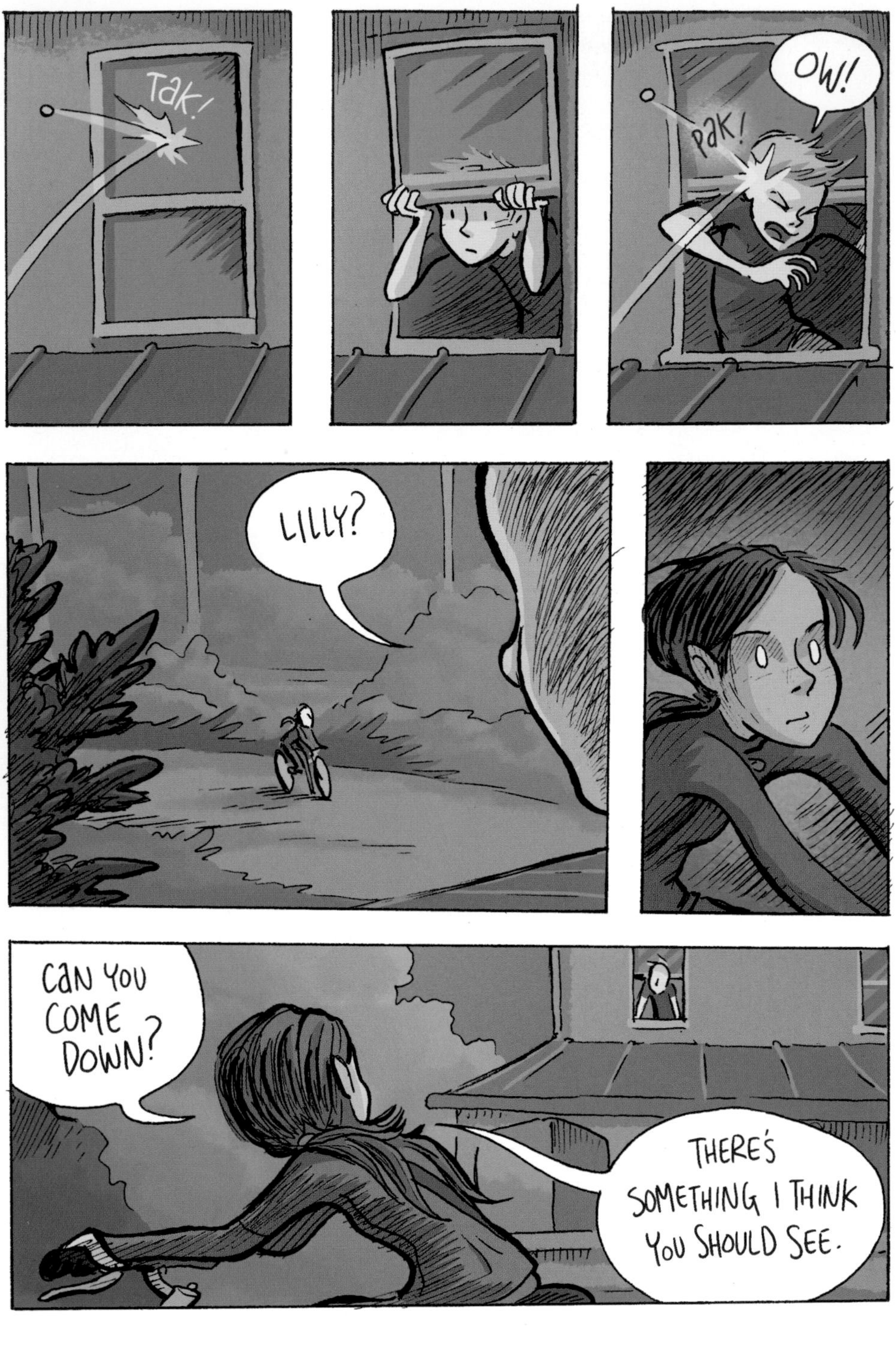
TAK!
OW!
PAK!
LILLY?
CAN YOU COME DOWN?
THERE'S SOMETHING I THINK YOU SHOULD SEE.

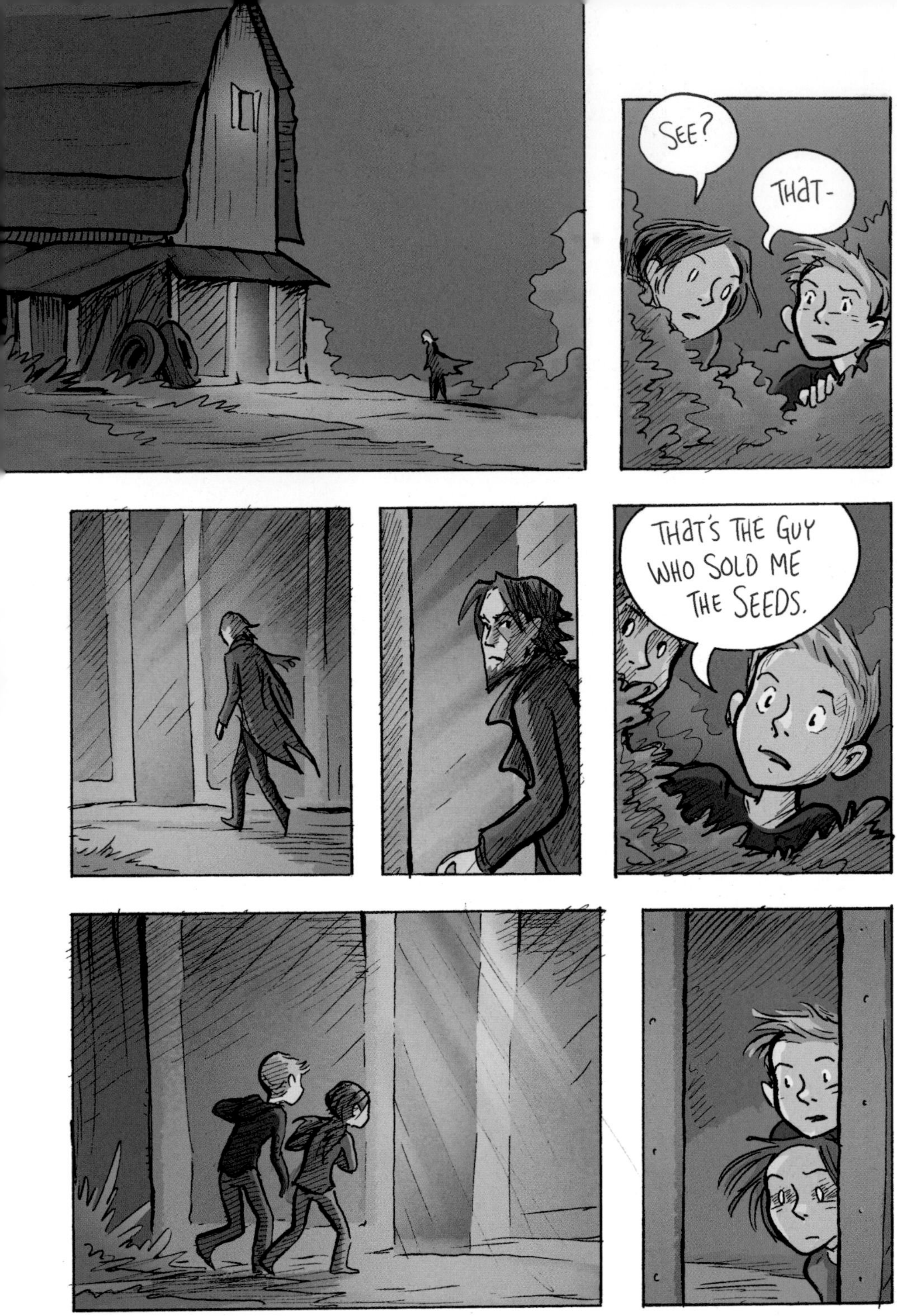
SEE?
THAT-
THAT'S THE GUY WHO SOLD ME THE SEEDS.

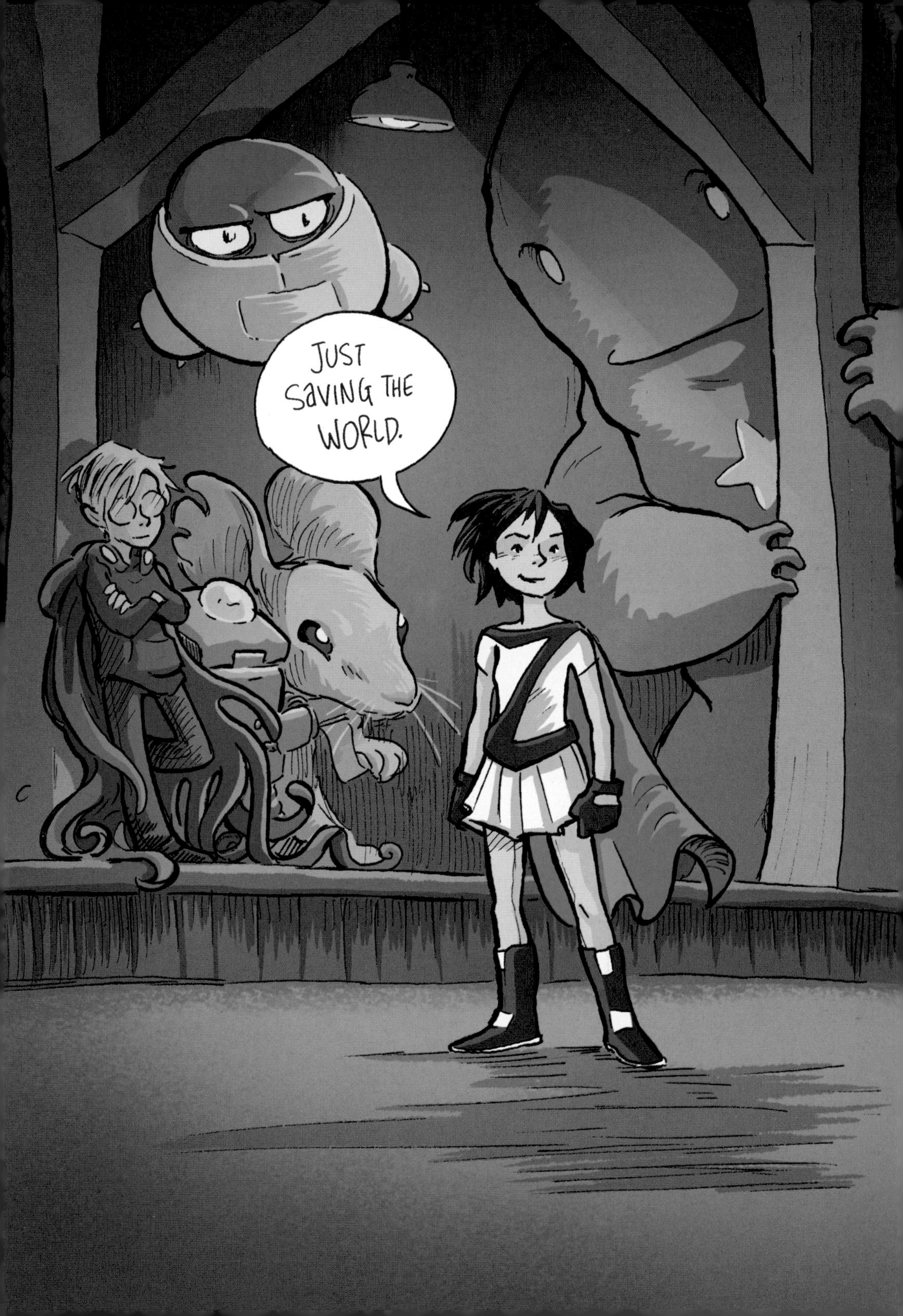
JUST SAVING THE WORLD.

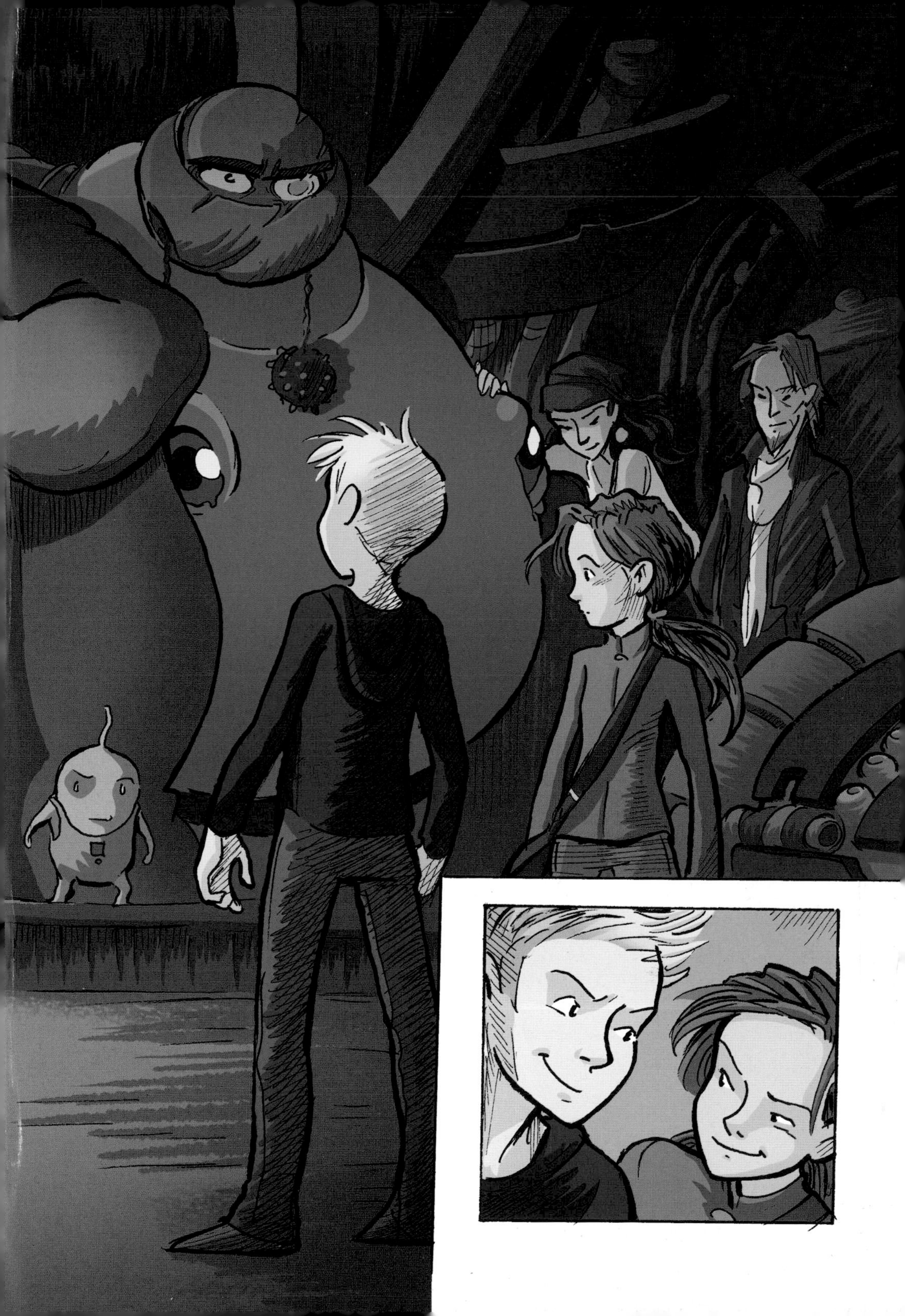

Library of Congress Control Number: 2016961549

Hardcover ISBN: 978-1-62672-267-5
Paperback ISBN: 978-1-62672-266-8

Our books may be purchased in bulk for promotional, educational, or
business use. Please contact your local bookseller or the Macmillan Corporate
and Premium Sales Department at (800) 221-7945 ext. 5442 or by e-mail
at MacmillanSpecialMarkets@macmillan.com.

The art for this book was drawn on laser printer paper with Sakura Pigma
Micron pens (sizes 005, 01, 05, and 08) over light colored pencil. Colors were
accomplished digitally using Photoshop.

First edition 2017
Book design by Joyana McDiarmid
Colors by Alex Campbell and Hilary Sycamore of Sky Blue Ink
Printed in China by Toppan Leefung Printing Ltd.,
Dongguan City, Guangdong Province

Hardcover: 10 9 8 7 6 5 4 3 2 1
Paperback: 10 9 8 7 6 5 4